THE UNDERGROUND

THE UNDERGROUND

BOOK ONE OF THE DERIVATES RISING TRILOGY

LIV EVANS

The Underground
First published by Liv Evans in 2020
ISBN 9780648812203

© 2020 by Liv Evans

All rights reserved.
No part of this book may be reproduced in any form or by any electronic or mechanical means, including information storage and retrieval systems, without written permission from the author, except for the use of brief quotations in a book review.

For any enquiries please visit www.livevans.com.au

Cover: Piere d'Arterie (Instagram @piere_d_arterie)

Editing: Chelsea Visser (Fiverr)

For my husband.
For the long nights spent writing, reading, and debating. Thank you for helping me keep a rebellious cast of characters in line, in The Underground, and in real life.
This story wouldn't be here without you.
Xx

1
KC-847

KC-847 GRASPED a handle to steady himself when the slick, chrome-coated van rocked as it passed through the protective electrostatic field surrounding the Hub. It was the first sign that they had left the bustling capital behind. He had only been permitted outside the Hub on three occasions, but this was his first mission as Team Captain. The woman he was ordered to retrieve had seen fit to flee the city, so he had no choice but to follow.

All seven people in the van, including KC-847, snapped to attention as the communication panel in the back corner of the vehicle let out a piercing ring. The crisp, functional interior of the van was bathed in soft blue light as KC-847 reached over, pressing his palm against the smooth glass to answer the call.

The face of a middle-aged woman filled the screen. Her lips curved into a smile as she surveyed the assembled group, her blonde ponytail bobbing as she nodded in approval. "KC-847, the GPS tracking tells me you're just about to cross over into Ground Zero territory, is that correct?"

KC-847 squared his shoulders and nodded. "Yes, Commander Hemwell. Crossing over in thirty seconds. All officers have their anti-radiation devices, body armour, and weapons."

"Excellent. Given the nature of your mission, we are setting your search and rescue time for nineteen-hundred hours. Please remember to report in if you require an extension. I don't want to waste resources sending the drones to check on you. Any final questions?"

"No, ma'am." KC-847 had spent countless hours preparing for this moment, for his first command mission. He knew everything he needed to about what the team were walking into. "We are ready. VC-825 and I will report once we have completed the primary objective."

"Very well." She nodded at him with a spark of amusement in her eyes before she looked past his shoulder. Her critical gaze fell on the six Citizens in the transport, all dressed in mottled grey Government fatigues with protective flak vests over the top and dull silver command visors lowered over their eyes. "Officers, today you are trailblazers. I know the Government's decision to place Derivates in charge of retrieval operations has been a point of contention, but KC-847 is highly qualified for the role. I expect you to follow his orders as you would those of any Citizen Officer. We are counting on you to prove that this initiative is successful. Is that understood?"

There was a general murmur of agreement behind KC-847, peppered with two 'Yes ma'am's and one deep, amused snort. The team was composed of Citizen Officers: ordinary, everyday humans. As a Derivate, a human with psionic abilities, he was a lesser being, nothing more than a tool for the Government to use to keep law and order. This mission was an exception; his powerful telekinesis was exactly what the team needed to overpower the runaway Derivate, whether the Citizens wanted to admit it or not.

"Excellent. See you for a full debrief at oh-nine-hundred tomorrow." Hemwell raised her hand and, as she saluted, she said "For the good of all."

The rustle of combat fatigues filled the space as everyone in the truck saluted their Commanding Officer and repeated "For the good of all" with unanimous enthusiasm. When the screen faded, KC-847 turned to those gathered and cleared his throat. The faces looking back at him were filled with a mix of anticipation and apprehension.

The transport hit another pocket of turbulence as they switched from the smooth Hub roads to the cracked asphalt of Ground Zero. KC-847 held his hand up, sending a wave of telekinetic energy out to hold himself steady. Once he had his footing, he ran a hand through his short cropped, mousy-brown hair and straightened up.

"Alpha team, we are going live in T-minus fifteen minutes. I am going to do a roll-call now so we can all focus as we transition from the Hub to Ground Zero." KC-847 let go of the handle by the back door to flick the switch on his visor. The names and personnel photos of the team members appeared on the HUD. He read their names aloud as he checked them off. He knew they were all present, but it was a necessary formality. It wasn't until he reached the second-to-last name that the standard call and response of 'Sir!' was replaced by something else:

"Yep."

KC-847 blinked and turned to face Anderson. The surly man was on the older side of middle-age and wearing a look of distaste that reflected his flippant disregard for protocol.

"The standard response is 'Sir'," KC-847 said, voice firm.

Anderson snorted. "For a Citizen Officer, perhaps. But you're no Citizen."

Beside him, Rogers rolled her eyes. McWilliam fixed him with a cold glare. Technically, Anderson was right. As humans with mutated genes, Derivates were not allowed to be registered as Citizens in any Government-controlled city.

"That is correct, but I am the ranking officer on this mission, and protocol requires the correct response." KC-847's voice was smooth and unperturbed. He squared his shoulders and gave the Citizen a second chance. "Anderson."

"Yup, still here."

A tense silence filled the van, the other Citizens chafing at Anderson's brazen disrespect.

There was no point arguing. KC-847 opened the Disciplinary Reporting module in his visor's interface and dictated, "Begin Report: Officer Anderson. Failure to adhere to Government protocol as outlined in Special Operations Policy Three-A on two occasions. End report."

Anderson's gaze flicked away from KC-847's red eyes to the deep black Government logo tattooed on his neck; two cupped hands holding a trio of interlinked circles. The symbol branded him as a Derivate. He was used to how Citizens sneered at the tattoo, a reminder of his place at the bottom of the social hierarchy. It wasn't the look that bothered him, just Anderson's lack of respect for protocol.

Anderson's gaze was steady, challenging him to do more than just make a report. KC-847 let it go. He understood why Anderson resented his presence. Having Derivates leading any operation was a new development. Many Citizens rallied against it. KC-847 wouldn't have been surprised if Anderson was one of the Citizens protesting in front of the Government's Headquarters in Centre One a few weeks earlier.

KC-847 continued down the list. "Chang."

"Sir!" Chang's salute was stiff, as if he was trying to make up for Anderson's lack of one.

"Thank you." KC-847 retracted the visor display so he could look at his team without obstruction.

"Our mission today is to retrieve a Derivate that has gone AWOL. She was last seen on surveillance drone footage four hours ago, entering the old subway tunnels. The reconnaissance team in the other van, led by VC-825, will enter the tunnel system first to find the fugitive. When they do, we move in and apprehend her. Is that clear?"

KC-847 looked around, pleased to see the officers nodding.

He reached over, tapping the screen on the wall of the van and bringing up a picture of their target. "KD-035 is a thirty-two-year-old telekinetic that spent most of her career working with the Metropolitan Law Enforcement Squad. We need to exercise caution during her retrieval, as she has excellent working knowledge of weapons and the use of telekinesis to trap and disable single targets. She is considered desperate and dangerous. To recap: we will wait outside the tunnels for confirmation that VC-825 and the reconnaissance team have located the fugitive, and then we will move in to apprehend her. Understood?"

"Yes sir," came five of the expected six voices.

KC-847 looked over at Anderson. "Is that clear?"

The ageing man surveyed his nails and scraped some dirt from under one as he shrugged. "You're not telling us anything we don't already know."

Once again, KC-847 ignored the Citizen's impertinence. It wasn't the natural order for Citizens to be reporting to a Derivate; the new system would take time to sink in. He flipped his visor down and settled into the jump seat secured to the rear door of the van. Using the control device on his wrist, he sent maps of the old subway system to his visor, deciding to use the remainder of the trip to study the wire-frame layout of the tunnel network.

The Citizens engaged in light conversation to pass the time. He tried to ignore the muttering, but a few angry phrases burrowed through his concentration.

"It's not right, reporting to those mules!"

"It's the new policy for retrievals—"

"Yeah, first retrievals, then law enforcement, and before we know it, the bastards'll be running the place."

"Anderson, I hardly—"

"Think of it like this—" Lee's hushed whisper made the others lean towards her, their armour creaking. "They're cannon fodder. They send them in because they have the clout to deal with deserters. If they die, we get a new one for the next mission. We're just here to make sure they don't get any grand ideas of escaping themselves. Simple."

KC-847 stiffened, the lines of the map on his visor merging as his eyes glazed over. Citizens often spoke about Derivates as though they were just mindless, deaf robots, so that wasn't new to him. But...

Cannon fodder.

He had never heard that one before. All Derivates were raised from birth to protect and serve the Citizens on behalf of the Government. He had been given his orders, and he would follow them to the best of his ability.

The van slowed and then sank, wobbling as the engine powered down and settled the craft onto cracked asphalt. KC-847 and his team filed out of the vehicle and into the jagged shadows of Ground Zero. The waning afternoon light peeked over the top of the rundown towers, leaving the team standing in the cool, crumbled space.

The buildings, once glorious skyscrapers at the epitome of an age of architectural technology, had been abandoned over a century ago. A battle between the newly evolved Derivate population and the era's government had ended in nuclear contamination, rendering the area unliveable. The Hub, the new, splendorous city that had risen to the east, replaced Ground Zero as the pinnacle of civilisation.

KC-847 ran his hands over his dark grey body armour, checking the buckles and clips. He made sure the gun on his hip had full power before he turned off the indicator lights. He didn't think he would need the weapon, given his telekinetic abilities, but policy stated that he had to have it as back-up.

"KC-847, are you and Alpha team good to go?" A soft voice interrupted his pre-mission checks and he looked up to see the smiling face of VC-825.

KC-847 and VC-825 were born in the same facility within a couple of months of each other, but the only features they shared were their red eyes and matching Government tattoos. She stood half a head shorter than him, and her curly blonde hair was tied in a neat bun at the nape of her neck. They spent their early years in the same training facility, though she clearly did not pay as much attention to their lessons as he did. She spent far too much energy on unnecessary facial expressions, like the smile she had just given him.

"Yes, all present and accounted for. What about Bravo team?"

"Affirmative. All present and accounted for." VC-825 straightened and tugged on the collar of the light black bodysuit she was wearing. It was form-fitting and made of advanced chameleonic fibres to help her blend into her surroundings. Her team of four reconnaissance officers stood behind her, shuffling their feet. "We'll go in. I'll keep you updated."

"Of course, on your lead," KC-847 said, and then saluted. "For the good of all."

"For the good of all." VC-825 gave him a half-hearted salute. She looked as though she wanted to say more but thought better of it. Instead, her narrow shoulders sagged, and she held up a hand. Her team fell in behind her and she led them over to the edge of the subway entrance. Before reaching the gaping mouth of the tunnel,

VC-825 gestured for radio silence as her four operatives faded into the shadows and out of view.

Alpha team formed ranks to wait for the recon team's signal. Standing beside KC-847, Chang shuddered. "Man, this place gives me the creeps."

2
FLIT

"I'VE GOT EXCITING news for you," Flit announced as she walked down an abandoned subterranean maintenance tunnel. Each step was more of a bounce, her dark brown ponytail swinging from side to side as she looked up at her best friend, Hawkeye. Even in the low, flickering light of the tunnel she could see a spark of curiosity in his deep green eyes.

"What is it?"

Flit grinned. "Pfft! You think I'm going to tell you that easily? Guess!"

Hawkeye rolled his eyes at her and sighed. "Ok, fine. Let's see... You finally beat my score on Virtu-ball 8000?"

Flit's snorted laugh echoed through the tunnel. "That's old news. I did that two weeks ago."

Hawkeye let out a frustrated groan and ran his hand through his hair. "And you didn't tell me?"

"Nah, I was waiting to see the horror on your face when you realised my name was above yours on the leader board. But there's no chance of that now. Keep guessing."

"Ummm... You got promoted at work?"

"Why would that excite me?" Flit rolled her eyes. She hated the drudgery of her day job in the Hub, where she aspired to achieve as little as possible. A promotion would make it harder to get away with daydreaming the hours away.

"You have a long weekend and you're gonna spend an extra day in the Underground?"

"Nope, better."

"Flit!"

"Alright, alright, spoilsport," Flit sighed, knowing his patience had reached its limit. If she didn't put Hawkeye out of his misery, he would sulk all night. "My request to transfer to the Underground was approved."

Hawkeye grabbed her shoulder and pulled her to a stop. "Seriously?" The excitement in his eyes was guarded, as though he didn't quite trust her. She couldn't blame him.

"Yep."

"That's awesome!" Hawkeye gave her a back-breaking hug.

Flit knew he would be happy for her. She had grown up living between the shining Government-controlled metropolis of the Hub and the dank tunnels of the Underground resistance. Whenever she was in the Underground, Hawkeye still had to go about his normal duties. She joined in where she could, but they rarely got to spend a good chunk of time together outside of mealtimes or patrols.

"We can't stand here and hug all night," Flit chuckled.

Hawkeye let her go and looked up at the manhole cover above their heads. "You're right. The sooner we get this patrol over, the better." He jumped up and grabbed onto a small iron handle in the ceiling. He pulled the cover out of the way. A rusted metal ladder clattered down in front of them. "So, when are you moving?" he asked as he started to climb.

"Two weeks," Flit called after him, lazing back against the wall.

"Two weeks?" There was surprise in the echo of his voice.

Flit chuckled as she watched Hawkeye haul himself into the tunnel above and step aside to make room for her. She didn't bother climbing the ladder. Instead, she looked up the shaft, concentrated for a nanosecond, and teleported herself to a point just above where the manhole cover had been. In the instant she reappeared in that empty space, she noted where Hawkeye was, and blinked to his side. Some teleporters hated the feeling of falling that accompanied jumping into places above floor height, but Flit loved the adrenaline rush that came with it. Like many others with her ability, Flit could only teleport to places she could see. She hoped that moving to the Underground full-time would allow her to train towards reaching locations outside her line of sight.

"Yeah. They don't want to rush the transfer to Eastport in case it looks suspicious. So, I'll pretend to go through the transfer application process at work, do a fake interview—all that crap. Hopefully the Government won't pick up on it," Flit informed him.

"Well, at least the transfer was approved." Hawkeye shrugged. The news must have been welcome enough for him to hold back his usual comment about it being lazy to teleport up a level instead of using the ladder. Flit enjoyed the reprieve from his judgement.

As Hawkeye pulled the ladder back up into the crawlspace between tunnels and closed the manhole cover, Flit walked over to a small round grate to her left. It was rusted in several spots with a worn symbol stamped into the metal on the circumference. To an untrained eye, the stamp would look like nothing more than an old manufacturer's logo. To Flit, it was a marker. There was a B in a small triangle with two lines underneath it. The letter told her they were in sector B. The direction of the triangle indicated that the tunnel ran north-east to south-west, and the two lines meant it was a mid-level tunnel.

Flit pulled a small metal tag off her utility belt and held it over the grate. After a moment, it beeped softly. The space beneath the grate glowed with blue light in the shape of a U with a downward facing arrow in the middle. The direction of that arrow showed the fastest route back to the Underground base. Flit knew her way around the Underground, but the grates didn't just give directions. If she and Hawkeye didn't come back from patrol, their supervisor would know this was the last checkpoint they had reached.

"The extra time will give my parents a chance to cool off before I have to move here. That's a good thing, I suppose," Flit said as they resumed their patrol.

"So, they still aren't on board with it all?" Hawkeye asked as he smoothed back his sand-coloured hair.

"Not even close. Well, Dad doesn't seem to mind, but Mum's furious. We argued about it for the entire trip here. But it doesn't matter, they'll get used to it. And I need to do something, Hawk.

Being up there, not doing anything to help—it's killing me!" Flit's hands balled into fists at her side. "There has been so much crap on the news about how they want to implement more restrictions on the Registereds' abilities."

That was another reason Flit hated her job in the Hub; being forced to take part in a system that she loathed. Under the Government's control, Derivates were registered, assigned a serial number, subdued through hormonal manipulation and used as public servants. They were treated like property. Flit, her family, and most members of the Underground were Derivates who flew under the Government's radar and lived without their punitive control. With their broad range of powers, they would be hunted on the surface and registered.

Or worse.

"As if they don't control them enough." Hawkeye shook his head as they turned and made their way down another tunnel. Lit by flickering emergency lighting, it would have been a tight squeeze for four people walking abreast.

"Exactly," Flit snapped. "It's bullshit."

"I know you want to escape seeing all that, but once you transfer you won't get to see the sun. Shit, Flit, I'd kill to spend a day outside in the fresh air and sunlight," Hawkeye lamented, his eye grazing over the tanned olive skin of her arms and neck.

Flit bristled at his comment. "The Underground's gotten too comfortable. We've forgotten that we aren't meant to live in tunnels. We need obliterate the Government so we can live up there as ourselves, not in hiding. Forget tans and fresh air, I want freedom."

Hawkeye shook his head as he led them over to the first control panel of the sector. Concealed behind a rusted ventilation grate, the screen lit up as he brushed his fingertips over it. He gestured for Flit to bring up the maintenance list while he flipped his visor down to find the checks and balances for that part of the system.

"In-Pipe Pressure?"

"Normal," Flit replied, scanning over the readout.

"Out-Pipe Pressure?"

"N-o-r-m-a-l."

"Air Quality?"

"You can breathe, can't you?"

Hawkeye sighed. "Air Quality?"

"Starts with n, ends with ormal."

"Bloody hell, let me do it." Hawkeye nudged her out of the way with his elbow. "I should report you for this, you know."

"For what?"

"For not taking the checks seriously."

Flit rolled her eyes. "If you had to put me on report for that you'd also have to add that I'm not taking your stupid haircut seriously either."

He patted his freshly styled coiffure self-consciously. "And now you're bullying me."

"Bullying? Shit, Hawkeye, you're such a child sometimes."

"Me? You're the one—" Hawkeye stopped when the mischievous glint in Flit's eyes warned him that he was playing right into her trap. He shook his head and turned back to the panel.

Hawkeye went through the rest of the balances on his own as she teleported around in half a dozen impatient hops. When Hawkeye finished, he slid the cover back over the panel, flipped up his visor, and looked at her. "So, what happens after two weeks?"

"Well, after the transfer is finalised, you're getting a new full-time patrol partner." Flit flashed him a dashing grin.

Hawkeye stopped dead in his tracks. His smile dropped. "Oh, shit. They haven't put us together, have they?"

"You bet your arse they did. How great is that?"

Hawkeye stared at her in horror. Flit stubbornly held his gaze. Seconds slipped past. Then, with a sudden splutter, Hawkeye doubled over with laughter. "Oh hell, those poor naïve fools. What a terrible decision." Shaking his head, he straightened up and draped an arm around Flit's shoulder. He pulled her against his side as they ambled through the tunnels together. "Although, you're a real pain in the arse. I should ask for a reassignment."

"Hey!" Flit bumped him with her hip, the flame grenades and pistol on her belt clattering. She teleported out from under his arm and started walking backwards so she could watch him as they approached a fork in the tunnel. One side led towards the border of this sector and terminated at a dead-end. It was a long, boring walk, and the ventilation was bad enough that the smell of mildew and stale air was always overwhelming. It would be quicker and less painful if she did it alone. "Want me to check this one? I'll be back in a flash, promise!"

"No, Flit, we're supposed to stick—" Before Hawkeye finished his sentence, Flit was off.

Each teleport took Flit deeper down the despised tunnel. Once she reached the end, she groaned. Dozens of giant, mutant roaches swarmed over the panel she needed to access. Each one was about as big as a domestic cat, their dark carapaces glinting in the flickering emergency lighting. Flit walked closer, but they didn't scatter like they usually did.

"Hey—shoo!" She stamped her feet and waved her arms around in attempt to scare them away. The roaches weren't dangerous, per se, but they had a gross habit of swarming over the warmest thing in the area. In this case, that would be her.

Flit sighed. "Of all the bloody days... Fine! If you want to be stubborn, then I have no sympathy for you."

Flit teleported several metres away before she plucked a smooth metal ball about the size of a nectarine off her utility belt. She squinted, judging the distance, and then lobbed it towards the roaches. It exploded with a flash of blinding flames. Roach shells and entrails splattered the tunnel walls. Flit's arms flew up to cover her face. She was far enough back to avoid the worst of it, but some stray bits of muck oozed down the cuffs of her cargo pants and over her boots. She whined and tried to shake it off as she walked towards the viscera-covered panel.

"Flit! Is everything ok?" Hawkeye's panicked voice was backed by the frantic beat of his feet slapping against the concrete as he ran towards her.

Flit scrunched up her nose as she skirted around a pile of flaming bug-guts. She flipped the panel open and checked that the emergency protocol was still intact. "Yeah, all good!" she called over her shoulder as she tapped her metal tag against the chip reader before closing the panel.

Flit turned, teleporting back to Hawkeye in three jumps. He

skidded to a stop, leaning over and putting his hands on his knees as he caught his breath.

"Together, Flit. We're supposed to stick together," Hawkeye panted, his frustration blunted by relief. He never could stay angry at her for long. He let out an amused huff of laughter as he took in the state of her boots. "Just roaches?"

"Yeah. Annoying little bastards refused to get off the panel."

"Probably liked the warmth of the electronics. We need to talk to Cogs, get her to look at it. It shouldn't be running hot enough to draw the roaches. It may be malfunctioning," Hawkeye hypothesised as they followed the other fork off the main tunnel.

Flit nodded. "We'll have to remember to do that when we get back."

Hawkeye looked at Flit out of the corner of his eye.

Flit knew what he would say before he said it, so she cut him off. "Yeah, yeah, I shouldn't have gone off on my own. I'd rather not waste our time making you walk that tunnel. I just want to get back to base and catch up with the others."

"No more running off, ok? I think I shit myself when that grenade went off."

"Alright, fine. Whatever. Won't happen again. To prove I'm sorry I'll buy you a new pair of underwear when I get back to the Hub. Brown, this time, so you won't notice the shit stains," Flit teased.

Hawkeye snorted. Neither of them believed that she was even remotely sorry. "Ugh, I'm gonna regret encouraging you to transfer. Come and do patrol with me, I said. It'll be fun, I said..." He shook his head.

Flit and Hawkeye continued their patrol, and Flit behaved herself. For the most part. Whenever she got restless, she teleported instead of walking, making one short jump for every four of Hawkeye's steps as though it were a game of leapfrog. It was a testament to the length of their friendship that their conversation still flowed smoothly.

It wasn't until the pair reached the uppermost levels of their patrol that Hawkeye reached out and put a hand on her shoulder to pull Flit to a stop. "Alright, crossing into surface-level tunnels now," Hawkeye warned her.

Flit shrugged. "So?"

"No more joking, okay? You never know what you'll run into in these parts." Hawkeye's tone was serious: he was genuinely concerned. He had good reason to be. The surface-level tunnels were where they were most likely to run into Government agents.

"Fine," Flit sighed, her shoulders falling. "I'll behave."

Hawkeye's expression softened in relief.

"Race you to the top!" Flit taunted as she teleported away, leaving Hawkeye groaning in her wake.

3
KC-847

AS HE WAITED outside the abandoned subway entrance with his team, KC-847 got his first real chance to look at the ruins of Ground Zero. The air in the city was still and stale, dust motes dancing on the dying sun rays in the deserted streets. The once towering brick and steel buildings had fallen into a crumbling state of disrepair, but some parts, like the subway entrance, remained eerily intact. It was an out-of-place portal of concrete and industrial solar tiles that cast ghoulish shadows on the cracked asphalt. The tunnels beyond were rumoured to house any number of mutated animals that evolved well after the Government stopped cataloguing them.

"Alpha team. Come in!" VC-825's voice burst through KC-847's musings. Her overly chirpy tone elicited a grunt of disgust from one of his team members.

"Copy, what is your status?" KC-847 focused on the info feed on his visor, noting that his fellow Derivate had forgone the gesture communication.

"We have located a mangled corpse in the first eight-way junction. It's wearing the right gear, but we need to get closer to confirm it is our mark. Requesting bac—"

KC-847 was just about to signal for his team to follow him when VC-825's transmission cut short. "Bravo team, report!" he snapped.

"Immediate back-up req—" VC-825's frantic call was interrupted by the staccato tattoo of gunfire.

"Shit, they must be close, I can hear the gunfire from here," Rogers hissed under her breath. KC-847 pulled out his earbud and grimaced as he confirmed Rogers' assessment.

"Alpha team, we are going in," KC-847 ordered, breaking into a run. He didn't need any further requests from VC-825.

The retrieval team's feet pounded against the broken ground, following KC-847 as they raced into the cavernous mouth of the tunnels. KC-847 switched his visor to dark-vision and superimposed the map of the tunnels over his view. Using the linked tracking module, he spotted the circular junction that VC-825 had referred to a level deeper in the subway system.

"We're overwh—" VC-825's plea was drowned out by a low, guttural chittering before the transmission cut off.

"Double-time," KC-847 barked. "Alpha team incoming. Bravo team, pull back. I repeat, retreat!" His words were steady through the hard pace he was keeping; the officers beside him were panting already.

Down and around, winding through the dark labyrinthine tunnels they went. Without the map on the visor, even KC-847's remarkable sense of direction would have been stumped. Between the consuming blackness and acrid, wet stench of the stale air, any normal person would turn and flee.

"Bravo team, we are approaching your position now." KC-847 skidded to a stop as he and his team entered the junction.

The blinking trackers for Bravo team were attached to limp bodies, buried beneath surging mounds of fur, teeth, and claws.

"What the hell?" Lee gasped from behind KC-847.

While KC-847 agreed with Lee's crude assessment of the situation, they didn't have time to waste. Instead, he raised his weapon, just as hundreds of pairs of black, glittering eyes turned to face them.

"Open fire."

The glow of their laser pointers lit the tunnel, bringing the true horror of the scene to life. The undulating mass of mutant rats screeched with each round fired towards them. Splattered with fresh blood, torn skin, and ligaments, the creatures surged towards the new arrivals. The burning acid tang he smelled before was stronger here, radiating out from the dozens of decomposing carcasses and mutant rat droppings that littered the ground. The stench clung to his nostrils as he sucked in deep, steady breaths. All in various states of decomposition, the corpses made sick squelching sounds beneath the mass of giant, mutated rats that scampered over them. Closer and closer the rats surged, unperturbed by the constant rain of bullets falling around them.

"Sir, we need to retreat!" Lee's cry was barely audible beneath the roiling thunder of weapon fire.

KC-847 grimaced as he raised his hands. He focused his mind on the surrounding targets, and *pushed*, throwing half a dozen of the mastiff sized rodents into a wall. There was the sickening crunch of spines snapping as their bodies sagged down onto the muck-slicked stone floor. As his team provided covering fire, he scanned the area, finding two vital signs from Bravo team's tracking markers.

"Negative, hold position. There are two officers alive under that swarm." KC-847 flung his arms out, sending more furry bodies flying as he helped to thin the tide. But, like any true wave, this one was unstoppable.

"There are more coming from behind us!" Anderson yelled.

KC-847 turned to see a whole new swarm of the monstrosities surging towards them, coming from the tunnel they had used to get there. He was just about to order the rear three officers provide cover when the first wave of rats leapt, taking down Anderson with a sickening tear of flesh and a splatter of hot blood.

Alpha team gave the rats everything they had, but they just kept coming. Lee, Anderson and Antonios were gone, buried beneath the ravenous aberrations. Out of the corner of his eye, KC-847 saw McWilliam and Rogers sinking beneath the swarm. He stumbled back against Chang and the two fought, side-by-side, backs against the grimy junction wall. It was short-lived. Chang's gun spluttered as it ran out of charges. The rats took advantage of the pause and lashed out, jaws snapping shut around Chang's legs and dragging him under. KC-847's body shook as he summoned all the power he could muster to keep the creatures at bay, but there were just too many of them. They climbed over each other, their teeth and jaws flashing ravenously as they surged towards him.

Death, it seemed, was inevitable.

4

FLIT

FLIT HAD ONLY BEEN TEASING Hawkeye when she teleported away from him. She stopped at the next junction and waited for him to catch up. When he did, he doubled over, holding onto his side as he struggled to catch his breath.

"That was the last of it, sorry. It's out of my system now," Flit promised, crossing her heart.

"One day Flit, I swear..." Hawkeye trailed off, muttering something Flit wasn't sure she wanted to hear. He had been making threats like that since they were kids, but he never followed through. Despite all the bickering and trickery, they still had each other's backs.

Hawkeye straightened up, and the two continued up the sharp incline of the tunnel. It had a surface-level exit at the end, so the dying evening light slanted in at just the right angle that it didn't require artificial lighting. If they walked to the end of the tunnel, they would get an amazing view of the ruins of the old city from the decrepit rail-bridge that spilled out of it.

Even though the view was lovely, the chance to see it came at great risk. Getting too close to an unprotected entrance meant that the Underground Derivates may be picked up on Government drones. But that was why remote viewers like Hawkeye were so useful for security patrols.

"Here's good," Hawkeye said, stopping a fair distance off from where the last of the light faded into sheltered shadows. Flit looked ahead, judging the distance and whistling with appreciation.

"Oh wow, really testing your limits, huh?"

"Flit, shut up," Hawkeye groaned as his eyes glazed over. Flit knew that he was using his ability to project his field of view right outside of the tunnels. Normally the process only took a few seconds, but after he had been silent for almost a whole minute, she felt restless.

"Hawk? What is it?" Flit's whisper was low as she put her hand on his shoulder. He shook his head and covered her hand with his own to shush her, but he still stared purposefully off into the distance. "Hawk, come on, don't mess around. I'm sorry about befo—"

Flit didn't get to finish before a cacophony of gunfire thundered through the area. Her eyes widened and her entire body sizzled with adrenaline.

"Two Government hover-trucks, both unguarded." Hawkeye snatched her hand and looked at her, suddenly very alert and very much present. "Down on the corner of old Sixth and Norton, just outside Town Hall station."

Flit swore under her breath as more weapons fire echoed through the tunnels. "Shit—that's right near The Nest! Don't those idiots ever learn?" Flit pointed at the end of the tunnel, hand shaking. "We have to get down there."

Hawkeye tensed. "No, we need to get back to an emergency shelter and let base know what is going on."

Flit froze. She narrowed her eyes at him. "They'll die before we can get a team together to handle The Nest."

"I won't risk your life for whoever is stupid enough to be down there."

Flit frowned. Hawkeye sure was sweet when he wanted to be. She looked back at the tunnel entrance and let out a frustrated groan. "Fine. Whatever. Here—" she stepped forward, wrapping her arms around him. He yelped and jumped back.

"No way! Every time you teleport me, I throw up all over my shoes. We're running."

"Running?" Flit cried. "We don't have time for that. I'm

jumping ahead."

"Fine. Just watch out, ok?" Hawkeye gripped her shoulders and refused to let her go until she nodded.

"Come on, we don't have time to stuff around." Flit stepped back and teleported down the tunnel. She made one jump to the first bend. He started running towards her. When he got part of the way, Flit whispered an apology under her breath before she teleported right back to the spot she had just left. With any luck, he would think she had gone on ahead. He wouldn't realise what she had done until it was too late.

Flit grabbed her pistol in her right hand and a fire grenade in her left before teleporting to the entrance of the tunnel. When she arrived, she groaned and threw her forearm up to cover her eyes. After the dim artificial lighting of the service tunnels, the searing rays of sunset were blinding.

When the burning in Flit's eyes subsided, she lowered her arm and looked around. The tunnel dropped off at a dizzying angle, the supports for the bridge continued into the distance, but the tracks twisted back on themselves at odd, broken angles. To the east, she spotted the two chrome Government vehicles Hawkeye had mentioned. There was no sign of movement in or around them. She bit her lip. A quick jump to the vehicles and one into the tunnel below would allow her to avoid any eyes if they left guards behind. It was almost two blocks away. Even with direct line of sight, it was a risky distance. Spending so much time in The Hub meant that Flit's long-range teleportation was rusty.

But she didn't have a choice.

The firefight was even louder from her vantage point. She steeled herself; gunfire was proof that there was someone still alive down there. Even if they were Government personnel, they didn't deserve to be mauled to death by those hideous rats.

Flit teleported. When her feet hit the fractured road, she stumbled for a step, but she was already looking into the shadowy tunnel beyond. These surface-level tunnels didn't have emergency lighting activated as a default. It gave the rats an advantage; they had adapted to the darkness. Flit teleported a dozen metres inside the tunnel entrance. Shafts of warm orange light from the setting sun bled into the gloom, far enough for her to locate the right fake ventilation cover. She pushed it aside, turning the emergency lighting in the sector on before slamming it shut and moving on.

In a flurry of teleports, Flit covered the distance between the tunnel opening and The Nest in a matter of seconds. When she arrived at the circular junction that everyone in the Underground despised, she was unprepared for the horror that met her eyes. The mountains of dead and rotting corpses were not new to her. What was new, however, were the cries of the dismembered and dying Government Officers as they lay prone at the opposite side of the vault. A single agent remained standing amongst a carpet of living, breathing death. She swore; the emergency lights hadn't been enough to scare them off their feeding frenzy.

As Flit tried to figure out what to do, a flicker of red caught her attention.

The sole remaining agent was a Registered Derivate. His eyes flashed in the flickering lights as he threw his hands up, holding the creatures back with telekinesis.

The circle of rats closed in around him like a noose as his body trembled and sagged with the strain of keeping them abreast. Overwhelming anger at the Government roiled through Flit. Nobody deserved to be used as heinously as Derivates were.

With a pang of pity for her fellow Derivate, Flit's right hand flew to her belt. She snatched one of the flame grenades and lobbed it towards the surging tide of rats.

With a loud bang, an inferno exploded in the cavernous junction and lighting the warbling shadows with a sickly orange hue. The screeching of the rats was ear-piercing as dozens of the creatures caught fire. Without so much as a second thought, Flit threw another three bombs into the swarm. More explosions and screeching ensued, but it took the detonation of the fifth flame grenade to send the swarm fleeing towards the nearest exit.

The only sound left was the crackle and hiss of the flames as they hungrily devoured the last of the screeching rodents. Warily, Flit picked her way over the unsteady pile of bodies towards where the Registered Derivate was slumped against the wall, panting.

She hoped she wasn't too late.

5
―――
KC-847

KC-847 GROANED when the lights in the tunnel flared and the night-vision filter seared into his eyes. He flipped the visor up with one hand and kept the rats at bay with the other. Every muscle in his body burned and sweat drenched his clothes. His stomach dropped as he realised that the extra lighting didn't deter the rats. They had gotten a taste of blood, and they wouldn't stop until they got more.

Just when KC-847 thought it was all over, there was a loud bang and a blinding burst of light as flames lashed towards him. He threw his hands up to cover his eyes and stumbled back. More explosions rocked the ground at his feet. Through the ringing in his ears, he heard the rats screeching, their long, curved claws skittering against the damp stone floors as they tried to flee. They were not fast enough. The flames engulfed them.

The heat licked at him through his protective armour. KC-847 pressed himself against the junction wall and watched as the vermin raced past him. Some managed to escape, squealing as their flaming bodies lit the tunnels they hurtled down; others succumbed to their injuries and fell where they were standing, writhing and squeaking. He coughed as the stench of smoke and burning fur threatened to choke him. His eyes watered. His lungs burned, each breath feeling like he was inhaling razor blades. His body shook with the effort of holding the rats back for so long. He knew without checking his HUD that everyone he came on this mission with was dead.

But someone had to throw those grenades.

KC-847 looked up, crimson eyes wide as he peered around the junction. Small fires still burned all around, but through the clearing smoke he saw the unmistakable silhouette of a woman.

It was hard to tell in the spluttering light of the junction, but KC-847 guessed that the woman was in her mid-twenties, like him. She had straight, dark hair tied up in a practical ponytail at the base of her neck. Even from a distance, he could see the wariness in her stance. Her hand brushed over her utility belt, with five empty slots and two small incendiary grenades remaining. Frowning, KC-847 took in the non-Government-issued belt. *Who had facilitated her escape?* He mentally compared the woman in front of him to the identification picture of KD-035. Some of her features looked off in the sub-par lighting, but it had to be her. Who else would be down here?

His team was gone, but he could still complete his mission.

"KD-035, by order of the Government, under section forty-three of the Derivate Act, you are under arrest. You will need to come with me. Should you resist, I am authorised to use whatever force necessary to detain you," he warned. He hoped she would listen to reason. "You are a telekinetic grade D; I am grade C. I out power you. It would be ill-advised to flee." KC-847 started towards her, his long strides stretching over the smoking rats.

At first the woman looked at him, blinking in confusion, but as he drew closer, her lips twisted into a grimace. "You... you want to arrest me?" Her eyes dropped to his combat fatigues and the weapons on his belt. "You're going to arrest me after I saved your arse from becoming rat-food? Are you frickin' kidding me?"

KC-847 kept moving towards her. "You went AWOL. You are to be returned to the Government Holdings for reconditioning."

The woman's face hardened, her dark brows furrowing. "I suppose you're right... I mean, you're a C and I'm only a D. I have no hope of escaping you." With a sigh of resignation, she cast her gaze to the ground. She put her hands out, wrists together.

KC-847 was told in his training that runaways would not come easily, but he had made several good points. And, surely, anything was better than this squalid place. He retrieved the magnetic cuffs from his belt and held them out, reaching for her slender wrists. They were remarkably clean for someone who had been rattling around in this junction. Somehow, he was dirtier than she was, with rat guts and blood splattered over his fatigues.

"Your swift compliance will be reflected in my report," he told her, reaching for the sleek silver inhibitor circlet at his belt. As he held it above her head, he noticed just how much shorter she was than him. And the fact that her eyes were hazel, not red. He knew that Citizens could have their eyes recoloured at certain clinics, so it was possible that she had done that. He thought back to the dossier that Hemwell had sent him. Something about her felt off.

"What I meant to say," she began, the tone of her voice conspiratorial enough that he leaned in closer to listen, "was that I'll come with you... if you can catch me."

In the blink of an eye, she disappeared. The magnetic cuffs clattered to the concrete. *A teleporter.* KC-847 straightened and scanned the area. She had to be around here somewhere.

"Over here big guy!" she called, voice laced with laughter.

KC-847 pressed his lips together in annoyance. He spun on his heel. She was perched on top of an old ventilation shaft that ran along the cavernous ceiling. She certainly wasn't KD-035. No, this woman was a teleporter. And now that he thought on it, she didn't have the Government tattoo that all Derivates had. He may have been looking for a run-away law enforcement officer, but he had a feeling he stumbled on something even more concerning.

"You are under arrest. Come quietly, or I will have to use force to apprehend you." He held his hands up in warning.

The woman just laughed. He had no choice but to stretch his arms out, one hand closing into a fist as he used his telekinetic power to hold her in place. He felt the pressure of it wrap around her small form as he took slow steps towards her. Restraining her drained his already depleted energy levels. He hoped she couldn't see how his hands were shaking with the strain.

"Please, is that what they teach you in training? You're gonna have to try harder than that if you want to catch me," the woman scoffed.

KC-847 felt a sudden push against his psychic force and the woman teleported away.

"Over here." Her voice came from just behind his right shoulder.

KC-847 whirled around, but she was already gone. Then, a whistle from the other side of the junction had him spinning. He tried to grasp at her again with his abilities, but she was a slippery one, shaking off his grapple and disappearing again.

"Oh, come on. You can do better than that!" she teased from somewhere to his left.

KC-847 gritted his teeth.

Was she playing with him? Well, if she wanted to fight dirty, he could do that. Instead of focusing on trying to catch her, he used his ability to grasp some bone fragments and rat entrails. The next time he heard one of her teasing calls, he flung his hand in her direction, sending the scraps hurtling towards her. There was a gasp of surprise, but she teleported away before the debris hit her.

"You're a clever one." The whisper came from right behind him. KC-847 jumped as her warm breath brushed the back of his neck. He whirled around, but she had already moved on.

He'd trained with teleporters before, but this one? She was quick.

There were no tell-tale sounds of her landing in a new location, so he turned in a slow circle as he scanned the junctions and tunnel entrances. He finally noticed her leaning against a shadowed wall beneath an arch, picking some dirt from under her nails. He continued to scan, pretending he hadn't seen her. Just as a smug smirk cracked her lips, he flung some metal shards from a broken sewer grate her way.

"Ouch!" Her cry was cut off as she teleported, an arc of blood splattering the space where she just stood.

"Alright, one point to you."

She was behind him.

"It hurts like a bitch!"

Now she was clinging to a pipe on the ceiling.

"May even need stitches."

On top of a stack of old crates.

KC-847 stopped and took a breath. Even injured, she was still playing with him. What was her game? His mind reeled back to his training. If he couldn't grapple her, and his ability was too slow to cast items at her, he had to find another way.

The buzz and static of the emergency light above his head made him look up, giving him an idea. She may jump around like a dimension-hopping frog, but she wouldn't be able to do that if she couldn't see where she was going.

As the woman continued to dart about, KC-847 turned in a slow circle, taking in the locations in the emergency lighting in the ceiling. He would need to take them all out in one quick move. He looked at the pile of broken rail sleepers to his right and reached out with his telekinesis, brushing over the hefty tracks, testing their weight and density. Even though he was exhausted, he had to find the energy to move them.

"What, giving up already? Come on, this was just getting fun." The woman popped into place right in front of him and he gasped, flinging the sleepers in all different directions.

"Ha!" she laughed with a cocky expression on her face.

The sound of smashing glass echoed through the tunnels and the lights fizzled out. She made one final jump as the world went dark.

With a loud grunt, KC-847 stumbled forward. A set of arms and legs wrapped around him in a tight hold. He found his feet, even with her unexpected weight on his back.

"Clever Mr. Officer," she breathed, her amusement mixed with annoyance. "You took out the lights so I couldn't see where to teleport. Well played."

KC-847 tried to shake her off. Even though he was strong and broad, she had a good grip on him. He considered using his abilities to cast her off, but stopped himself. At least she was close to him. He gritted his teeth and used his telekinesis to pull the spare handcuffs slowly and silently off his belt, moving them up towards her wrists as she nattered on.

"So, here's the deal. You make one more move, I'll jump to

whatever spot in this darkness I find most appealing, and I will take you with me," she warned him, her voice taking on a sharp edge. "I'd also stop moving those cuffs up higher too, if I were you."

KC-847 froze, the cuffs hovering just in front of his chest as she caught on to his plan.

He replayed her threat over in his head. Surely she wasn't that crazy? If she misjudged her teleport, they could end up spliced with the ground, or a rail sleeper, or even some bloodied rat corpses...

The woman went to speak when shouting from further down one of the tunnels interrupted her. "Flit? Are you down there?"

KC-847's ears rung as she yelled back, "In the junction. I've got one of them!"

"We're coming!"

KC-847's heart hammered in his chest. He struggled in her grip, trying to shake her off. He had to escape before her reinforcements arrived.

"Don't make me teleport," she grunted as she clung to him.

He paused, not sure what to do. She was obviously somewhat unhinged, and he didn't want to end up with half of his body merged into some concrete wall. Maybe when her colleagues came, she would ease up enough for him to escape.

It was only another couple of seconds before lights appeared in the distance. They bounced, growing as they drew closer. The footsteps of what had to be half a dozen people echoed through the tunnels, and soon the junction was blazing with the light from their flood lamps. The woman's nails dug into the flesh of his chest as she clung to him. Hot sticky blood from the gash on her thigh soaked through the side of his shirt.

Five strangers with torches ran to surround him. Between them and the woman on his back, he knew he had to be careful. He narrowed his eyes as he inspected the newcomers. No red eyes, no tattoos, but given the appearance of the woman on his back, he couldn't take anything for granted.

"Flit, over here, now," barked an older man with buzzed grey hair and stern sky-blue eyes. He raised his gun at KC-847.

KC-847 sucked in a long breath of relief as the woman's weight disappeared from his back. He straightened up, assessing the situation and trying to figure out the best way out of it. The woman reappeared behind the stern-looking man. A younger, tawny blonde-haired man at his side frowned at her and muttered something KC-847 couldn't hear. She jutted her head towards KC-847, and the man refocused his attention and raised his weapon.

"What's your name, officer?" the gruff, greying one asked.

KC-847 bristled at the order in his tone. He pressed his lips together and stood straighter, rolling his shoulders back.

"I believe you were asked a question, officer," a middle-aged woman with salt and pepper hair said smoothly, stepping into the circle. Unlike the others, she wasn't wearing deep grey and black camouflage fatigues. Her warm brown skin was draped in a casual dress, but there was a gun clipped to the belt cinched at her waist.

"If you don't come with us quietly, we've been authorised to use force," Flit said, an almost sing-song quality to her voice. KC-847 looked at her, his eyes narrowing.

KC-847 tore his eyes away from the odd group and scanned the surrounding area. He gritted his teeth when he noticed a pile of rubble from a collapsing archway just to his left. He wouldn't be able to get all of them, but he could distract them enough to make an escape. His fingers flexed at his sides, and just as he was about to act, the middle-aged woman stepped forward. Her eyes caught his and, in a moment of concern, her psychic energy pushed into his mind.

"Time to sleep, officer," she whispered, the very words swirling in his mind and settling over his consciousness like a warm blanket.

KC-847 groaned and tried to resist, but she was too powerful. Blackness pulled at his consciousness, and his body swayed before he collapsed to the ground.

6

FLIT

FLIT'S LEG hurt like a bitch. The moment that they neutralised the Registered Derivate, her companions turned on her with matching looks of concern.

"Shit, are you alright?" Hawkeye rushed over to slide his arm under hers to help her stand. Her thigh was still oozing blood down the front of her pants.

"Yeah, just a scrape," Flit lied, downplaying what clearly needed immediate first aid.

Posthoc rounded on her. "You're bloody lucky you didn't lose the whole leg. Or worse!"

Flit flinched at the anger in his tone. Not much more than an hour ago she was in a meeting with him, promising she would be a model Security Team member. "Look, I know it was risky, but we didn't have time to stuff around. If I hadn't gotten down here when I did then he'd be dead." Flit squared her shoulders as she met Posthoc's eyes.

"Better him than you," Hawkeye muttered under his breath as he guided her over to sit on an empty barrel.

"You wouldn't have been stuffing around, you would have been following protocol," Posthoc pointed out. "It's escapades like this that'll see you put onto maintenance duties, Flit. If it wasn't for the fact your mother is on duty in medbay"—he nodded towards her thigh—"I'd have to discipline you. But I figure dealing with your mother is punishment enough."

Oh shit.

Her mother.

"Surely someone else is on duty, can't I see them?" Flit asked, dread churning inside the pit of her stomach.

"Nope. Patch wasn't feeling well today and Physie has too much paperwork. Besides, you deserve it." Posthoc holstered his pistol. Reaching into a pouch at his hip, he fiddled around in there until he found a bandage, pulling it out with a low '*ah-ha!*'. He threw it to Hawkeye. "Get some pressure on that while we sort out this Registered. We need to get out of here before those blasted rats come back."

Hawkeye squatted down and peeled open one end of the bandage. He took Flit's foot and gingerly rested it on his knee.

Flit rolled her eyes and held her hand out for the bandage. "I can do that."

"No, don't be stupid, you won't get enough pressure on it," he snapped as he started wrapping it around her thigh.

Flit gave in. He was already sulking; it would only get worse if she refused to let him bandage her. She understood that he was frustrated, and while she didn't regret doing what she did, she had hoped he would understand. "Hawk—"

"Don't, Flit," he warned, exasperated.

Flit ignored him. "Look, I know you're pissed, and I'm sorry I ditched you—"

"You think I'm pissed because you ditched me?" Hawkeye growled with a firm tug of the bandage.

"Ouch! Hawk, I'm sorry I lied—"

"It isn't even that!" Hawkeye ran his fingers over the edge of the bandage to seal it. It had contained the bleeding, but now all she could feel was the agony as her thigh throbbed in time with her heart.

"Well then... I'm sorry, alright? For whatever pissed you off, I'm sorry!"

"Bloody hell, Flit. You just don't get it," Hawkeye groaned, getting to his feet and running a hand through his sandy hair irritably. "You lied, you ditched me, whatever. I'm used to that. But you put yourself in danger—again! If you keep making stupid decisions, you're going to get yourself killed." By the time he stopped ranting, his chest was heaving.

Flit was stumped. For once in her life, she didn't know what to say. Her mouth opened and closed several times while Hawkeye stared at her, anger burning in his eyes. "I—well, the gunfire was crazy, if I didn't—"

"You've been so reckless ever since Ro—"

"We don't have time for this," Posthoc snapped, turning and glaring at them over his shoulder. At his side, Bookworm, the woman who used telecoercion to force the officer to fall sleep, shifted uncomfortably. Posthoc wasn't the only one eager to get out of there.

"I'm good to go," Flit said, groaning as she got to her feet and flicked Hawkeye a narrow-eyed look of warning. Hawkeye kept his arm under hers, helping her hobble after their leader as he turned and walked away.

AN HOUR later Flit was lying on a bed in the medbay, trying her best to block out the endless stream of nagging from her mother. She knew that this would be the first of many telling-offs for what she did to save the officer, and she figured it would be the worst. If she could endure this, she could endure anything. She looked up at the white painted ceiling, trying to count the many flecks and imperfections.

"You could have been killed! What if he sliced your femoral artery instead, huh? Did you think about that? He would have dragged you up to the Hub and you'd be sent to one of their top-secret facilities. Do you know what they do to people there, Flit? No? Well, that's because no one does. Because no one ever comes back alive!" Tinker tugged hard on the bandage she was applying to Flit's leg. She had used her microkinetic abilities to knit the skin over the wound closed, and once the bandage was fastened, she would work to fix the internal damage.

"It's fine, Mum. I had it under control," Flit sighed with a dismissive wave of her hand.

Tinker cocked an eyebrow at her as she settled her hand over the wound. "Really? And is that how you ended up hurt?"

"I was just toying with him, ok? I could've ended it earlier if I had to, but I needed to drag it out until the others arrived. If I didn't let him get a hit in, he would've exerted himself more, and then he'd be dead."

Tinker's soft hand went rigid and she narrowed her eyes at Flit. "You let him hit you?"

Flit shrugged. "Yeah."

"Then you can let yourself heal," Tinker snapped, snatching her hand back and turning on her heel.

Flit's jaw dropped as her mother walked away. "Are you serious?" Flit sat up straighter, wincing as her leg smarted.

"You bet your butt I'm serious. If you're silly enough to let yourself get hurt, then you can deal with the reality of it healing." Tinker started tapping away at the computer in the data station of the room, at the end of the row of five beds.

Flit rolled her eyes. She should have known her mother would do something like this. "Right, if that's the case, can I go now? No use hanging around here." Flit swung her legs over the edge of the bed.

The glare her mother gave her was enough to make her sit back down. "No. I don't know what was on those sleepers he flung at you. You're staying here until I can clear you of any contamination."

Flit could tell by the way that her mother crossed her arms and turned away that she was just being petty. She groaned and brought her forearm up to cover her eyes as she flopped back onto the stiff bed. She could just leave. Escape to somewhere—anywhere—else. But that would be a bad idea. She was already in far too much trouble, and she didn't want Posthoc to drop her from his team because of the drama.

Flit's gaze kept landing where the officer was laying, bound to the medbay bed by the wrists. Her mother had stripped him of his bloodied body-armour and weapons and settled a thin metal inhibitor over his brows to block his access to his abilities. Now that he was lying on his back in a simple pair of Government-issued cargo pants and a fitted white t-shirt, Flit could appreciate the condition his body was in. He was well built; tall and athletic, but also well-proportioned. In the bright white lights of the clinic, the tan on his exposed forearms, neck, and face stood out: a sign that he spent time above ground. His flaxen hair was close-cropped in the standard, practical style of all male Registereds. Her eyes then settled on his neck and her lips curled in distaste. A symbol of two hands cupping an oval holding three interlocking circles was tattooed into his neck. The Government's symbol. She remembered the deep, unnerving crimson colour of his eyes.

"He seems to have come through relatively unscathed," Tinker announced, her tone somewhat softer. Flit's eyes snapped to her mother, embarrassed that she was caught looking at him so closely.

"Yeah, well, he put up a good fight. With abilities like that he must be high ranking for a Registered. I can't remember what he said he was, B or C, maybe," Flit observed, thinking back to how fast he was able to fling heavy objects about.

Tinker frowned. "We'll have to keep that inhibitor on him for a while then." She walked over to the Registered and gently tilted his head so that his face was looking away from Flit. She pressed her fingers to the back of his neck, over the small bump of skin that covered his control chip and closed her eyes.

"What are you doing?"

"I've told you before about the extra restrictions they place in Derivates control chips, haven't I?" Tinker asked. She had slipped into what Flit always thought of as her doctor voice.

Flit nodded. Every Citizen and Derivate had a control chip in them. It was used for identification, and to make payments, check-ins, and the like. For Derivates, it included extra programs that suppressed their psychic abilities, hormones, and emotional responses.

"Yeah?"

"Well, they often come with a... Well, I suppose it's a kill-switch, for lack of a better word. If the chip goes unscanned for more than a certain period, then it will short-circuit the autonomic nervous system. The time varies depending on the Derivate's position, but this fellow here would only have"—Tinker fell silent for a few moments, her fingers shifting on the chip—"maybe another twenty hours or so. You were right, he must be a valuable asset."

"He's not an asset!" The Government might have referred to the Registereds as assets, but her fellow Underground Derivates should have known better. Derivates, like Citizens, were human and deserved to be treated as such.

"I know, I know," Tinker sighed as she opened her eyes and looked at her daughter. Despite the anger between them, her face softened. "But now it won't be an issue. I've tampered with it a bit and figured out how to deactivate it. Luckily, the Government don't account for microkinetics with medical knowledge. Ideally, he wouldn't be down here, but since he is, we have to give him a chance to make his own decisions."

Flit smiled at that news. Registereds didn't come to the Underground often, but when they did, they were always given a choice to return to the surface with their minds tampered or to remain with the Underground.

Tinker made her way back over to the data station where she started entering her medical notes. Flit sat back and let her eyes slide closed. It had been a long day, and she'd been too excited waiting to hear about the outcome of her transfer to sleep much the night before. The reassuring, low buzz of the medbay machines soon had her drifting off to sleep.

"I MUST INFORM YOU, Madam, that if you do not release me, I will be forced to arrest you."

The stern, clipped words roused Flit from her shallow sleep. She rubbed her eyes as she sat up, squinting in the bright lights of the medbay. For a moment she forgot what she was doing on the crisp sheets, but then her thigh flared with pain and everything came back to her. She looked over to where her mother was standing, beside the officer, and frowned.

"Right, well—" Tinker said gently, pausing and looking over at the officer to supply his name so she could continue.

He didn't.

"What's your name?" Tinker asked.

The officer's brows furrowed at the question. "I don't have a name."

"Your designation then," Tinker corrected, the tension at the edges of her voice letting Flit know that she was struggling to keep her patience.

"My designation is KC-847."

Flit snorted.

Both her mother and the officer looked over, realising she was awake. The officer's brows knitted into a single thick line when he saw her. His eyes flicked between her still-sooty face and her neatly bandaged thigh. He seemed to be thinking for a moment before he turned back to Tinker. "Have you performed any medical procedures or scans on me?"

"Yes, I—"

"Then apart from my designation, the only thing I am required to inform you is that you and your colleagues are in violation of the Derivate Act, section seven, which details the improper treatment of Government Property. Of course, that is assuming that you have not obtained permission from the Government to treat one of their assets?"

"Assets? Damn it man, you're a human, not a bloody asset!" Flit snapped, unable to stop herself. She sat a little straighter as her mother glared at her.

But... what was she supposed to do? They had brainwashed the poor guy to think he wasn't even entitled to have his life saved without their stupid permission. It made her wonder how many Derivates had died while waiting for the Government's bureaucratic wheels to decide if the benefits outweighed the costs.

"As you are in breach of section seven, I must arrest you and any co-conspirators to face trial in the Hub."

"Oh, for fuck—"

"Flit!"

Flit rolled her eyes. "Sorry. For goodness' sake. How do you intend to do that while you're strapped to a bed with an inhibitor on, huh?"

The officer looked at the cuffs on his hands and ankles and then back at Tinker. "Please be aware that anything you say or do may be used against you in a court of law," he continued, unperturbed.

Flit just stared at her mother, dumbfounded.

Tinker wasn't so surprised. "Very well officer, I appreciate the warning." Tinker tugged a nearby stool to the bedside, settling onto it so she was at the same height as him. "Now, when Flit and the others brought you in, you had some internal injuries and strain related damage from excessive use of your ability. I worked with that to the best of my ability, but it will still take some time for you to heal fully."

"Doctor, when you say, 'to the best of my ability', what do you mean?" the officer asked. From his tone, it sounded almost like an interrogation.

"Oooh, better not answer that Doctor... He might use it against you in a court of law," Flit said with a slow, mocking nod.

"Flit," Tinker groaned, pinching the bridge of her nose.

"Sorry," Flit said, even though she wasn't sorry at all. "Why don't you sign that release form for me, and I'll be out of your way, yeah?"

"Not a chance."

Flit pursed her lips together and slumped back against the pillows, mumbling, "It was worth a shot."

"Although she is right. Your answer may be used against you," the officer said.

Laughter spluttered from Flit as she doubled over.

Tinker sighed. "My name is Tinker. I'm a microkinetic healer. I used my abilities to muster the natural healing faculties in your body before I interfaced with the control chip, removed the kill-switch protocol, and begun the process of incrementally reducing your hormonal controls."

The officer sat in silence for a moment as he processed that information. "You do not have the authority to do that."

"No, I don't. But given the fact that there are no Government representatives here to provide that consent, I assumed that responsibility. Sorry, KC-847, I know the kill-switch is a way out for officers that get captured, but we don't agree with that down here."

Flit watched the officer's red eyes closely and frowned as this realisation dawned on him. He looked almost… disappointed?

He should be grateful, or at the very least relieved.

"How long do you intend to keep me prisoner?" he asked.

"You're not a prisoner here. You will be our guest until you've learned enough to decide whether you want to return to the Hub or remain with us," Tinker informed him.

"I already know my answer. I am required to return to the Hub immediately, thank you."

Tinker shook her head. "I know you feel that way now, but it's our ethical imperative to give you a chance to shake the emotional and hormonal controls forced on you before you can make that decision."

"And who are 'we'?"

Tinker looked over at Flit as she balanced her options.

"Welcome to the Underground, KC-847." Flit smirked as she met his eyes. He frowned. They had a hell of a lot to teach him.

7

KC-847

"THE UNDERGROUND?" KC-847's brows furrowed as he looked around the room they were in. For the first time, he realised that there were no windows on any of the walls. He had no way of knowing whether she meant that figuratively or literally.

"It just so happens that your precious Government isn't the only organisation that exists around here." Flit shrugged, but there was a smug smile on her face.

KC-847 tried to process what he had learned since entering the tunnels earlier. He had never met a Derivate that wasn't registered before. These ones did not have any order or rank about them. Dressed in a mismatch of fatigues, scrubs, and every-day Citizen clothing, he wasn't sure what to make of them.

"What is it that this 'Underground' does?" KC-847 asked Flit.

Flit looked as though she was about to answer, but Tinker stepped between the two beds. Her eyes, strikingly like Flit's hazel ones, settled on KC-847. A few strands of her light brown hair fell out of her braid and fluttered over her cheek.

"There'll be plenty of time to learn more later, KC-847. For now, you need to rest," Tinker explained.

KC-847 was about to tell her he felt well-rested enough to learn more right away, but she reached out and put her hand on his temple. Before he could pull away something in his mind shifted and he slumped back against the bed, swallowed by a deep, dreamless sleep.

WHEN KC-847 WOKE AGAIN, the unruly Flit was gone. The small room was much quieter for it. The rustling of his sheets as he sat up got the medic's attention. She walked over, gracing him with a gentle smile and reaching out to take his wrist. He did not fight her as she slipped two fingers between the handcuff and his skin. After a few moments she nodded to herself and returned to the computer system to type in some observations.

"I think you might have blown the ability cap of your control chip if Flit hadn't found you when she did," Tinker informed him.

KC-847 sat up a little straighter, every one of his muscles feeling strained well beyond the point of comfort. He shook his head. "That is not possible. It is a cap, an upper limit."

"Well, in normal situations it is. But the amount of adrenaline running through your veins meant that your abilities were straining against it. Given what Flit reported, and the damage that Posthoc and the others told me about, I think you probably have quite a high level of natural talent."

The Government capped the ability of Derivates. It was for their own safety. Young Derivates with little control over their abilities were prone to exerting themselves to the point of death or disability. It was one way the Government ensured that its assets remained healthy. He had known some Derivates to have their caps raised if they were promoted, but it was done carefully and followed by rigorous training.

"Well, if I do, I do not wish to find out. Experimenting with psionic abilities without proper training is dangerous," KC-847 said matter-of-factly, watching Tinker tap away at the screen of the console.

"Or so the Government tells you. It isn't that bad. If you didn't have the control chip you would've been even more effective against those rats. Part of the reason you feel like you've been run over by a hover-truck is because your body had to fight against the control chip as well as the rats."

"Or I would have exerted my abilities and killed myself in the process."

"Potentially, but I think it's unlikely." Tinker turned, leaning back against the console and looking over at him, "When we've all gotten to know you better, I can adjust the settings on your inhibitor so you can test your ability. In a controlled environment, of course."

KC-847 didn't intend to stick around for long enough to get to that point. No, he would escape at the first opportunity and report back to the Hub. He would be reprimanded for failing his mission, but he would accept the punishment. It was the least he deserved, and he respected that. Unlike Flit. She clearly had no respect for her superiors.

"Who is in charge down here? I need to speak to your superior," KC-847 asked, feeling bold with his request. He knew it was a long-shot, but if he had useful information to take back to the Hub, his mission wouldn't have been a complete waste of resources.

"We have two leaders. There are a few levels between me and them, though. What are you hoping to achieve? I am sure I can find you the right person to talk to," Tinker replied.

There was a genuine interest and kindness in Tinker's tone that KC-847 had not received from any medical officer in the Hub. Or any other person, for that matter. He wasn't used to being treated like anything other than a machine.

"I would like to know more about this... band, or group you have. And where we are."

For all intents and purposes, the room KC-847 was in could have been a medical bay in any building in the Hub, save for the lack of windows. The only things here that marred the walls were the monitors and intermittently placed ventilation shafts. The air that came through them had a stale, dank quality to it that was at odds with the vivid, sterile white of the walls. There were five beds; three on the wall that his was against, and two on the one opposite, which also held the clinical console and a door that KC-847 had seen that led to a small storage room.

"Well, luckily for you, I've arrived."

KC-847 looked up as a balding, fifty-something year old man stepped in through the door.

"Oh, Acumen, you're early." Tinker smiled at the newcomer. It wasn't the professional smile someone would give a colleague or acquaintance; there was more relief and friendliness behind it.

"Yeah, I got bored of hanging around the office, so I figured I should come and meet our new guest."

KC-847 looked between the man's bright blue eyes and the wrist restraints holding him to the bed. He felt like more like a prisoner than a guest. He wondered if they treated all their guests this way. Not that he would be around long enough to find out; he would escape before then.

"Guest, prisoner, much of a muchness. Let's not get hung up on semantics, yeah? And good luck with the 'breaking out' thing. No one else has managed it before. But hey, who knows, you may just be the first," Acumen said with a smirk as he leaned back against the door frame.

KC-847 froze, feeling violated. The man had to be a telepath. A strong one, too, as he had read KC-847's thoughts without him even noticing.

"Acumen! What happened to your manners?" Tinker tutted, shaking her head. "I swear, the whole Underground has gone mad." She turned and made for the storage room, rustling through some neatly stacked boxes.

"Ah, you're right. My apologies. Let's start again." Acumen walked over to KC-847's bed. "Good morning, I'm Acumen. I'm a mind-reader. I work in the security department. They've asked me to come here and show you around and teach you more about our fine establishment." Acumen then held out his hand, as if offering for KC-847 to shake. He then let out a soft 'oh' as he remembered the wrist cuffs and leaned in closer.

KC-847 looked at the clock, shocked to see it was morning. He must have been out all night. Nevertheless, he stretched the straps on the cuffs until he could shake the man's hand. Acumen had a firm grip, but nothing that implied he was trying to take control in the relationship. "My designation is KC-847. I'm not authorised to tell you more than that." KC-847 attempted to keep his mind free of any compromising information.

"Don't bother trying to hide it from me, buddy. You aren't thinking anything I haven't seen before." Acumen winked.

KC-847 frowned. Had Acumen come by when he was asleep? If he had compromised anything while he was resting, the Government would not be forgiving. Although KC-847 realised it didn't matter. He just needed to worry about what he could control; and that meant following procedure. He straightened up, just about to recite Acumen's rights when the man interrupted him.

"I'm in breach of Section Seven of the Derivates Act, yada yada yada, yep. What I say might be used against me, blah blah. Got it. Don't care." Acumen shrugged.

KC-847 clamped his mouth shut. There wasn't much point talking when Acumen would just pluck the thoughts right from his head before he could decide whether he wanted to voice them.

"Yeah, you're right buddy I can read it all," Acumen laughed, tapping his forehead. "And yes, I've been told it's highly annoying."

Acumen leaned over, and KC-847 caught a glimpse of what looked like normal street clothes, like any Citizen in the Hub might wear. Like the others, he didn't have red irises or a Government tattoo. KC-847 thought all Derivates had red eyes.

"Well, you're wrong there. The Government use genetic manipulation to change your eyes. They figure it'll make you stand out enough that Citizens won't accidentally mistake you for one of their own," Acumen informed him, once more plucking a question out of his head before he had asked it.

It seemed like a waste of resources for the Government to do that. Though everyone he had seen since meeting Flit had normal eye colours, including Acumen, with his icy blue irises. It made more sense for the Government to have the resources to change eyes than this bunch of misfits.

Acumen strolled over to the monitor Tinker had been working on and leaned over, scanning the screen before shaking his head. "Ah, who am I kidding? I got no idea what any of this gibberish means. Tinker?" He looked over his shoulder, the woman poked her head out of the storeroom. "Can KC-748—"

"847," KC-847 corrected.

"Sorry. 847. Can he go for a stroll? I'm sure his arms and legs could do with a stretch."

"That's a good idea. My shift'll be over soon, I'm sure Tonic will appreciate some time to get his head around the handover notes before diving in." Tinker nodded. She walked over and unfastened the cuffs on KC-847's wrists.

With the use of his hands returned to him, KC-847 saluted her. She may have treated him illegally, but she was still a doctor and deserved the respect that came with the title. "For the good of all," he recited crisply.

Tinker froze, her fingers hovering over the cuff on his left ankle. She looked up at him warily. "We don't say that in the Underground. That is the Government's motto, not ours."

KC-847 was shocked. Everyone said it on the surface. "Is there a rule against it?" he asked, wondering why anyone would eschew such a basic sign-off.

Tinker frowned. "Technically, no, but—"

"Yes," Acumen interrupted, ignoring the warning look Tinker shot him. "It's this whole big rule down here. Saying that is the fastest way to get yourself into trouble. Best avoid it, hmm?"

KC-847 considered this revelation. If he was going to have anything useful to report when he escaped, getting into trouble would only get in his way. He could stop saying it, if it meant getting more intel.

Tinker finished undoing the last cuff, and with a sense of resolve, KC-847 sat up and swung his legs over the edge of the bed. He looked at Acumen, still amazed they were going to let him walk around their base. Were they mad? What was to stop him from trying to escape, or from hurting their people?

"This'll stop you." Acumen tapped his head again. "And the inhibitor. And the fact that you don't know how to get out of here. It's a veritable labyrinth out there. It'd be wiser to sit tight for a while, gather as much intelligence as you can, and then make your escape once you have fooled us into trusting you."

KC-847 could not argue with that.

THE FIRST THING KC-847 noticed as Acumen led him through the tunnels was that the entire complex was underground. He had not seen a single window as they wound through the twisting maze. He had tried to keep track of the turns, but between the mental strain and the vigilance required to stay safe in a hostile place, his mind just couldn't manage it.

"Don't worry, these tunnels are even confusing for us sometimes," Acumen supplied.

KC-847 looked at the man out of the corner of his eye. He seemed to read minds almost like a reflex. Back in the Hub mind-readers were kept on a tight leash. Their abilities represented an invasion of privacy that ordinary Citizens couldn't tolerate. KC-847 had never come across someone capable of Acumen's level of skill before, but he now understood why it was an issue.

"To be fair, I don't read everyone's mind. I'm very well behaved if I stumble on something secret. Unfortunately, I need to be in your head, given how you came to be with us. But you're a smart guy, I'm sure you understand that," Acumen told him in a calm, casual tone as they turned from the grey lined corridors into ones painted a gentle light blue.

KC-847 wasn't in a position to disagree; even if he was, he didn't think he would. He was too distracted by the sound of youthful laughter and footsteps echoing down the tunnels. A moment later a coloured streak shot out of a corridor further down and to his left.

"Seeker, come back!" a voice called.

The pitter-patter got louder as the streak, a young boy, zigzagged towards Acumen and KC-847. Acumen smirked at the child and stepped back, flattening himself against the wall and gesturing for KC-847 to follow suit.

"Acumen!" The child skidded to a halt and flung his arms around the man. Acumen chuckled and patted the child's back before holding him at arms' length.

"I'd love to stay and chat, but I'm on duty, buddy. Gotta show the new guest around," Acumen apologised, gesturing to KC-847. "I know, it sucks. But I'll come and play chess with you in the Mess after dinner. Promise."

The child looked disappointed for all of a breath before he turned to KC-847. "You... You're... Woah!" The child's eyes widened with awe. He stepped even closer and stared up at KC-847's neck tattoo.

"Seeker, get back here," a woman cried out as she jogged down the corridor. When she reached her child, she dragged him away from KC-847 as though he were some rabid, saliva-slathered mongrel. The woman cast Acumen an angry, reproachful look.

"But Mum, he's a—"

"A Registered. Yes, Seeker, he is." From the way she spat the words it sounded as though she held as much animosity for KC-847 as any of the Citizens in the Hub. Clearly, not everyone in the Underground was as tolerant of his presence as Acumen and Tinker pretended to be.

"That. Is. So. Cool!" The child bounced from foot to foot.

The mother's frown deepened. "Come on, Seek, we need to go. You've got an appointment with Patch. We shouldn't keep him waiting." The woman tried to lead the child away by his shoulders, but after a few steps he wiggled free of her grip and dashed back to KC-847.

"What's your name?" Seeker asked, looking up with wide eyes.

"Ah—" KC-847 stopped, not sure Seeker's mother would appreciate him interacting with the child. He had seen Citizen children being reprimanded for talking to Derivates in the Hub, and he did not want to get this child into trouble.

"Go on," Acumen urged, earning another angry glare from the mother.

"My designation is KC-847."

Seeker scrunched up his face. "That's a weird name," he said as he chewed it over. After a moment he shrugged and held his hand out for KC-847 to shake. KC-847 looked at the mother with an apology in his eyes as he gently shook the boy's hand. "My name's Seeker. I'm a postcog. Cool, huh? You're so tanned! I've never been above ground. Is that where you're from? Oh wow, maybe after I see Patch, I can find you and you can tell all about what it's like up there. I would give up all my ice-cream for a week to see the sun. Is it really as bright as—"

"Woah, slow down, Bud," Acumen chuckled, patting Seeker's shoulder. "KC-847 is new, we don't want to scare him off, do we?" Seeker sighed and shook his head, his shaggy black hair tousled by the movement. "You'd better get going before your mother has a panic attack and needs mouth-to-mouth from Patch to revive her. Again."

The boy cackled with laughter, but the woman's entire body stiffened as Acumen winked at her.

"I swear Acumen, one of these days I'm going to—"

"Oh, come now, you don't want to say that in front of polite company," Acumen tutted, shaking his head. "Oh, by the way, where's your appointment with Patch? Tunnel Forty-Two?"

"Acumen!" The woman's face went as red as KC-847's eyes, and he worried she might burst a blood vessel.

Acumen howled with laughter before putting his arm around KC-847's shoulder. "Alright, we've lingered long enough. See you both later!" Acumen ushered KC-847 down the corridor, away from the woman who was still fuming. He was chuckling to himself and muttering under his breath about young love. KC-847 did not understand what he had just witnessed.

KC-847 was silent for the longest time, thinking over the encounter he'd just had. Thankfully, Acumen left him to his thoughts. There were so many new people, and so many of them were self-professed Derivates. Everything he had ever been taught pointed to the fact that the Government controlled Derivate breeding. It wasn't possible that there could be so many of them hiding in the Underground. He thought about the woman he had been on a mission to capture. Clearly, she had known where to go. She may have chosen a terrible route through the tunnels, but if Flit had found KD-035 before KC-847 and the others had arrived, they may have brought down here. Is this what happened to the Registered Derivates that went AWOL?

"Sometimes." Acumen's voice split through KC-847's musings like a warm knife through butter. KC-847 looked over at him as they slowed to a stop in a four-way junction. It was a large space with a few seats, a drinking fountain, and a tech console in the middle. Several people were relaxing on the seats and taking turns passing a tablet around with some game on it. They were so absorbed in their activities that they didn't notice Acumen and KC-847 walking by.

"We don't usually find Registereds like the one you were after soon enough, unless they are sent to us by one of our operatives and we have warning. Navigating those tunnels is a dangerous exercise. There's a reason that most of us don't step outside of the Residence." Acumen gestured around them with a slow sweep of his arm.

"So that child was telling the truth? He's never been to the Hub? Never seen the sun?"

Acumen nodded with a grim expression on his face. "That's right. A lot of the younger generation haven't had the pleasure of getting surface-side. We used to try and get as many families living part-time in the Hub as we could, but in recent years it has gotten more… dangerous."

"When you say, 'a lot of the younger generation', what do you mean? How many children are there down here?"

Acumen's lips twisted, his eyes drifting up to the right as he seemed to think about it.

"I don't know the exact number. Between security protocol and the fact that new ones keep cropping up all the time, I can't say," Acumen explained. As far as KC-847 could tell, he was being honest.

In the Hub they only allowed the birth of ninety-nine Derivates per calendar year. If the residents of the Underground bred unchecked the results could be catastrophic. "How many of them are Derivates?"

"Almost all of them. We have a few Citizens that had gotten on the wrong side of the law for helping us or whatever, but we're mostly Derivates down here."

KC-847 was stunned into silence. Not only were these people living in these tunnels, apparently in reasonable comfort, but there were entire generations of them. How did they not destroy themselves with their powers as they matured? How did they not destroy each other?

"If a child grows up being taught how to harness their abilities, the risk of them losing control is significantly reduced. We believe in empowering people, not restricting them."

"That sounds dangerous."

"A weapon's only as dangerous as the person holding it." Acumen shrugged and then gestured to a tunnel to their left. "Let's keep moving. I'll show you the residential area. I think you'll find it much nicer than what you're used to."

8

FLIT

THE HOURS SPENT in the medbay dragged by slowly after Tinker knocked KC-847 out. Flit wasn't sure if it was because of the continuing ache in her leg, or the frustration of having to see a human being who was so complicit in his own suppression. She understood that Registereds' had little say in their complicity, but the fact that he believed the lies wholeheartedly made her want to break something.

By the time Flit's mother tired of her complaining and 'discharged' her, it was the early hours of the morning. She teleported her tired self to the temporary quarters her family shared in the Residence and fell asleep the moment she collapsed onto her bed.

Later that morning, Flit woke to the horrid, high-pitched mewling of her alarm. She peeled her gritty eyes open and groaned as she looked at the clock. She'd only gotten two hours of sleep. She would have ignored her alarm, but she didn't want to miss out on training. While slaving away in a boring admin job in the Hub, she daydreamed about her weekend training sessions. There was no way she was going to miss out because of the fuss of the previous night.

Flit got up and went for a shower. The pressure of the spray through the waterproof dressing was enough to make her groan in pain. If her mother had healed the wound properly, it would have been nothing more than an irritating itch by now. But no, when Tinker wanted to teach Flit a lesson, she went all out.

When Flit emerged from the bathroom, dressed in her training gear, her mother was standing there waiting in the hallway.

Tinker looked tired, but that was normal after a full day of work in the Hub and a night shift in the medbay. Her hazel eyes scanned up Flit up and down before narrowing. "And where do you think you're going?"

Flit gestured to her fatigues. "Training."

"You're on light duties."

"Since when?"

"Since anything more will tear that open." Tinker nodded towards her thigh.

Flit's hands balled into fists at her side. "I can still train."

"Not according to the report I submitted this morning. Sorry, Flit, but you won't be training again until I grant you medical clearance."

Flit's teeth ached from how hard she gritted them. Her mother wasn't sorry, she did it on purpose. She knew how much Flit loved training. "That isn't fair." It took every ounce of control Flit had to keep her tone civil.

"No, but life isn't fair. You made a dangerous decision yesterday, and today you face the consequences. You need to learn, Flit; you're good, but not invincible."

Flit didn't bother answering. She teleported right through the open door before her mother could close it. Her leg hurt too much to walk, so she teleported the rest of the way through the tunnels that led to the training grounds. Light duties or not, she would train.

"I CAN'T LET you in here with that."

Flit's nails bit into the palm of her hands as she looked up at Posthoc. He stood in the doorway to the training room, between her and the others, and pointed at her leg. Her normally fitted training pants were bulkier where she had the bandage wrapped around her already shapely thigh. "Why not?"

Posthoc rolled his eyes. "Flit, please. Your mother sent your medical report through before I got out of bed this morning."

"But I'm a teleporter. I don't even need to walk to get around!" Flit argued. She was grasping for excuses, but she had to try. She refused to let this mess impede her progress. "Please let me train."

"No, sorry. But you can watch." Posthoc gestured to the bench seat outside the training room window. He stepped back and the door slid shut between them with a definitive *schlick*. Flit looked between the door and bench a few times, trying to figure out how far she could push the issue.

"Flit, you're out. How are you?"

Flit turned, thigh burning at the sudden movement. Her shoulders hunched as she looked at Hawkeye. "I'm pissed off. Mum put me on light duties."

Hawkeye winced. There wasn't a single member of the security team that would be content with light duties. He walked over and pointed to the bulk around her thigh. "She didn't heal it, huh?"

"Nope. Apparently, I need to learn from my mistakes," Flit snapped.

"I can't say I blame her. What you did could've gone so wrong—"

"Whose side are you—"

"I'm not taking sides." Hawkeye raised his hands at Flit's accusation. "You made a reckless decision. You went into the Nest alone, even when we knew there were Government agents there. You could have been killed. Or worse!"

Flit groaned and slumped against the wall of the training room. She should have known he wouldn't let it go so easily. "I had it under control."

"Your injury suggests otherwise." Hawkeye gestured to her thigh.

Flit stood taller, putting weight on her leg and ignoring the pain. "I knew what I was doing, Hawk. I kept him busy while waiting for you guys to arrive. If I didn't let him think he could hit me, he would have overdone it. What's the point in saving him from the rats if he died from exertion?" Flit asked, her voice low with frustration. She looked over her shoulder and back into the training room where their teammates had formed a wide circle and started their warm-up stretches.

"That is, quite literally, the worst excuse you've ever made." Hawkeye sighed, shaking his head. He peered past Flit to look into the room behind her. The rest of their team had formed a circle and started stretching to warm up. "I have to get going, but maybe after this we can catch up over a snack, ok?"

It was the closest thing to a peace offering that Flit was likely to get. She sighed and nodded, teleporting one step to the side to let him pass. He reached out, squeezing her shoulder reassuringly before he disappeared into the training room. Flit jumped over to the bench and flopped onto it. Even if she couldn't take part in the session, she could still learn from it.

9

KC-847

ACUMEN AND KC-847 continued their tour of the Underground. They passed by a dozen different people who all seemed to be up for the morning, ready to get their days started. Every now and again, KC-847 caught sight of his own reflection in a screen or metal panel, and he saw the thin circlet over his brow. The Government only ever used restrictive devices on unruly Derivates. He had worked hard to behave and avoid the visible shame of wearing one. It was no wonder the various people they walked past gave them a wide berth.

Just as KC-847 was about to conclude that the Underground was nothing but tunnels, Acumen broke the silence that had fallen between them.

"Welcome to the Residence."

The wide passage they were walking through opened into a cavern that was nothing short of immense and chaotic. It held an entire apartment building in it that was as wide as any in the Hub and soared well above the warm glow of full-spectrum sunlamps that lit the cavern up like daylight. Greenery spilled from every join of glass in the building, almost as if nature was trying to reclaim the block. Expansive hydroponic gardens wrapped around the building in a ring of sweet-smelling nature. It looked, for all intents and purposes, like a normal apartment building. Except for the out-of-control weeds strangling the exterior.

"It's a vertical garden. We use the plants to help control the air quality," Acumen explained.

That knowledge didn't make it look any less unkempt.

Somewhere between rows of leafy greens, the laughter of children echoed through the cavern. KC-847 stopped and looked over, surprised but not sure of what to make of it. He never thought a settlement like this would exist, let alone one so well-equipped. A few rag-tag Derivates who had escaped the control of the Government, maybe. But this? They were living full lives down here, sustaining themselves. Right under the nose of those they sought to escape.

"Impressive, huh?" A smug smirk tugged at Acumen's lips.

KC-847 shook his head. "I did not say that."

"No, but you were thinking it. Don't worry, your fascination with us will remain strictly between you and me." Acumen gave him a melodramatic wink. He clapped his hands and rubbed them together as looked around, as if trying to figure out where to start.

"Is there enough food to feed everyone down here?" KC-847 asked, gesturing to the generous ring of gardens around the Residence.

"Yes." Acumen nodded. "We have a few other gardens and some areas to maintain livestock. We don't feast every night, but we do well enough. You'll enjoy the food down here. Much better than that tasteless, lab-grown junk the Government feeds you."

KC-847 frowned. The Government catered for all his nutritional needs. Adding in extra flavours and textures wasn't efficient or necessary.

"There is more to food than basic nutritional requirements," Acumen told him, exasperated. "Come on, let me show you the living quarters." Acumen led him down a stone path laid into real grass.

Children squealed and giggled as they chased each other through the rows of the gardens close to the apartment building as KC-847 walked past. One boy picked up a handful of dirt, ready to throw it at the girl on the other side of a fern, but she stomped her foot and yelled, "No! Throw it at him!", pointing at a boy beside him. The psionic coercion in her tone was strong enough that even

KC-847 felt it. At the last second, her attacker's hand jerked to the side, and he dumped the dirt all over his friend. The girl giggled maniacally, while the muddied child whined, "No fair! We said no powers!"

KC-847 shook his head. As a child, he had been on a strict regimen of academic education and telekinesis training. He had powers and was therefore responsible for learning to control them. Using powers flippantly was punishable by a reduced cap or solitary confinement. He had never seen Derivate children playing like that before.

When they reached the large double doors of the Residence, Acumen pressed his hand against a security panel to the side, and they slid open. The interior of the building was just as visually over-stimulating as the outside. Used to the crisp, utilitarian design preferred in the Hub, the splattering of screens and bursts of colour on every wall made it impossible for KC-847 to figure out what to look at first.

"Welcome to the lobby. This whole first level is a dedicated community space. Over there we have some commons seating." Acumen gestured to his right where three dozen sets of plush, comfortable looking sofas of all different shapes, sizes, and colours were arranged in various configurations.

The next gesture guided KC-847's eyes to a large transparent data screen against the outer wall of the building, surrounded by close to a hundred seats, all with arms that had their own datapads attached. "That side is where we hold some of our smaller, unofficial community briefings and meetings.

"To the rear, we have a recreation space: gym, spa, sauna, that sort of thing; and on the other side is a set of casual meeting and activity rooms. During the day they're used as school rooms for the kids while their parents are out on duty, but in the evenings, everyone is free to use the AR systems for fun." As Acumen spoke, he pointed to the walled-off section beyond the bank of elevators in the middle of the lobby.

The Underground Derivates had access to almost every luxury available to Citizens. The focus on recreation and socialisation in the space was clear, and most of the screens flashed photos of various people talking and laughing with each other. It was such a contrast to what KC-847 was used to. If these people had enough time to mess around, they clearly weren't working or training hard enough.

"Here, come on," Acumen said, guiding him over the elevator. Once more he used his handprint to activate the switch panel. The elevator arrived in an instant. They stepped inside. The button for level six was glowing softly, but Acumen chose the seventh-floor instead.

"Most of the living quarters are taken, but we've got a couple of empties on level seven. One's being prepped today for a new resident—"Acumen stopped and looked at KC-847, understanding dawning on his face. "Oh, of course. You've already met her."

KC-847 thought back to the brown-haired, hazel-eyed woman who had taken him prisoner. His lips pressed together in disapproval as he remembered the haphazard way she had played with him in that junction. Almost like a cat playing with a trapped mouse. Except, he hadn't realised he was the mouse. She was cocky, that was one thing he could say for her. And outspoken. He couldn't imagine how she had survived for so long without running her mouth and getting herself into trouble.

"Who said she hasn't? Flit's the reigning queen of trouble," Acumen chuckled as the elevator shot up. "She is a handful, and cocky to a fault, but her heart's in the right place. In all fairness, if she wasn't such a firecracker, you would've been rat food."

KC-847 gritted his teeth as the elevator doors opened, his cheeks burning and his stomach churning uncomfortably. He had forgotten that the telepath was spying on his thoughts. He regretted that Acumen has witnessed the ones about Flit. He didn't know her well enough to judge her.

Acumen walked KC-847 down the main corridor, past a common room and communal kitchen, to an apartment at the back of the building. When he pushed the first door open, KC-847 was impressed. Bright and airy, with enough room for a comfortable sized bed, a desk, storage space, and a private bathroom, it was something that not even the highest ranking Derivates in the Hub would dream of living in.

"All of this space is for one person?" KC-847 asked, turning around as he took it all in.

"In this apartment? Yes, although there are some people who share apartments on this level."

"Why would they need to share? Do you not have enough room for everyone?" KC-847 asked, wondering just how many people must live in the Underground if that was the case.

"No, we've got more than enough apartments. Some people want to live together." Acumen gestured to the bed at the back of the room. There were two pillows on it, and enough room for two bodies.

KC-847 furrowed his brows; it made little sense. Citizens only shared beds in order to reproduce. Derivates did not need to do so, as they were bred using artificially inseminated surrogates in a laboratory setting. They felt no natural inclination towards intimacy.

Acumen laughed out loud.

KC-847 looked at him, not sure what was so funny.

"Sorry." Acumen cleared his throat before continuing. "Sometimes I forget the lies they feed you Registereds. We don't—ugh—we don't call it breeding down here. People don't breed, animals do. People have one-night stands, or casual sex, or they fall in love... they create families, even generations. And the people who share a bed? Well, they do it because they want to."

Acumen stopped and waited for that to sink in.

KC-847 blinked. "They... You... feel the desire to engage in physical intimacy?" KC-847 asked. "That can't be right. The genes activated by the Derivacy mutation reduce emotions and desire. Only Citizens reproduce sexually."

Acumen sighed, looking away for a moment as he wrestled with what he wanted to say next. "No. It's the control chip that the Government implants in Registereds that controls emotions and sexual desire."

KC-847's cheeks flushed at the thought. He pressed his palms up against the unusual warmth. His stomach churned at the thought of intimacy. In the past, speaking about Derivate or Citizen breeding had just been a fact of life. His head spun with the realisation that maybe, for the first time, he felt something other than unswerving obedience. He reached behind his head and rubbed the small bump where the control chip rested beneath his skin.

"I know it is a lot to take in, but it's true. Tinker is reducing the regulation of your chip. She can't let it all go at once—that would be enough to overwhelm even the most sensible person—but she is giving you yourself back, a bit at a time."

Tinker had told KC-847 that she had reduced the level of the chip's control, but he hadn't understood the consequences of that. He thought back to his time in the Hub, the years he spent in the Law Enforcement Department chasing after the Citizens who had lost control of their emotions; the rage, lust, greed, jealousy, hate…

"KC-847, please, take a breath." Acumen's deep voice held a steadying sway as it washed over him. "I know this is overwhelming, but we'll be with you for the entire process. If you decide that you can't live with your natural hormone levels, then we can get you back to a point you're comfortable with. All we ask is that you try. Right now you're just following orders. We want to give you a chance to live."

KC-847 could have sworn he had been living a full life in the Hub. A simple life. He had never wanted for more. Or had he? And had those desires been suppressed by the Government?

10
———
FLIT

FLIT WATCHED AS HAWKEYE, Swipe, Link, Clarity, Tweak, and Sway went through the training exercise that Posthoc had laid out for them. He'd set the training hall up to look like a random four-way rail junction teeming with holographic foes in the form of Government Officers. It was one of those rare sessions where the whole team was available to work together; normally, they had one pair working patrol, but Posthoc must have asked the Red or Green team to cover for them.

The scenarios were always valuable exercises, but from what Flit could tell, the team were missing her ability to jump around and take out enemies quickly and quietly. Hawkeye was doing his best to get a good visual gauge of the situation and relay it to the others. Tweak, their microkinetic, was messing with the lighting systems to give his team an advantage. When the lights went out, Clarity stood to the side and called out orders into the darkness, adjusting their movements based on what her precognition showed her.

Flit changed the viewing window to night-vision to watch the fight progressing just in time to see Swipe throw her arms up, pushing a dozen enemies away at once. Beside her, Hawkeye was engaged in hand-to-hand combat with some projections, with Sway at his side. Sway's power of telecoercion was useless again holographic enemies, but he, like Hawkeye, was a strong fighter.

"Swipe, come around from behind. Tweak, start thinning the

crowd." Link, Sway's girlfriend, called out adjustments to Clarity's orders based on what she read from the different team member's minds. Together, they functioned as synchronised parts of one team, instead of half a dozen people fighting on their own. Flit's team, the Blue team, was well balanced as far as powers went. Their patrol pairs were based on what abilities best complemented one another, and her being out on medical leave threw the whole balance off.

Halfway through the session, her nails were digging into her thighs and her toes were tapping a rapid beat on the concrete floor. It was difficult to resist the urge to teleport into the room to help them out, but she was already on shaky ground with Posthoc. Still, if she wasn't on light duties, the exercise would already be over with.

"Ooh, light duties, huh? Your mother is tough."

Flit startled, turning as Acumen sauntered into the observation area. She frowned at his familiar face, lined with subtle crow's feet and framed in grey hair. Beside him was—

"I believe you've already met KC-847. I'm just giving him a tour of the facilities," Acumen informed her with a grin.

Flit rolled her eyes as she got to her feet, trying not to wince as the movement put pressure on her thigh. "Please forgive Acumen. He has a habit of stating the obvious to sound wise and important. But don't let him fool you, he's neither of those things," Flit stage-whispered to KC-847. The poor scarlet eyed guy looked between Flit and Acumen, uncertain of what to make of the banter.

"Don't worry, buddy, Flit's joking," Acumen reassured the officer.

KC-847's shoulders fell. Flit could swear she saw relief in his eyes.

"So, they stuck you with Acumen, huh?" Flit asked, feeling sorry for KC-847. Acumen may have had a good sense of humour, and be a generally fun guy to be around, but he was one of the best telepaths in the Underground. Nothing slipped by him. "I hope he has been polite and kept out of your mind."

"Telepaths in the Hub aren't permitted to intrude without authorisation or suspicion of serious risk of harm," KC-847 recited.

Flit was about to write it off as him being a robot when Acumen spoke up. "Well, you're not in the Hub anymore, and the crew down here love my comforting presence in their minds." Acumen patted KC-847 on the shoulder.

Flit snorted a laugh and shook her head. "We do not." She looked over at KC-847, briefly overwhelmed by just how tall he was. Most people towered over her, but she guessed that he had to be at least fifteen centimetres over Hawkeye's one hundred and seventy-five. "Look, if you stick around, maybe I'll teach you some ways to keep that bugger out of your head."

KC-847 looked between Flit and Acumen, eyes wide at the offer. Acumen shrugged; he would not block her reaching out a metaphorical hand of friendship. Flit was about to say something when KC-847's eyes flicked past her to focus on the fight going on inside the training room. His expression hardened.

"Your simulator renders Government Derivates as training targets?" His voice was stiff.

Flit nodded, lifting a shoulder in half a shrug. "And Citizen Officers, hostile Citizens and mutant fauna." Her explanation didn't soften the look on KC-847's face.

Acumen cleared his throat. "Government Officers, Derivates or not, are a real threat down here. The last conflict between their forces and ours resulted in the loss of three good people. We need to train for every eventuality, even if it means fighting against those who are just doing their jobs."

Flit frowned as she realised what KC-847's concern was. "We don't *want* to fight anyone," she told him. "If it were up to us, we would all live on the surface, equal with the Citizens in both responsibilities and rights. We were forced down here by Government laws and the threat of genocide."

"Because you are dangerous. We are dangerous. Our powers are an environmental aberration that creates an imbalance between us and the Citizens," KC-847 stated in that robotic tone of his, reciting what they had drilled into him since birth.

Flit rounded on him. "Has anyone harmed you since you've been down here?"

"Well, no—"

"Have you been locked in a cell without any sustenance?"

"No, I—"

"Oh, what about torture? Has anyone strapped you up to some horrid machine that makes you realise that some things are worse than death?"

"Not to a machine, but—"

"Have you seen anyone spontaneously combust because they weren't in full control of their powers?"

He pressed his lips together. "I've only been down here for—"

"So how can you say we're inherently dangerous when you have witnessed none of that? When we are allowing one of our greatest threats to walk among us? Would your precious Government do that? No, they'd kill us on sight—even the kids!"

KC-847's shoulders tensed. "Do you always interrupt people?" he snapped.

Flit's eyes widened. KC-847 stepped back, brushing his fingers over his inhibitor self-consciously, as though he was as surprised by his sudden outburst as Flit was. Flit and Acumen looked at each other for a drawn out moment before they both laughed, the tension slowly draining out of the space. Flit had to hand it to KC-847. He had guts.

"I only interrupt people when they try to tell me that my friends and family don't deserve to be treated like humans."

KC-847's posture softened as he looked at Flit, his red gaze catching hers. The intensity of the curiosity in his eyes made her suck in a breath. Acumen's head cocked to the side with interest, picking up the tension. Flit cleared her throat and tore her eyes from the Registered's. "We're all human, and we deserve to be treated as such. Not like mutant rodents, left to rot underground without ever seeing real sunlight."

Flit's words were the softest she had ever spoken in front of KC-847, her righteous fire simmering back to a moderate smoulder. She scooted over on the bench so there was enough room for Acumen and KC-847. "Why don't you two sit down? I assume you're here to watch the training."

Acumen beamed, walking over to her and patting her shoulder before he sat on the opposite end of the bench. KC-847 had no choice but to sit between them. Given that he wore an inhibitor but no cuffs, it was a risky move on Acumen's behalf. Flit didn't mind. If he tried anything, she could get away from him, injured or not. Somehow, she doubted KC-847 would take that risk.

KC-847 sat down on the bench and the three of them watched as a swarm of mutant spiders skittered through the holographic tunnels towards Blue team. Clarity and Tweak raced back to the fire-door control panel and started fiddling with it, while Hawkeye relayed numbers and positions to Swipe. Swipe, the blonde bombshell, flung the large, dog-sized spiders into one another.

"Your macrokinetic has a very high power yield," KC-847 commented quietly as he followed Swipe's exploits.

Flit chuckled derisively. "And a huge ego to match."

The simulated spiders' bodies made sickening crunching sounds as they slammed into the walls. Clarity yelled out a warning, and everyone ducked. A moment later, one of the pipes that the spiders had been skittering along creaked, snapped, and fell, plummeting towards the team. Swipe had it, though, throwing her hand out and stopping the heavy metal as Hawkeye unbuckled his pistol and provided cover fire.

"I'm sure she won't mind," Acumen said, speaking out of the blue. It wasn't unusual for him.

Flit didn't take her eyes off the fight, wishing she was in there to cull the rear of the swarm.

"I, uh… Miss?"

Acumen snorted at KC-847's formal attempts to get Flit's attention.

"Shut it, Acumen. At least KC-847 has manners." Flit leaned forward to cast Acumen a glare. When she leaned back, she looked up at KC-847 with a polite smile. "Yes?"

"Why are you watching this?" he asked. "I've been told that most people have jobs down here."

Flit frowned, biting back a bitter response. "I should be in there." She gestured towards the training room. "I'm part of Blue team. We usually go on patrols or train. But I'm on light duties because some guy threw a jagged railway sleeper into my thigh."

KC-847 looked down at her leg, studying it with an intense

furrow of his brow. Flit shifted uncomfortably under his scrutiny, as innocent as it was. "None of the doctors healed your wound?"

Flit shook her head. "No, Mum—ah, Tinker—decided that I should learn from my mistakes. So, she cleared out any contaminants and knitted it together to prevent bleeding. The rest has to heal naturally."

KC-847 looked shocked. Whether it was because Flit let it slip that Tinker was her mother, or because she was refused advanced healing, she wasn't sure.

"Yeah, Tinker may have a great bedside manner, but you don't want to piss her off. You can see where Flit inherited her hot-blooded personality from," Acumen said.

KC-847 looked down at his hands for a few moments before returning his gaze to Flit. "I am sorry I got you restricted to light duties. I know it is not ideal to be side-lined and miss out on training."

Flit looked at him, the natural shields she kept around herself because of his red eyes and Government tattoo softening at his concession. She shrugged as if it was no big deal. "You can't apologise for it if I let you hit me."

"You... let me hit you?" The disbelief in his tone was palpable.

"Yeah. I had to keep you busy while I waited for the others to arrive."

"I doubt that," KC-847 said matter-of-factly, making Acumen smirk "I saw the shock on your face when I hit you. I was close to capturing you."

Flit laughed. "You couldn't get a hit on me if you tried." The idea was preposterous. "And there is no way you could have caught me."

"I almost had you. Without the lights you would not have lasted much longer."

"Oh, really?" Flit turned towards him, forgetting the fight in the training room. She sat up a little straighter. "I tell you what, when you decide that down here is the right place to be, and you get that inhibitor off, you and I will go for round two. Deal?"

Flit reached out, offering him her hand.

KC-847 grinned as he took her hand and shook it. "Deal."

11

KC-847

KC-847 SPENT his first two weeks in the Underground learning his way around and trying to understand the size and structure of the population. Even though the tunnels were nothing short of labyrinthine, he got a good idea of the layout the main areas, and every adventure with Acumen resulted in him meeting new people. Acumen explained that everyone worked a range of different shifts to keep the Underground running and protected.

KC-847 never got past the residential tunnels and caverns, but he discovered the most frequented entrances and exits by noting the directions that people heading out on patrols took. Still, he couldn't formulate an escape strategy while Acumen was around, and he spent almost all of his waking moments with the man.

After watching that first training session with Acumen and Flit, Acumen took him to more, because he saw how much KC-847 enjoyed watching the team at work. Flit wasn't at any of the sessions because she was either in the Hub or on light duties. It was a double-life that still shocked KC-847. He didn't know how unregistered Derivates like Flit escaped the notice of the Government, but he wanted to find out.

KC-847 tried as hard as he could to remain resistant to the obvious charms of the Underground. Most people were cautious around him, but they had all been polite with only a few exceptions —namely, the people who couldn't hide their disgust at his red eyes and Government tattoo. The food was even more delicious than Acumen had suggested, and after being discharged from Tinker's care, he was assigned his own room in one of the nearby tunnels. Even though Acumen claimed it was more of a cell compared to the suites in the Residence, he had his own space with a bed, a bathroom, and more creature comforts than he would ever have on the Surface.

KC-847 was sitting in his room, catching up on the Hub news on his datapad, when a crisp knocking stole his attention. "Come in," he called out.

As usual, the door slid open to reveal Acumen.

Until KC-847 decided whether he wanted to join the Underground, and his decision was approved, he required supervision to leave his room. It didn't bother him; he could understand the logic, and now that he was used to the invasiveness of Acumen's abilities, he'd grown to appreciate the man for his easy manner and open-mindedness.

"Naww, you're in a sweet mood today. I appreciate you too, buddy," Acumen teased with a smirk. "I said yesterday that we'd check out the Red Team's training session, but the plan has changed." Acumen looked at KC-847 after he said this, watching for a reaction.

Assuming he had not stated the plan right away because he was dragging out the big reveal, KC-847 prompted, "And?" He was curious about the change in their routine, but not surprised.

"We're meeting with Harmony and Divvy instead."

KC-847 straightened and his brows knitted together as he looked at Acumen. Up in the Hub, no one knew who the true leaders of the Government were. They worked in conclave, handing decisions to the department heads without ever identifying themselves. KC-847 had assumed the leaders in the Underground were the similar, except people knew who they were. He'd never seen either of them, not even in passing. The sudden announcement of a meeting with them made his gut churn. He gritted his teeth; he never got nervous like that on the Surface.

"That's because your control chip prevented unnecessary anxiety. Your chip was set up high, too. It's a new feeling for you, but not an unreasonable one. I mean, shit, I still get nervous when I have to see those two. But you'll be fine. They may be our leaders, but they're reasonable." Acumen shrugged, trying to put KC-847 at ease.

Arguing that it wasn't anxiety would have been a defensive lie. He was torn between escaping and sticking around to gather more information. He didn't think he would have a meeting with the leaders before he figured out what he wanted to do for himself.

"Come on, best we don't keep them waiting." Acumen's grin faded as he stepped back. KC-847 took one last look around his room and nodded. It hit him for the first time that he may not be there tomorrow, and he wasn't sure how he felt about that.

This time when Acumen led him through the tunnels, they took a right down a passage that he'd never been down. The residential areas of the Underground had light blue walls and the tunnels around the service areas like medbay and the Mess hall were grey, but the new tunnel was stark white. Once they reached the end, they found a solid metal blast door with a control panel on it. Acumen completed a handprint scan, a retina scan, and tapped a password into the panel before the door slid open smoothly.

Behind that door, there was a large, open plan war-room space. Transparent information screens were attached to complex consoles, each one attended by a harried looking worker. The spaces not dedicated to consoles were home to holographic projector tables displaying various mesh tunnel maps that their operators were surveying. KC-847 didn't recognise most of the faces, and they all continued their work without looking up to see who had arrived.

The perimeter of the large room was lined with a variety of doors and glass-walled offices. Acumen walked to the back and pressed his palm against a reader beside a non-descript empty wall panel. The panel pulled back and slid into a hidden cavity in the wall itself, and he gestured for KC-847 to follow him. The corridor behind was plain, the concrete that same stark white as the outer tunnel. The lights overhead buzzed in a way that showed an isolated generator was powering them. They passed several unmarked, dull metal doors before Acumen stopped in front of one. Just as he was about to reach out to scan his hand on the reader, the door slid open to reveal a middle-aged woman with fiery red hair that had just started greying around the temples.

Upon seeing them standing there, the woman nodded politely. "KC-847, thank you for coming. My name is Divvy, and I am one of the two leaders of the Underground. Please, come in and take a seat." She gestured to the table in the middle of the room.

There was another woman sitting there. That one was older, her light blue eyes surprisingly warm beneath her severely cut white fringe. She stood up and smiled at KC-847 and Acumen. "KC-847, it's lovely to finally meet you. My name is Harmony."

KC-847 looked over at Acumen, who gave him a slight nod before he took a seat, gesturing for KC-847 to do the same. Once they were both settled, Harmony looked between them and smiled. "So, Acumen tells me you have taken all of this in stride. How have you found the Underground so far?" she asked, relaxing back into her seat.

Apart from Divvy's keen eyes watching him, KC-847 could almost believe that this was just a casual conversation. "It is not quite what I expected," he admitted, feeling his cheeks heat at the intensity of the attention they were paying to him. He was used to answering questions for his superiors, but she had asked for an opinion. He wasn't authorised to have those.

"Given that Acumen said you weren't aware of our presence, I assumed as much. What sort of things have surprised you about the Underground, then?" Divvy said, her tone only a touch lighter than her glare.

"The set up you have is quite sustainable, and I am yet to see a single person who has been injured by reckless use of their powers." KC-847 spoke slowly, trying to gather all his thoughts together efficiently.

"Reckless use of their powers?" Divvy asked, arching a perfectly manicured eyebrow in question.

"Oh, nothing reportable, I'm sure," KC-847 assured her. He thought about the people he'd gotten to know over the last few weeks and didn't want to get them into trouble with their leaders. "Perhaps the word I used was wrong. Flippant is more appropriate. Macrokinetics using their abilities to get themselves a drink, teleporters who don't walk so much as hop, mind-readers who don't know the difference between personal thoughts and a conversation."

Beside him, Acumen chuckled.

"So, what you're saying is that it's a surprise to see Derivates using their abilities as part of their everyday life?" Harmony clarified with a patient smile.

KC-847 looked over at her. He hadn't thought about it like that. He nodded. "Yes, ma'am."

"Have you found our people accommodating?" Harmony asked, watching him with her keen blue eyes. For a moment, KC-847 wondered what her abilities were. It was possible that she was attempting to read his mind.

"Yes, Acumen in particular. The others, those from the Blue Team, have made it their mission to ensure I sit with them at dinner time and try all the spicy food." KC-847 scrunched up his face as he remembered how they all howled with laughter at his first taste of fresh chilli. "Although perhaps that isn't so accommodating."

Acumen smirked and there was a sparkle in Divvy's eyes, but it was Harmony who spoke. "Well, down here that is just about the best accommodation you can get," she said, nodding with approval.

KC-847 didn't understand. His scorched taste buds certainly didn't appreciate their version of accommodation.

"It's about the fact they're joking with you, not feeding you spicy food," Acumen supplied.

KC-847 let out a hum of understanding. That reasoning sounded more logical. There was a burgeoning sense of camaraderie between him and some members of the Underground as they learned was more about him, and he learned more about them.

Divvy cleared her throat and leaned forward, steepling her hands on the table. "The reason we've asked you here is to let you know that you have a decision to make."

KC-847 sucked in a breath. He wasn't ready to decide.

"Relax, you still have time." Harmony's voice immediately calmed him. "We have decided to extend your privileges to help you get a more balanced opinion of the Underground before you choose your path."

Divvy looked at KC-847 seriously. "We would like you to start training with the others and pitching in around the Residence. Acumen said that he sensed your growing restlessness and figured it would be good for you to get a proper taste of life around here."

KC-847 looked over at Acumen, who winked at him, the corner of his lips curling up in excitement.

"Starting tomorrow, we've assigned you to team training sessions with the Blue Team in Security," Harmony explained, smiling when KC-847 sat a little straighter. "It will begin with some one-on-one sessions with their macrokinetic, Swipe, and once you get used to your unfiltered powers, you can train with the others individually. When you're not training, you are welcome to help in other areas. What you do will depend on the day, but I'm sure Acumen will keep you busy."

KC-847 couldn't believe it. They were allowing him to train with their people? To work within the vulnerable walls of their home? Nothing like this would ever happen within the structure of the Government, but despite the looming sense of responsibility it brought, it was flattering. He thought about how he got to this point, and then realised he hadn't counted any of the doorways on the way into this space. He hadn't tried to look over Acumen's shoulder to learn the passwords. When was it exactly that had he stopped looking for a way out?

"That sounds acceptable, thank you," KC-847 said, having to force the strength into his voice as his heart tightened. The show of trust made his eyes sting. He pressed his lips together and looked away from the women opposite of him, not used to dealing with these kinds of emotions. Although, unlike many of the new feelings he had, this one was easy to name.

He was grateful.

Not only for the opportunity to spend more time interacting with their teams, but because they had taken him in in the first place, even at great risk to their establishment.

"Excellent. You'll find some new clothes in your room that'll be more suitable for training in," Divvy informed him.

Harmony leaned in, smiling. "As for today, I believe the Blue

Team are having a party to celebrate Flit's permanent position with them. You should join them."

KC-847 sat up straight and gave Harmony and Divvy a crisp salute. He had never been to a party before, but he was not about to ignore his first official order from them. "That sounds perfect, thank you ma'am," he said, returning to the rank and formality of his Government training.

Harmony smiled at him and shook her head. "Please, just call me Harmony. No need to salute or stand at attention here."

"Yes ma'am—" KC-847 started before he could catch himself. "Uh, sorry. Yes, Harmony. Thank you."

Divvy got to her feet and walked over to the door, opening it to see them out. "We hope you like it down here. We've been watching you settle in, and it would be a shame to lose someone as talented and adaptable as you."

KC-847 blinked, caught off guard by the compliment. He cleared his throat. "Thank you, ma'am."

Unlike Harmony, Divvy didn't correct him.

"Great!" Acumen rubbed his hands together excitedly. "Let's go to this party thing. I heard Flit brought down some proper dairy-based ice-cream with her. We'd better get there before those vultures devour it all." Acumen's chair scraped along the concrete as he got to his feet. KC-847 thanked both leaders again before he followed Acumen out of the room, too busy thinking about what all of this would mean to keep track of the route they took.

12

KC-847

WHEN ACUMEN AND KC-847 ARRIVED, the party had already started. The Blue Team had appropriated their favourite training room for the event. Instead of using the holographic projectors for scenery or enemies, they had set them to scatter beautiful rainbow fractals of light around the room. The patterns shifted in a mesmerising, pulsing rhythm that matched the tempo of the low music playing. Flit, Swipe, Hawkeye, Clarity, and Tweak were seated around a table in the middle that was loaded with a range of foods. From the observation window, KC-847 watched them chatting and laughing how only friends could. He hovered at the threshold of the room hesitantly, but Acumen had no such qualms.

"Flit!" Acumen called over the music, commandeering the attention of the group. They turned around, cheering and whooping at his arrival. "I hear congratulations are in order. I must also sadly announce my application to transfer to the Hub. If you're down here full time, I gotta escape!"

KC-847's eyebrows rose. Who would watch him if Acumen was gone? He'd rather not be left to someone else's devices. While KC-847 was concerned about this, the others all looked at the telepath and then broke into an appreciative roar of laughter. Flit, sensing the teasing slight, picked up a cup and threw it at him. It hit his shoulder, but Acumen caught it before it fell and pegged it back her. Flit teleported out of the way, and the next instant she was standing right beside KC-847 in the doorway. He jumped, his heart thundering in his chest at her unexpected appearance.

"Hi!" She gave him a smile so bright he should have shielded his eyes.

KC-847 blinked as he took her in. Her small, yet powerfully built frame was draped in a beautiful, deep green dress. The straps that held it up were no thicker than his fingers, and it ended at her mid-thighs. It was so different to her normal tank tops and cargo pants that he couldn't help but stare, especially at the way the neckline of her dress dipped in a most distracting V-shape.

Acumen snorted a laugh.

Perhaps it was more than the fact that she wasn't in her fatigues that kept him looking. It might have been how her glossy chestnut curls fell over the smooth tanned skin of her shoulder. Or that he saw the shape of her in a whole new light. She even smelled different; gone was the feminine scent masked by the grime of these tunnels, replaced by a fresh, flowery fragrance that wasn't at all unappealing.

"KC?" Flit tilted her head to the side when he didn't respond. Hearing the new, shortened version of his designation that people were using snapped him out of his thoughts. Initially, he disliked the nickname they had given him, but apparently his full designation was too much of a mouthful. He had begrudgingly accepted it, but only because there were no other KCs in the Underground. He inwardly cursed himself as Acumen barely managed to stifle a laugh.

"Oh, yes. Hello, Flit." KC-847 spoke far too quickly, shaking his head and wondering why he was so distracted. Flit smiled at him brightly, unperturbed by his lack of eloquence. "Uh, congratulations... So, you are in the Underground full-time now?" he asked, searching for something to say to her; some reason to justify the fact he couldn't take his eyes off her.

"Yeah! Great, huh?" She stood straighter and squared her shoulders. "Although this is a double celebration. We heard you got clearance to train with us, so we figured why not kill two birds with one stone?"

Speechless, a tingling warmth rose in KC-847's cheeks and

chest. A double celebration? They knew he was joining their team and they wanted to celebrate?

"Don't look so surprised, Stud, we're happy to have you," the tall blonde macrokinetic, Swipe, said as she walked over and leaned against the training room doorframe.

"Stud?" Flit's previously amicable tone turned incredulous as she narrowed her eyes at Swipe over her shoulder.

KC-847 tore his eyes away from Flit to look at Swipe. Just like Flit, she was wearing a dress, but hers was slinky and clung to her in a way that Flit's didn't. For a moment, KC-847 realised that he had a perfect outline of Swipe's form through her dress. "Uh, yeah, that's right. I have been told I will start training with you tomorrow, Swipe." KC-847 nodded, taking a low, deep breath, telling himself to focus.

"It's already on my calendar. I'm looking forward to seeing what you've got." The way that Swipe raked her eyes up and down his fitted t-shirt made KC-847 wary. "Don't worry, I'll go easy on you." Her deep red lips curled into a smirk as she patted his chest. She settled her hand there for a heartbeat, her palm hot even through the fabric of his t-shirt. KC-847 looked down at her hand before she stepped back and winked at him.

Flit frowned, casting Swipe an acidic look. "He doesn't need someone to go easy on him. That's an insult, given his level of power." Flit shook her head. After a moment, she straightened up and put that bright smile back on her face. "Come on, there's still plenty of food. And ice-cream! Do you like ice-cream?" Flit turned on her heel and led the way to the table without waiting for an answer.

"I do not know," KC-847 admitted as he followed her, watching the people at the table as they feasted on foods he had only recently tried for the first time.

"Well, there's only one way to find out. Come on."

"What are its nutritional values?"

Flit snorted. "High sugar. High fat. Extra high awesomeness."

KC-847 frowned. That did not sound good. Nevertheless, he sank down in the empty seat between her and Clarity.

"So, Flit, did your folks come around to the idea of you moving down here?" Clarity asked. She was a tall, willowy young woman with long black hair and deep brown up-turned eyes that made KC-847 feel like she could read his mind. When he first met her, he mistakenly assumed she was a telepath rather than a precog.

"They didn't have much of a choice, although my mother is yet to approve me for active duty. I'm mostly healed though, so she's running out of excuses." Flit picked up an empty bowl and scooped some thick white ice-cream into it. Without a word, she slid the bowl and a fresh spoon over to KC-847.

With a surprised 'thank you', he took it from her. KC-847 tried ice-cream for the first time, and even though the first two mouthfuls were delicious, the third left him with a headache that split his frontal lobe in half. He put the ice-cream aside; the pain was not worth the sweetness.

"Well, I'm sure you'll give her another one soon enough," Tweak teased, making the others laugh. Even KC-847 joined in. Tweak was right: from all the stories he had heard, Flit had a way of finding trouble.

At the sound of KC-847's laughter, Acumen turned around and smiled. KC-847 cleared his throat and pursed his lips together. It was, most likely, a result of the reduction in potency of the control chip, meaning he had started to feel proper emotions for the first time.

"Oh, shut up." Flit picked up a salted peanut and threw it at Tweak, but the microkinetic was too quick. With a wave of his hand, the peanut exploded, showering Flit and Swipe with crumbs. Swipe groaned and brushed the debris off her shirt.

"We all know it's true. Even KC laughed."

At Tweak's comment, all eyes turned to KC-847. His cheeks heated at the attention. He shrugged and Flit leaned over, playfully elbowing him in the ribs. "Remember, it was this troublemaker that saved your arse from being rat food."

Her tone was light, so KC-847 assumed it was a playful comment. "From the stories I heard, you can hardly pin your reputation on me," he retorted without a second thought.

Flit's smile widened and she doubled over with laughter; the sound of it was so pure and unfiltered that KC-847 watched her in awe. The others joined in, and KC-847 realised that he had just returned the same sort of jibe that they all used to communicate. He smiled, finally understanding how things worked.

"Oh, man. Swipe, please train him fast so I can get some on-one-time with him and kick his arse," Flit said when she caught her breath.

"As much as I'd like to see you try, I want to take my time with him." Swipe's voice was a low purr that made KC-847 shiver. The intensity of Swipe's blue-eyed gaze signalled a deeper meaning to her words. Even though his body seemed to like the idea, there was something in his head telling him it wouldn't end well.

Acumen leaned forward, blocking KC-847's view of Swipe. He looked like he was about to say something when cheers erupted from the table. KC-847 turned to see two more people walking into the room. It was Sway, a charismatic telecoercionist and Link, the caramel-skinned telepath.

"You two are late!" Tweak jeered. "Get stuck in Tunnel Forty-Two on the way?"

The group erupted with laughter, except for Acumen who just shook his head, and KC-847, who didn't understand what was so funny.

Link blushed, but Sway draped his arm over her shoulder and smirked. "So what if we did? You jealous, Tweak? It's been a while since you've been to Forty-Two."

"Ha! Hardly, I'm simply better at fitting it into my schedule so I'm not late for the good parties."

Swipe reached out, using her telekinesis to pull a bench over from against the wall over. She settled it at the end of the table. Sway and Link sat down next to each other, close enough that their arms were touching.

"Is Tunnel Forty-Two a regular patrol?" KC-847 asked. Acumen had referred to it when he spoke to Seeker and his mother on his first morning in the Underground.

Everyone at the table turned to look at KC-847. Their laughter grew even louder, spurred on by their earlier amusement.

"Only if you're lucky," Tweak chuckled.

KC-847 frowned. "Do you need certain clearance to complete that route?"

The roar of laughter only got louder. Except for Flit, who stopped laughing and pursed her lips together, shaking her head at the others.

Sway sniggered. "That, and a partner."

Link, who couldn't stop a small spurt of giggles, elbowed him.

"Unless you're Acumen. He has to go solo," Tweak added, dodging the empty cup Acumen lobbed at him.

KC-847 turned to Acumen. He was missing something, but he trusted the telepath to be honest with him. "Why do you have to go solo? Is that a punishment?"

The laughter was so loud it blocked out the hum of music from the speakers.

"Stop, stop!" Flit wiped tears of amusement from her eyes. "Guys, that isn't fair. Give him a break."

Sway rolled his eyes and smoothed down his slick blond hair. "Sheesh, Flit, loosen up! Maybe you need to go to Forty-Two yourself. It's been over a year since Ro—"

The laughter snapped to a stop so fast that it gave KC-847 whiplash. Flit stiffened beside him. He wondered what was so special about Forty-Two that it would help Flit lighten up.

He was about to ask when Link muttered "Sway!" and elbowed her boyfriend in the ribs.

Sway threw his hands up and sat back. "What? It's true, it's about time she moved on."

"Too soon, bro, too soon." Tweak glared at the other man from across the table, shaking his head.

KC-847 was no expert in reading the mood at social gatherings, but even he sensed the amusement frost over with tension.

"Well, I think you've all had too much to drink. Half of you are on patrol tonight, you need to keep your wits about you." Acumen leaned forward to break up the direct line of sight between Flit and Sway.

Even though the group agreed to stop drinking their moonshine, they didn't stop eating. The mood lightened, but KC-847 couldn't shake how quickly it had turned after a few small comments. Flit was sullen and silent for a while, but Hawkeye slid his seat in between hers and Tweak's. The sandy-haired man spoke to Flit in low, smooth murmurs that KC-847 couldn't hear, and soon enough she was smiling and talking to the others again.

The discussion around the table flowed, and even though some small rifts between the various people were becoming obvious, the most interesting thing was that they all treated KC-847 like one of them. He didn't even mind. There were worse things than being assimilated into such a lively group; after that party, the thought of going back to The Hub was one of them.

13

FLIT

TINKER WASN'T HAPPY.

Flit sighed. "What sort mother would be upset that her daughter's wound healed?"

Tinker stood back and tapped some notes into her datapad. "The sort that knows the trouble her daughter will get up to the moment she's granted medical clearance."

"I told you she was dreading this." Flit sat up straighter and looked over her mother's shoulder at Hawkeye, who had come along to the check-up. She had been in the Underground full-time for a week, stuck on light duties that entire time. Her thigh had healed, and she was itching to get back in the field.

"Is it any wonder I'm concerned?" Tinker turned, looking at Hawkeye.

He raised his hands in a show of wariness. "Don't pull me into this. I learned the hard way that I shouldn't get between the two of you."

Tinker and Flit laughed.

"So, does this mean I'm cleared for duty?" Flit asked, bouncing on the edge of the bed with anticipation.

Tinker rolled her eyes. "Yes, alright, fine." She stepped back so that Flit could stand.

"Good, because I was about to seek a second opinion," Flit

teased. When she stood, she leaned over and pulled her reluctant mother into a hug.

"Flit?"

"Yes?"

"Please be careful. I don't want to put you back together again."

Flit hugged her mother a little tighter. "I'll be fine, I promise. Someone has to end this stalemate between the Underground and the Government."

"There are so many parts of this fight we don't see. I know you have big, brave ideas about how you want to change the world, but things like that take time, blood, sweat, and tears," Tinker warned her.

"I know Mum," Flit promised as she pulled back out of the embrace. "But for now? I believe the tunnels down around the Catacombs need checking. I'll see you for dinner—"

The medbay door slid open, cutting Flit's reply short. Flit teleported away from the gurney as two pairs of workers, each carrying a bloodied and broken Green security team member between them, rushed in.

Tinker was already in medic mode. "What happened?"

"Collapse in Y-twenty-two," a woman carrying the security officers declared.

"Get them on the beds, I'll call—"

"Already on it!" Flit interrupted Tinker, teleporting over to the wall and tapping an emergency alert for more medics on the comm screen. She then jumped into the stores and grabbed an armful of cleansing swabs, bandages, and other vital items before reappearing at her mother's side.

Without being asked, Flit and Hawkeye launched in to help. Their medical skills did not extend beyond basic first aid, but they put their hands to good use. The two Green Team members were critically injured, but they helped to stabilise them until medical reinforcements arrived. While the medics worked, Flit and Hawkeye tidied the medbay before leaving for their afternoon patrol. As they did, Tinker looked at Flit with a pleading expression. Flit nodded almost imperceptibly: a promise to be careful.

LATER THAT EVENING, Flit and Hawkeye made their way back to the Residence after their patrol to change out of their grimy, tunnel-scum soaked gear before dinner. They had just stepped into the refreshing light and life of the gardens around the apartment building, when Flit brought up a concern Hawkeye had dismissed on their patrol.

"I still don't like it," Flit grumbled.

"It was a tunnel collapse. Two people got injured. Of course, you don't like it. Neither do I."

"Tunnels don't just collapse. You and Swipe patrolled that sector last week and it was fine." Flit narrowed her eyes at him.

"It was a freak accident."

"You say that, but—"

Hawkeye stopped in his tracks and turned to Flit, grasping her shoulders. "Flit, don't do this. You're manufacturing drama. If you're that bored, we can go over the Intelligence training manual together or spend some time in the VR suite. But don't do this. Don't make the collapse into something it isn't."

Flit gritted her teeth and clenched her hands tight enough for her nails to dig into her skin. She heard what he was trying to tell her, but there was a swirling suspicion inside her that refused to be tamed by his logic. It had been years since there was a collapse, and even then, it was because the maintenance was shoddy, not because of some magical coincidence. "I know you don—" Flit stopped, her brows furrowing as she turned away, looking down the rows of hydroponic gardens.

"What is it?" Hawkeye peered around, concerned.

She took his hand and pulled him between the rows of vegetables. "Look." She pointed down the row of freshly sprouted spinach.

The pair's eyes fell on KC and Acumen as they tended to the irrigation drains below the garden-beds. Beside them were Seeker and Kindling, two of the younger residents of the Underground. The kids were watching the repairs with interest while grilling KC about all things above-ground.

"KC-874, what do you think of the Underground?" Kindling

asked, her fingers curling as she stopped herself from reaching out with her microkinetic abilities to help mend the pipes.

Seeker rolled his eyes. "It's 847."

Kindling frowned. "That's what I said!"

"No, you said 874, dummy," Seeker groaned

"Seeker..." Acumen's voice held a warning as he looked up from the pipe he was working on.

Seeker met his gaze with a pout of defiance.

"Well, sorry, I'm not used to calling people numbers," Kindling grumbled, stabbing some grass with a stick petulantly, upset at being called a dummy.

"It is alright. If it helps, you can call me KC like the others do," KC offered.

Flit's smile widened. She and the others had taken to shortening KC's designation in the past couple of weeks, for ease of conversation. Initially, he had bristled at the informality, but he came around to it. Flit was glad. Having a nickname was part of being in the Underground. It meant that the others accepted him. It was a good sign in her books.

Seeker wasn't ready to let it go. "What kind of name is KC-847, anyway? Why would your parents call you that? It's weird."

Flit wondered if it would annoy KC. Instead of snapping back, or reciting some protocol, he smiled at Seeker.

"I guess you are right. It makes for a strange name, but it is not really a name, it is a designation."

"A designation?"

"Yes. Each letter and number means something. It is a way for the Government to track its assets—its people," KC corrected, the look of confusion on the children's face softening when he replaced the word assets. "The first letter denotes my ability classification and the second is my power cap. K is for macrokinetic, and C gives everyone a rough idea of the things I can do. The eight shows that I was born in the year one-hundred-and-eight, and the forty-seven represents my birth order. There are only ninety-nine of us born in the Hub each year."

The kids took it all in with the innocence only children had. "So, if your cap is C, what can you do?" Seeker asked.

"That is something we have yet to determine. I do not have that cap anymore, so that letter should be changed, I suppose," KC mused as he wiped some soil from his brow with the back of his hand.

Kindling frowned. "Then your name is wrong, isn't it? What are we supposed to call you, now?"

KC pressed his lips together in a thoughtful line. He sat back, looking at his hands as he considered Kindling's question. Flit leaned in closer, but she stepped on a twig and the sound of it snapping made KC look up, startled. His eyes widened and his shoulders set back when he saw Flit and Hawkeye standing there. "Oh, hello."

"Sorry, we heard your storytelling and took a detour on our way back to our rooms." Flit bit her lip as she hunched her shoulders in apology, feeling bad for eavesdropping.

"Oh." KC looked back at the kids and smiled. "Yes, these two like stories." From the surprise in his tone, Flit assumed he'd never had much of a chance to interact with kids.

"Yeah, but your name is still weird, even with the story," Kindling muttered, poking a stray rock with a stick.

"I have never given it much thought. My designation has always been fine for me. How do people down here come up with names like Flit or Seeker?" KC rocked back on his haunches and looked at the others.

Seeker groaned. "Our parents name us, duh!"

Hawkeye, Flit, and Acumen laughed. KC look confused, clearly having trouble figuring out why that was funny.

Acumen took a deep breath to stop his laughter and gave Seeker an amused look tinted with a gentle warning. "That's not a very constructive answer."

"It's true—"

"When we're born, temporal sensors use their abilities on the babies. They record what they see about their powers and share it with the parents who select a name based on that information," Flit explained, not wanting to confuse poor KC anymore.

KC frowned. "That is a gross misuse of their powers."

Coming from an ex-Registered that used to use his abilities to hunt down other Derivates seeking refuge, Flit found that quite a contradiction. But she couldn't compare the situation, and it wasn't like he had much of a say in the matter. "It's tradition. A new life is important. A little self-serving decadence is one way we can celebrate that."

He accepted her answer in that brooding, thoughtful way of his, chewing over his words before he spoke again. "So, why did your parents choose Flit?"

Flit didn't bother answering with words. Instead, she teleported around the gardens in a dozen short, fast jumps. For her, it was like taking a tiny jump to the left, but to KC, she would be flitting around the place faster than a blink. When she stopped, she put up her hands and waggled her fingers, as if saying 'tadah!'.

Understanding dawned in KC's eyes. "You do kind of flutter around, don't you?"

"Exactly." Flit nodded. "Everyone tends to teleport a little differently; at least, from an outsider's perspective. My father, Stride, looks as though he teleports between steps. The leader of Intelligence, Shadow, quite literally fades in and out of the shadows. It's so cool." Flit's voice took on a dreamy quality as she talked about Shadow's style of teleporting. She had admired him for as long as she could remember. He was such a powerful teleporter and a total enigma to boot.

Lips pressing together in a thoughtful grimace, KC looked down at his hands as he considered Flit's words. "I see." KC sighed heavily. After a moment he shook off whatever thoughts were troubling him, and he turned to Seeker and Kindling. "I suppose you are right. My name is out of place down here."

"Don't worry, you can pick a new one!" Without warning, Seeker snatched up KC's hands.

"Seeker!" Acumen launched forward to pull Seeker away, but the child's face contorted in horror and he scrambled away from KC. Acumen sighed and shook head as he watched the poor child cowering against a row of spinach.

"Seeker, you should know better than that!" Hawkeye reprimanded the child.

KC sat a little straighter and looked at the boy. "What did you see?"

"Rats, all the rats! And your friends, the rats ate them all!" Seeker whimpered.

Flit teleported over and tucked the child against her side. "See what happens when you jump into things, buddy? The temporal sensors who help with names have years of experience pinpointing a moment in time. You'll get there one day, but not like that. Next time, ask permission before trying that, ok?" Flit kept her voice low, not wanting to embarrass Seeker in front of the others. Publicly shaming him for trying to help wouldn't achieve anything.

"Maybe we can call you Rat-Killer," Kindling gasped, eyes wide with awe as she looked at KC. Her comment was accurate yet irreverent in the way that only a child's could be.

"Nah, that sucks." Seeker peeled away from Flit, horror of the rats forgotten in favour of trying to find his friend a new name. "What about Exterminator? That's way cooler."

Flit snorted with amusement and shook her head. "I don't think that's the image KC is going for." Flit looked over at KC as he sat, his brows knitted together as he took all the chatter in. She felt sorry for him, having to deal with so many new things. "If anything, his name would be more like Scraps," she teased, wanting to ease the tension.

KC looked up at Flit, his head tilted to the side in question. "Scraps?"

"Yeah, you weren't so much exterminating those rats as throwing scraps at them." Flit winked, letting him know that she was just joking.

Instead of getting annoyed, KC's lips turned up in a half-smile. "It is also what I threw at you before I almost caught you." He smirked at her, crimson eyes shining with competition.

Flit cocked an amused eyebrow at him. "You were nowhere near catching me."

The two looked at each other, neither one wanting to back down. After a moment, KC nodded and said, "Scraps seems like a good name. I will go with that."

"You don't have to do that buddy; she was only teasing you." Acumen patted KC's shoulder.

"No... Scraps is good." His tone was firm enough that Acumen didn't bother arguing the point further.

There was silence as the adults read into his decision. If KC took a new name, he was one step closer to wanting to stay with them. To being one of them. For whatever reason, he had decided that his new name suited him better than his designation.

Hawkeye shifted beside Flit and cleared his throat. "Flit, we should get going. We need to get clean before dinner, remember?"

Looking down at herself, Flit frowned. Her light-grey shirt was almost black with grime. "You're right. I guess we'll see you at dinner, Scraps." Flit smiled as she used his new name for the first time.

He returned her smile with equal enthusiasm. "See you at dinner, Flit. Hawkeye."

Flit beamed at Hawkeye as they turned to make their way towards their rooms. "I guess that means he's planning to stick around for a while." She was excited that he was breaking free of the Government's brainwashing.

Hawkeye just shrugged. She wasn't sure what his problem was, but he clearly wasn't in a talkative mood. It was unusual for him; she wondered what she had done to piss him off enough to warrant the silent treatment.

14

SCRAPS

SCRAPS STOOD outside the training room with Acumen and watched Heft and Swipe finishing up their session through the observation window. The difference in their technique was evident; Swipe was gifted with the ability to move items precisely at lightning speed. Small objects had the same impact as bullets under her influence. Heft's advantage was in brute strength. He shifted heavy items like lockers and steel beams without breaking a sweat. Watching the two sparring was mesmerising. They must have worked together before, as they seemed to predict what the other would do. Every now and again one would get the upper hand, but the other countered it without much fuss.

"Swipe and Heft work well together," Scraps commented.

Acumen nodded. "They've been regular training partners ever since Swipe moved to the Underground seven years ago."

"Why are they not in the same team? They would be a formidable pair in the field."

"We try and balance the teams out. Sure, they would be great in a full-on fight, but that would leave them ill-matched for a range of other situations."

"Talking about people again? Don't you ever learn not to gossip?" Swipe asked, shaking her head as she stepped outside of the training room, draping a towel over her shoulders. Her body was covered in a fine sheen of sweat that caught Scraps' attention and made his face flush with heat. He had never taken much notice of how a thin layer of moisture could highlight the curves and dips of a woman's neck, shoulders and—

"I'm too old to learn new tricks. You should know that by now."

Swipe laughed and turned her attention to Scraps. "So, you ready for training, KC—or should I call you something else now?"

"Yes." Scraps brightened, smiling as he nodded. "I changed my name to Scraps. I no longer feel like my designation suits who I—"

A loud snort interrupted Scraps as Heft pushed past Swipe. "That was nice of you Acumen, giving your new pet a name."

The chatty mood of the group turned cold. Scraps frowned, his eyebrows furrowing as he tried to figure out what Heft had meant. Swipe's face hardened, and Acumen's eyes clouded with confusion.

Swipe turned to the tall, bulky man. "What the hell?" She swatted his chest.

"I'm only saying what we're all thinking."

"No you're not," Acumen said firmly, stepping closer to Scraps. If anyone would know, it was the mind-reader.

"Then you're lying to yourselves. We don't need any mules in the Underground. Flit should have put it down instead of dragging its sorry arse back down here."

The words hit Scraps like a punch in the gut. He was still processing the comment when Acumen put a hand on Heft's shoulder. The larger man glared at the mind-reader and shrugged his hand off.

"Where the hell did that come from?" Acumen asked.

"Stay out of my damn head." Heft gave Acumen a hard glare before storming off.

Scraps, Acumen, and Swipe stood in the doorway to the training room, staring after Heft's retreating back. Scraps' gut churned as the harsh words tumbled over and over in his mind. Since coming to the Underground, he had not encountered such open hostility.

"Hey, Stud, how about we go train?" Swipe reached out, patting his shoulder and interrupting his musings. "And while we're at it, you can tell me all about your new name."

Shaking away his thoughts, Scraps looked at Swipe. "Oh, uh,

sure." Scraps nodded a farewell to Acumen before following Swipe into the training room.

"So, where d'you get 'Scraps' come from? It isn't what I think of when I look at a strapping guy like you," Swipe said over her shoulder as she tapped commands onto the holographic synthesiser.

"I was talking to Acumen, Kindling, Seeker, Hawkeye, and Flit about the naming conventions here. I find designations much more practical, but if I want to fit in, I figured it was time for a new name," Scraps explained as he stretched his arms and legs to warm up for the session. Talking was easier than focusing on the aggressive feeling gnawing at his gut. "Kindling suggested Exterminator because of my efficient destruction of the rats in The Nest."

Instead of laughing in amusement as he thought she might, Swipe scrunched up her nose.

Scraps continued, making a mental note that what he thought would be a humorous comment had missed the mark. "Although, I did not kill the rats. Flit did. She joked about the fact that all I was doing was throwing scraps at the rats, and I thought it fit."

"You mean, Flit gave you a sarcastic new name and you just took it?" Swipe's face set in what Scraps recognised as annoyance.

"No." He shook his head. "There is more to it than that. I just… I felt like it worked, and I had hoped that others would look past my eyes and my tattoo if they did not have to use my designation." He also liked it because he had been trying to rebuild himself from the scraps of his past ever since he arrived in the Underground, but that felt a little too personal to share with Swipe.

Swipe let out a quiet sigh, looking out the training room window towards the passage Heft had stormed off down. She shook her head slowly before squaring her shoulders, "Come on Scraps, let's train."

SWIPE WORKED Scraps hard that session. By the end, he was exhausted. A low, throbbing headache lingered behind his eyes, and he decided it would be safest to skip dinner and go straight to bed. When Acumen opened the door to the training room, Swipe made her way out with a word of farewell.

Acumen leaned against the doorframe and crossed his arms over his broad chest. "You look like you could do with a break."

Scraps draped a towel around his shoulders and stood up. A wave of vertigo swept through him and he froze, giving his body a moment to adjust. "Yes. I am not used to pushing my powers this hard." He pressed his lips together.

On the surface, Scraps didn't even break a sweat during training sessions, but the amount of concentration required to control his abilities without the control chip was utterly exhausting. He had to work hard for every little bit of progress.

Shrugging as he walked over, Acumen said, "You're still getting used to everything." He took an apple from his vest pocket and placed it on the ground at his feet. "Try putting that back in my pocket."

Scraps frowned. Swipe was supposed to be working with him on his fine control skills, but she focused on using his abilities to block and redirect whatever she threw at him instead. His initial frustration at the change of purpose was short lived as was forced to focus on what he was doing rather than Heft's comments. When the session was over, he was too exhausted to care.

Despite being tired, Scraps looked at the apple. He had never rejected a command before, and he wasn't about to start now.

He reached out, focusing on the apple and lifting it off the floor. It shot up a little too quickly at first, but he got it under control. It was like turning on a tap but having the water pressure up too high. His default was an overabundance of energy. He narrowed his eyes as he focused his power, controlling the speed and moving the apple back towards Acumen. With his free hand, he motioned at Acumen's vest pocket to open it. Keeping the two actions smooth and steady, without putting too much power into them, was a challenge. Just as he was about to settle the apple into the pocket, his head throbbed, and his concentration slipped. The apple exploded and splattered all over Acumen's shirt and hair. Scraps let out a frustrated sigh as his arms fell to his side.

Why was such a simple task so difficult to achieve?

What was wrong with him?

Acumen chuckled and shook his head. "Scraps, buddy, I did

that to show you how far you've come. A week ago, you couldn't pick up the apple without exploding it. That's great progress, especially given that headache you've got coming on," Acumen said with a genuine smile.

Scraps shrugged, feeling uncomfortable accepting praise he didn't feel he deserved. "I am not used to being so incompetent."

"You're not. You're just learning to control yourself without that stupid filter the Government forced on you."

Even though the words were light, Scraps felt an uncharacteristic pang of annoyance at how the Government had controlled him. Even now, his greatest fear was hurting someone else by accident; he deserved to have his abilities restricted. He owed it to the others to keep them safe.

"Let's get you back to your room, I'm sure there is something in your bathroom that'll fix that headache."

When they got back to Scraps' quarters, they found painkillers in his vanity cabinet. They helped with the headache, but exhaustion still dragged at his every movement. After sitting down and chatting about mundane topics with Acumen for fifteen minutes, Scraps said that he wanted to turn in for the night. After such a big day, sleep would be the only thing that would restore his energy.

SCRAPS HAD JUST SUNKEN into a dark, oblivious state of dreamless sleep when there was a loud knock at his door. He sat bolt upright; his eyes bleary. He glanced at the clock to see he'd only been asleep for an hour and a half.

"Acumen?" he called out. The telepath was the only person who ever stopped by. Although, it made little sense that he was at the door when he had told Scraps to get some rest.

"No, it's Flit, I brought you some dinner."

Scraps froze.

Why would she do that?

He slipped out of bed and stepped towards the door when the fabric of his boxers shifted, and he was alerted to a familiar uncomfortable sensation. He looked down. It was the same problem he'd had every morning for the past three weeks. From what Tinker said, it was normal for some males, but it wasn't normal for him.

"Ah, just a minute—" he called out, hurrying over to his wardrobe and fishing out a shirt. He tugged it down over his head and pressed his lips together as the pressure refused to subside in his shorts.

"Don't take too long, you don't want your food to get cold."

He gathered from the way Flit chuckled that she was joking. If anyone could get a meal from the Mess to his room before it got cold, it was her. "Sorry, I just got out of the shower. I will be there in a moment," Scraps lied.

Scraps closed his eyes and tried to stamp out anything that was encouraging his hardness. Oddly enough, the thought of Flit walking in made his task more difficult. However, the fact she had brought him food made up for that when his stomach rumbled like angry thunder before a storm.

The aching hardness waned, and Scraps once more cursed the control chip. He didn't know how people got anything productive done when their bodies were determined to work against them. He walked over to the door and tugged it open. Flit let out a squeak as she tumbled forward.

On instinct, Scraps reached out with his telekinesis to catch her, but winced as the inhibitor zapped the power off at the root. Scraps needn't have worried. After the first flailing step, she disappeared from in front of him and he heard the light thump of her feet hitting the floor behind him. He turned around to see her standing there, trying to look collected. It was convincing, too. If he hadn't seen her tumble, he would never have known what she saved herself from.

"You did not have to bring me food, I was just about to go to bed," Scraps said, looking between her face and the tray of food she was holding. Although, the aroma was rather enticing.

"No, I didn't, but Acumen told me about your headache, so I thought I'd drop something off. After a hard training session, your body needs the nutrients." She held out the tray with a smile that made her eyes sparkle.

Returning the smile cautiously, Scraps took the tray. "Thank you." He carried the tray to his table, setting it down and then turning back to her.

She didn't seem to be leaving.

"I am not permitted to be alone with a member of the Underground without Acumen present," Scraps warned.

With a flippant wave of her hand, Flit said, "Oh, I know." She sank onto one of the two dining chairs in his small room.

His brows furrowed as he took in that information. "Then perhaps you should go, I would hate for you to get into trouble on my account."

Flit snorted. "What they don't know won't hurt them." She winked.

Was everything a joke to her?

"You are aware that I spend my days with a telepath?" he asked, standing beside his seat but not settling onto it.

"Well, obviously, but even if Acumen figures it out, he won't say anything. He's a big softy. Besides, if he didn't want me to bring you dinner, he shouldn't have told me how worn out you looked after training, and how we should all make sure you're taking care of yourself." Flit shrugged. "Come on, sit. Eat. It's better hot, I swear."

Scraps stood there for a moment, looking between her and the food. His stomach grumbled in protest at the delay, and he sighed in resignation as he sat down. "Aren't you worried I might hurt you?" he asked before taking his first spoonful of soup.

"Nah, you couldn't if you tried." She tapped her temple.

He reached up, brushing his fingers over the thin metal wire of the circlet inhibitor around his head. He had gotten so used to its presence that he had forgotten about it. It was only ever off for training. "I have other ways of neutralising targets."

Flit shrugged. "You'd have to catch me first. We've already established that you can't do that. I think I'm safe."

Scraps was about to argue when he saw a flicker of amusement in her eyes, almost like she wanted him to bite back. "When we have our rematch, I will catch you, do not worry about that. I am better trained than you think I am."

Flit was cocky, but she wasn't the only one who knew how to handle an adversary. He was looking forward to showing her what he was capable of, especially with his telekinesis getting stronger by the day. He continued to eat, and they sat in companionable silence until he was about half-way done.

"So, I heard that something went down before training today. How are you feeling about that?" Flit asked, leaning in a little.

Scraps put his spoon down and looked up at her, remembering Heft's angry words. That now familiar, biting anger gnawed at his guts. "I do not know what you are referring to." His tone was more curt than he intended it to be. He had spent his entire life working for the Government, having Citizens hurl worse insults than that at him. It had never bothered him before, so he refused to let Heft's comments get to him. At least, he tried to, but it was another thing he was failing at.

"Sure, you do." Flit rolled her eyes. "You've seen how fast rumours get around this place, there's no point pretending it didn't happen."

Scraps pressed his lips together as he caught her gaze. He was not sure why she was pushing the issue. "I have dealt with worse."

Flit frowned, her hazel eyes filling with sadness. "I'm sure you have, but I just wanted you to know that Heft doesn't speak for all of us."

The painful frustration inside Scraps ground to a halt at Flit's words. "You do not think I am a mule that should be put down?"

Anger radiated off Flit in hot, roiling waves as her face went pale and her hands balled into fists at her side. "That's what he said to you?"

"Yes."

"Arsehole." Flit shook her head and her mouth flapped open and shut several times before she spoke again. "Look, I don't want you to think I am justifying that idiot's attitude, but the Underground is a small place. Some people have been stuck in these tunnels for their entire lives, never seeing the sun. They live, breathe, and feel this darkness. This is their home—their refuge from the threat up there." Flit pointed to the ceiling, but Scraps knew that she was referring to the city that he assumed was above their heads.

Flit leaned forward, putting her elbows on the table and resting her chin on her clasped hands. "These whispers have nothing to do with you as a person. It's what they feel you represent. They're scared, Scraps. Not of you, but of the reminder that what we have down here is bloody fragile."

"They think I will ruin that?" Scraps asked, disappointment curling the edges of his tone.

"You, someone else, something else... who knows?" Flit shrugged. "But they'll get over it. You're not the first Ex-Registered we've had down here, and hopefully, you won't be the last. They just need to learn to see you for who you are, to see past your eyes and tattoo like the rest of us do."

"So there really are others like me in the Underground?" Scraps had heard the others speak of it before, but without seeing it for himself he did not feel that the claims held much weight.

"Yes, and they are living full lives, loved and respected by the people around them. They have jobs, families, and they have gotten used to living without the control chip holding them back."

An unexpected flutter of hope bloomed in Scraps' chest. Surely if they could do it, he could too.

"Regardless of what fools like Heft say, we've got your back. You have a home here now, and the Blue Team are your family. Don't forget that, ok?" As Flit spoke, there was a fire in her eyes, the one she got whenever she was talking about Derivate rights, or her passion for the Underground.

Scraps felt like he was truly seeing Flit for the first time. He remembered how frustrating he had found her during his early days in the Underground. Since then he'd discovered that there was an interesting person beneath all that blustering confidence. She was passionate; out of everyone he'd met in the Underground, he would put his bet on her to lead a revolution. He'd never met anyone quite so tenacious; and strangely enough, he found it fascinating. He looked forward to running into her, because he always learned something new when she was around.

The anger in his Scraps' gut ebbed away. Flit's words wrapped around him like a warm coat. With someone that cared enough to check on him like she had, he was confident he would be able to work through whatever challenges arose. He cleared his throat of the unexpected surge of emotion and gave her a solemn smile. "Thank you Flit. It means a lot to have your support."

Flit teleported so that she was standing beside the table. She patted his shoulder gently. Her touch was soft but reassuring, and he gulped at the unexpectedly pleasant contact. "I'm here for you whenever you need to chat. Stupid seclusion rules or not, ok?" She winked at him.

Scraps chuckled and shook his head. She was incorrigible.

"See you tomorrow at breakfast, yeah?" Flit meet his eyes with such a look of warmth and confidence that he could not deny her.

"Of course."

Watching the ever-surprising woman walk out of his room, Scraps sat back, his soup all but forgotten. Despite what Heft said, and those angry whispers and looks he had noticed in the tunnels and the Mess, he had people on his side in the Underground. A smile tugged at his lips, and he returned to his meal with renewed enthusiasm.

15

FLIT

FLIT WAS SETTLING into her permanent role in the Underground well, but there was one thing that she would never admit to anyone but herself:

She missed the sunlight.

She had heard some other half-halfers complain about how much they dreaded the dank, artificial flickering lights of the Underground. How natural light was almost as important as oxygen. Hell, even her mother had warned her that there was no adequate replacement for genuine sunlight. At least the Underground had a good handle on making sure the lights encouraged a healthy sleep cycle. Still, as she made her way to the training room to meet Hawkeye after his training session with Scraps, she couldn't help but feel some remorse over her dwindling tan. Her rich olive skin was something that had set her apart from everyone else who lived in the Underground, and she liked the way it looked on her.

Flit stopped in front of the training room noted on Hawkeye's schedule. A frown tugged at her lips as she peered through the window. The tables and chairs were stacked to the side, the crash mats rolled up and piled in a corner, and the holographic training system was shut down.

Hawkeye must have changed venues. She walked up and down the corridor, checking all eight training rooms. Three were being used by members of other Security teams. Flit knocked on the door of the one Clip, Oculus, Heft, and Switch from the Green team were training in. Clip looked up from the simulated computer console he was working on. He smiled when he saw Flit and teleported over to open the door.

"Flit, what can I do for you?" he asked.

"Hey, Clip, I'm just looking for Hawk and Scraps. They should be in training room three, but they're not. Have you guys seen them?" Flit tucked her hands into her pockets as she looked at the others.

"No, we've been knee-deep in sim training all afternoon." Clip frowned, leaning out into the hall and looking down the corridor. He turned back to his team. "Anyone seen Scraps and Hawkeye this afternoon?"

"They were in three when I arrived for training," Oculus said, turning her piercing blue eyes towards Flit.

Flit bit her lip. "Hmm…"

"Hawkeye and the mule went that way—"

With a flinch, Flit turned, narrowing her eyes at Heft. "Excuse me?"

"I said, I saw Hawkeye and the mule go that way," Heft repeated slowly, pointing down the corridor that led to the gymnasium.

Flit balled her hands into fists inside her pockets. "What's your problem?"

"Guys, please." Clip stepped between Flit and Heft.

Flit teleported so she was standing in front of Heft. She was a head-and-a-half shorter than him, but she knew she could take him if it came to that.

"Me?" Heft scoffed. "I don't have a problem. You're the idiot that brought that creep down here."

Rage surged through her veins.

Clip teleported to Heft's side and put a warning hand on his shoulder. "Heft, enough."

Flit glared at Heft, every breath angry and ragged as it rattled out through her lips. "Never let me hear you call him that again. Do you understand?" She wanted to punch the nasty bastard, but the last thing she needed was to be reprimanded for getting into a fight.

She teleported back into the corridor, and Clip's shoulders sagged in relief. He mouthed 'sorry' before Flit slapped her palm on the access panel, the door sliding shut between them.

Flit stood outside for a moment, catching her breath as she talked herself down from going back into the training room and sticking her foot up Heft's dumb arse. She didn't want to leave Hawkeye waiting; their patrol was more important than teaching Heft a lesson.

HEFT, the bastard, was right.

When Flit walked into the gym, Hawkeye and Scraps were in the weights section at the far end. Scraps was on the bench with Hawkeye spotting for him. Flit calculated the weight on the bar and she let out a low whistle of appreciation.

Hearing the impressed sound, Hawkeye flicked his attention to her for a moment and grinned. "We had enough of the hand-to-hand stuff for today," he called from across the room. "I figured I should get Scraps in here and see what all these muscles are good for."

Hawkeye loved his hand-to-hand combat. Being a remote viewer, he couldn't rely on physical powers to help him out of a tight situation like a teleporter or telekinetic might. Instead, his ability gave him a kind of tremorsense that allowed him to sense his opponent's next move as they made it. Combined with his intense physical training, it gave him quite the edge in a fist fight. Between his speed and his ability, it was hard for anyone to get a hit in on him. Given that Scraps was well built, but unused to fighting, she supposed Hawkeye wanted to see what he could do with all that bulk.

Flit was curious too. As she watched, it became clear how well those Government-enforced chest and arm muscles were working through Scraps' sweat-slicked singlet. "Don't let me interrupt. You've still got time. I'm early." Flit shrugged, leaning casually against the wall.

"Are you just gonna watch, or do you want to come over here

and join in?" Hawkeye asked, helping Scraps settle the bar back onto the holder.

"Nah, weights aren't my thing. I'll just observe and take notes."

Hawkeye snorted a laugh as he offered Scraps his hand and pulled him up into a seated position. Scraps used his telekinesis to summon his water bottle. He took several thirsty gulps before he set it down and got to his feet, letting Hawkeye take over the bench. He used the opportunity to give the remote viewer some advice on lifting and breathing technique. Flit was pleased to see that Hawkeye and Scraps were getting along. The more people the Ex-Registered got to know, the more likely he was to form bonds strong enough to keep him in the Underground.

Scraps looked at Flit over his shoulder, his brows furrowing. "Are you taking notes? I do not see a data pad."

"No data pad required, they're all up here." Flit tapped her temple.

"That does not sound like a reliable way to store your notes," Scraps grumbled as he returned his attention to Hawkeye.

Flit chuckled. She was never the kind to get all excited about gym-style workouts, but she was more than happy to watch this one.

"They're getting along well."

Acumen's voice made Flit jump. She swore under her breath and turned around, not sure how the telepath managed to sneak up on her.

"You were too busy watching that fine display of masculine prowess over there to notice me," Acumen supplied.

Flit rolled her eyes. "I'm taking notes."

Acumen chuckled. "Oh, I bet you are."

"You're right. They do seem to be getting along," Flit said, changing the topic. "Must be the mutual love for weightlifting. It's an excellent excuse for them to get to know each other better while doing something cooperative, rather than trying to punch each other in the face."

Training together or not, Flit figured it was impossible to dislike Hawkeye. He was a good guy, and heaps of fun to be around. Unlike her. She rubbed people up the wrong way.

"You're not so bad. Some people just have trouble comprehending the monumental amount of conviction you carry in your small frame," Acumen explained.

Flit looked over at him as a grimace tugged at her lips. "I don't know whether to take that as a compliment."

"It was meant as one. Even Scraps has come around to you."

That piqued Flit's interest. "What do you mean, 'even Scraps'?"

"Only that your zealousness used to make him wary, but now he enjoys listening to your sermons."

"I don't give sermons."

Acumen cast her an amused look and she turned her nose up at him. She resented that he referred to her sharing her opinions as giving sermons. She just wanted to make sure that people understood why what they were doing was important. Where would they be if the first generation of Derivates had not fought tirelessly to carve out their safe space in the Underground? If everyone in the Underground stuck to basic Supply shifts? If they didn't work hard to better their abilities?

Flit's mind slammed to a stop. Damn, maybe she did give sermons.

Acumen choked out a laugh.

She playfully elbowed him in the ribs. "You're such an arse."

"Someone has to tell the truth... I'm sure it also has something to do with the dinner you took him last night."

Flit looked at Acumen out of the corner of her eye.

"Oh yes, I know about that little rendezvous. And the inspiring chat you had while you were there." Acumen tapped his head and winked at her.

"Someone had to make sure the poor guy didn't starve," Flit muttered.

"Hmm..." Acumen said nothing else about it as they watched Scraps and Hawkeye set the weights back in place and wipe down the benches before walking over, sweat dripping down their bodies, and dabbing at their faces with towels.

"Why so early, Flit?" Hawkeye asked with a broad smile.

Flit glared at him. "What is this? Pick on Flit day?" she snapped.

He raised his hands in defence. "Just making an observation. I take it you're ready to head out for the evening, then?"

"Yeah, ready whenever you are."

"Great. I'm just gonna head back upstairs to take a shower and get changed. Want to come?" Hawkeye asked.

Flit's eyebrows shot into her hairline. Acumen's laugh was poorly concealed by clearing his throat. "To the shower or just upstairs?"

Face flushing, Hawkeye narrowed his eyes at her. "What do you think?"

Flit waved a hand dismissively. "I'll meet you at the armoury. I thought you'd be ready to go, but since you're not, I might skip ahead and restock our belts."

"Alright." As Hawkeye turned to leave, he reached out, patting Scraps on the shoulder. "Good session today buddy."

Flit looked at Scraps again. With the sweat making his singlet cling to his chest like a second skin, she could see just what Hawkeye was referring to. Scraps had a well-cut figure that spoke of years of training. "How are you finding the hand-to-hand combat?"

Scraps shrugged. "I know that you value it in the Underground, but I see little point in it. Without the inhibitor, I can use my abilities to achieve much more than my physical muscles ever will."

"What about with an inhibitor? What then?" Flit asked, cocking an eyebrow.

"Well..." Scraps reached up and touched the slender metal band around his brow, frowning as he realized that she had just mentioned the exact situation he was in. "I have never been in a situation before where I've had to resort physical combat. But, if I am in the future, I suppose the training will be useful."

Flit smiled as she nodded, reaching out and putting her hand on his shoulder. "Hopefully it doesn't come down to that. So, do you know what your plans are yet? When do you have to decide whether you'll go back to the surface?"

"I am not sure." Scraps' gaze darted to Acumen, who conveniently ignored his look. When he looked back at Flit he shrugged. Flit took her hand back, her fingertips still warm from where they had touched his skin. "I am not used to making decisions for myself without parameters; there are a lot of factors I need to consider. I am enjoying my time here, but my concern is that the others won't accept me, no matter how long I have been down here. I know you said that there are other people like me, but I have yet to see evidence of that."

"Flit's right," Acumen chimed in. "We've got quite a few ex-Registered Derivates down here. You've met some already, but they haven't made themselves known to you. It's a part of their lives that they have made a conscious decision to leave behind. Some of them had a tough past, so they're in no rush to put themselves or their families at risk, just in case you go back up."

Scraps turned to Acumen, surprised. This, apparently, was something he hadn't expected to learn. Flit made a mental note to see if she could sweet-talk any of the ex-Registered's into having a chat with Scraps. She had a feeling that, deep down, he wanted to remain with them, but his duty to the Government kept him from making that choice. She couldn't think of any reason that someone would leave the Underground for the Hub.

Acumen looked at Flit. "Don't you have a patrol to go on?"

Flit shrugged. She was in no rush to leave. "Yeah, but Hawk takes forever in the shower."

"Well, we have a few places to get to before dinner. I promised Scraps I'd give him a tour of the archives, show him more of the history of this place," Acumen explained. Scraps brightened at this prospect, eager to learn whatever he could about how they lived.

"Right. I'll see you both around, I guess." Flit was about to walk off when realised she hadn't been assigned training sessions with Scraps, even though most of the others had. She stopped to turn around and ask Acumen about it.

"You can start that tomorrow if you like. You can take Hawkeye's time slot for a while. Posthoc's already approved it, but apparently he hasn't gotten around to telling you yet." Acumen answered her question before she even asked it. As usual.

Flit perked up. "Awesome, see you tomorrow, Scraps. You'd better bring your A-game if you want to catch me," she called over her shoulder as she walked down the concrete-lined tunnels.

16

FLIT

FLIT AND HAWKEYE knew something was wrong when they reached the gardens surrounding the Residence on the way back from their patrol. There was a quiet, piercing alarm echoing through the tunnels. Something about the sharp pitch made Flit wince with discomfort. She could not remember the last time she had heard the emergency alarm outside of drills. It was concerning.

It was late enough that most people should have been in bed, yet the Residence was abuzz with activity. The emergency-level lighting in the garden made night look like late afternoon, and there were people gathering by the front door, talking to each other in hushed voices. Flit looked at Hawkeye, confused, as they picked up their pace. They joined the back of the crowd just as it filtered through the doors and towards the sizeable meeting space in the atrium that acted as an emergency assembly area.

"Killswitch. What's going on?" Flit asked as they slipped past an athletically built man who was chatting in a group with some senior residents.

His deep etched frown-lines were more pronounced than usual. "There was a tunnel collapse in G twenty-eight about an hour ago. We're still waiting for information, but Harmony and Divvy have called for an urgent meeting in the Commons," he explained, in his low baritone.

Flit turned to look at her best friend. "G? Hawk, who was patrolling G tonight?"

"Green Team, I think."

"Shit, I hope they're ok." Flit took Hawkeye's hand and dragged him through the people gathered in the meeting area. Everyone who wasn't on duty or called out to help would attend the meeting. Several dozen chairs had been added to the forty that were there for their regular meetings, and they were filling fast.

"Flit, Hawk, over here." Clarity jumped up out of a seat in the middle of the mass and waved them over. She, Sway, and Link were all seated together, and Sway had taken it upon himself to kick his legs up onto the two seats beside them. Flit couldn't help but smirk at how his lack of manners worked in their favour for once. She and Hawkeye made a beeline for the group and settled into the spare seats.

Link leaned past Sway and pulled Flit into a tight hug. "Gosh, I'm glad you two are safe! I was so worried about you."

"I told you they would be," Clarity sighed, stony-faced. Flit didn't need to see her to know that the black-haired beauty was rolling her eyes.

"You can't blame her for not trusting your tired precognitions. We all know how inaccurate they are when you haven't had enough sleep," Sway snapped, defending his girlfriend.

Link ignored the other two. "What happened, did you guys hear anything?" she asked, raking her fingers through her silky smooth hair as she tried to cut off further dispute.

"No, we just got back." Hawkeye shook his head and looked around. After a moment he sighed, then his eyes glazed over in the way they did when he was using his abilities, no doubt bouncing his vision off various points around the room to see if he could gather any more information.

"We don't know anything yet, either. We tried to ask Posthoc, but he wasn't answering at any of his usual stations." Link gestured towards the communicator on the wall nearby.

Flit nodded grimly. "That makes sense. He's probably managing the emergency response team."

"None of the Green Team are here," Hawkeye supplied, his shoulders slumping as he returned to his own senses. "A few of the more evasive Control and Intelligence officers are though. Trojan and Lucky are chatting about something behind that divider." Hawekeye pointed to the retractable screen that could be pulled across the space to separate it into smaller meeting rooms.

"They never leave their cave," Flit mused, using her own term for the high-security Intelligence and Control zones of the Underground.

The others muttered in agreement. If the Control and Intelligence crews were here, the situation couldn't be good. Flit was about to ask where Sway and Tweak were when a hushed silence fell over the room. Instead of the chatter of many concerned voices, the rhythmic click-clack of Harmony's heels sounded through the room. Flit sat up straighter, eager to know what was going on.

Harmony didn't waste time setting up. She went straight to the lectern at the front of the meeting space and pressed a button that opened a 3D mesh map of the Underground in the lobby void above their heads.

"Thank you all for coming. I apologise for the lateness of the hour, but we have declared a state of emergency. Tonight, one of the Security teams was patrolling Sector G, carrying out a routine inspection of the lifeline support systems. While they were there, an explosion rocketed through the network."

Flit gasped with the rest of the group as an extensive area of the projected map fill with red lines.

"The area affected was large. Some critical oxygen supply lines were crushed in the explosion and resulting tunnel collapse. Maintenance teams are working where they can to ensure oxygen supply remains sufficient in critical living and working spaces."

The red areas all dipped downwards in the centre, showing roughly where the explosion had been, and just how many tunnels would be inaccessible because of it. Flit looked over at Hawkeye with wide eyes and he reached out, taking her hand and lacing their fingers together.

"What about the people on patrol?" Flit called out, unable to stop herself. Hawkeye squeezed her hand in reprimand.

Divvy's face hardened as she looked at Flit. "They have yet to report in."

A ripple of horrified whispers undulated through the crowd. Flit's stomach dropped and her head spun. Everyone knew what Divvy really meant. If the reinforced supply lines couldn't survive the explosion and cave-in, what hope did two delicate human bodies have?

"Given the magnitude of the collapse and the risk posed to our life-support systems, we've had to divert many of our active team members to damage control in the affected areas. Therefore, we have reassigned some of you to better help us investigate this disturbance."

Another murmur went through the crowd. It was rare that reassignments or jobs were forced upon anyone without consultation, but Divvy's words didn't imply any choice in the matter. Lucky and Trojan stepped in behind Harmony, each one looking sombre.

"Lucky will take the new recruits for Control, and Trojan will look after those in Intelligence. When I call your name and assignment, please meet them at the back of the room, behind the divider." At Harmony's words, Trojan and Lucky moved around the outside of the group to where she said they would be.

"Shit, this must be bad," Flit whispered to the others. They all nodded in agreement. Sway slipped his arm around Link's shoulders. A twang of sorrow tugged at Flit's heartstrings as she saw them offer each other comfort. It wasn't all that long ago that she had someone to hold when times were tough. Even though she was independent enough to go without it, it sure would have been comforting in such a moment.

Harmony started rattling off names and assignments. Those called got up and shuffled towards the right person without a word of protest. "Ratchet, Control. Cogs, Control. Bookworm, Intelligence. Hawkeye, Intelligence. Smalls, Control."

Flit froze. She, Clarity, Sway, and Link all turned to look at Hawkeye. He sat there, just as stunned as they were.

"Hawk..." Flit whispered as she turned to face him. He took a slow breath and looked over his shoulder at the growing group of people gathering around Trojan. His grip on her hand was so tight it ached.

"Shit, I... I wasn't expecting that." His gaze snapped between Trojan and their group.

"Dude, get back there! This is what you've been wanting for ages," Sway hissed, leaning in closer. Link elbowed him in the ribs. "What? It's true."

"Have a bit of tact, will you?" Link scolded him. He just shrugged.

Hawkeye didn't seem to hear any of it. He just looked at Flit, his fingers untangling from hers.

He got to his feet and she stood with him. "Hawk—" Flit's voice caught in her throat. It was a different situation, but memories flooded back, casting her to other farewells that didn't go so well. Her chest rose and fell raggedly, each breath harder to suck in than the last.

Hawkeye put a gentle, warm hand on her shoulder. "I'll be careful, I promise." He pulled her into a hug. His familiar scent overwhelmed her. It took all her self-control not to cling to him. To cling to the best friend who had been there with her through thick and thin. The friend who had dragged her out of her darkest moments.

Hawkeye pulled back out of the hug when Harmony finished reading from her list. His eyes burned into Flit's. "I'm sorry, I know we were supposed to do this together..." He leaned closer, and Flit clung to him.

In that moment, Flit couldn't have given less of a shit about the deal they had made when they were young and naïve. That they would only move into the Intelligence team as a pair. The tunnel collapse and the fact that two people, perhaps more, might be dead overrode any vow they had made. She knew that. So why was her chest hurting so much?

"It's ok. Go. They need you." Flit took a deep breath. A chasm of unspoken words yawned between them. Hawkeye nodded and took two backwards steps before turning and making his way to the back of the room.

"Damn... that was close," Clarity whispered to Link and Sway.

The comment shook Flit out of her stupor. "What was?" She tore her eyes away from the screen that Hawkeye disappeared behind. The three all straightened up and tried to look innocent.

"Oh, nothing." Clarity was a terrible liar. Flit was about to press her for more, but Harmony cleared her throat to draw the attention of those in the room.

"That is all I have for the moment. Please, everyone, return to your rooms and try to get some sleep. We will update the live news feed with any information as we get it, but the most important thing we can do is prepare ourselves for the days ahead. Get some rest. We'll need you all in peak condition to deal with this situation swiftly and safely."

Surely Harmony was joking. Flit didn't think a single person in the lobby would get a wink of sleep that night.

DESPITE FLIT'S EARLIER CONCERNS, she did eventually fall asleep. A day of training followed by an evening patrol was enough to wear her down. Her dreams were more like nightmares, though: tunnel collapses, invading Government Officers, waking up to find her friends and family were gone. She was grateful when a knocking broke her out of her restless slumber.

Flit snapped awake. She sat bolt upright and looked at the door. There was another knock. "Who is it?"

"It's me." Hawkeye's voice came through her door.

Flit jumped out of bed. She forgot that she was wearing little more than a pair of boyleg briefs and a singlet as she hit the panel beside the door. "Hawk, how is everything? Is there any news?" Flit asked, before the door finished sliding open. Remembering what had happened the night before only made it easier for Flit to feel alert.

Hawkeye stared at her for a moment as if he had forgotten what he wanted to say. His eyes snapped up to hers and he cleared his throat. "Ah, no. They're still unable to get into Twenty-Eight, so the chances of Clip and Simmer getting out are next to none."

Flit gasped, pressing her hand against the doorframe for support. Clip and Simmer? Before they both got assigned to different teams, she would train with them on the weekends she spent in the Underground. Clip had been one of her first teleportation trainers. She had been talking to him less than twelve hours ago. "Shit! Hawk…"

"I know," Hawkeye whispered, but there was something detached in his voice. It was the same tone so many people in the Underground used when they became desensitised to the horror of a situation. "But Flit, there's more."

Fuck, what more could there be? Flit thought, her hands balling into fists at her side.

"They asked me to accompany a surface-bound team on a surveillance mission. There are some suspicions—and please don't tell them I told you this, but—there are some suspicions that the collapse wasn't an accident."

"No, Clip and Simmer would never—" Flit took a step towards Hawkeye, conviction burning in her eyes. He put his hands on her bare shoulders. His skin felt like a fiery brand against hers.

"I know, I know. That isn't what they're thinking. But we need more information. I have to go."

Flit's eyes stung. Her throat ached. "When?"

"Now. I just came back to get my stuff. I wasn't supposed to stop by, but I had to tell you. I couldn't leave without saying goodbye."

Without saying another word, Flit pulled her best friend into a tight embrace. She rested her head against his chest. His entire body melted into her arms. The base tattoo of his heartbeat echoed against her ear, and even though it should have calmed her, there was something so temporary about its rhythm. Something so humanly fragile.

"How long?"

"I don't know. Two weeks at least. They won't say much. Too big a risk. All I know is that I had to say goodbye." Hawkeye gently pulled himself from her embrace, holding her at arm's length. He looked deep into her eyes, and just as his lips parted to say more, his gaze wandered somewhere past her shoulders. His fingers tightened against her skin as he took a ragged breath. He bit his lip, shaking his head.

"Hawkeye?"

"Flit, I—" He stopped himself as he dragged his gaze back to her eyes. He sighed, leaning his forehead against hers as he held her close. "Please don't do anything stupid while I'm gone."

Flit smiled. Even in a moment like this, he felt the need to issue a pointless warning. "Me? Stupid? I never do anything stupid. I make calculated decisions."

"The only calculation that factors into your decisions is how to piss off the most people in a single course of action." He sighed, sounding resigned. He pressed a soft kiss against her forehead.

Looking at him with concern shining in her eyes, Flit asked, "Hawkeye, what is it?"

His eyes flicked behind her shoulders again. He shook his head. "Nothing, I just... Please promise me you'll be here when I get back. I need to know that I have someone to come back for." His words were filled with such an ache that Flit clung to his hands.

"Where else am I gonna go?" Flit sighed, biting her lip. "Of course, I'll be here. Just hurry back, ok?"

"Yeah, of course..." Hawkeye nodded as he stepped back, letting their hands untangle as their arms fell to their sides. "Goodbye Flit."

"Don't you dare say goodbye," Flit warned. She had already said goodbye to too many people. She wouldn't say it to him too. "Say catch you later."

"Sure... Catch you later, Flit." Hawkeye turned and walked away; his steps slow as he reached the corner that would take him to the elevator. He hesitated, shoulders tensing as he resisted the urge to turn and look back at her once more before he resumed his journey.

In a matter of moments, he was gone. Flit clutched at the doorway, her heart pounding. One risk of living in the Underground was that you never knew which goodbye would be your last. All she could do was hope that she and Hawkeye had many more left in them.

When Flit shut the door and went back to bed, she saw the photo that had settled on her comms unit screensaver. It was a snap of her and Rook, just over a year ago. About a month before everything went to hell. Her heart ached at the sight of it, and even though she had worked so hard to bury her feelings, tears sprung to her eyes. Hawkeye had been the one to see her through her darkest hours, to help her rediscover her purpose, to make her feel worthy again. And now? If she lost him, it would shatter her beyond repair.

17

SCRAPS

THE NIGHT of the tunnel collapses showed Scraps what the Underground was made of. Any doubts he had about the training and restraint of the rogue group were wiped out when he watched their response to the tragedy. Everyone pulled together as a unit; they took their orders, they worked hard, they made sure that their friends and families were safe, and they did everything they could to make sure they wouldn't be caught off-guard again.

The people in the Underground weren't just a rag-tag bunch. They were a tight-knit community. Even though they had their interpersonal squabbles, the needs of the collective took precedence, and their pride for their cause only got stronger after the disaster.

A few days after the incident, Scraps sat in his room after dinner, reading one of the emergency procedure manuals on the Underground's public database, when there was a knock at his door. Acumen had made a point of saying he was heading to bed early to catch up on rest because of the double shifts he had been pulling, so Scraps wasn't sure who it was. Still, when he got up to open his door and it slid aside to reveal Flit, he wasn't entirely surprised.

He looked down at her, pressing his lips together in a frown. "You know there are procedures for this, right?"

"I think we both know by now that I believe procedures are nothing more than optional guidelines." Flit waved her hand dismissively and winked at him.

Scraps' lips twisted into a disapproving frown. With everything going on in the Underground, he didn't know how she still had the energy to joke around. "And what reason do you have for ignoring procedures tonight?" he asked, still not closing the door or stepping back to let her pass.

"You mean, apart from the fact that it's stupid you still need a minder? Or because, I don't believe you'd hurt me, even if you could catch me. Not that you could, by the—"

"Flit!" An exasperated sigh from the corridor behind Flit made Scraps jump. A woman stepped into the doorway beside Flit. "Please excuse her, she forgets her manners sometimes."

Scraps looked at the woman. Her deep black hair was greying around her temples, and her brown eyes held a warm, reddish undertone. Even though her face was thinning, her skin starting to show the signs of age, her smile was kind as she reached forward to shake his hand.

"My name is Bookworm," the woman said. Scraps took her hand and shook it, even though he wasn't sure why she was standing outside his room. She looked back over her shoulder, and then at Scraps again. "I know it is against the rules, but do you mind if I come in? I was hoping to introduce myself."

Scraps tried to remember where he had seen her before. He nodded as he racked his brain, stepping aside so she and Flit could come inside. As the two walked past, Flit's footsteps had an extra excited spring to them. When the door slid shut behind them he gestured for the two women to take a seat at his small dining table and he settled onto on the end of his bed.

"Thanks for letting me in, Scraps. I know you're probably worried you'll get in trouble for having us in your room without Acumen, so I won't stay for long," Bookworm promised.

There was something about her voice that tickled a memory at the back of his mind. She also seemed to know just what he was thinking. "Ah, so you are a telepath, then?" Scraps asked, wondering why Flit would want to bring another telepath in to meet him. Was she concerned he was scheming behind the Underground's back?

"Far from it," Bookworm chuckled softly as she shook her head.

Then Scraps remembered. On his first day in the Underground, in the Nest, she was with the group of people who captured him. She was the one who rendered him unconscious.

"They called me TE-8266 for much of my early life."

Scraps' eyes widened and his heart skipped a beat. "TE-8266?" An Ex-Registered telecoercionist? He peered deeper into her eyes. He had noticed the warm red undertone to them, but they were nowhere near as bright as his. His gaze dropped down to her neck, where the skin showed only a thin white ghost of a tattoo. "You... You were..."

"Like you, yes," Bookworm confirmed, "I was reluctant to come and talk to you, as I'm not sure where you're at with your own experience down here, but Flit convinced me it might help. I know what it's like to be in your shoes."

He wondered if Bookworm would regret her decision to visit him if he asked all the questions that had been brewing in his mind over the past couple of months. "I would appreciate that very much. Can I get you a drink, a cup of tea or anything?"

"No, thank you for the offer." Bookworm graced him with a warm smile. "Why don't you begin by telling me how you wound up in the Underground? We can go from there," Bookworm suggested when Scraps struggled to figure out what to ask first. His eyes dipped to the faint outline of the tattoo on her neck as he began his story.

Bookworm was an excellent listener. She didn't jump in to ask questions while Scraps was explaining things. Flit did her thing and added in minor facts or anecdotes here or there. Scraps found that most of them were helpful, filling in things from an Underground perspective about his time with them. When Scraps got to the part about the influence of his control chip, Bookworm nodded knowingly.

"At first, I was displeased about having the control chip tampered with. So many emotions and thoughts that I was protected from poured in. I wasn't ready for them," Scraps admitted.

"I don't think anyone could be," Bookworm acknowledged. "Even me. I sought this place out after having some issues with my CO. He... I needed to escape. I was lucky to stumble across one of the Intelligence Team's Outreach workers. They told me about the Underground, about everything I had been missing out on. After a bit of drama I made my escape, fully aware of what was going to happen. But even that didn't prepare me. It was... strange and so intense."

Scraps didn't show his surprise at the fact that Bookworm had willingly escaped. He wondered how she found the Underground Operative, but that was a question for another time. "So, how did you deal with it all?" he asked.

"Honestly? Most days, I didn't. Not very well, at least. The team down here were amazing; they were patient with me through the early days of the emotional rollercoaster. They were all experienced with handling their own emotions and gave me great advice during the transition." Bookworm tucked some greying wisps of hair behind her ear. "Who is your doctor?"

"Tinker."

Bookworm smiled at Flit. "Tinker is lovely, very helpful. Although I imagine there are some things you'd prefer to speak to a man about. If that is the case, please ask to see a male doctor. This isn't the Hub; you're allowed to make requests like that. My son, Patch, he is a doctor too. I'm sure he can fill you in on some nuances of the transition, having grown up with me as his mother."

There were so many things to consider in that statement that Scraps took a good few beats to digest it. The first was that it was fine to request a new doctor. It wasn't that Tinker was unsuitable; he had a healthy amount of respect for the woman. But Bookworm was right, there were certain issues he wasn't comfortable discussing with her.

"So... you have a son?" Scraps asked, hooking onto the second part of her statement.

Bookworm's eyes sparkled with affection. "Yes, Patch is a micro. I also have a daughter; you've been training with her. Her name is Link."

Scraps' eyes widened. Link was the daughter of an ex-Registered Derivate? The entire Blue Team had been more than welcoming. Between Flit's progressive attitudes, and now Links' parentage, it all made sense. He thought of Link and Sway, the Blue Team's only couple. Flit's insistence that ex-Registereds could have children was true.

"But a life down here, away from the fresh air and sunlight, away from the conveniences and safety of the Hub… Is that an ideal way to live?" Scraps asked, voicing the concern he had ever since he stopped looking for the exits.

Bookworm shrugged. "Everyone will have their own answer to that, I have made my choice, and I have to live with it."

Flit bounced up and down in her seat, lips pressed together, almost as if there was a torrent of words she was struggling to contain.

Scraps admired her enthusiasm and how she never hid it. He liked it. He always knew where he stood with her. "Flit?"

Her words tumbled out. "What point is there to sunlight and fresh air if you aren't free to enjoy it? Or if they are the only joys in your life? Humans are such social creatures that we could be locked in darkness for a decade and still survive if we had another person. But put us in a cell full of sunlight and fresh air with no human contact? I know what I'd prefer."

Scraps frowned. "There were things I found satisfying in the Hub." It wasn't as horrible in the city as Flit thought.

"I'm sure there were. But when were you ever free to be you?"

Brows furrowed, he sighed heavily. "I don't even know who I am, not anymore."

Bookworm's head tilted to the side and she smiled in understanding. "You know the life you left behind. If you go back to the Hub, you know what your future will look like. Down here? Well, if you stick around wonderful people like Flit, Acumen, and the Blue Team, you'll figure out who you are on your own terms. And the future? It's yours to shape."

Going back to the Hub seemed like the simplest option: he knew what to expect from the people around him and he had a future laid out. One where he didn't have to spend sleepless nights wondering whether he was doing the right thing. He just did what he was told, no questions asked… He had thought the simplest option was the best one.

Scraps wasn't so sure anymore.

"I've just got one more question for now," Scraps said. "How many Registered Derivates have returned to the Hub?"

Bookworm smiled as she got to her feet, smoothing down her linen pants as she looked at Scraps. "That's a good question." Her terracotta lips quirked in a mysterious smile. She reached out to shake his hand one more time before stepping back. "It's been lovely to meet you, Scraps. Please come and find me if you ever have any questions. Or even if you just want to chat."

Bookworm patted him on the shoulder before she made her way out of his room. She was long gone by the time he realised that she hadn't answered his last question. Flit teleported off her seat and reappeared by the door.

"Flit," Scraps called out after her. She turned around to face him. "Thank you."

Flit's smile was brighter than any of the artificial lighting in the Underground. "It was nothing," she said with a cavalier shrug before she teleported out of his line of sight.

Scraps sighed as he sank back onto his bed. He had so much to think about.

SCRAPS DIDN'T KNOW when Harmony and Divvy would call on him to make his decision. He figured the tunnel collapse had bought him extra time. But a week after the event, life started to settle, and Scraps had decided what he wanted to do.

"Scraps, buddy, what is it?" groaned Acumen as he answered Scraps' call on the comm unit.

Acumen yawned and scratched his stubbly beard. Normally he wouldn't arrive to pick up Scraps for another hour, but Scraps figured the call was warranted. He didn't want Acumen to make plans for the day and then have to rearrange them.

"I've made my decision. I wanted to see if it is possible to meet with Harmony and Divvy." Scraps squared his shoulders so he would look as confident as he felt.

Acumen rose one of his bushy eyebrows in surprise. "You're

sure? You don't have to decide until they call you." For once, there wasn't even a hint of a joke in his tone.

"I'm ready now. I've wasted enough time."

Acumen hesitated for only a moment before nodding. "I'll see what I can do."

RIGHT AFTER BREAKFAST, Acumen and Scraps made their way over to the high security tunnels of Control. He had been there only once before, when he met with Harmony and Divvy for the first time. This time, as he walked through, a few of the people he recognised from around the complex waved or nodded as he passed.

Acumen led them right to the same room they used that first time. The door opened as they approached, and the two were invited to sit down right away.

"Scraps, I'm sorry. We intended to touch base with you earlier, but as you know, things have been rather chaotic," Harmony said.

Divvy slid two glasses of water that she had just finished filling over to Scraps and Acumen. She must have known when they would arrive.

"I understand. I hope my request to see you has not come at an inconvenient time?" Scraps asked respectfully. He had observed both leaders managing the crisis, and they had shown admirable integrity and empathy.

"Not at all. We're glad you reached out. Now, why don't you tell us about the decision you've made?" Divvy clasped her hands on the table and looked at him expectantly.

Scraps took that as permission to speak freely. "A few months ago, I didn't even know the Underground existed," Scraps began, using the words he had rehearsed all night. "I did not know that such a complex and coordinated organisation could survive outside the Government's control. When I first came down here, I intended to return to The Hub with whatever information I could find."

Harmony and Acumen shifted in their seats, leaning in closer.

"I spent every moment I had alone memorising the layout of the tunnels, the names of the people, descriptions, information about anything that I could take back to my superiors in the Hub. But, well, I guess I got distracted."

Divvy's lips curled into a knowing smile.

"I never thought of having a life before. I mean, a real one: one with options. I just followed orders. The control chip kept whatever natural curiosity or rebelliousness I had in check. And then Tinker reduced the control it had on me."

"Those chips are hideous." Harmony shook her head, sitting back in her seat. The others hummed in agreement. "We understand that coming off the control chip can be overwhelming. We're impressed at how well you've handled it."

Scraps blushed at the compliment, but his chest swelled with pride. "It was—is—challenging. I have felt things that I never felt before. Then I met Bookworm, and I realised that I could either accept or reject the feelings I have been having. I can learn to live with them or run back to my old life because it's familiar." Scraps stopped, his brows furrowing as he rested his palms on the table. "Feeling so many things... It made me feel alive for the first time. Seeing the way people live down here made me curious. Watching the Blue Team training sessions inspired me, tasting the real food down here made me hungry for more. Hearing people like Flit speak made me angry—"

"Scraps, buddy, hearing Flit ranting would make anyone angry," Acumen chuckled.

"No!" Scraps blurted, sitting up taller and shaking his head. "Not that kind of angry... A different kind. It is hard to find the right word for it. It is just that everything she has said is true—"

"Oh, hell..."

"Acumen." Harmony shot the man a warning glare. "Scraps, please, continue."

Scraps sat back in his seat, frustrated that he was no better at expressing himself than a belligerent child. "It is a good kind of angry. What she said about the Government treating us like machines—it's true. They lied to us, none of it was 'For the good of all'. They were just using us. They told us we were not capable of feelings, or deserving of things like freedom, or free will, or friendship, or love, or even common dignity. Yes, she is overwhelming in her passion, but she inspired me to think about things in ways that would never have been possible without her."

As Scraps spoke, he could not believe just how many words tumbled out of his mouth. Gone was his carefully rehearsed speech. Instead, he spoke his mind and connected some thoughts he didn't know he had. "So yes, I am angry, but I refuse to let it fester. I am ready to do something with it, to make something of myself. And"—Scraps hesitated, his gut twisting with what he had come learn was anxiety—"if you will have me, I am ready to help the Underground. Just tell me what to do and where to go, and you will find I am excellent at taking orders."

"And you're aware that making this decision constitutes outright resistance against Government laws?" Harmony's words were slow and careful.

"When freedom is a luxury, resistance is inevitable," Scraps told her. "They have made their decisions, and now I am making mine."

Harmony and Divvy looked at each other. After a moment, their faces split into matching smiles.

"We were hoping you'd come to this decision." Harmony extended her hand across the table and Scraps shook it. "We're happy to have you on our side."

"In fact, we already have a few jobs in mind for you," Divvy added as she reached out to shake his hand, too. Scraps had no doubt that he had just made the best decision of his life.

Acumen grinned and patted his shoulder. "Welcome to the Underground, Scraps."

AFTER A LENGTHY CONVERSATION with the leaders, Acumen and Scraps made their way to the Mess for lunch. It was the peak time for that meal, so the large room was buzzing with conversation. As usual, the Blue Team had taken their favourite table in the far right corner. Scraps and Acumen wasted no time making their way over.

The Mess was one of Scraps' favourite places in the tunnel network. It was always a tangle of life and laughter. Like the Residence, the walls were covered in screens that flashed photos, news reels, and notices. There wasn't a single matching bench or seat, and people had taken to decorating the middle of the tables with handmade sculptures or items collected from treks in the deep cave system. The table that the Blue Team favoured had a mix of different coloured split geodes and leafy green plant cuttings that Link liked to collect on her patrols.

Seeing Acumen and Scraps approaching, Flit and Link slid apart to make room for them. Swipe's eyes lit up, and she gave Scraps a little wave from across the table like she always did when she saw him.

As soon as they were settled, Acumen sat a little straighter and looked over at Sway. "No way! I wouldn't have picked it. I can't believe you won that bet." His voice was an odd mix of curiosity and disappointment.

Sway laughed, dimples appearing on his cheeks as he flashed a dashing smile. "Come on," he slammed the back of his hand onto the table, "pay up old man."

Acumen muttered something under his breath and reached into his pocket, pulling out a candy bar and handing it over reluctantly.

"You know, for a telepath you suck at figuring out when people—"

Acumen silenced Sway with look of warning.

Flit, never one to miss a beat, leaned in. "When people what? What was the bet this time? Come on guys, spill!"

Acumen and Sway looked at each other. Scraps knew for a fact that these bets were commonplace, the same candy bar had been traded between Acumen and Sway for the past two weeks. He wondered why one of them didn't just eat the thing.

"Nothing, just a stupid idea that Sway had." Acumen waved his hand dismissively.

"Liar. It wasn't a stupid idea, we've been arguing about it for months!" Sway snapped, tucking the candy bar into his top pocket with a cocky smirk.

"If it wasn't a stupid idea, then it certainly bears discussing with the group." Flit sure was relentless when she wanted to be.

Clarity reached out across the table and patted Flit's hand. "Why don't we talk about something else instead?"

"I'll tell you what," Flit dug her hand into her cargo pants pocket and pulled out a small silver pack. She slid it onto the table. "I see your candy bar and raise you some gum."

Acumen and Sway looked unimpressed.

Flit sighed and reached down her top and retrieved a datastick from... somewhere. From the way her shirt shifted, Scraps could only imagine it was in her bra. He frowned. He didn't know those things had pockets.

Acumen spluttered with laughter beside him, and Link covered her mouth with her hand as her cheeks turned rosy with a blush.

"What?" Scraps asked.

"No, they certainly don't have pockets in them." Acumen's face twitched as he tried to turn his grin into a more serious expression.

Flit looked at Scraps, head tilted to the side, but she couldn't seem to figure out what she had missed. She shook her head and then slid the datastick onto the table. "The gum, and a copy of the latest Leda Polaris VR from the Hub. Do you know how hard it was to get?"

Both Acumen and Sway looked at the contraband drive with renewed interest.

Link sighed, reaching out and snapping both items off the table. "Flit, trust me, you don't want to know what this one is about." Link threw the two small items back to her.

"Oh, now I need to know. Name your price!"

Scraps shook his head along with the others. It was so typical of her to pursue something harder the moment someone told her not to. He'd only known her a brief time, but it was long enough to know that.

"Hey!" Acumen's tone was bright enough to cutting through the thickening tension at the table. "Enough of this childish bickering, yeah? We've got news. You know, actual, important news."

The others looked at Acumen with renewed interest.

"Scraps, tell 'em." Acumen elbowed Scraps in the ribs. Scraps looked at him, his brows furrowed in confusion. "About you-know-who joining the you-know-what." Acumen winked and tapped his brow.

Scraps reached up, brushing his fingers over the wire of the inhibitor. "Oh, yeah." He didn't think it warranted an announcement, but then again, he wasn't the best judge of those things. "I have decided to stay in the Underground. After lunch, I will meet up with Tinker to have my inhibitor removed, and then Acumen is helping me move into the Residence. I was given a few options for my first assignment, but I chose to join the Blue Team."

There was an uncharacteristic silence as the team processed the news, and then the table exploded into a roar of jubilant cheers and clapping. Scraps' cheeks burned as other diners in the Mess turned to look at their riotous table. Promotions in the Hub were never celebrated like this. You got a new assignment and you moved on. But now? All concerns that Scraps had about the team not wanting him to join the Underground were blasted away.

"Scraps, that is amazing!" Flit threw herself at him, pulling him in for a tight embrace. Her long chestnut hair was down, and as she pressed herself against him and he caught the fruity, playful scent of her shampoo. It differed greatly from the practical, unscented ones that the Underground provided for him. She was also far softer and far warmer than he had imagined.

Scraps' heart seized with emotion. He had never been hugged before. What was a hug, but a useless display of human affection? Or at least, that was what he had been told. Even though he just sat there in her arms, not knowing how to respond, he enjoyed the emotional physical contact more than he ever imagined he would.

"I'm so excited you're sticking around." Flit pulled back, her hazel eyes glittering in the mess lighting as she smiled up at him.

Tweak and Sway reached over to shake his hand. Acumen patted his shoulder companionably. Link and Clarity gave him excited hugs, and Swipe clung to him for far longer than any of the others. When it was over, Scraps realised he smelled of several kinds of perfumes.

18

FLIT

"SO, how was that for improving my range?" Flit asked smugly, leaning against the doorframe of the monitoring room. Posthoc and Beam looked over at her.

Beam, her father's childhood best friend and fellow teleporter, frowned. "You need to slow down. Don't push yourself too hard."

"Too hard? I don't think so. It was easy enough"—Flit held her hands up and wiggled her fingers—"and I'm all here. Nails and everything."

Beam sighed and tapped the console in front of him. A holographic vitals chart was projected above it with a record of Flit's heart rate and blood pressure from her last teleport. Flit noted the spikes peaking higher and higher as she pushed her boundaries.

"One of these times, you will push yourself too far. We talk a lot about splicing, but the danger of over-exertion is always there. See this spike"—Beam pointed to the highest peak on the chart as he looked at her—"most people would go into cardiac arrest if they hit that level."

Flit rolled her eyes. "I know my limits."

"Then you know that you need to stop pushing them."

Flit narrowed her eyes as she looked from Beam to Posthoc.

Posthoc stood back, raising his hands. "Don't look at me. I know better than to get into the middle of an ego-fight between two teleporters."

"Ego fight?" Beam snapped.

"Yeah, Flit's vitals are spiking, but she's only a few metres off your long-range record. If I were you, I'd be cautioning her off progress too. How long have you held the record for? Twenty years?"

"Twenty-five!" Beam corrected automatically. Flit smirked at the exchange, but Beam wasn't so impressed. "Did you come here to undermine my experience, or is there another reason you're still talking?"

"Actually, there was something else," Posthoc admitted, turning to Flit. "Flit, you've got a new assignment."

Flit's eyes widened. Could this be it? Was she finally being assigned to Intelligence? "I've gotten a reassignment?"

"No, an additional assignment. You'll still be in the Blue Team, but we wanted to offer you the chance to be Scraps' training mentor."

Flit couldn't believe her ears. "You want me to be Scraps' mentor? Are you serious?"

"Acumen and I discussed it and, surprisingly, we both agreed that you're best for the role. So, is that a yes or a no? There are others I can ask if you—"

"Yes!" Flit interrupted. She thought she would be the last choice. What kind of role model was she, compared to people like Link and Tweak, who were the epitome of well-disciplined Security members? Flit wasn't sure what the deal was, but she wouldn't question a good thing. A thrill of excitement ran through her at the extra responsibility, and she wondered what Scraps would think.

AFTER WANDERING AROUND for a while in search of Scraps, Flit ran into Acumen, who told her that he was with her mother having his inhibitor removed. She paced up and down the corridor outside her mother's consultation room, though instead of walking she teleported in stepping-distance hops. Back and forward, wondering where she was supposed to start with the whole 'mentoring' thing.

"Flit? What are you doing out here?"

Flit turned at the sound of her father's voice and her face split into a pleased smile. "Dad!" She teleported down the corridor to stand in front of him and threw her arms around him in a warm hug.

He chuckled and patted her back with his good hand. "Here I was thinking I wouldn't see you until dinner."

Flit shrugged. "I need to talk to Scraps. He's in with Mum." As they walked back towards the consultation room, the limp in her father's gait echoed down the corridor, adding an off-beat rhythm to her own regular steps. She was used to it, though; he'd had the limp since before she was born. "You'll never guess what happened in training today."

"What?" Her father's face softened into a smile at her enthusiasm.

Flit was about to tell him of her near-record breaking teleport when the door to the medical suite slid open to reveal her mother and Scraps. Tinker looked out and her eyes widened with surprise. "Stride? Flit? What are you both doing here?" Her shocked expression quickly morphed into a wary, narrow-eyed look.

"I just thought I'd come up and wait for your shift to end. I got through the cold-stores maintenance early," Stride explained, "and then I ran into this scallywag along the way." He reached out and ruffled Flit's hair. Well, at least he tried to. She teleported a metre away before he could touch her.

"Hey Mum," Flit said brightly. "I'm actually here for Scraps."

Flit looked at the red-eyed macrokinetic and her smile widened. She had gotten so used to seeing the thin silver inhibitor over his brow that it seemed like part of him. Now it was off, she realised just how ingrained he had become in the Underground. If it weren't for the red irises and the tattoo peeking out the side of his jacket collar, she might have thought he had been with them all along.

"Me? Why?" Scraps noticed the intensity of her inspection and his cheeks reddened.

Flit teleported closer to him. "I've got great news for you."

He looked at her, immediately wary. "I think I've had enough great news for the next couple of weeks, if I'm honest."

Whenever Flit stood that close, she noticed just how tall Scraps really was. "Ha, nice try. But this news comes from above," Flit said, pointing upwards. She stopped as he looked worried. "Oh, not that kind of above. I meant above us in the ladder of authority."

"Flit?" Tinker prodded; her tone edged in impatience. Her mother often stepped in when she rambled. Tinker was a much more efficient conversationalist.

"I'm gonna be your mentor. Lucky you!" Flit watched Scraps' face as her news sunk in.

Scraps furrowed his brows. "What is the role of a mentor?"

"I'm taking over for Acumen. Not the creepy, stalkery kind of stuff. I won't be watching you sleep or anything—"

"Flit!"

Flit winked at Scraps when Tinker protested. He smiled back at her.

"I'll be overseeing the organisation of your training and all that. Now that you're officially part of the Blue Team, I'll make sure you get enough time with all of us. You're also my new patrol partner," Flit explained. There was more to it than that, but she would tell him later without her folks hanging about.

"Oh."

Flit rolled her eyes. "Ouch. I mean, you could at least pretend to be happy."

"No, I did not mean it like that. I just…" Scraps trailed off, struggling to find the right words. "I have grown accustomed to Acumen's presence."

Flit shrugged. "Yeah, he kinda grows on you. But with everything going on down here, they need him back in his normal role, so you're stuck with me."

Scraps nodded, taking a moment to consider this news. Slowly a smile tugged at his lips. Flit thought it suited him. "I guess it is only fitting, since you are the one that brought me down here."

Scraps looked down into her eyes. Flit was about to reply when Scraps looked past her shoulder and his stance stiffened. He stepped around her and offered his hand to his father. "Sorry, I forgot my manners. My name is Scraps; I do not believe we have met before."

"No, we haven't, but I've heard a bit about you already." Stride didn't take the offered hand. Flit bit the inside of her lip and hoped Scraps wasn't offended. "I'm sure I'll see more of you since you're sticking around. Now, I'd hate to run, but Tinker and I need to have dinner before it gets too late."

Scraps let his hand drop and nodded. "Yes, of course, Sir."

Flit winced at the formality in his tone. He hadn't talked like that for few weeks. Stride walked forward and took Tinker's hand as they made their way down the corridor.

"Wait," Flit called after them. "I didn't tell you my good news."

"There's more?" Tinker asked, surprised.

"Yeah. I'm only a couple of metres off breaking Beam's long-distance jump record!"

Tinker's face dropped while Stride's brightened. "No way!" In the blink of an eye, he teleported in front of his daughter and pulled her into a firm hug. "That's my girl! After that upstart broke my record, I was hoping you'd be the one to take it back."

"Stride!"

Stride made a show of clearing his throat and straightening up. "Now, Flit, you need to be careful when you do such big jumps. You shouldn't stretch yourself so far so fast," he recited, the words forced and robotic.

Flit waved her hand dismissively. "Yeah, yeah."

Stride winked at her before he turned and, between steps, teleported back to Tinker's side.

"See you at dinner, darling!" Tinker called back over her shoulder.

As Tinker and Stride walked away, Flit turned back to Scraps and sighed. "Sorry about that."

"About what?"

"My father not shaking your hand. It wasn't anything personal. At least, I don't think it was. It's just that he was in an accident about thirty years ago and spliced his right hand and foot into a tunnel wall. So, he doesn't like handshakes because they don't feel genuine for him with his prosthetics."

Scraps winced.

"Yeah, it was how he and my mother met. She was the first medic on scene and had the very unfortunate duty of freeing his wrist and ankle from the wall he spliced into. I think it's the reason she freaks out every time I do something other than sit still. She's terrified she'll be called to a scene involving me and a wall."

"That is understandable," Scraps said with a frown as they started walking.

"Yeah, but also frustrating. It would be nice if she were a little more enthusiastic about my training. I mean, I'm the only one that's even come close to breaking Beam's record in the last decade, and she can't even break out a smile for it."

"What is Beam's record? How far can you teleport? From what I've seen you are probably classification C," Scraps said.

Flit frowned. She'd heard him talking to others and trying to measure their abilities by the Government's yardstick. "You know that the Classification System is bullshit, right?"

Scraps stiffened. "It is a very useful way to measure and understand Derivate abilities and—"

"Yeah, but it's bullshit," Flit repeated, rolling her eyes. "Their restrictions are based purely on their own control measures. We don't classify abilities the same way. Some people are amazing at some aspects and not so good at others."

"So, it is harder to label them because everyone is different?" Scraps asked.

"Yep." Flit nodded, her high brown ponytail bouncing. "I'm... let me think... I'm closer to a B with a dash of AAA."

Scraps stopped walking and looked at her. "How is that even possible?" he scoffed.

Flit couldn't help but grin. "See, told you the system was bullshit. You've only ever seen me teleport alone, but I can also take others with me, so that makes me B. I can teleport small items without going along with them, so long as I have line of sight. That ability is—"

"AAA." Scraps completed her sentence.

"Exactly. And right now, my line-of-sight jumping is about to exceed known limits. Once I've nailed that, I'll likely begin translocation."

"You mean, teleporting outside of your line of sight? I know that is a classification, but I have never once met someone who could do it. Even when I worked for the more covert departments."

"Not many people can translocate," Flit acknowledged. "There are a handful down here. Shadow, the leader of Intelligence, can apparently teleport anywhere. Like, you name it, he can go there. Beam can do it too, but only if he has a solid, three-dimensional visual reference point. That's why he's overseeing my training. I also suspect that there are a couple more amongst the Intelligence team, but as soon as a teleporter reaches that level, they get reassigned quick smart."

"Which is why you are working towards it?" Scraps may be the strong and silent type, but he was observant. He also had a logical mind, as Flit had seen time and time again in group training.

"Exactly. I want to get back up there." Flit jabbed her finger towards the ceiling. "I'm ready to make a difference."

"That sounds rather dangerous."

Flit shrugged. The Underground would never get anywhere if they didn't start taking more risks. If she had to put herself on the line to work towards freedom, that was a sacrifice she was prepared to make.

"So, no control chip, no inhibitor… How does it feel?" she asked, changing the topic back to him as a good mentor should.

Scraps looked down at his hands and his lips twisted as he mulled over his thoughts. "I think I've gotten used to not having my abilities," he admitted. "It was a rather humbling lesson in what it would be like to be a Citizen."

"Well now you've got them back, you'll get used to them again soon enough. I know the feeling, though. Living between the Underground and the Hub meant I had to be very careful to not use my powers. I got used to walking everywhere. But now I'm down here permanently, I'm getting around like the others, teleporting about just because I can. But it's always good to remember what life's like without your abilities. It's so easy to get complacent and rely on them."

"That is true. In the instance you're caught flat-footed, you need to know how to get along without them," Scraps agreed.

Flit stopped walking and looked up at him. He frowned as he

turned back to her. "Does that mean you're missing your sparring sessions with Hawkeye?" Flit asked in mock surprise.

Scraps pressed his lips together and shook his head, clearly sensing the playfulness in her tone. "I am merely saying that there is value in learning other skills."

"Naww, you do miss him!" She patted his shoulder. "Never mind, Scraps. I miss the goofball too."

Scraps didn't argue. Flit figured he was learning the difference between playing and genuine disagreements. "So, I've got to join my parents for dinner, but I can find you after and help you get moved into your new room if you like. At lunch you did say something about moving, didn't you?" Flit asked as they approached the large double-doors of the Mess.

"I am in the Residence now. Two doors down from you," he announced with a wide, proud smile.

Flit imagined that it felt like quite the achievement to move out of the holding rooms and into the Residence with everyone else.

"Acumen already helped me move though. I do not have many possessions. Just some clothes."

"Ok, I suppose I'll give you your first night in peace then, but I'll be knocking on your door first thing in the morning with your new training schedule," Flit warned, stuffing her hands in the pockets of her cargo pants as she smiled at him.

"I'm already looking forward to it," Scraps replied without an ounce of sarcasm.

19

SCRAPS

"WAIT, WHAT? YOU'RE HIS MENTOR?" Swipe snapped, looking between Flit and Scraps in disbelief. Along with Link, they had just finished a group simulation exercise. Scraps and Flit were going to remain behind for their first one-on-one training session together.

"Uh, yes..." Scraps intoned. He wasn't sure what he said to annoy Swipe, but he knew that tone well enough to understand that she was angry about something.

"I am. What's the problem?" Flit asked, taking off the interface gauntlets for the projection system and settling them on the console.

"I hardly think you're a suitable mentor for anyone, let alone our newest member."

Scraps stood, shocked. Swipe and Flit did not get along, but the blonde woman was being unnecessarily hostile about a decision that had nothing to do with her.

"That isn't fair," Link interjected, narrowing her eyes at Swipe in reproach.

"It's true! She's a terrible—"

"Oh, what, and you're any better?" Flit teleported closer to Swipe.

Swipe stepped back from the smaller woman. "Yes, I am. I don't understand why they chose you, when you couldn't follow a damn rule to save your life."

Link sighed. "Scraps has a better handle of the rules and regulations down here than any of us do."

"That is probably true," Scraps conceded.

Although Swipe's complaint did make him wonder why Flit was selected to be his mentor. They should have picked someone who would set a good example. She was outspoken, determined, and unapologetic about her beliefs. She was everything he wasn't.

Maybe that was the point.

Swipe looked between Flit and Scraps and her face hardened. "You know what, I've got better things to do," she snapped, throwing her hands up in the air and storming out.

Flit snorted and shook her head, teleporting over to the bench against the wall and picking up her water bottle, leaving Scraps and Link alone in the middle of the large room.

Link let out a loud sigh and rested her hand on Scraps' forearm. "Look, Flit may not be the best at following orders, but she is pretty much everything every kid in the Underground wants to be when they grow up. Well, before we have the hope battered out of us. They made her your mentor for good reason," she promised.

"I trust Posthoc and Acumen. I didn't mean to question their wisdom," Scraps said, not sure why his assigned mentor was such a hot topic.

"See you this afternoon at the service." Link patted his shoulder before she turned to leave. Scraps saw her whisper something to Flit on the way out, who just shrugged in response.

Scraps replayed the conversation in his mind as he stepped into a lunge, beginning his warm-up routine. Swipe and Flit had clashed on so many occasions. While he did not expect everyone in the Underground to get along, there seemed to be an added level of the friction between the two women.

"What is going on between you and Swipe?" Scraps asked. "You are always fighting."

"We've got history," Flit said, refusing to turn around as she set her water bottle back on the bench. Her posture was tight.

Scraps frowned at the rare show of tension in Flit. There was something inside of him that stirred at the tone of her voice. He didn't know what was bothering her, but he wanted to make it stop. "What history?"

Flit turned around and looked up at him, her hazel eyes meeting his. Scraps could see her weighing up her thoughts, biting her lip as she considered her words more carefully than he had ever seen her do before. "We're not here to talk about that. Swipe and I will never get along. We've burned too many bridges for that to happen. And today…" Flit hesitated, her shoulders hunched. "Today we have the service for Clip and Simmer, the two people lost in the tunnel collapse. We're all on edge. I'm sorry you had to see that."

Scraps was disappointed as Flit had neatly skirted around his question. Before joining the Underground he would have been grateful to be left out of the fuss, but now? He thought of both Flit and Swipe as friends and wanted to help them repair their relationship. It was frustrating that Flit didn't trust him enough to confide in him. He thought they were closer than that.

"We're working on co-teleporting today." Flit straightened up as she changed the subject.

Scraps understood why she did it. Lingering on hurtful feelings could be consuming. Training was an effective distraction.

"I figure that since we're patrol partners, it's the best place to start. If we run into a messy situation, I'll be able to get us out, fast, but I've heard that teleporting can be" —Flit tilted her head from side to side as she struggled to find the right word—"unpleasant for those who weren't born to it. You need to get used to that."

"What do you mean?"

"Co-teleporting makes most people nauseous. I've had people pass out before, and I've had a good pair of shoes ruined because someone puked on them. Never could get the smell out." Flit scrunched up her nose at the memory.

Scraps chuckled. "You are talking to an ex-Government Officer. We do not puke on our shoes because of a little of teleporting."

It was Flit's turn to laugh; the sound tinkling off the walls of the training room warmed Scraps' heart. The smile on her face also brought out that sweet dimple on her cheek that she got whenever she laughed. When she could muster a straight face again, she shook out her shoulders and stepped closer to him. He moved back, not used to having someone in his personal space.

Flit winced. "Sorry, I should've warned you. I need to get close to bring you along with me. The closer we are, the safer it is."

Scraps' cheeks flared with a blush. He could feel the warmth of her already; having her even nearer did strange things to his body. He cleared his throat. "How close is close?"

"If this makes you uncomfortable, we can move on to something else." Flit's tone was gentle. "If you want to give it a go, I have to touch you, otherwise it won't work." She held her arms open, giving him the chance to step into them if he wanted.

A part of him that was eager to walk right into her waiting arms. But what if there was something about him that repelled her? What if she got close and decided that she didn't want to touch him? Scraps didn't have much experience touching other people outside of combat situations, and he certainly did not want to fight Flit.

After a moment, Flit gestured towards him. "May I?"

He nodded stiffly. "Yes." The word was clipped with anxiety.

Flit closed the distance between them, and he felt the smooth skin of her arms brushing over his as she wrapped them around him. She lined her body up against his, and she was much softer than he had imagined she would be. She looked up at him, her hazel eyes bright with encouragement.

"Please don't hold your breath. If you faint in our first session, the others will never let you live it down and it'll reflect poorly on me as a trainer," Flit teased, easing the tension in him a little.

Scraps took a slow breath to settle the strange churning in his stomach. He was a trained operative, a little teleportation didn't intimidate him. So why was he feeling so anxious? As he looked down at Flit, he caught a whiff of that lovely perfume of hers and the churning returned. Teleporting wasn't a problem, but being close to her?

That was an issue.

"Ok, breathe. Copy that."

Flit chuckled, shaking her head. She rested one hand against the base of his neck, and settled the other against his lower back. Scraps sucked in a breath at her touch. His body was reacting to her proximity, and he didn't want her to feel it. "Flit, I—"

"Don't worry, I won't let you get hurt," Flit promised in a reassuring tone.

Scraps gritted his teeth in frustration; that wasn't his prime concern in that moment. He knew she would never hurt him. "I know, I—"

"Just remember to breathe. I will teleport a tiny step to your left, alright? On the count of three. One… Two… Three."

A wave of vertigo overwhelmed Scraps as his entire world shifted one step to the left. His arms instinctively flung out to wrap around Flit, clinging to her as his vision swam. She may have been much smaller than him, but she was solid enough to quell the nausea. Scraps groaned. "Unpleasant is one way to describe it." He closed his eyes and made a concerted effort to steady his breathing. As the dizziness subsided, he removed his arms from around her, blushing. "Sorry, I did not mean to—"

"It's fine. Hold on to me if you need to. It'll make it easier for the both of us," Flit assured him.

"Ok." Scraps squared his shoulders and held her again, glad for the excuse. Anything to steady his shaking hands. "How often will we be doing this on patrol?"

"It's not a regular thing. We're working towards achieving a distance that will get us out of any immediate danger," Flit said as though it was no big deal.

"Did you have to do this with Hawkeye?" Scraps asked, trying to buy himself some recovery time. He would go again, but he needed to catch his breath first.

Flit chuckled. "Yeah, he puked all over my pants the first few times, so you're already doing better than him. Are we ready to go again?" she asked, her hands resuming their position on the base of his neck and his lower back.

Scraps took a deep breath to steel himself for the next gut-churning jump. On a positive note, he realised the side-effects of teleporting were enough to distract him from the way Flit's entire body was pressed up against his. "Ok."

Scraps hoped he would hold on to the contents of his stomach over the next two hours. He wished they could just have that rematch she had been threatening for months, but he supposed co-teleporting was the more practical option.

AN HOUR AND A HALF LATER, Scraps slumped onto the bench against the wall in the training room, panting. Somehow Flit was still standing, bouncing from foot to foot as they cooled down. He marvelled at the fact she still had energy left when all he wanted to do was collapse.

"So, will that be enough distance for us to get out of danger, or do we need to do this again?" He tried not to sound too averse to the idea.

"It should be enough to go on patrols. A little more training wouldn't hurt, but I think our next session should be that rematch we're both waiting for."

Scraps leaned against the wall and looked at Flit. Once she finished gulping down some water, she set her bottle on the ground and pulled the elastic out of the bottom of her braid. During their training session it had all come loose. She ran her fingers through it, the movement drawing his eyes to how the feathered ends of her hair fell over the swelling of her chest. The smooth tanned skin there was slightly flushed and covered in a fine sheen of sweat that highlighted just how curvaceous that part of her body was. "I like that idea." Scraps tore his gaze away from Flit and her exposed skin along her neckline. He looked at the level of water in his bottle instead and found it much easier to concentrate on conversation.

Flit picked up her water bottle again and looked down at herself, frowning. "The service is in an hour down in the Catacombs. If you haven't been down there before, I'm happy to show you the way, but I need to go back to my room and clean up first. I stink."

Scraps frowned. He had been close enough to smell her for the entire training session and she did not stink in the slightest. However, he couldn't say the same about himself. "I should clean up too. Is there a dress code for this kind of event?" He looked down at his sweat-soaked training fatigues.

"Not so much. Just something clean'll do. Unless you'd like me to find you something more casual? I'm sure I could dig something up."

Scraps thought of all the different outfits he had seen other males wearing. He considered taking Flit up on her offer, but it wouldn't make a difference. He was comfortable in the clothing the Underground had provided him with, and he had a clean set in his wardrobe. That should be enough. "No, I will be all right, thank you. But a shower would be nice." He stood, tucked his water bottle under his arm, and led the way to the door.

Flit and Scraps walked back to the Residence in companionable silence. When they got to their level, they split off at Flit's room, as it was first.

"I'll meet you out here in half an hour?" Scraps asked.

Flit opened the door and his eyes widened. The room beyond was nothing short of chaotic. Clothes and other items were strewn around haphazardly. They covered almost every available surface. Even the floor. He pressed his lips together and his brows furrowed. How did she walk in there without treading on something?

Flit chuckled sheepishly as she looked over her shoulder. She cleared her throat. "Please ignore the floordrobe. I brought a lot down from the Hub. I've been meaning to sort through it all, but it's been busy around here." Flit pulled the door shut behind her as she spoke.

Even though Scraps had come down to the Underground with nothing, he still would never have had as much mess as Flit had in her room. Such clutter and disarray attracted a strict penalty in the Derivate Quarters. "All right, I'll see you in half an hour."

As Scraps turned and walked away, he shook his head. He shouldn't have been be surprised. The chaos in her room represented her flighty nature quite well. He only hoped she would have a better handle on his training schedule.

20
———

SCRAPS

THE CATACOMBS, Scraps learned, were the cavernous archways beneath the heart of the Underground that served as a graveyard. They were lit by dim, moody bulbs tucked high in the cave roof, and a nearby subterranean river filled them with unearthly wailing sounds. It was easy to see why they were reserved for the fallen; the Catacombs had a certain hushed reverence about them.

By the time Flit and Scraps descended into the space, it was already teeming with people, more than Scraps had thought he would see down here. There were plenty he recognised, but some faces were foreign. He wondered at how the labyrinthine tunnels kept so much of the thriving society sheltered.

Flit and Scraps joined the crowd of people streaming through the main entrance down a walkway marked by a runway of small round stones. At the end of the path was a ring of benches carved from rocks and boulders, surrounding a central pulpit. All around the gathering space, graves of the deceased spread into the dark recesses of the cavern, marked by headstones hand-carved with varying levels of artistry, and punctuated by towering stalagmites and looming stalactites. Scraps wasn't sure how far the cavern went, but the headstones Scraps saw made him wonder just how long the group had been underground for. In the Hub, they had moved to more space- and environmentally-friendly options for their dead, such as cremation and vertical-forest grave sites. The remaining energy in the bodies were harnessed to grow new life or to better balance the biome. Scraps wasn't sure what the decomposing remains did for the tunnel biome, but he hoped that the sheer number of graves didn't destabilise the ground.

"How long has the Underground been operating?" Scraps whispered to Flit as they joined the procession of people making for the ring of benches.

"Ever since the war. It was the only place the founders could escape to when the tide turned against them. Those injured by the Government or fleeing their growing regime came down here. They were just meant to regroup and catch their breath before taking the fight back to the Government." Flit stopped, frowning as she looked around them. When she spoke again, her voice was barely above a whisper. "Almost a hundred years later, and you can see we kinda hit a snag on that last part."

Hit a snag, indeed. Given that no one in the Hub seemed to know about the Underground, they had strayed far from what Flit said their initial briefing was. Scraps wondered how they had lost that along the way. Then again, maybe the resting remains all around them were proof enough.

Flit and Scraps found some space on a bench towards the back. Scraps noticed that Flit had lost a little of the bounce in her step, and by the time they sat, her ever-present smirk was gone. He looked around and saw some familiar faces in other rows, but no one was getting up or moving about to sit with their friends. In the shadows of the catacombs, respect and calmness reigned supreme.

The stream of people shuffling in dwindled into a few stragglers when Harmony and Divvy arrived, leading the funeral procession. The two caskets floated smoothly after them, with Heft walking behind, his hands raised and face stoic. The last people to walk in were members of the Green Security Team and some older people who were clinging to them for support. As the caskets were hovered down the aisle, the people on the benches rose to stand. It was a wave of movement, a ripple of respect for their fallen comrades. Harmony and Divvy continued forward until they both stood behind the pulpit, and the two caskets settled down beside them.

The family and team members took their places in the first, empty row of seats.

Scraps had never been to a funeral before. When Registereds died, they were cremated; their items redistributed or disposed of; their designation in the Hub Database was deactivated. That was it.

The ceremony for Clip and Simmer was an emotional affair. Harmony and Divvy took turns to speak about the two: their contributions to the Underground, their unfailing devotion to maintaining the safety of their fellow Undergrounders, that they were doing their job right until their last moments. They spoke about the families they left behind; the spouses crying on the front seat, held in the arms of their grieving children, the team-mates that felt their absence keenly, the wider community who would be poorer for losing them.

Scraps was surrounded by a community in mourning; tears and whimpers flowed freely in the catacombs. He knew his control chip was no longer active, but he was unable to connect with the correct emotions for the situation. Was something wrong with him?

He had only met Clip and Simmer once or twice, and while their deaths were unfortunate, the tunnel collapse was a horrible accident. It was just a mix of poor timing and terrible luck.

As friends and family members of the fallen moved to the pulpit to make speeches and farewells, a small sniffle made Scraps turn to look at Flit. Her shoulders shook with silent sobs as tears streamed down her flushed cheeks. Scraps frowned, biting his lip as he witnessed the show of emotion from someone who always seemed so strong. He shifted uncomfortably in his seat, wanting to help but not knowing how.

Scraps looked around, seeing shows of physical comfort being shared between friends; hand holding, hugs, shoulders leaned against one another. After being hugged by his female comrades when he announced he had joined the Underground, he understood the intimate power of physical gestures. So, Scraps reached out, settling his hand on Flit's shoulder. She turned to him, her bloodshot eyes wide at the uncharacteristic gesture. It only took her a moment to process what he was doing before she let out a soft, shaking breath and leaned against him.

Scraps wondered what it was like to be in her shoes. To have lost someone that he cared about.

Then it hit him.

VC-825.

He hadn't thought about her since he was captured, but now her face hovered in the shadowy edges of his memory and he realised that he should have felt something about her death. They had spent their childhoods training side by side. She offered him smiles when others barely looked at him. Even in the minutes before her death, she tried to squeeze some semblance of humanity from him; a sign that he was thinking or feeling too, beneath all the brainwashing. He remembered how her shoulders and smile fell before she led her team into that tunnel and to their doom. Scraps' eyes stung, but he blinked rapidly to clear the uncomfortable sensation. The connection to his own kind was something that the Government had deprived him of for too long. He may have been too late to reach out to VC-825, but he had a whole new group of friends in the Underground he could learn to support. With that resolution, he held Flit to his side a little tighter.

As the ceremony ended, each row stood in an orderly fashion and filed past the two caskets, their fingers brushing over the surfaces as they whispered their last goodbyes. When it came to their row Flit rose, taking Scraps' hand and leading him over with the others. He stood behind her as she placed her hand on one casket after the other, whispering something. When it was his turn, he was not sure what to say or do, so he bowed his head before moving on.

Scraps and Flit joined the stream of people making for the exit, but just before they reached the tunnel that would lead back up to the main habitation levels, Flit took his hand and pulled him off to the side.

"I can't leave yet," Flit said, her voice trembling as she bit her lip and looked at the ground.

"I can stay here if you like," Scraps offered. "I don't have anywhere to be." He did not want to leave her alone in such a lifeless place when she was upset.

"Thanks, but no... I need to do this alone." Flit looked past him, searching the line until recognition flashed in her eyes. She waved her hand, and Link and a man around the same age as her stepped out of the group. The man looked just like Link, with the same deep caramel skin and black hair. Scraps had seen him around the Mess and medbays, but never learned his name.

"Hey guys," Link said, nodding at them both.

The man looked between Flit and Scraps and then smiled. "Hi. I don't think we've been introduced. I'm Patch, Link's brother." Patch reached out, offering Scraps his hand.

Scraps gave it a quick, firm shake. Then his eyes widened in recognition. Bookworm mentioned him when she visited Scraps. Now that they were standing close enough, Scraps could see the family resemblance.

"Flit, are you ok?" Link asked, her own eyes still red-rimmed from crying. She reached out and rested her hand on Flit's shoulder. Link looked into Flit's eyes for a moment and then nodded at whatever thought she must have picked up on. "That's fine. Scraps can come back up with us. I'll tell the others you won't be at dinner and I'll get something sent to your ro—"

Flit looked as though she was about to argue.

"Don't you dare. You're eating dinner, and that's final. I'll feed you myself if I have to," Link warned, her eyes narrowing as she looked at her friend.

Scraps wondered what Flit had thought to Link.

Flit sighed. "Fine." She turned to Scraps. "I'll see you in the morning after your training session with Swipe, okay?"

Scraps nodded mutely. He wanted to ask Flit what was wrong, but before he could, Link grabbed his forearm. He turned to face her. She shook her head and Scraps kept his question to himself. "All right. See you then." He let Link lead him out of the Catacombs, turning to look back over his shoulder as Flit slipped into the shadows between headstones.

"She'll be okay, she just has a visit to make while she's down there," Link assured him, letting go of his arm and tucking a stray strand of hair behind her ear.

Scraps frowned. "Did she lose someone else?"

Patch nodded. "We all did, but Flit felt his loss most keenly."

When Scraps went to ask something, Patch continued, his tone laced with apology, "I would tell you more, but it isn't my story to tell."

As much as Scraps wanted to know what made Flit so sad, he respected Patch's decision. Flit was always so open with him, but as curious as he was, he could be patient. So, he filed away his concern and concentrated on following Patch and Link through the labyrinthine tunnels on their way back to the Mess.

21

FLIT

THE PATH between the headstones was well worn, but not because of Flit. It had been a long while since she had ventured to this part of the Underground. It stirred up too many bad memories that threatened to unhinge the precarious mental balance she had found. She had spent most of the past two days trying to decide if she would delve further into the Catacombs after Clip and Simmer's funeral. In the end, the lure of his 'resting' place was too strong to resist.

Rook.

In the back corner of the cavern, in a natural archway shrouded by stalactites, she would find his headstone above a place where he would never truly rest. Perhaps that was why Flit hated coming down here. It was a farce. If his body was beneath the gravelly earth, maybe she would feel some connection to him. But not all those who were lost could come home, and Rook was one of them.

The haunting whistle of the subterranean river turned to a gushing roar, and Flit knew she was close. She turned left down one path, and right down another. It was an arduous task to walk past dozens of names she knew to find the one she was truly after. As she got closer, the breathing she had tried so hard to hold steady wavered. Even though she had cried plenty of silent tears for Clip and Simmer, she still had some left when her eyes fell on Rook's name, carved on a tall shard of rough-cut marble.

Flit teleported the last few metres, her feet stumbling as she fell to her knees on the gravel in front of the stone. Her chest ached, like she had been stabbed with a dagger of ice; the frostbite of loss sunk deep into her veins, spreading through her limbs with every painful spasm of her heart. She doubted she would ever get used to seeing his name on stone.

There were still some days where she swore she would wake up and find him laying beside her.

"Oh Rook," Flit whispered, trembling fingers reaching out to trace the name. It was the only physical connection she had to him anymore, symbolic as it was. "I'm s-so sorry... I know I haven't come down here, haven't talked to you." Tears burnt fiery trails down her cheeks, a startling counterpoint to the frigid pangs of loss pulsing inside her.

Flit shifted to her side, making herself more comfortable in front of the headstone. She tried to figure out what to say. What words could encompass how she felt in that moment? She felt silly, talking to the stone above an empty grave, but in the shadowy reverence of the Catacombs it somehow felt right.

"It's been a crazy few months, babe. I'm sure Clip and Simmer will tell you about it over a glass of moonshine. They're with you now. At least, I hope they are..."

Flit took a deep breath, bringing a shaking hand up to wipe away the tears that were falling down her cheeks. "The tunnel explosion that took them from us set this place right off. Hawkeye got pulled into the Intelligence team. The little shit left me behind. Would you believe it?" Flit chuckled, shaking her head.

"I haven't heard from Hawk in weeks. I'm worried. I miss him. He was the one who kept me together when you—when you—" Flit stopped and groaned in frustration. Even with the genuine evidence she had to prove he was gone, saying it out loud was still the hardest thing to do.

"I'm scared, Rook. He has to come back! I can't.... I can't lose him too." Flit reached out, running her fingers over the dips and curves of his name, closing her eyes and just letting her feelings guide her.

"You always told me I'm the strongest person you knew, that I'm capable of so much, but I don't cope well with a broken heart. With Hawkeye gone, I feel like I'm losing the people I love one by one. I mean, I'd never admit it to them, but I didn't realise how much I would miss my folks. Crazy, right? But only seeing them once a week... it's hard."

Flit shifted so she was sitting side on to the stone, resting her head against it. The hard marble was a cold substitute for the warmth of Rook's carved chest, but it was all she had. She sighed as she pressed her wet cheek against it, the coolness soothing the swelling of her tear-stained eyes.

"If you were still here, and Hawkeye wasn't gallivanting around in the Hub, I'd almost say things were going well. Apart from the explosion, of course. I'm in the Underground full-time now. An unrestricted member of the Blue Team. You'd be so proud of how well we're working together. I know you used to ride us hard to get us to cooperate, but we're so in sync now. Even with Scraps."

Flit stopped speaking as she thought of the Underground's newest recruit. A gentle smile tugged at the corners of her frown and she opened her eyes. "Scraps is new. An Ex-Registered I saved from being rat-chowder in the Nest. Those Government Agents never learn, do they? When he first came down, he was so... so... robotic. For a while I was concerned he wouldn't be able to work past all that brain-washing, but he's doing so well now," Flit said, dashing away her tears with the back of her hand. "He's stopped referring to protocol all the time and is starting to see how crazy the Government is. He tried to crack a joke at dinner the other night, too. It was terrible."

Flit chuckled at the memory of the poorly executed joke and how, when it had fallen flat, Scraps had announced that he needed to study more to make the next joke more effective. "But he's trying. It's kinda nice to see, you know? And under all that stiffness and rule-following, he's turning out to be a great gu—"

"I should've known you'd be here."

The sharp voice that cut through the soothing whooshing echo of the river startled Flit. It was edged with such anger that her shoulders instinctively tensed and her heart raced. She turned towards the newcomer. "Swipe, please, not now." Flit's voice was clipped. Suddenly, she was so exhausted. She didn't have the energy to fight with Swipe. Not here. Not now.

"Do what, Flit?" The venom in Swipe's words stung Flit and made her hands shake. "Remind you that it's your fault that there we're looking at an empty grave with Rook's name on it? Because it is your fault, you know."

"Swipe—"

"No! I'm not finished with you. You always run away when I try to hold you accountable, and now there is no one here to jump in and pretend you're too fragile to hear it!"

"Swipe!"

Tears poured down Swipe's face, and the sense of loss in her eyes was the only thing that stopped Flit from smacking her pretty face. Emotions were running high because of the funeral; neither of them were thinking straight.

"Why do you always have to do this?" Swipe asked. Her long nails dug into her arms as she crossed them, making small white crescents on her porcelain skin. "If it's not bad enough that you stole Rook from me, you're doing the same with Scraps, too."

Flit felt as though a bucket of ice water was dumped over her head. "What?"

"You know what I mean. Rook was my best friend, you took him from me!"

"I didn't steal anyone! For fuck's sake, how could I take a friendship from you?" Flit got to her feet, trying to hold her ground as she stood in front of Rook's headstone.

"The moment you started seeing him, he didn't have time for me anymore. Oh sorry, Flit wants to go here—or ooh, sorry, I'm eating dinner with Flit tonight!" Swipe said, the tears falling faster. "I didn't even get to say goodbye to him that day—"

"Who did?" Flit cried, her voice echoing through the caverns. Her broken heart pounded in her chest as she thought back to the last time she saw him. "Name one person who knew what was coming when he—"

"Don't turn this on me!"

Flit could feel the retort about to roll off her tongue, but she snapped her mouth shut and took several deep, unsteady breaths.

The headstone loomed at her back, a reminder of where she was. It was not the time or place to get into it. As much as she wanted to set Swipe straight, nothing good would come of it. Neither of them were in the right headspace for any sensible discussion. Flit may be impulsive, but she had enough respect for those who had passed to avoid letting angry fights tarnish their memory. "Give me five minutes, then I'll go," Flit offered with a sigh, looking back over her shoulder at the headstone.

"Why? So you can sob more about how great Scraps is? About how you're enjoying your time with him so much?"

Swipe was crazy. "What the fuck are you talking about?" Flit stepped closer to the blonde. She had only just decided not to fight her, but the resolution was already wearing thin.

"You know what I'm talking about. You're always fluttering around him and throwing yourself in his face. If it wasn't bad enough that you got Rook killed, you're going to mess around with Scraps until we lose him too! You destroy everything!"

Flit's vision swam red with rage. "Swipe, if you don't shut up—"

"No!" Swipe yelled, her voice bouncing off the stones around them. "You know what? Screw you and your bullshit. I came here to talk to my friend, but you're in the way. You're always in the way!" She threw her hands up in the air, a spray of gravel pattering across the nearby headstones as she struggled to contain her anger. "Whatever! You can have the stupid fucking stone. He's not there anyway."

Before Flit could teleport over there and punch Swipe in the face, the blonde turned on her heels and fled, her unbound hair streaming behind her as she ran. Flit let out a shuddering gasp and fell to her knees, fumbling blindly through fresh tears until she pressed her forehead against Rook's name once more. It had been so long since she had felt so lost and confused, and this time, there was no one there to help her break free.

22

―――

SCRAPS

SCRAPS WAS SHOCKED WHEN HE, Patch and Link turned and made their way down the tunnel that led to the Mess and heard the buzz of conversation and music. There seemed to be a party going on inside. Scraps frowned, unable to comprehend the mood shift from the Catacombs to here. "What is going on?" he asked, leaning closer to Patch and Link.

"After every funeral we hold a wake. It's a chance to spend time with others and remember the good times we shared with the fallen. It must seem crass, but if we focus on the mourning and forget to celebrate the lives of those we lost, then we aren't doing their memories justice," Link explained, smiling over at him. She looked like she was about to say more when someone called her name.

Sway pushed his way through the stream of people making for the Mess. The moment he reached Link, he wrapped his arms around her; she let out a soft sigh and seemed to melt into his arms. He kissed her smooth hair and looked down at her. Some silent communication seemed to pass between them, and she nodded. He cupped her cheek for a tender moment and looked deep into his eyes before he slid his arm around her waist.

"I suppose we do things different to what you're used to," Sway said, looking over at Scraps as the group started walking again.

Scraps nodded. "Yes, I am still trying to understand the protocol surrounding this situation."

Sway tilted his head, confused. His spikey blond hair flopped to one side. "What did you do when you lost a team member up there?"

"Nothing."

Sway cocked an eyebrow in disbelief. "What do you mean, nothing?"

Not many people in the Underground knew what life was like for Registereds. Scraps wasn't bothered by Sway's surprise. "If we lost a team member, we moved on. Their CO's filled in the formwork and we went about business as usual without fanfare." Scraps gestured around them, to the people gathered.

"Fanfare? Fuck, what do they think we are, robots?" Sway threw his hands up in frustration. Scraps could see the same fire building in him that Flit would get when they talked about how Derivates were treated in the Hub.

"Sway," Link hissed in quiet reprimand. "We've talked about this."

Sway rolled his eyes. "So, you never used to feel anything? Even if someone died?"

Link elbowed him in the ribs.

Scraps winced at the disdain in Sway's tone, but he didn't blame him. Scraps could understand how he would seem inhumane if he never mourned the loss of a comrade. At least, he could see it now. He liked that Sway asked him, rather than just assuming he knew. It gave him a chance to express himself. "I did feel some things. My emotions were just muted. Not the... extremes I am used to now."

Sway chuckled. "You? Extreme?"

"It feels like that some days. I used to get frustrated from time to time, if there were delays at work or unnecessary obstacles... but that was about it," Scraps explained.

"And how about now, then?" Patch asked in a hushed tone. He looked around and waited until a group that was walking next to them moved ahead before continuing. "I assume Tinker deactivated your chip?"

"Now? I feel a lot. Too much, sometimes. There are still so many emotions I am trying to get used to. Frustration, confusion, anger, loneliness, regret, lust, sadness, joy.... It's endless."

Sway stopped walking pulling Link to a halt as he looked over at Scraps with mischief glinting in his eyes.

Link's eyes widened with horror. "Sway! Don't you da—"

"Woah, wait a second. I heard sadness and anger and all that... but did you say lust?" Sway asked.

A hot flush creeped up Scraps' cheeks.

Link shot Sway a disparaging look. "You don't have to answer that."

"I was told it is normal," Scraps said defensively, not wanting to let Sway's teasing tone go unaddressed.

It only made Sway chuckle again, earning him glaring looks of disapproval from Sway and Patch. "Oh yeah, it's normal. The question is, what are you going to do about it?"

Scraps frowned as he considered Sway's question. It was a good one. He had just been ignoring his desires, but that method was proving ineffective. From his understanding of the way the human body worked, abstinence and intimacy were the only options to deal with those feelings. Abstinence was not working, but he didn't know where to begin with intimacy. "Well, if you must know," Scraps began matter-of-factly.

"Oh, hell! Scraps, no, you don't have to tell him that. It's none of his damn business." Link waved her hands at him to warn him to stop.

Sway groaned. "Come on babe!"

"Don't 'babe' me. You're being a jerk." Link snatched Sway's hand and dragged him ahead, the sound of her reprimands getting lost in the crowd.

Patch sighed and patted Scraps on the shoulder. "Sorry about that, I don't think people like Sway understand what they're doing. He's never spent any time on the surface. He doesn't understand what Registereds are forced to go through," Patch said quietly, guiding Scraps out of the stream of people that were heading through the open double doors.

"Why was Link so annoyed?" Scraps asked, watching them disappear into the Mess.

"We generally don't quiz people about things like lust in public spaces, especially not when walking between a funeral and a wake,"

Patch explained. "If you ever need advice or information or anything, and you don't feel comfortable asking Tinker, come and find me."

Scraps appreciated the offer. There was a calm, measured quality to Patch's tone that made Scraps feel comfortable talking to him. Like he would not use Scraps' words as the punchline of a joke. Patch was also male and around his own age, it would be more comfortable discussing such issues with him than Tinker. Especially as Tinker was Flit's mother. It just seemed strange. Not that Flit had anything to do with it, of course, but it was awkward all the same.

"Thank you, I appreciate your offer," Scraps said earnestly.

Patch nodded and waited until a group of older women walked past before continuing. "Also, I should warn you that there are some women in the area that are interested in you. Some of it is because you're new. New faces don't crop up around here that often. It doesn't mean they won't like you for you, but don't let anyone rush you into anything you're not ready for. Give yourself time to get to know the women you like—" Patch stopped, seeming to catch himself. "If you like women. Sorry, I shouldn't make assumptions."

Scraps tilted his head to the side as he thought about it. None of his steamier dreams had featured men, nor had his eyes glued to male assets quite the way they had to female ones.

"I like women." Scraps could say it with absolute certainty. It was not something he had explicitly considered before, but as he said it, he felt like some part of his newly forming identity clicked into place.

"Okay. Just ignore what guys like Sway try to tell you. You need to consider what you want from relationships. Exploration? Connection? Relief? Most of the people our age have had time to consider that. So, if you're thinking of jumping into the dating game, take your time to figure that out so thing don't get messy."

Scraps wished he could have written that information down. It was more guidance on the topic than he had received before. Tinker had been excellent ensuring he understood the biological mechanics, but she never told him about the social side.

"Sorry." Patch looked at Scraps out of the corner of his eye. "I am smothering you with information. I know you're probably overwhelmed with everything you're had to take in so far."

"No, this is good. I am always eager to learn more." Scraps shook his head and smiled at Patch. "Is there any other important protocol I should know?"

"Well... Not protocol, per se, but before getting into a relationship of any sort it is important to consider what could happen if it ends. If you're thinking of someone on your team, there will be social ramif—"

"Hey, mule!"

The sneered call cut through Patch's words and the medic winced. He straightened up, eyes narrowing as two people walked towards them. One male and one female, both with their shoulders tensed and hands balled into fists. Scraps recognised the man as Heft, the Green Team member who had been rude to him a few weeks earlier. The woman spat at Scraps' feet as they drew close. Scraps was used to behaviour like that in the Hub, but it felt different down here. More personal. His heart beat faster, and heat rose in his face.

"Guys, this isn't the time or place," Patch warned, stepping beside Scraps.

"When is the time or place? When this mule drops more tunnels on our people?" Heft snapped.

A lump formed in Scraps' throat. They thought he caused the tunnel collapse?

A few people walking past slowed to watch. Their curious gazes made Scraps' skin burn. How many people blamed him? "I had nothing—"

"Yeah, I'd say that too, you mule," Oculus sneered. Her eyes flicked over his red irises and the tattoo on his neck. "They may have taken your inhibitor off, but we're not stupid. We can see what you're here for."

"That's enough," Patch growled, moving between Scraps and the pair.

Heft rolled his eyes. "Of course you're on his side. Your mother is one of those bastards, isn't she?"

Scraps did not have time to intervene before Patch's fist

slammed into the side of Heft's face. The people who had stopped to watch gasped and jumped back as Heft fell into Oculus. Heft raised a shaking hand towards Patch's face.

"Patch!" Scraps jumped forward, hands up, ready to protect Patch. He had seen Heft training with Swipe, he could stop him if need be. Scraps would not allow Patch to get hurt on his account.

"Hey, cool it!" Acumen's voice sliced through the tension as he and Posthoc pushed through the thickening crowd. "What the hell is going on?"

"We didn't do anything! They just attacked us—" Oculus started.

"Let me be the judge of that." Posthoc held up a hand to silence Oculus. His eyes glazed over as he used his postcognition to ascertain the truth of her statement. He shook his head as he snapped back to the present time. "You should know better than to lie to me by now."

Oculus glared at him. Heft spat some blood on the ground nearby and pressed the palm of his hand against his split lip.

"Acumen, you take those two idiots and I'll deal with this pair," Posthoc stepped in front of Patch and Scraps. Once Heft and Oculus had been frog-marched out of the hallway by Acumen, Posthoc sighed and looked at Patch with disappointment glimmering in his eyes. "Of all the days to punch that idiot, you chose today?"

Patch had the good sense to hang his head. Scraps looked equally contrite, his heart slamming against his ribs as he wondered if this would be it. If this is would get him kicked out of the Underground for good. His position with the rebels was built on shaky ground, and the thought of leaving the group filled him with dread.

"I'm sorry, I shouldn't have—" Patch started.

"Oh no, you should have. He was being an arsehole. You just needed to pick a better time. And a place with fewer witnesses. And maybe a different day." Posthoc sighed and pinched the bridge of his nose. "You two had better come with me, I'll need you to sign the incident report."

Scraps and Patch wore matching looks of disbelief as Posthoc led them back towards the tunnels of the Warren, where most of the administrative and support services were. Scraps had thought for sure that he would get into trouble, but Posthoc seemed to understand the scuffle. More than that— he supported it.

Scraps sighed and shook his head as he followed the leader of the Security department. This place got stranger by the day.

23

FLIT

"SO, I heard you were in a punch-up yesterday," Flit said to Scraps as she buckled her utility belt on over her loose black cargo pants. They were in the Security armoury, surrounded by four walls of weapons and equipment, preparing for their first patrol as a pair.

Scraps frowned. "I would hardly call it that," he muttered, looking through the equipment on his belt.

Flit ran her eyes over it too, to make sure he had the standard array; eight fire grenades, a pistol, and an emergency communicator beacon. "Honestly Scraps, I leave you alone for five minutes and you wind up in a fight," Flit teased, smiling at him and trying to lighten the mood.

"It wasn't me!" The exasperation in his tone told Flit it was still a touchy subject. "I didn't start it, nor did I throw the punch."

Flit sighed. "I know, I know, Patch explained this morning. Sorry Oculus and Heft are such jerks. I hope Posthoc went easy on you."

"He took our statements. That was it." Scraps looked up, furrowing his brows in confusion. "Well, after saying he did not blame Patch for punching Heft. Is that a normal reprimand procedure in the Underground? Your superiors encourage you to fight?"

Flit choked on a laugh and shook her head. She leaned back against the metal table they used to prepare their gear and looked at Scraps. Even though he still had the red eyes and Government tattoo, there was something different about him. Something had changed since that first time she saw him. She didn't know whether it was the more relaxed set of his shoulders or how he seemed to think rather than regurgitate protocol. Whatever it was, it suited him. There was something refreshing about being around him; he didn't blindly accept the things that she herself had become accustomed to. Like her superiors saying it was ok that someone had been punched.

"No, fighting is discouraged. I think the issue here is the intentions behind the fight," Flit explained with a shrug. "Heft and Oculus will get into trouble for the way they carried on. Saying that kind of stuff… That's not ok. And while Patch shouldn't have punched Heft, he was standing up for someone else's rights, trying to protect you and his mother before either of those idiots did something worse. I'm sure Patch will be reprimanded too, but privately."

Scraps chewed over her words before he spoke again, his tone more hesitant. "They said the tunnel collapse was my fault. People down here do not trust me, do they?"

Flit frowned and couldn't meet his eyes. He was trying so hard, and had changed so much, but she understood why others who didn't know him were scared. "Some people down here have lost a lot to the Government. They see Registereds as traitors. People out to destroy their own kind—"

Scraps pressed his lips together and stood straighter, ready to defend himself. "But—"

Flit raised a hand to cut off his argument. "You had no choice. You were brainwashed. Logically, I know that. But we've all lost best friends, family, lovers—" Flit's voice caught in her throat, her eyes burning with emotion. She took a slow breath. "You just… You need to know that some people have more trouble seeing past that than others."

"What about you? Can you see past it?"

Flit froze, looking up at Scraps like a rat caught in a torch-beam. Her initial instinct was to blurt out 'of course,', but he deserved better than that. He deserved the truth. "I have my days," she admitted, not breaking eye contact, "but I've lived in both worlds. While I wasn't Registered, I saw how the Government and Citizens treated them. I've heard horror stories from others. No one would choose that life. The fact that you ended up in the Hub and I wound up down here is nothing more than an accident of birth."

Scraps seemed taken aback by her honesty. He tore his eyes from her and looked down at his hazy reflection on the surface of the stainless-steel bench. It was times like these that Flit wished she was a telepath.

It was almost a minute before he spoke. "Then why did you rescue me?"

"Because you needed help." Flit reached out, putting her hand over his where it rested on the edge of the bench. His skin was warm and smooth, another reminder of the fact that Registered and Underground made no difference. They were both just human. "When you're down here you help first and judge later. It's what we do. Or, at least, what we're supposed to do."

"So, you've helped me, is now the time when you judge me?" Scraps asked, his eyes meeting hers once more. "Was I worth it?"

Flit's heart ached at the uncertainty in his tone. The stoic set of his shoulders might have fooled someone into thinking he was approaching the question objectively, but there was vulnerability in his eyes and a concerned waver in his voice.

"Yes. You are."

There was no hesitation. No uncertainty.

Scraps shifted, rolling his shoulders back and giving her a sharp nod of understanding. She didn't bother qualifying her answer; she had no intention to treat him like some list of pros and cons. She took a chance on a stranger that day, and she didn't regret it. In fact, the better she got to know him, the more pleased she was to have him on their side. He had shown such honesty, openness, and understanding that she knew he would succeed in the Underground.

"Now." Flit took her hand off his and poked a grenade on his belt. "Do you know how to use this?" Her eyes rose over his body to meet his again. It was an effort to not let her gaze snag on the way his tight t-shirt clung to his toned chest.

Scraps knew what all the weapons were, and they were both aware of it. However, the question provided a change of topic which allowed them to clear their mind. Scraps gave her a quick run-down of how to use the items in his arsenal. When he was finished, they both made for the door but had to step aside as it slid open to reveal Tweak and Clarity. They looked exhausted; their fatigues covered in dark but dried splatters of what looked like blood.

"Hey, you guys heading out?" Clarity asked, smile bright despite her exhaustion. Clarity always found energy to smile at her friends.

"Yeah. Where did you guys come back from? You're a mess," Flit asked, her eyes scanning over them to make sure they weren't injured.

Tweak sighed as he dumped his weapons belt onto the metal prep table with a loud clank. "Cleared out a roost of bats that were chewing some wiring in Sector Q."

Flit scrunched her nose in disgust. "That explains the blood." Most of her team members detested the rats the most, but the bats were her least favourite Underground inhabitants. Damn things hid high in the ceilings of caves and came down in a flurry of razor sharp, rabies-infected teeth if you got too close.

"So, Scraps, this is your first patrol. That's exciting." Clarity turned to the red-eyed telekinetic.

"Yes, I am looking forward to it. It is good to feel like I am being productive again." Scraps squared his shoulders and stood a little taller, looking every bit the professional officer.

"Don't forget to ask Flit to take you by Tunnel Forty-Two on the way back. I think you'll like that one," Tweak said, a smirk tugging at his lips.

Flit choked on a cough and Clarity rolled her eyes.

"Where is Forty-Two?" Scraps asked, "I have heard so much about it. I would like to see it. What sort of tunnel is it?"

"Oh, only the best kind." Tweak winked.

"The architecture down here is fascinating. Flit, can we stop by—"

"No!"

"Oh, Flit, don't be slack." Tweak's lips fell into a playful pout.

"Bloody idiot," Flit muttered under her breath, rolling her eyes. "Go get cleaned up, Tweak. You must've stepped in bat shit on your way back, you stink." Flit pushed past Tweak as he looked down at his fatigues and frowned.

"Have fun, you guys," Clarity said as Flit left the room with Scraps following behind her.

Just before the door shut between them, Flit overheard Tweak ask Clarity, "I don't stink, do I?"

"Is Forty-Two restricted?" Scraps asked as they walked down the corridor.

Flit was tempted to go back and murder Tweak. "No. Well, yes. Kinda. Look, I—just forget it, ok? Tweak was being an idiot. He shouldn't have said anything." Flit waved dismissively. She remembered how the topic came up at her party months ago, and what Tweak thought about her. He suggested it was about time she moved on after Rook. The thought didn't twist her gut quite as painfully as it did before, but that didn't mean she wanted to discuss it with Scraps.

When Flit and Scraps left the tunnels of the Warrens behind, their first patrol went without incident. Sector A was the closest to the living areas of the Underground and the least problematic section of all the tunnels. It was a good test for rookies, but Flit was disappointed. She had reached the surface-level sectors with Hawkeye. Being back within sniffing distance of headquarters felt like a demotion. But she liked Scraps, so she figured his company was worth it.

Flit spent the monotonous walking time of the patrol explaining about various creatures they could run into and how to deal with them. She taught Scraps about the layout of the tunnels and how to look for the markers showing the way to base and the nearest emergency shelters. When they walked past one such shelter, she opened it and allowed him to look around. He was impressed by how well hidden it was behind a nondescript panel of concrete.

It had been a long while since Flit had seen these sights with fresh eyes, so it was reassuring to know they were inconspicuous to the untrained observer. Scraps soaked up all the information eagerly and asked questions that made her reassess what she knew. He seemed to want to learn everything he could, and she was happy to talk about the organisation she was so proud of.

24

SCRAPS

AFTER THEIR FIRST PATROL, Scraps and Flit fell into a routine. He spent alternating mornings in one-on-one and group training. His afternoons were dedicated to patrols with Flit. Even though she didn't spend much time with Scraps when he first arrived in the Underground, she more than made up for it once their patrols started.

The long, often uneventful treks through the monotonous tunnels did not provide much entertainment, but Scraps looked forward to them. After Flit had run out of facts and protocols to teach him, she told him about her life. She explained what it was like to grow up living in both worlds; that of a Citizen and an Underground Derivate. She explained the discomfort of enjoying incredible privilege (albeit with a constant tinge of risk); of having access to excellent education, food, and living conditions. She saw the Registered Derivates being treated like animals. Every time she came down to the Underground, she was reminded of the life for those who did not wish to live under the thumb of the Government. There was lingering guilt, she told him, to having that double life and not doing anything to help better her kind.

But talking would only get them so far. Scraps used to be fine carrying out routine assigned tasks without issue, but now that he had more motivation than ever before, he wanted to make sure he was still learning and growing. Flit seemed to grow listless after a week or two of just talking. Scraps wondered how she ever committed herself to the patrols. It was at the start of their third week as partners that she showed him.

The skittering sound of mutant rats was something that Scraps would never forget. The scratching of claws against concrete, the thump and drag of their meaty bodies...

"Flit." Scraps put a hand on her shoulder to pull her to a stop. They were standing just before a T-junction in a tunnel at the very border of their assigned patrol.

Flit froze under his grip and looked over at him, nodding. She heard it too.

Scraps steadied his breathing and focused on the scurrying. The sound was coming from the tunnel to the right; from the amount of noise, he could picture their dirty, mastiff-sized bodies writhing over one another. Flashes of the carnage from the day he was brought to the Underground seared through his mind and he shuddered.

Suddenly, the hand Scraps had placed on Flit's shoulder fell through thin air. If it were anyone else, he would be concerned, but he was used to Flit disappearing and reappearing without warning. She often did it during their patrols to save them from having to go down dead-ends or into tight places. He was not comfortable with her shirking protocol, but he found out quickly that he couldn't deter her, so he didn't bother fighting about it.

"There's about a dozen of them," Flit whispered as she snapped into place right beside him.

Scraps frowned. "That's a lot. There are only two of us."

"Yeah, I suppose we could call for back up... but where's the fun in that?"

"Fun?" he mouthed.

Flit's thoughtful, neutral expression turned to a smirk that spoke of mischief. Scraps' narrowed his eyes at her. He had seen that look before during their team training sessions.

"What part of clearing those rodents alone would be fun? It sounds risky to me. Besides, according to the policy in the Security Patrol Handbook, we are supposed to stick to our own sector unless there is a risk of serious harm to the Underground. Sway and Swipe are patrolling that sector in the morning, we should report the disturbance to them," he whispered as the chittering edged nearer.

Flit leaned in, gesturing for him to come closer. Scraps leaned down so his face was next to hers before she whispered, "Five to one."

Scraps looked at the time on his wrist device. It was only nine-thirty. He frowned. Flit was very odd sometimes. "Pardon?"

"Five to one," she repeated, her warm breath brushing against his cheek in a rather distracting manner. "I bet I can exterminate five in the time it takes you to kill one."

Scraps pulled back, cocking an eyebrow at her. There was something about her presumptuous tone that rankled him. He did not think her estimation was a cooperative or professional way to approach the issue. Even if it was, she was a teleporter. She could not destroy so many creatures when all she could do was hop around. Really, it seemed like the odds were in his favour. "Challenge accepted."

A roguish smirk tugged at the corner of his lips as Flit bounced on the balls of her feet in excitement. That mischievous look came back with an edge of competitiveness that made him straighten up.

"Wait," he whispered. "What's in it for me?"

Flit tilted her head to the side. "What do you mean?"

"Well, I've observed many bets being made in the Underground, and they all hinge on the mutual wager of desirable goods and or services."

Nodding with approval, Flit said, "I see you've been learning. Good." She looked back over her shoulder as there was a squeak and a scuffle from the tunnel with the rats. "I've got three sour straps in my room, good surface quality. I'll give you those if you win."

Scraps frowned as he realised the error in his plan. "I do not have anything to offer you in return."

Flit shrugged. "That's okay, we can just say you owe me one." Her shrug was nonchalant, but her words were almost as ominous as the sound of the rats scuffling about around the corner.

Scraps did not want to let such a favour go undefined. "I do not feel comfortable with that."

Flit huffed as she considered it. "Next time I challenge you to something, you do it without mentioning the words policy, procedure, or protocol," she suggested.

Scraps looked at the hazel-eyed woman as he considered this. Flit had a reputation for flying by the seat of her pants and getting into sticky situations, but she was never outright dangerous. However, despite her bravado, she seemed to have the best interest of others at heart. If he gave her his word, he could trust she would not make him do something despicable. After all, this was the woman who had put herself at grave personal risk to rescue an unknown enemy.

"Deal." He extended his hand to shake on the wager and make it official. She took it. Her palm was warm, soft, and much smaller in his grasp. He held onto it as his red eyes met hers. "So, when do we—"

"Wahoo!" Flit's voice echoed from the other tunnel as she jumped mid-word. It took Scraps a moment to realise that she had gotten herself a head start. The tunnel filled with a flash of blinding light and the squealing of large rodents as a fire grenade went off. "One! Better hurry." Another grenade went off, followed by a joyful whoop. "Three!"

Scraps didn't waste any more time. He raced for the edge of the tunnel. His feet slid as he rounded the corner, but he used the momentum to turn and assess the situation. He reached out with his right hand and used his abilities to stabilise his drift. He threw it up in a swiping movement to knock a rat off the top of the seething pile that was cascading towards Flit on the other side of the tunnel.

"Four!"

Scraps gritted his teeth as he skidded to a stop. He pushed forward with both hands, slamming a wall of force into the rat-pile that knocked them down into a thinned-out carpet. Two of the rats turned on him and his arm tensed, his hand making a grasping motion as he picked up the creature on the right. He could feel the resistance of its skin and bones, and just as he was about to snap its neck—

"Six! Two for one. Hell yes!" Flit's jubilation was so loud, Scraps wouldn't have been surprised if it echoed back to the Residence.

Scraps didn't hold back after that. His telekinesis whipped around wildly, battling Flit for the last five rodents. It was a challenge. He had seen Flit in training, but there was something about being in the field with real enemies that gave her a chilling edge. She darted around, daggers flashing in her hands as fire grenades exploded, dropping rats all around her. She was so quick the critters didn't even know she was there to deliver their death.

The last of the rats let out a loud squeal as Scraps brought an overhead concrete manhole cover down to crush it. Scraps slumped against the tunnel wall, sweat pouring down his face. Flit reappeared at his side and looked up at him, arms crossed over her chest, with the smuggest smirk he'd ever seen on her face.

"Ten to five," she huffed, "and I got six before you got your first. Looks like you owe me one."

Scraps was still trying to process how Flit got one, let alone five, up on him so quickly. "You have won our wager. Congratulations," he replied, voice gruff.

Flit laughed and elbowed him playfully in the side. "Oh, I would've won even if I didn't beat you. That was the most fun I've had in months."

"It wasn't—" Scraps stopped mid-sentence.

He was about to argue that what they had done was duty, not fun. But that wasn't true. The surge of adrenaline that rushed through his body as he used his powers to destroy the rats made him feel more alive than he had in months. Coupled with the healthy competition, he found the last five minutes more gratifying than any of his training had been. Instead of disagreeing with her, he wondered at the smile that broke out across his face.

Flit was right. It *was* fun.

Scraps had always been competitive when it came to training and his duties. It was what helped him climb through the Government Derivate ranks with ease. Since coming to the Underground, that natural competitive streak was overshadowed by the ever-growing amount of information that he just didn't know. There was too much for him to learn to feel like he was accomplishing anything with distinction. Flit, it seemed, was just as driven as he was. It was good to spend time with someone who wanted to push him and add new meaning to his learning, rather than to just build up his already competent abilities.

"You are right," Scraps conceded with a nod, "that was fun."

Flit's eyes widened and she let out a loud whoop, jumping up and down on the spot and pounding her fist in the air. She was so excited that even Scraps had to laugh. When she finally settled down, she looped her arm through his elbow and guided him past the twitching rat carcasses.

"So, we can do it again, then?" she asked, voice bursting with hope.

"If the opportunity presents itself?" Scraps mused, "I would like that."

"Oh, thank goodness." Flit groaned, her body sagging melodramatically against his side, making him stumble to regain his balance. "It's been ages since anyone down here has had enough spirit to play that game with me."

"You mean Hawkeye didn't?" Scraps looked at her as they walked and making no attempt to remove his arm from her hold. Normally, he would withdraw from physical contact on instinct; it was a survival mechanism for Registereds. Any sort of non-professional physical touch was severely punished by their superiors. But he had no desire to withdraw from Flit. He put it down to the adrenaline rush from their skirmish.

Flit snorted with laughter. "Ha, no! Bloody Hawkeye just whines about his boots getting messy. 'Let's just do it quick with a fire grenade and get home'." The last part was done in a perfect impersonation of Hawkeye's exasperated tone.

"It presented an excellent opportunity to test our skills."

"And…?"

Scraps heaved a heavy sigh. "And to have fun."

Flit's smile was bright enough to light the dim tunnel they were in three times over.

25

FLIT

THE WEEKS BLED INTO MONTHS. Flit missed Hawkeye like hell, but her patrols with Scraps became an excellent distraction. She found that the Underground's latest recruit had a way of making her forget about her other concerns.

At least, until her parents brought them up at dinner. As she sat at the table with Tinker and Stride, pushing the last of her food around on her plate with her fork, her father leaned in. "How are you coping without Hawkeye being around?" he asked.

Flit stopped mid-fork-shove and looked up at him. She sighed before answering. "Fine, I guess. I just wish they could make contact, so I know he's all right."

Tinker reached across the table and squeezed Flit's hand. "I'm sure they'll be fine. They're all clever and well trained. They'll be back before you know it."

"Mmhmm..."

Being clever and well trained did not make them impervious to the Government. Flit put her fork down and leaned back in her seat. Her parents were just being caring, but the last thing she needed was people promising her Hawkeye was fine when they knew as little about the situation as she did. She didn't need platitudes. She needed her best friend back. Talking about the fact he wasn't back only made Flit miss him more.

Tinker sighed. "Flit, we just want to make sure you're ok. With Hawkeye away, and the anniversary of Rook's de—"

"Oh my, is that the time?" Flit interrupted, looking at the clock and trying her best to appear crestfallen. "I better get going. I've got a patrol tonight." Flit stood, stretched her arms and legs, and then picked up her dinner tray.

Tinker's expression fell with disappointment at how swiftly Flit cut off the conversation. "I thought you weren't on night shift for another week?"

"We had to change the schedule around a bit because Silver-tongue and Heft have training with Control this week. It was easier for us to take the shift a week early than swapping every second night over."

Her parents didn't argue with that. Everyone knew messing around with the body-clock and sleep cycles was a terrible idea. Even though Flit would do her week of late shifts early, it was better than being exhausted by a week of alternating afternoons and nights.

Flit's terrible attempt at reassurance made Stride's face contort with concern. Flit laughed and ruffled his thinning hair before she walked around and gave her mother a hug goodbye. Now that dinner was over, the two of them would head back up to the surface to get some rest before returning to work in their Hub jobs the following day. It was a tiring way to live their lives, never getting a day off, but they were committed.

Flit deposited her empty tray on the cleaning trolley before she teleported over to the Blue Team. Sway, Tweak, Swipe, Clarity, and Scraps were having dinner at their usual table in the back corner of the Mess. Or, as Acumen called it, the 'naughty corner'.

Sway was mid-sentence when Flit appeared beside him.

"She told me that—Ahh! Bloody hell, Flit," Sway choked, almost falling out of his seat in fright.

Clarity reached out and moved his drink aside just in time to save it from his flailing arms.

The others at the table laughed as Sway righted himself and turned to glare at Flit, his face bright red. "Dinner with Mumsy and Popsy all done?"

Flit didn't bother biting back. She just smirked at him cockily; they both knew he was grasping at straws to cover his embarrassment. "Yeah, time for a patrol. Some of us have work to do, you know," Flit said before looking at Scraps.

"I'll put my tray away and be right with you." Scraps got to his feet.

Sway let out a low whistle. "Woah, Scraps, my man. Looks like Flit's in one of her moods. If you're lucky, she'll take you to Tunnel Forty-Two after your patrol to blow off some steam," Sway crossed his arms over his chest and smirked at Flit in smug, silent victory.

Scraps looked over at Flit, red eyes wide and dancing with excitement. "Could we? I have been wanting to see Forty-Two for a while now."

Everyone at the table burst into laughter at his expense.

"You're all jerks!" Flit huffed. She looked at Scraps. "No, Scraps. No Forty-Two."

Scraps' face fell, only prompting further laughter. Sway seemed proud of himself. Flit wanted to punch his stupid face.

Scraps frowned and checked at his watch, pressing his lips together as he tried to find a solution. "I am sure we can make time if w—"

"Can we talk about this la—"

Swipe's voice cut through the laughter. "Don't worry, stud, if Flit won't take you to Forty-Two, I will. Drop by my room after your patrol and we can make it happen."

In an instant, the amused mood around the steel table turned to shocked silence. A surge of anger roiled in Flit's gut.

"Oh, thank you Swipe, I would appreciate that!" Scraps said, surprised but grateful.

"Shit, I bet you will," Tweak muttered under his breath with a suggestive eyebrow waggle at Swipe. She threw a piece of her leftover bread at him.

Flit glared at Swipe. "No, you won't, because Swipe is full of shit. She won't be taking you to Forty-Two. No-one down here will be until you're good and ready."

Scraps shifted uncomfortably on his feet as the discussion turned heated. "But Flit—"

The high-pitched scraping of Swipe's chair interrupted Scraps' protest. Swipe got to her feet and turned her back on Scraps to look at Flit, eyes narrowed, plump red lips pursed. "Who the hell said this had anything to do with you? Mind your own business."

Flit wasn't sure if Swipe stood between her and Scraps as a protective gesture, or an attempt to hide her hissed words from Scraps. "This became my business when the joke went too far."

"Too far? I don't see him complaining."

Scraps peered around Swipe's shoulder and caught Flit's eye. "I really would like to go to—"

"Scraps." Clarity reached forward, pressing her hand against his forearm and shaking her head. He looked frustrated, but he didn't protest further.

Flit gritted her teeth. She had so many angry words for Swipe that she couldn't pick which to spit at her first. After a failed attempt to speak that had Swipe cocking an arched eyebrow at her, she clenched her fists at her side and grasped at the first thing she could. "Why don't you see what Harmony and Divvy think of your offer, huh? This is the Underground, not the Government. We treat people with respect," Flit hissed, low and angry.

Swipe's eyes widened and she stepped closer so she could get right up in Flit's face.

"Oh no, no, no," Clarity groaned, jumping out of her own chair and wedging herself between Flit and Swipe.

"Clarity, you don't want to get into the middle of this," Swipe warned.

"No, you don't want to get into this. I can tell you right now that you'll both end up in the medbay for a week, and nobody will get to go on patrol—or to Forty-Two—with Scraps."

Being a temporal sensor, Clarity could predict that Flit and Swipe were just moments from blows. Clarity was usually hesitant to use her powers to intervene in social situations, so Flit gritted her teeth and stepped back. Swipe, however, did not seem willing to back down.

"Swipe, sit down please. This joke's gone too far." Clarity put her hand on Swipe's shoulder. Her voice was soft and coaxing.

Swipe looked at her, her entire body quivering with rage before she shook Clarity's hand off and stormed out of the Mess.

"Come on Scraps, we've got work to do," Flit sighed, looking over all the heads at the table at Scraps. The poor guy's eyes were wide with surprise as he took in how fast things had escalated. Rather than arguing further, he just nodded, leaving his tray behind as Flit turned on her heel and led the way out.

THANKS to the drama at dinner, Flit and Scraps' patrol was quiet. Flit attempted to make conversation with him several times, only to have him reply with clipped, one-word answers. It reminded her of the way he had spoken when he first came to the Underground, and the more time that passed, the more concerned she became. She was trying to figure out what she could say to fix it all when he broke the silence.

"Flit?" he asked, slowing their brisk pace to a stop as he looked over at her.

Flit stopped too, turning to face him. "Yeah?"

"Do you think I am a competent member of the Security team?"

Flit's eyebrows creased as her confusion showed on her face. "Of course." Scraps may be new to the role, but he could teach most of the Security team members a thing or two about how they should do their job. Herself included, particularly when it came to policies and procedures she didn't read.

"Would you trust me to carry out whatever task I was assigned?"

"Absolutely." She narrowed her eyes at him, not sure where he was taking the conversation.

"Then why do you to refuse to take me to Forty-Two?" A light blush dusted his cheeks as he glared at her.

Flit closed her eyes and took a deep breath. So that was where he was going with all of it. "Look, Scraps, I don't think you're incompetent—"

"But you must! If you won't take me yourself, why did you stop Swipe—"

"Sex, Scraps," Flit spluttered, her voice echoing down the tunnels. "Tunnel Forty-Two means sex."

Scraps' mouth snapped shut and he looked at her, his expression frozen between shock and disbelief. "W-what?"

"When the others are talking about Tunnel Forty-Two, they are using it as a euphemism for sex." The anger Flit had leashed at Swipe's actions strained to claw free again. "They've been keeping it as a stupid joke between themselves because they find it amusing. Their small minds can't come up with anything more entertaining."

"Sex? No. That is not possible." Scraps shook his head. "Weren't Sway and Link late to your party because they were doing some urgent maintenance in Tunnel Forty-Two?"

"Tweak only said that to make fun of them. There is no Tunnel Forty-Two. It doesn't exist. Even the naming convention is wrong."

That seemed to be the confirmation Scraps needed to realise Flit was telling the truth. His shoulders slumped and he looked away from her. "I did wonder about that..."

Flit rubbed her eyes and shook her head as Scraps took the time to process what she had told him.

The more Scraps seemed to think about it, the further his face and shoulders fell. "So, they have been joking with me this entire time?"

The hurt in his tone made Flit want to go back and punch them all in the face. She nodded. "Like I said, they were being idiots."

"And when Swipe offered to take me to Tunnel Forty-Two, you stopped her?"

Now it was Flit's turn to shift uncomfortably and look away. "Scraps, I want the best for you down here, I really do. If that involves having sex, that's great. But I won't stand by and let people take advantage of you. If you want to go back to Swipe's room tonight and learn all about that—" Flit stopped and shuddered at the thought of Swipe and Scraps together. An unfamiliar emotion clawed at her gut. She pushed it aside. "Then... fine. Just don't let her drag you in under false pretences, ok?"

Truthfully, Flit was *not* fine with Scraps and Swipe having sex, but she kept that to herself. Scraps was only just getting used to his hormones, and if he needed to explore that, then that was his prerogative, even if it involved Swipe.

"No, I will not go to Swipe's room tonight," Scraps said as he resumed their journey down the tunnel, his expression unreadable.

Flit let out a sigh of relief as she followed him. They only got a few metres before Scraps turned to the side to look at her. His crimson eyes caught Flit's, and she could see warmth in them.

"Flit?"

"Yes?"

"Thank you."

Flit's cheeks flushed pink. She broke the intense eye-contact with him and shrugged. "It's fine. I'm just looking out for you. It's my job."

"It is," Scraps said with a smile, "But you also did it because you are a good person."

Flit's heart melted. Given Scraps' natural honesty and innocence in the way of social norms, that was the most genuine compliment she had ever received. She patted his arm, trying to ignore the feel of his muscled arms beneath her palm. "You're welcome. You know I'm here—"

Scraps held his hand up in a stop motion and Flit froze. She held her breath, looking around for whatever threat he had spotted. What was it, more rats? Or, in these parts, it was more likely to be roaches. She leaned closer to him. "What is it?"

"Shh!" Scraps looked around, his red eyes scanning the tunnel first before narrowing and settling upon a pipe a few metres from them.

"Did you hear that?"

"Hear what?" Flit had to hand it to him; he was much more perceptive than she was.

Scraps strode over to the pipe he was looking at, leaning in close and running his fingers over the joins. When he muttered something disconcertedly under his breath, Flit's heart leapt into her throat. She teleported to his side. The moment her feet touched the ground, a low wheeze came from the pipe's straining joints. A foul odour clouded the air and Flit stumbled back, covering her nose as she looked up further down the tunnel. In the dim lighting, the ripples of straining joins were clear along the length of the pipe.

"Shit," Flit muttered. She searched along the concrete walls for the nearest pressure panel. It was on the opposite wall, further down the tunnel. She teleported over, flicked it open.

"How bad is it?" Scraps' voice echoed down to her.

Flit scanned the pressure gauges. Her stomach dropped and adrenaline flooded through her system. "Bad. The readings are all in the red." She flipped the panel shut and teleported back to Scraps' side. "We need to get to a shelter to report. Now."

Flit stepped even closer to Scraps until the heat of his body warmed hers. She held her arms open for him. Understanding flickered across his features. Scraps nodded, leaning closer and closing the distance between them. She wrapped her arms around him and took a moment to steady herself. This was serious; she had to remain calm. "The nearest shelter is two levels up. Don't forget to breathe."

That was the only warning Flit gave Scraps before she started teleporting them. After two jumps, she stopped beneath a manhole cover. She pointed up at it and with a wave of Scraps' hand the cover popped out of place. She teleported them to the next level. From there it was another five rapid jumps before they were standing outside the emergency shelter.

Scraps pressed his palms against the wall and leaned over, sucking in steady breaths as he tried to get his bearings. Flit used the time to find the access panel and get the shelter open. It was one of the smaller ones. There two metal-framed bunks, one against either side wall, with a communications console on the rear wall next to a door that led to a small bathroom.

Flit teleported over to the communication console put a call through on the emergency frequency. Control answered within seconds.

"You've reached Control. This is Divvy. State your emergency."

"This is patrol team Blue C in shelter E-zero-nine. Sewage pressure readouts in Tunnel E-twenty-three are in the red. Pipes are bulging at the seams with gas leaking out. Requesting immediate maintenance."

"Copy that, Blue C. Remain in shelter E-zero-nine until the maintenance team clears the area. They will teleport up with," there was a pause and the sound of fingers tapping against a glass screen, "Beam. ETA five minutes."

"Good. Thanks Control." Flit ended the communication and sagged back against the metal-panelled wall.

"So, now we wait?" Scraps asked.

Flit nodded, her heart still hammering in her chest.

The next five minutes passed with agonizing slowness. Instead of checking the clock, Flit passed the time by counting her short-hop teleports from one side of the room to another.

"You know that will not make the time pass any faster, don't you?" Scraps asked, his eyes flicking back and forth with every jump she made. He had settled onto the edge of the bed, his hands clasped on his lap. The only visible sign of tension was in the rigid set of his well-muscled shoulders.

"Obviously, but I hate just sitting here and doing nothing."

"You aren't sitting down."

Flit groaned and threw him a warning look. Scraps' mouth snapped shut.

He didn't stay quiet for long, though. "We have done everything that protocol has dictated, what is the purpose of—"

"Blue Team C? This is the Emergency Maintenance team. We've arrived on location and are beginning our investigation now." Beam's confirmation crackled through the comms unit and Flit breathed a sigh of relief. The poor quality of the communication meant Beam and the others were using short-range devices. Usually, those on patrol didn't bother with communication devices. The sheer amount of steel and concrete between most of the tunnels and the Underground Control base prevented most wireless transmissions. With only two levels and about a hundred metres of horizontal displacement between them, the devices worked. Flit slid open a panel beneath the comm screen and retrieved two earpieces that were there. She nestled one into her ear and threw the other to Scraps, just in case something went wrong and they needed to flee the shelter.

"Great, thanks guys. Let us know how it goes." Flit flopped onto the bed behind Scraps and let out a huff of relief. The Emergency Maintenance team had some of the best microkinetics in the Underground. Whether it was Ratchet, Cogs, or Killswitch, they would figure out whatever was going.

"How long will this take? Can we still complete our patrol afterwards?" Scraps asked.

"Yeah, if it's a minor issue it'll be fixed soo—"

A sudden boom thundered through the very concrete of the tunnels. The emergency shelter shook, dust raining out of the joins in the ceiling and walls, showering Flit and Scraps in powdery debris. There was a loud, low groan of steel and concrete from somewhere outside the shelter and the floor vibrated. It rippled up Flit's spine; her teeth chattered and her stomach roiled.

"Fuck." Flit's hand flew to her ear, pressing in the earpiece harder. "Beam, are you there? Requesting contact."

"Flit, the pipe expl—Cogs, watch out!"

Someone screamed.

Flit winced as the wailing of bending steel pierced through the earpiece. It was cut off by a shuddering crash that sent adrenalin surging through limbs. "Beam? Beam! Do you copy?"

Flit's desperate plea was met with radio silence. She teleported back to the comms screen and pressed the red emergency indicator.

"Blue Team C, report!" Divvy's crisp voice demanded.

"There's been an explosion. We were cut off mid-communication from Beam."

"I'm calling the engineers. Hold for further instructions."

Flit let out a frustrated groan and slammed her hand against the wall beside the panel. "We need to get out there!" Flit whirled around to face Scraps.

Scraps frowned so deep, his brows furrowing. "We were told to await furth—"

Another bone-shaking rumble undulated through the shelter. Flit huffed with impatience. "Control are making orders remotely. We're here in the field. You can feel how bad this is. It could take the engineers a quarter of an hour to decide what to do. We don't have that much time. I can be there and back in forty-five seconds." Flit teleported to Scraps and held her hand out for him to take. He pulled back from the offer and looked up at her, shaking his head. Flit's shoulders fell. "Please. I may need you to help me dig them out."

"We were told to await further instructions," Scraps reiterated, determined to follow orders.

Flit narrowed her eyes at him, giving him a chance to reconsider, but he refused to capitulate. She took a deep breath before she teleported to the door. She pushed it open and looked back at him over her shoulder. He gave her an almost imperceptible shake of his head, his crimson eyes set.

"I'll be back," Flit snapped before she left the shelter.

26

FLIT

TWENTY SECONDS and six jumps later, Flit knew things were bad.

She made it all the way back to the tunnel above E-zero-nine, but the floor had collapsed. The affected area, at least ten metres across, was a concave mess of concrete and splintered steel sleepers. The solid edge she was standing on rumbled and shook beneath her feet. Flames crackled as they licked at the broken edges of the tunnel. The sound made her skin crawl as adrenaline sizzled through her.

"Beam? Someone? Report!" Flit barked, her eyes darted over the scene as she tried to find an entry point.

"Beam?" Flit's hands balled into fists at her side as she waited for a response.

"Flit, call control. Beam is down. I'm trying to stop the leak, but every time I plug it up it pops somewhere else. I'm not sure I can fix it. This pipe could burst at any moment." Cogs was one of the most experienced microkinetics in the Underground, and her voice was cool and professional despite the dire situation.

"Cogs, I'm right above you—"

"Get back to the shelter!" Cogs ordered.

"Not without you."

A metallic groan echoed from beneath Flit's feet. The floor shook again and the odour of gas seeped through the cracked concrete. "It's spreading to this tunnel. We need to get out of here before the flames cause another explosion," Flit warned them.

The familiar voice of Heft came through the comms. "Flit's right. Cogs, we can't save this."

Heft might be an arsehole, but that didn't mean Flit wanted to see him get hurt. Her top priority was making sure everyone got out alive. "Heft, move some of those beams. I'm above the collapse on the south side. Get me line of sight. I'll get you out."

Flit stumbled back as the ground beneath her feet shifted. Debris and dust rained through the gaping chasm like sand through an hourglass, measuring the time they had left before they reached the point of no return.

"Watch out!" Heft called as a steel sleeper slid out of place and the groaning mountain of rubble toppled. Flit fell to the side, her shoulder slamming against the wall. A deafening pop sounded, and the hissing of gas intensified.

"Fuck!" Cogs yelled.

Flit coughed and spluttered, sewage gas and concrete grit plastering to the walls of her throat. She waved a desperate hand in front of her face. Cog's swearing was enough to make her teleport to the other side of the chasm. The moment her feet touched the ground, she fell to her stomach on the floor, distributing her weight across the unstable concrete and peering through the settling dust.

Flit's gaze landed on the familiar greys of Underground fatigues as Cogs plastered herself against the pipe. Her vibrant red braid was black with dirt and grease. Heft was at her back, sweat shining on his forehead as he held his arms out, supporting the precariously balanced concrete beneath Flit's stomach with telekinesis. Beam's prone form slumped against the opposite wall, a trickle of blood running down his creased forehead. His eyes were closed, but his chest was rising and falling raggedly.

"Hurry," Heft groaned, his face pinched and pale with the effort of holding up so much weight.

Just as Flit was about to teleport, an intense whine vibrated through the air and a loose steel sleeper beneath her gave way. "Heft!" Flit cried.

Heft cast his hand towards the sliding steel support, falling to his knees under the strain. "I can't—hold—"

The steel sleeper slipped free of Heft's grasp and rocketed downwards, slamming into Beam, crushing him with a sickening squelch.

Flit gasped, her eyes wide as she looked down at the scene below in horror. "No!"

"Flit, I can't hold this much longer."

Flit swallowed her anguish, burying it beneath adrenaline and her drive to survive. She wanted to take Beam too, but he was already gone. She had to concentrate on the living. Flit teleported to the level below, landing square between Cogs and Heft. She wrapped her arms around their shaking, sweat-soaked torsos. "Heft, the second your feet touch the ground, run. I'll get Cogs clear and come back for you. Teleporting on three. One. Two. Three!"

Flit steeled herself and teleported herself and the other two up to the level above. Her lungs burned and an iron fist clenched around her brain at the strain on her powers as she dragged their bodies across folded space.

But they made it. As they landed, Flit loosened her grip on Heft's waist and he bolted. Flit tightened her grasp on Cogs and teleported her ahead as another explosion rocked through the tunnel. The uncontrolled gas metastasised, mingling with the flickering embers and sending a new hurricane of flames and debris their way.

Flit cried out, twisting her body to shield Cogs. A large shard of concrete pounded into her side and sent the two women flying.

Flit slammed into a wall. A wheezing breath whistled between her clenched teeth as the air was knocked from her lungs. She slumped to the ground, each breath piercing her lungs with increasing levels of agony. Her head spun, her vision splattered with black spots.

"Flit! Flit, we need to move," Cogs cried.

Flit could barely hear Cogs over the ringing in her ears, could barely think beyond the struggle to suck in another breath. She looked down the tunnel as the heat of the inferno singed her fatigues. Her vision swam; the tunnel swayed from side to side like a hapless boat on stormy seas. Flit grunted and pushed aside the pain. She concentrated on the single stable point in the chaos and cast herself and Cogs to that space.

The roaring and snapping of the flames retreated as Flit kept moving. She relied on Cogs to help keep her standing between jumps. It wasn't much further, but it felt like an eternity as each breath got harder to take. They overtook Heft somewhere between the second and third jump, but Flit wasn't worried. If the tunnel collapsed around him, he could prop it up long enough to escape. Cogs couldn't do that.

Finally, Flit and Cogs reached the door of the shelter. Flit slumped against the wall, wheezing as her comrade slapped her palm against the access panel.

"That was longer than forty-five seconds," Scraps commented the moment the door slid open.

Flit couldn't summon enough breath to put together a witty comeback.

"Call Control and tell them that there's a live gas leak and ongoing cave-in in E-twenty-three," Cogs ordered Scraps as she turned her piercing blue eyes on Flit, her lips pressed together in concern. "You're pale and shaking. Sit down."

"I'm f-fine," Flit gasped.

Cogs rolled her eyes. "Sit down!" she snapped, stepping so close to Flit that she instinctively shifted away. The back of her knees hit the bed and she fell onto it, groaning as her injured ribs sent shock waves of agony through her entire body. Cogs pressed her hand against Flit's sweating forehead and closed her eyes.

Heft skidded around the corner of the shelter, sweat pouring off his face. "Flit? Cogs?" He slammed his hand on the panel and the door slid shut behind him.

Then, Heft's eyes settled on Scraps as he stood at the other side of the room. The space between them crackled with tension. There were only a few metres between them in the small shelter.

"What the fuck?" Heft growled upon seeing the Ex-Registered.

Scraps froze as he ended the call with Control and looked at Heft warily. "Heft?"

Heft flung his arm out, his energy slamming the unsuspecting

Scraps against the rear wall and pinning him there. "What the fuck are you doing here?"

"Stop." Flit struggled to her feet. She was about to teleport herself between them when Heft threw his free hand out, pinning her in place with his powers. On any other occasion, she would resist his grasp and teleport anyway, but his invisible force squeezed around her torso and her knees buckled, her body writhing in pain as her lungs burned.

"Flit!" Scraps' voice boomed through the room as he sent a burst of telekinetic energy towards Heft, knocking him off balance and breaking his hold on Flit. "We were ordered to hold position."

"Fuck orders. Beam died out there, you coward!"

"Heft, enough." Cogs stepped between the two men and narrowed her eyes at Heft.

"If you like following orders so much, you mule, I'll give you a fucking order." Heft lunged to the side, sending the steel-framed cot opposite to the one Flit was on flying towards Scraps.

Flit used the distraction to teleport across the shelter, charging into Heft and knocking him to the ground. He grunted and rolled, using the momentum to fling her away. She tried to teleport back to her feet, but the force of Heft's blow sent her sailing towards the comms console.

"No!" Scraps leapt over. He turned mid-air and slid his body beneath Flit's as they crashed into the console together. He cushioned her from the worst of the impact, but the force exacerbated the pain in her ribs from when the concrete hit her earlier, and she coughed as she struggled to catch her breath.

Heft jumped to his feet, his hands frozen before him, his eyes wide as blood oozed from the corner of Flit's mouth. She let out a wet cough, splattering blood across the floor. Her eyes felt heavy. Everything would be easier if she just fell asleep.

"Shit." Cogs ran over and fell to her knees in front of Flit. Her hand was burning hot as she pressed it against Flit's cold and clammy forehead. "Flit, stay with me. Don't fall asleep. Please, stay with me."

Flit tried, she really did, but no amount of willpower could stop her world from going black.

27

SCRAPS

THE MOMENT FLIT PASSED OUT, a tense silence filled the shelter. Scraps and Heft, still panting from the exertion of their fight, glared at each other.

Cogs closed her eyes, concentrating hard enough to make her forehead crease. "I think she's gone into shock. Call Control and get a medic up here immediately," Cogs muttered, letting her hand drop.

Scraps wasn't a medic or a micro, but even he could see that Flit was injured. Her normally tanned skin had taken on a ghostly pallor; her chest rose and fell erratically as she struggled to breathe. The blood that oozed out of the corner of her mouth gurgled with each gasp.

Scraps used his physical and telekinetic strength to ease Flit onto the metal cot while Cogs called Control. Control agreed to send a team up and relayed instructions to Cogs to help her stabilise Flit while they waited. Scraps stood aside, watching and waiting, knowing there was nothing he could do. He'd never felt so helpless before in his life, and an odd sense of guilt clawed at his gut.

Scraps was so busy trying to figure out how he could help Flit he didn't notice Heft walking over until the barrel-chested man stepped in front of him. "If you were there, she wouldn't be injured. If she dies, that's on you," Heft spat.

Scraps' heart seized in his chest. He felt like an ice-cold bucket of water was dumped over his head. He knew Heft was angry, but that accusation hit him hard. "I wa—"

"What? Just following orders?"

"Enough!" Cog's voice cut through the simmering tension. "You idiots need to shut up. I'm trying to concentrate. Heft, get outside and keep an eye out for the others. Scraps, just—" Cogs stopped and shook her head, raking a hand through her hair in frustration. "Just sit down and shut up."

It was a long five minutes before the emergency medical staff arrived. Scraps was relieved it wasn't Tinker running in. Flit did not look good, and the moment that the microkinetic healer arrived they announced that she had broken ribs and a pierced lung. In a flurry of movement, they got Flit stable enough to move, transferred her to a stretcher, and then she was gone.

Everyone made it back to base without further incident as emergency teams scrambled to contain the leak in the collapsed tunnel. Scraps wasn't sure what to do with himself, but he didn't have to think it over for long. He was pulled aside for an immediate debrief with Harmony, Acumen, and the head of Intelligence, Shadow. Scraps gave them all the information he could. On any other day it would have been reassurance enough to know that he had followed orders, but Heft's words rang through his mind. If he had gone with Flit, as she had asked, would the outcome be any different? Would Beam still be alive? Would Flit be there in the debriefing with him instead of in the medical bay?

When the debriefing finished, they asked if Scraps had questions. He could only think of one: "Is Flit ok?"

Harmony picked up the datapad she had set on the table when they sat down and tapped the screen a few times. "She's still being tended to. It'll be a lengthy operation. You should go to bed, try to get some rest." Harmony tucked the datapad under her arm as the group stood.

Scraps nodded and trudged back to his room. He wanted to wait in the medical bay until the operation was finished and he could ensure Flit was ok, but he didn't know if he would be in the way. Besides, Harmony had told him to go to bed, and she was the leader. He had followed harder orders in the past few hours, so there was no point trying to resist that one. After he got back to his room and took a shower, he collapsed onto his bed, exhausted. As he laid back, the events of the evening replayed over and over in his mind and, for the first time in his life, he couldn't will himself to sleep.

A LOUD KNOCKING on his door woke Scraps the next morning. He jolted awake with a groan, rubbing his eyes and looking at the clock. It was after ten in the morning. He wasn't sure when he fell asleep, or how he slept through his alarm, but his eyes were full of grit and he had a pounding headache. He got up from his bed, stumbling over to his dresser before taking a shirt out and slipping it on.

When Scraps opened the door, Acumen's familiar face greeted him. "Rough night, huh?" Acumen hummed.

Scraps nodded and stepped back, gesturing for Acumen to come in. "Yes."

Acumen walked right over and sank onto Scraps' desk chair. "I came to see how you're doing."

Scraps stopped mid-step as he turned to join Acumen at the table. How *was* he doing? He wasn't even sure. He had spent the night tossing and turning, the events after his arrival in the emergency shelter haunted him. There were so many things that nagged at him: Heft's accusation, how injured Flit was before they carried her out, the fact that Beam didn't make it out alive... That he might have been the one to prevent all the pain and loss if he had just gone with Flit like she asked.

"I'm fine."

It was a lie and they both knew it.

Acumen sighed. "You were following orders. Whatever happened was not on you. It was an accident. A horrible, tragic accident, but an accident all the same."

Scraps pressed his lips together and nodded. Acumen was right. But... why did Scraps feel so torn?

"Buddy, take it easy on yourself. Look, why don't you take the day off, get more sleep, and I'll drop by again later so we can chat more."

Scraps shook his head. "No, I have training with—" Scraps stopped as a realisation knocked the breath out of him.

Flit. He was supposed to have training with Flit. He didn't even know if she made it through the night, let alone if she was well enough for training.

"She's in the medical bay now. They repaired the puncture, but they didn't knit her ribs back fully. They think the last part will heal best naturally." Acumen took the question right out of Scraps' mind. "She's stable, though. She'll be all right. If you want to see her, I'm sure she'd like it."

Scraps was grateful for the information. "That sounds like an excellent idea. I will clean up and then visit Flit."

Acumen got to his feet and patted Scraps on the shoulder before he made his way out of the room.

Scraps scrambled to get ready and was in the medical bay within fifteen minutes. When Scraps arrived, Flit was still out cold. But she was alive. He stayed by her bedside all day. Various members of the Underground dropped in and out to check up on her. When they saw him at her bedside, some did a double take. He could see the accusation in their eyes: the weight of the same suspicions Heft had flung at him. Scraps refused to let it bother him. He could handle their suspicious looks if it meant staying by Flit's side. He didn't leave until her parents arrived just before dinner.

Dinner was another issue altogether. All the suspicious looks Scraps had gotten throughout the day were magnified in the Mess Hall. The Blue Team was more than happy to sit with him, but Flit's absence was painfully obvious. After dinner, he considered retreating to his room, but he knew he wouldn't be able to sleep. So, Scraps returned to the medbay to see Flit awake and chatting to Tinker and Stride. When he came in, they gave Flit a kiss on the cheek and excused themselves so they could get dinner, leaving him alone with her.

Scraps wasn't sure what to expect when Flit saw him for the first time after waking, but she gave him a small, pained smile. "Hey," she croaked, her voice raw and raspy.

"Hello." Scraps walked over and gestured to the chair beside her bed. She nodded and he sank down into it. He looked at her closely; she had gotten a little of her colouring back, but the bags beneath her eyes were dark and puffy, and every breath was a laborious rattle.

"Long night?" Flit frowned as she took in his appearance.

Scraps straightened, trying to smooth out his clothes. "Shouldn't I be the one asking you that?"

Flit tried to shrug, but she winced at the effort and sighed. "It hurts to talk, but I hate silence. Please... talk to me."

"What would you like me to talk about?"

Flit's eyes darted around the room and rested when they fell on the medic on duty, an older woman Scraps hadn't met before. When Flit looked back at him, there was sadness in her eyes. She looked down at her injured hands and fiddled with a bandage on one. "Anything..."

Scraps didn't expect Flit's quiet request. He was sure she would be angry at him, that she would have yelled. If he had followed orders, things might have turned out different. But... She didn't yell. She didn't rage. She just asked him to talk, to keep her company.

So he did. He lied and told her that things were going well outside. Everyone was taking the tragedy in stride. He told her what chapters of the Maintenance Procedure Manuals he was planning to read next. She let him talk without interruption. She didn't even roll her eyes as he talked about policy. It was a welcome distraction from the events of the previous night, but all the distractions in the world couldn't stop the conflict raging in Scraps' mind as he wondered if he had made a mistake by not going with Flit.

WHAT HAD STARTED out as whispers turned into fully fledged rumours. Despite the changing perceptions of him, the Blue Team had Scraps' back. When it was time for Beam's funeral, he initially refused to attend, but Flit had shown up at his door and insisted he go with her. What seemed like half of the members of the Underground turned to glare at him when he arrived in the Catacombs, but Flit stood at his side, unflinching. It was a touching display of support that showed her thoughts on the matter loud and clear: she put no stock in the rumours and accusations.

Flit cried at the funeral, just as she had the previous one, but this time, Scraps did not hesitate to put a comforting arm around her shoulder. Swipe had also become more protective of him. She snapped at people several times for whispering as he walked by. While Scraps appreciated it, he assured her it wasn't necessary. Arguing only made it seem like he had something to feel guilty about.

Once more, the Underground rerouted their scarce resources to investigate the fallout of the explosion. The Security department was an entire team down, so they combined the Green and Red Teams to make up for lost or reassigned members. The Blue Team wasn't complete either. Flit was put on light duties. Well, she was put on bed rest, but the medics soon learned she would never stay still and gave her something to do to avoid her getting into more trouble. Hawkeye was yet to return, so Scraps was bounced around to various partners to fill empty spots in the over-scheduled patrol roster. The frequency of training sessions had decreased out of sheer necessity; everyone was just too busy trying to keep their home safe.

Scraps relished the extra work. Focusing on that was easier than ruminating on his place in the Underground and wondering if they would ever accept him the way they had accepted Bookworm. He found it difficult to believe. Either way, it relieved him to have Flit on his side. He visited her every day for at least an hour. They talked about anything and everything to fill the time. The only thing they hadn't talked about was the tunnel collapse. Scraps wasn't sure why. Everyone else was more than willing to tell him their opinion about it, but the only person who was there with him was resoundingly quiet on the topic.

Every time Scraps looked at Flit's face, his mind dragged him back to when she passed out in his arms. He had never been so worried about anyone before in his life. Seeing her hurt and knowing he could have prevented it filled him with guilt. He looked forward to seeing her, but was frustrated on her behalf when she complained about being held back because of her injuries. He was unhappy with the situation, too, as he missed their patrols. All the time they previously spent together was now filled with extra study that, while informative, didn't make him smile the same way spending time with Flit did. Still, keeping busy meant Scraps had less time to think about how odd it was that previously treasured activities didn't seem as rewarding anymore if he wasn't doing them with Flit.

"Hello, earth to Scraps," Swipe's voice cut through Scraps' musing and he jumped with surprise, the weighted medicine ball he was holding dropping onto—"Ouch!"—Swipe's foot.

"Swipe?" Scraps raced forward. He swept her off her feet and carried her over to the metal bench in the training room. Once she was settled, she made no move to take her arms from around him, so he slipped free of her hold and straightened up.

"What the hell was that? It's like you were on another planet." Swipe's face crinkled in a mix of annoyance and discomfort.

"I am so sorry. I do not know where my mind was." Scraps got to his knees and reached for her boot. She left out a soft hiss. "Let me look." He loosened the laces.

Swipe gritted her teeth as she watched, her hand reaching out and grasping Scraps' shoulder. "Ouch, shit! Stud, do you know what you're doing down there?" she asked as he put her boot aside and peeled off her sock.

"First aid is part of every Registered's training." Scraps experimentally ran his fingers over her foot, putting pressure on the red parts and testing for her reactions. "Can you put any pressure on it? Wiggle your toes?"

Swipe pressed her foot against his thigh, and she let out a low groan, but it didn't seem to be anything too sharp. She wiggled her toes and shrugged. "I don't think it's broken," Swipe said as she leaned over to get a closer look.

"Nor do I. But it will need something for the swelling."

Swipe nodded and reached her hand out. In the corner of the room, the door to the first aid cabinet slid open. She sat a little straighter as she looked over. "Shit. There's no cold pack in there. I swear, I'm gonna find who used that kit last and kick their arse—"

"There's no need for that." Scraps helped her set her foot on the bench and stood up. "I can go get one. Where are they kept?"

"In the cold rooms. Do you know where they are?"

Scraps nodded. "I'll be right back," he promised before racing out of the room.

Luckily, cold storage was only a short distance from the training rooms. Scraps navigated the intervening tunnels without needing to think about where he was going. Finding his way around his new home was second nature to him. A few people paused to watch him suspiciously as he raced by, but he didn't bother stopping to explain. When he reached the entry to the storeroom tunnel, he pressed his palm against the access panel of the first cold room, but it didn't open. He was about to turn around and go to the medbays instead when he noticed one of the freezer doors was slightly ajar. He dashed in and skidded to a halt when he saw Flit standing there.

"Floor's slippery, slow down!" Flit looked up from her datapad, her wide eyes softened as they settled on him. "Oh! Hey Scraps. Aren't you supposed to be training with Swipe?" She tucked the datapad under her arm.

Scraps smiled back at her as she stood there in an oversized, puffy, insulated jacket. It looked silly on her, like she was wrapped in several black tyres, but he supposed she needed it in cold storage. The frigid air was already biting into his skin, rapidly cooling the sweat on his brow. "I was. She got hurt. I came down to get a cold pack, but I don't have access to the other storage vaults," Scraps explained, the words forming soft white steam puffs in front of his face.

"Oh, right. The ice packs are on that shelf over there. There are fifty-six. Fifty-five now, I suppose." Flit sighed, taking the datapad back out from under her arm and tapping the screen with a huff.

Scraps nodded and reached back to pull the door shut to keep the chilly air in.

"No!" Flit yelped, "Don't shut the"—the door groaned as it closed. The lights flickered off and the automatic locks clicked into place—"door."

The whirring overhead fans went into overdrive and filled the space with a tempest of icy air.

28

―――

SCRAPS

SCRAPS FROWNED. "We are locked in, aren't we?"

"This freezer's broken. That's why I'm down here, counting stock before the rest of the team come and move it to another vault. There's some electrical glitch with the locking and cooling systems… Although you can probably see that now."

Indeed, he could.

From what Scraps saw before the lights went off the room was about five by five metres, with shelves along the two sides and the rear wall. The shelves were stacked high with supplies, but he doubted there would be anything that could help them out. Scraps turned in a slow circle and saw the control panel by the door. He took a step towards it, wondering if he could use it to get them out.

"It's broken." Flit's amused tone sliced through the chilly breeze blowing in the darkness.

Scraps frowned. "It can't hurt to try again before we both freeze to death." He tapped at the screen.

"Well, I'll be fine. I got this handy jacket to prevent that. Not sure about you though," Flit chucked. He could picture her shaking her head.

Scraps could not access most of the menu, but for the parts he could access, it looked as though the systems were performing within the 'normal' parameters. There was clearly a malfunction. He was just about to give up when the fiery brand of Flit's palm pressed against his shoulder. He jumped in surprise and looked back at her. The light from the panel let off a gentle glow in the space that illuminated the soft curves of her face.

"Let me try again. There has to be an emergency open function somewhere," Flit offered. She stepped up to his side, the puffy jacket she was wearing sliding along his arm and sending a shiver down his spine. He moved back and her hand dropped from his shoulder. He missed the warmth. The panel on the wall flickered to life as Flit tapped it. She fiddled with the menu, then bashed the screen with her fist a few times. "Bloody stupid piece of—" Flit's voice descended into a jumbled chain of muttering and cursing that Scraps wasn't entirely sure he wanted to decipher.

"I don't suppose you can contact the maintenance crew with your datapad?" Scraps suggested before she got too lost in her rant.

"I can, but there's no telling how long it'll be before they see the message. Their inboxes are flooded with maintenance requests on an hourly basis. I can't send it as an emergency, because they should be here within the next fifteen minutes anyway, to move the stuff."

Scraps groaned. "Fifteen minutes?" His hands shook and teeth chattered as the cold seeped through his skin.

Flit pressed her hand against his bicep. Her skin was so much warmer than his. "Damn...you're not dressed for this climate, are you?"

"Ah, no. Not really."

For a few moments, only the sound was the frantic whirring of fans.

"I have an idea... just let me send this message." Flit held onto his arm as she shifted around him. There was a rasping as she patted some nearby boxes with her free hand, trying to locate the datapad. She found it with a triumphant 'Aha!'. The activated screen lit up her face, showing her concentration in the way she bit her lip as she tapped her message onto the screen. In the darkness, Scraps was acutely aware of the sound of her steady breathing and the crisp citrusy scent of her perfume compared to whatever else was stored in the freezer.

"Scraps, I've got a way we can keep you warm while we wait. There's a small pile of flattened boxes on the ground about two metres to your right. Prop one or two of them up against the shelf on the closest wall and sit down on the others."

"I'll be fine," he assured her, even though his teeth chattered so loud she could probably hear them.

Flit sighed. "You won't get a bravery award for freezing to death. Please, just sit down." As she spoke the sound of a zipper opening tore into the darkness.

Scraps' breath caught in his throat and his eyes widened. He thought of Flit unzipping the jacket, wondering what would be beneath. The sound of that zip opening was one of the most arousing things he had ever heard.

"Scraps?"

"Oh, uh, yeah. Sorry. I... Uh, I will sit down," Scraps stammered, turning around and reaching for the boxes. He set them up as she suggested and hissed as he lowered himself to the floor and felt the sting of the icy surfaces against his bare calves. He had heard jokes at dinner about what people could do to stay warm at night, but surely that wasn't Flit's plan.

The rustle of clothing being shucked off and shaken out made Scraps doubt his conclusion. "Uh... Flit?" he breathed, his mind filling with the most delightful images. Ones that he should not be thinking in such a situation.

"Yes?"

Scraps pressed more of his bare skin against the cold room floor, using the iciness to distract from the fiery feeling growing in the pit of his stomach. "What are you doing?"

"We've only got one coat," Flit told him, oblivious to the discomfort in his tone. "So, if you stretch your legs out and spread them a bit, I can sit between them. We can use the jacket like a blanket and huddle up under it together."

"Oh." Scraps wasn't if he was disappointed or relieved by her plan.

Flit took a deep breath. "All right, I'm coming over now before I freeze my butt off." She shuffled her feet against the ground, sweeping over the cold floor until her toes knocked into one of his boots "Ah, there you are."

There was a scuffle, a flutter in the darkness, and Scraps felt the relative fire of Flit's skin on his icy calf. He moved his legs a little as she kneeled between them.

"Sorry, I don't want to sit on you." Flit gently grasped his calf and she shifted again.

Scraps' breath caught in his throat as Flit turned around and settled between his legs. She scooted towards him until the warmth of her back radiated against his chest. She shook out the coat, and the pre-warmed fabric settled over their bodies. It should have been a welcome relief, that toasty warmth, but he had trouble thinking beyond just how close Flit was to him.

"I'll tuck my knees up, that way you can cross your legs a bit. We'll fit under the coat better that way," Flit suggested.

With a bit of readjusting Flit was safely nestled within the boundaries of Scraps' bent knees. He let sighed with relief at how well the coat preserved their shared warmth. His skin started to thaw and, without thinking, he wrapped his arms around her waist to close the small wind tunnel between his chest and her back. She hissed with pain and he immediately let go, remembering her injury. "I am sorry!" Scraps' face flushed as he realised that not only had he hurt her, but he had touched her inappropriately.

First, he injured Swipe because he was distracted, and now he was touching Flit all over. He just could not get himself together. It was days like this when he resented that his control chip had been deactivated.

Scraps was broken from his self-chastisement when Flit took his hands and settled them a little lower around her abdomen.

"It's fine," she assured him, though he could still hear the hitch in her breathing. She didn't let go of his hands. Her palms were warm and soft, and her breathing made her shoulders rise and fall against his chest.

Once more, the sounds of the overactive fans filled the freezer. At first, Scraps told himself the silence was fine. That he was concentrating on letting his body return to a safe temperature. The problem was that, once they were warm, his mind started racing again. Scraps was captivated by his awareness of Flit's body; how she smelled, how warm her back was against his chest, how her breathing was slow, steady, and sweet smelling. He was aware of how his body would react if he didn't find some way to distract himself. He felt terrible about it; they were both stuck in the freezer because he couldn't keep his mind off how his decision on their patrol affected her.

It felt disrespectful to have such basic, carnal thoughts about Flit. She was his mentor and friend, and it was unprofessional of him to think of her in any other way. He hadn't had a chance to talk to her about the tunnel collapse until now, and even though he thought about what he would say many times, he couldn't find the words with her between his legs.

But Flit, as always, was perceptive. "What is it?"

Scraps' shoulders tensed. "What do you mean?"

"You want to say something, I can feel it. You're all tense."

Scraps wasn't sure how Flit had sensed his indecision, but she laid out the perfect opening and he had to take it. "Heft said that if I had been there, Beam would be alive, and you would not have gotten injured." The words slipped out of his mouth before he could find a better way to phrase them.

Hesitation thickened the space between them as Flit soaked up his concern. "Heft is an arsehole."

Well, that wasn't the response Scraps was expecting. "But… Is he right?" Scraps probed. Arseholes could be right or wrong. Or at least, that was what he had gathered from the times where Flit had called Sway one for the socially inappropriate observations he made at dinner.

"Yes? No? Who knows, hmm?" Flit sighed and rested her head back against his shoulder. "Scraps, there's no way to know what would have happened if you came with me. You did what you thought was right. You need to be confident that you made the best decision you could at the time."

"I followed orders. The people in Control know the correct protocol and procedures, and I accepted that. It is what I was taught to do. It is what members of the Underground are supposed to do." Even as he spoke, Scraps wondered why he spent so much time trying to rationalise what happened. He never second-guessed decisions he made in the field. Why was the tunnel collapse different?

"Who are you trying to convince? Me or you?" Flit's words were gentle, but they hit him harder than a speeding hovercraft.

"Why aren't you angry at me? You wanted me to go with you, I know you did," Scraps said. "You could have called in that payment I owed you, but you didn't."

"Well, that would have been a shit move. I wouldn't take advantage of your trust like that." Scraps' singlet scrunched against his chest as Flit shrugged. "You were doing what you thought was right. I can't tell you whether or not it was. We'll never know, and you'll only tie yourself in knots trying to figure it out. If I died out there, I would have looked like the idiot because I should have followed orders... but I did what I thought was right. We both did."

Scraps groaned with frustration at her non-answer. "So, am I supposed to follow orders or not?" A sore pounding started behind his eyes; the stirrings of a headache brought about by the infuriating complexity of his new life.

"It doesn't have to be an absolute yes or no. Every situation is unique. You just need to think on your feet and go with your gut."

"The Government said that gut feelings are nothing more than base survival instincts that ignore logic and evidence. They are not sound guides for decision making. Follow orders, follow protocol. It is that simple." Scraps' upbringing and rigid training came back to the forefront of his mind.

"The Government are arseholes too."

"Flit, not everyone is an arsehole," he tutted, unimpressed.

Flit let out a long sigh. "How have the Government's lessons worked out for you so far, hmm?"

Scraps pressed his lips together. She had a point. With each day that passed, he learned life wasn't as black and white as the Government made it out to be. He took a slow, steady breath and closed his eyes. Before the tunnel collapse, he thought he had gotten used to life in the Underground. It turned out he still had so much more to learn.

An unpleasant silence filled the space. Scraps made a personal resolution to think about things more critically from that point forward. He wanted to take advantage of the opportunity he had to reinvent himself in the Underground. He did not have the mental energy to keep replaying the tunnel collapse in his mind. It had made him clumsy enough to injure one of his colleagues, and he would be damned if he let that happen again. So, Scraps pushed those worries from his mind as he grasped for something else to talk about. "I haven't seen you much lately. How are you healing?"

Flit sagged against his chest. "I'm getting there, I suppose. I hate being on light duties, but it's better than nothing. Mum wanted me to be on bedrest for longer, but I was going stir crazy."

If the way she relaxed against his chest was any sign, she was glad for the break in the silence. Her silky hair brushed against his cheek and his breath caught in his throat. It smelled clean and fruity, so unlike the musty, frigid odour of the freezer.

"There is no harm in taking a break if your body is recovering, it is better than straining the injury."

Flit shrugged. "What's the point of recovering if I lose my mind in the process?"

Scraps chuckled. That was such a typical Flit thing to say. "Surely there is something else you could do to keep your mind busy," Scraps mused. "Whenever I had down time in the Hub, I would use it to get ahead on my studies. Are there any policies or procedures you can research?"

Flit chuckled, but not unkindly. "Oh Scraps, only you would think reading policies and procedures was a fun way to spend your downtime."

Scraps could imagine the amused half smirk she got any time their conversation turned to his respect for rules. It was the same smile that made his breath catch a little. "What? It is a perfect opportunity to brush up on policy. You should try it sometime. I have only just begun to explore the policies available down here. They are fascinating. For example, they updated the maintenance requirements for sewage treatment pipes last week. Given the explosion, you could look at—"

"Scraps, Scraps, I will not read policies," Flit laughed, her body shaking against him.

Despite the heaviness of their earlier conversation, a smile tugged at the corner of his lips. There was something about Flit's laugh that always made him happier. "I'm just saying—"

"Scraps," Flit wheezed, her hand crushing his as she held it against her ribs. "Please, stop making me laugh, it hurts too much."

Scraps stopped straight away, not wanting to cause her any pain. "I was being serious," he muttered, surprising himself with the petulance in his own tone.

"Oh, I know." Flit reached back and cupped his cheek. She patted it reassuringly. "I know you are. It's just not something that people down here do in their spare time. I've been so busy training you for patrols that I forgot to train you how to have fun."

Scraps perked up. "You can do that?" He wasn't sure how it would work, but he was definitely interested.

Flit sighed, leaning her head back against his chest. "No, I was being facetiou—" Flit began, but she stopped almost as soon as she started. Scraps was very aware of the fact that her hand was still cupping his cheek. No one had ever touched him like that before. It was rather intimate, but in a nice way. She shook her head. "You know what? Yes. Yes, I'll train you to have fun. We'll start this weekend."

"Is there any pre-reading I can do to prepare?"

Flit groaned and turned to the side, the top of her arm resting against him. His eyes had adjusted enough that he could see the shadowy silhouette of her face in front of his.

"No, there is no pre-reading for fun."

"But how will I know what is expected of me?"

"You'll just have to trust me. Do you think you can do that without a manual?"

Scraps' eyes skimmed over the familiar profile of her face as he thought about it. He supposed it was a fair question, given their discussion so far. "You may be unpredictable, but I know you have best the interest of your friends at heart. I trust you."

Flit's bottom lip puckered as she bit it. Scraps straightened as she shifted, turning to face him. Their noses were barely an inch apart. The coat slipped off his shoulders, but the feel of her so close, her sweet scent; it was enough to keep him warm.

"Scraps..." Flit whispered. The air between them zapped with the static electricity that he felt whenever he was with her. She was about to say more when—

Scraps threw up an arm to cover his eyes as the door was wrenched open with a loud screech. The light from the tunnel outside blazed in. Flit cried out in pain at the sudden brightness.

"What the hell?" a gruff voice grumbled.

Flit scuffled to her feet, swearing under her breath. Scraps suddenly felt so cold without her body against his. He hadn't realised how much warmth they had been sharing beneath the jacket.

"The uh, the freezer's busted," Flit stammered.

With the light streaming in, Scraps saw how flushed her face was. It was rather endearing.

"That's why I'm here... but what the hell were you two doing?" The man stopped and shook his head. "Actually, please don't tell me—"

"It's not like that!" Flit blurted, holding her hands up, trying to placate him.

Scraps frowned and he picked up the coat she dropped as he got to his feet. He set it on her shoulders.

"Really? Because you know what it looks like—"

"In a freezer, Twitch? What do you take me for?" Flit groaned, disgusted.

The middle-aged male shrugged. He frowned, the wiry hairs of his black moustache and beard overlapped.

"No, I was down here counting the stock before the transfer when Scraps came down for an ice-pack and let the door close."

Twitch didn't seem convinced. "Right."

Flit sighed, turning to Scraps. "You'd better get that back to Swipe before she sends down a search party," Flit suggested, not meeting his eyes.

Scraps' mind flashed back to that moment in the darkness before they were interrupted. He felt the loss of her warm touch. He wanted to reach out and caress her flushed cheek, but he shoved his hand into his pocket instead. "You are right. Swipe needs the ice." Scraps nodded stiffly, skirting around Flit and grabbing the icepack off the shelf. He gave the maintenance worker an even more awkward nod as he dashed past and left Flit to deal with the fallout.

29

SCRAPS

"GOODNESS ME, Stud. I thought you knew where the freezer was. I was just about to send out a search party!"

Swipe looked over the moment that Scraps walked through the door, ice pack in hand. He made his way over to where she was sitting at the far end of the room.

Scraps looked at the blossoming red patch on the top of her foot. "How is your foot feeling?"

"Still sore. I tried walking on it while you were gone. It didn't go well. I'll need help to get back to my room."

Scraps gave her an apologetic smile. "It is the least I can do."

Swipe's pretty face brightened, and a few loose wisps of blonde hair fluttered down over her eyes. "Thank you so much." Swipe said, grabbing his hand. Her skin was just as warm and soft as Flit's, but her touch didn't make his stomach churn the same way that Flit's did. Swipe used her telekinesis to summon her boot from further down the bench and got to her feet, with a hiss of pain through gritted teeth. Once she was upright, she draped her arm around his shoulder and leaned against him heavily. To keep them both steady, Scraps had to wrap his arm around her waist.

"So, what are your plans for the afternoon? Have you got any more training?" Swipe asked as they made their way out of the training room together.

Scraps shook his head. "I've finished training for the day, but I have supervision with Posthoc in about half an hour. After that, I might do my normal workout before dinner. When I saw Flit in the freezer, she said she wanted to start my recreation training on the weekend. I might see if I can do some research for it tonight."

Swipe stopped walking and looked sideways at him, her brows furrowed. "You saw Flit in the freezer?"

"Yes, it was malfunctioning, so she was in there counting stock before they moved it. When I walked in, I shut the door and we got trapped."

Swipe pursed her lips. "That's convenient."

"Convenient? Hardly. I would have frozen to death in there if it wasn't for Flit!" Scraps grumbled as they resumed walking. When would it ever be convenient to get stuck in a freezer?

"What did Flit do to stop you from freezing, Stud?" Swipe asked, a sharp edge to her voice.

Scraps shrugged. "Not much. We just talked to pass the time."

Swipe looked at him, her eyes dragging down his exposed biceps and then over his torso as though he was an appetizing meal. He looked away from her intense gaze.

"Talking alone can't stop a person from freezing." Swipe rubbed his bicep as she spoke, as if trying to warm him.

Scraps frowned at the awkward touch, but he couldn't pull away while he was helping her walk. "No, Flit took her coat off and we both sat underneath it. It was the best way to conserve warmth."

Swipe stumbled and Scraps had to turn and grab her with both hands. "When you said sat underneath it…"

"We both sat down on the floor and put it over us like a blanket." Scraps spoke the same way he did when he explained a complex concept to Seeker and Kindling.

"And that was all you did? Sit?"

Scraps confusion escalated. "Yes. What else would we have done?"

Swipe's expression softened. She started walking again, placated. They turned off the main junction in the training area and started down the larger thoroughfare that led to the Residence. They nodded or smiled at the people they passed. Swipe didn't talk again until they reached the hydroponic gardens surrounding the large, indoor apartment building. "So... you and Flit are getting along well."

Even though it sounded like an observation, Scraps picked up on something caustic behind the words. Swipe's blue eyes flicked to him as they walked. A surge of defensiveness welled up inside him. "Yes, we are."

"Do you like her?"

Scraps wasn't sure what that had to do with anything. "She's been an excellent mentor," he hedged, wondering if Swipe was checking if Flit was doing her job. From what he understood about the relationship between the two women, Swipe would report Flit for failing her duty if he told her of any transgressions. Flit was doing everything a mentor should and more, though, so he didn't want her to get into trouble. She did that well enough without his help.

Swipe sighed. "No, I meant—" Swipe stopped and shook her head. "You know what, don't worry. I don't want to waste our time together talking about her."

Annoyance flickered through Scraps at the way Swipe referred to Flit as 'her'. Although it wasn't the pronoun; it was the tone. Swipe was the one who had brought Flit up, why was she getting annoyed?

Women were confusing.

"All right." Scraps tried to brush it off. He pressed his hand against the entrance panel by the front door of the Residence and it slid open for them.

"I know you've got your meeting with Posthoc, but is there any chance you can help me up to my room?" Swipe asked.

Scraps nodded. "I was thinking of having a quick shower before I meet with him. I might as well help you to your room. You are on the level below me, right?" Annoyance aside, it was his fault that Swipe got hurt. That made him responsible for getting her back to her room safely.

Swipe's face brightened and her arm slid down his side as they made their way to the elevator. Soon enough they had ridden up to her floor, and Scraps stopped, making sure Swipe was steady on her feet when they reached her door. Swipe leaned back against the smooth white wall beside her door as she looked at him. "Thanks for seeing me to my room." Swipe reached out and rested her hand on his bicep. She bit her lip and looked up at him through her lashes. There was something oddly appealing about the pout that tugged at her plump red lips.

"You are welcome. It is the least I can do. I am sorry that I lost concentration earlier." Scraps gave her an apologetic look.

Swipe smirked. "I've been told I can be distracting."

He looked down at her lips again, noticing how they curved, how they puckered as she bit them.

"Are you distracted right now?" Her voice was nothing more than a soft whisper.

Swipe's sweet breath fluttered against Scrap's cheek as her eyes met his. She leaned forward, closing the gap between them. Her lips claimed his and she wrapped her arms around his shoulders. Scraps gasped into the kiss. Swipe used the opening to run her tongue along his lips.

By the time Scraps processed what was happening, he could taste Swipe. He yelped and stumbled back, freeing himself from her hold and shaking his head.

"Scraps?" Swipe reached for him.

"I-I'm sorry," Scraps stammered, backing up a few more steps before he turned and fled. His footsteps echoed down the corridor and he stopped, panting when he reached the elevator. He jammed his finger against the button in a rapid tattoo as he tried to get away. When he looked back over his shoulder Swipe was still standing in front of her door, her fingers pressed against her lips, her face a picture of dismay.

"SCRAPS, I haven't seen you in a while. What can I do for you?"

Scraps stopped in his tracks as he walked into the medical room. He had not thought about where he was going, he was too busy replaying the kiss with Swipe over and over in his mind. He blinked as he tried to figure out why he was in the medbay. "I, uh, I was hoping to speak to someone..." he said, looking up at—

Tinker.

Scraps' face flooded with heat. Of all the medics that could be on duty, it was Tinker? That just would not do.

Tinker gestured for him to take a seat on the nearest bed and smiled at him. "You look a little overwhelmed. What can I do to help?"

"Oh, nothing. I, uh—" Scraps stammered. Tinker would be more than willing to discuss his concerns with him, but with what happened with Flit in the freezer it would be an awkward conversation he was not ready to have.

"Scraps?"

"Sorry... I was hoping to see Patch." Scraps look around, wondering if the young man was on shift.

Tinker frowned, the lines either side of her hazel eyes crinkled. It was the same look Flit got when she was getting suspicious. "Patch hasn't seen you before, are you sure there isn't something I can do to help?"

Scraps shook his head. "No, but he said that if I ever needed to talk about— well— talk about things, to see to him."

Tinker stopped, the confusion in her eyes was blown away by a wave of clarity. Her face settled and she nodded professionally. "I see. I'll let him know you're here. He should be finished with his patient in a few minutes."

Scraps walked over to the bed but didn't sit down. He had too much restless energy to stay still. He pressed his fingers against his lips and could still taste Swipe's kiss. Everyone in the Underground swore that kissing was enjoyable, but there was a writhing knot in his gut. How was it possible that his body enjoyed her kiss, while his mind rallied against it?

"Scraps?" Patch's voice broke through his musing.

Scraps stopped pacing and looked over at him.

"What can I do for you?" Patch asked, a polite smile on his face.

Scraps felt silly. He was an adult; he should not have to rush to a doctor the moment something new and confusing happened. He should be able to handle something as simple as a kiss on his own. "Uh, nothing. Sorry, I should not be bothering you. I am sure you are quite busy." Scraps made for the door.

Patch stepped between Scraps and the exit and shook his head. "It's fine, I have plenty of time." He ran his eyes over Scraps, assessing him for physical injuries. "Why don't we go somewhere less clinical?" Patch offered.

Scraps hung his head and followed Patch out of the four-bed infirmary room and into a narrow concrete corridor behind the rear door. They walked past two marked storerooms before Patch pressed his hand against an access panel. A door slid open, revealing a small room Scraps hadn't been in before. It was compact but comfortable. There were two couches, a tall potted plant and a blank screen against one wall. Patch gestured for Scraps to take a seat, so he sank into one of the soft couches.

"I am sorry. I don't know why I came here, but I should not be wasting your time." The apology tumbled from Scraps' lips.

"You say you shouldn't be here, but you seem very confused about something. That is unusual for you," Patch observed, sitting on his own couch opposite Scraps and leaning against the armrest. When he smiled up at Scraps it was as if he had all the time in the world.

Scraps sighed, frustrated. "Well, yes. It is. But all of this is confusing for me." He sat up as straight as always, posture perfect, but his toes tapped on the floor.

Patch's eyes dipped down, taking the tapping in, before rising back to meet Scraps' gaze. "What is confusing for you?"

Scraps' foot tapped faster. The sound bounced around the room, an external rendition of how fast his anxious heart was beating. "All of it! Everything! Before Tinker deactivated my control chip, I was fine. I knew how to handle every situation, and I never wound up feeling so... so... so lost!" Scraps blurted. For a moment he was shocked at his outburst, but it had started, and he couldn't have stopped the words if he tried. "Ever since the chip was deactivated, I have been trying my best to keep things under control. I do not feel angry, I do not get sad, I make sure I try to enjoy the good times, but sometimes my brain snags on things and won't let them go."

Patch leaned back into his seat a little more. "What does your brain snag on?"

"I can't stop wondering what would have happened if I went

along with Flit after the explosion. Would Beam be alive? Would Flit have gotten out without almost dying herself? All these questions keep playing over and over in my head. During training, it was so distracting. I never get distracted like this!"

"Ah, I see..."

"And then I dropped a weighted ball on Swipe's foot. I had to go down to the freezer and get some ice for her, but the freezer was malfunctioning. I let the door shut and I got stuck in the freezer with Flit. After I came out, I walked Swipe back to her room— you know— to help her, and then she kissed me! Swipe kissed me!" Scraps let out a huff and sank back into the couch, breathless.

Patch looked over at Scraps, his head tilted to one side as he tried to catch up on the cascade of events. When he processed it all, Patch nodded in understanding, his face frustratingly neutral. "So, Swipe kissed you? How did you feel about that?"

Scraps' toes tapped so fast they were a constant buzz. "I do not know! That is the problem. I should have enjoyed it. She's attractive. I had the correct physiological reactions, but..." Scraps sighed heavily.

"You didn't enjoy it?"

Scraps groaned. "No! What is wrong with me? I like women, so I should have enjoyed it. It was my first kiss. Instead of savouring it, my gut twisted into knots. I do not want to see her again for a while. What am I supposed to say to her after that?"

"Just because someone kissed you does not mean you have to enjoy it. We are only human, Scraps. We have our preferences and we have to trust our gut sometimes."

There it was again. 'Trust your gut'. Flit had just gotten through telling him the same thing, yet he still didn't know what it even meant.

"I do not know what my gut is trying to tell me. Why can't this be simpler? Surely somewhere has written a manual about how to respond to situations like this." Scraps shook his head.

"There are no policy or procedure manuals for attraction and arousal. I wish there were, but they just don't exist. It's too complex."

Scraps pressed his lips together in frustration. Of course, there were no manuals. Most people wouldn't need them. Unless some stupid Government had taken away all their emotions during their formative years. Scraps groaned. Maybe Flit was right. Maybe the Government were arseholes.

Patch gave Scraps an empathetic smile as he struggled with his thoughts. "Why don't you tell me more about that the knots in your gut?" Patch suggested.

"They did not start until after Swipe kissed me. I was too shocked to feel anything else. But then I pulled back and I realised I did not want to kiss her. I've never thought of her in that way."

"You were shocked that she kissed you? You hadn't picked up on any signals she intended to do so? She didn't ask your permission?"

Scraps threw his hands up in the air in frustration. The pot plant in the corner of the room shook as a wave of unintentional telekinetic energy buffeted it. "No! It was out of nowhere. One minute we were talking about Flit and how our training was going, and the next we stopped at her door and she kissed me, just like that!"

Patch's eyebrow rose in interest. "You know, that's the second or third time I've heard Flit's name since we started talking," Patch pointed out.

Scraps looked over at him, his eyebrows furrowing. What did that have to do with anything? "Yes, but it wasn't Flit who kissed me. All of those events with Flit were context for the situation."

"Uh-huh." Patch sat back in his chair looking unconvinced.

There was something in his expression that set Scraps on edge; as though he knew something that Scraps didn't. Scraps didn't like it. "What? It is true. If I hadn't been thinking of Flit and the tunnel collapse, then I would not have dropped the ball. If the freezer was not broken, Flit and I would not have gotten stuck together. I would have had the ice pack back to Swipe faster and she wouldn't have been so annoyed about it being held up. And if Swipe wasn't injured, I would not have walked her to her room, and she would not have kissed me!" Scraps spluttered, even though he thought he had made it clear already.

"So, what you're saying is that this all comes back to you thinking about Flit?" Patch asked.

Scraps froze.

That wasn't what he was saying, but when he heard it reflected to him, he realised that Patch was right. But... he felt terrible. None of it was Flit's fault. She didn't ask Scraps to fret about her. It wasn't fair to let her shoulder the blame for something that she had no control over. "It is not Flit's fault that Swipe kissed me," Scraps said firmly, sitting straighter.

A flicker of a smirk tugged at Patch's lips. "No, it wasn't," he agreed. "But do you think she might have something to do with your reaction to the kiss?"

Scraps opened his mouth to answer, but his words got stuck in his throat. He thought about what would have happened if Flit had seen Swipe kiss him, and that knot in his gut bucked. His cheeks flushed with guilt. Then, another scenario came to mind. Instead of Swipe kissing him it was Flit. The knot uncoiled and swirled until it felt like some different; something arousing.

"Oh."

Scraps stared dumbfounded at Patch, who just smiled and shrugged. He straightened up, brushing some dust off his grey trousers. "It seems we've found a potential cause for your confusion."

"Are you... Are you suggesting that I like Flit? And that is why I did not enjoy Swipe's kiss?"

Patch shrugged.

"That is not possible. I do not have enough experience to like someone. Besides, Flit and I are very different people. She is fiery and instinctive in a way that I will never be. And she is so short. How would that even work, mechanically speaking? Wouldn't it be uncomfortable for her?"

Patch chuckled, shaking his head. "Stop thinking of this as a tactical operation and trust those feelings you're developing."

Scraps frowned. "I do not know how to do that. How does one even know when they are attracted to another person? I mean, apart from the physiological reactions?"

"Are those there? The physiological reactions?"

Scraps blushed. "Yes."

"Well, that is a start I suppose. Let me see." Patch tapped his chin as he sat back in his chair. Scraps waited with bated breath for his next bit of insight. Finally, he spoke. "When you like someone you look forward to seeing them again, you enjoy spending time with them and get a pang of disappointment when they are gone. Sometimes you may get upset or jealous if you see them with someone else. You look for ways to make them happy, no matter how small or silly. You worry about them if you think they may be unsafe... Does any of this sound familiar?"

Finally, someone gave him some solid parameters. Scraps considered what Patch said. He worried about Flit after that tunnel collapse, but the explosion itself would have been enough to set that off. He looked forward to spending time with her, more so than he did with others, and enjoyed seeing her happy. But he was never jealous; it was a pleasure to watch her interacting with others in that playful manner of hers.

"Some of it," Scraps conceded. "But there are bits that also don't match up."

Patch shrugged. "Not all of it will for every relationship. You just need to see what works for you." Patch leaned closer. "Next time you're with Flit, just let your instincts guide you. Listen to your body; does your heart race faster? Do your palms get sweaty? Is it harder to find the right words? Do you notice how she smiles? How she smells? How does it feel if she brushes past you? Things like that."

Scraps thought it over and did not think his feelings for Flit met all of the criteria. She was his friend, that was all. Still, he nodded, trying to store all the information away to review later.

"I can see you're trying to take all of this in, but please, be kind to yourself. Even the oldest people down here are still clueless about the laws of attraction. It's a funny thing. Don't let it get you down, ok? And if you ever need to talk, I'm here," Patch said.

Scraps' toes stopped tapping and he got to his feet. "Thank you, I appreciate you taking time out of your busy schedule to—"

Scraps stopped, his eyes widening as he thought about schedules. In particular, the schedule Flit had set for him, and the meeting he was supposed to have with Posthoc. He looked down at the time on his wristband and winced.

"Oh no, I'm late for a meeting with Posthoc. I'm sorry. I really do appreciate your time, though." Scraps turned and rushed out of the room. He barely heard Patch call out after him, promising to send Posthoc a message excusing Scraps for being late on medical grounds.

30

FLIT

RUMOURS SPREAD FAST in the Underground. After Flit and Scraps were discovered in the freezer, Flit spent the entire afternoon fielding suspicious and amused glances from the other team members in Supply. She knew, come dinner, everyone would be gossiping about the unfortunate 'coincidence'. She only hoped that her parents didn't hear about it.

Flit was acutely aware of how some members of the Underground were whispering about Scraps' role in the tunnel collapse behind his back, and it made her furious. They were quick to shut up whenever she was around, especially after she stood by Scraps' side at Beam's funeral. It touched her heart when Scraps asked why she wasn't annoyed at him. Those moments before she went rogue were vivid in her memory; yes, she'd given him an opportunity to go along with her, but he stuck to his own morals and she would never judge him for that. She hoped he would think more critically about it next time, but she would never force anyone to risk their lives against their own will. The real question that played over in her mind, though, was: what could she have done better, so Beam got out alive?

However, Flit had something else to occupy her mind as she worked her Supply shift. As she had promised Scraps, she considered how she could add some fun and leisure into his schedule. Not that fun and leisure was something she believed should be scheduled, but for Scraps she would make the exception.

By the end of the day, Flit had an excellent plan to introduce Scraps to the more recreational aspects of life in the Underground. Concerned that he might try and get out of it, she added it to his calendar as 'Recreation Training' and fluffed a few training outcomes for good measure: 'trainee comprehends the importance of recreation for enhancing overall wellbeing', 'trainee analyses and compares various leisure activities to determine which is more personally enjoyable,', and 'trainee creates work life balance by not studying all the time and allows himself to have fun once in a while.' She knew the last one might be a bit of a stretch for Scraps, but she'd like to see him weasel his way out of leisure time now it had outcomes and was on his training schedule.

Flit's plan started that night with an introduction to something she had been missing since Hawkeye went on his mission: Virtual Reality Gaming. She took Scraps to one of the training rooms and experimented with the menu. He expressed his concern about hacking into the system, but she assured him they were encouraged to do so after hours. She pulled up a fun puzzle-solving game that manufactured a holographic room around them. At first, he poked around, but once he discovered the connections between the logic and moving to the next stage in the game, he showed himself to have a very nimble mind. They worked together well, too. Hawkeye would have rolled his eyes at some of her more out-of-the-box ideas, but Scraps listened carefully and tried them.

A couple of weeks later, Posthoc called Flit and Scraps into his office for a meeting and informed them that Scraps would be required to complete his orienteering test. Scraps perked up at the idea of being examined, and although Flit wasn't surprised, she still shook her head at his eagerness. The orienteering test was a way for fresh Security recruits to prove they knew enough about the layout of the tunnels to go on further-reaching patrols. Given the labyrinthine nature of the Underground, Flit put dedicated study sessions into Scraps' schedule so he wouldn't use his newly allotted leisure time to cram for the test. It worked well, given that she was not on active duty, and it meant that they had something to do in the time where they would have been training together. Preparing for the orienteering test also gave Flit something else to focus on other than her growing conviction that the tunnel collapse wasn't an accident. Control claimed that it was a maintenance issue, but she didn't believe it. She couldn't.

Scraps made for an excellent student. His probing, inquisitive questions made Flit think about her own knowledge and she spotted some gaps she started studying to fill. He was also willing to listen to her when she would go off on her random tangents. Sometimes, when she was talking, she would catch him watching her with intense interest. Whenever he saw her notice his attention, he would blush and look away.

Given that the two were spending more time together Flit had a harder time ignoring the feelings that fluttered in her belly when she saw him. She told herself it was the excitement of making a new friend, but ever since being stuck in the freezer with him there was a new tension between them. She'd notice him looking at her from time to time, and he was quicker to smile at her than before. Swipe's accusations at Rook's graveside came back to haunt her and she worked to shake them off. Every time she thought of Rook, her heart broke all over again. Although, Scraps did make for a wonderful friend, and he was nice to look at… Flit pushed those thoughts from her mind. She wasn't ready for anything new and she highly doubted Scraps would be interested in her anyway.

"You're the queen of self-deception," Acumen tutted, resting his chin on his hand as he looked over at her.

Flit narrowed her eyes at him. *Nosy bastard.* "No, I just know my own feelings." Flit shook herself from her earlier train of thought and turned her attention back to the diamond shaped board on the table between them.

Flit and Acumen were sitting in the Mess just before the dinner session started, hunched over one of the metal tables. It was another half hour until the food would be available, so she figured that playing a game with Acumen was preferable to being bored. Or stewing in her musings about Scraps and Rook.

Acumen snorted. "Just quit your daydreaming and move your damn piece. Please."

Flit frowned as she looked down at the board once more and cursed. While she was distracted, Acumen moved his pieces up to surround hers. In two more moves he would have her, no matter what she did. With a heavy breath of defeat, she reached out, flicking her piece over one tile. "I still don't know why I play this game with you; you suck the strategies straight out of my mind," she muttered.

"It's because you're a sucker for punishment and you don't learn your lesson." A smug smirk tugged at Acumen's lips. "And I resent your implication that I cheat. I don't. You just have a terrible poker face. It's tragic."

Flit was about to make a snarky comment right back at him when the buzz of conversation at one of the other tables caught her attention. Flit turned around to see two of the members of the Supply team murmuring to each other in low voices.

"Three bags. We all counted it. I don't know how they disappeared. They were there one day and gone the next, even wiped off the inventory."

"You must have been hallucinating. Three bags of desiccant don't just grow legs and walk away. Those little sacks always look like sodium, perhaps that was what you counted by mistake."

Flit's brow furrowed. Something about that didn't sound right. She was just about to turn around and ask the workers for more information when Acumen tapped the table in front of her.

"Flit! For goodness' sake, just end the game so I can play with someone who has half a brain to spare!"

Flit rolled her eyes and shifted her piece one square to the side before she slid off her seat. She reached into her pocket and retrieved three surface candies, slapping them onto the table for Acumen before she made her way to the others. The two middle-aged men looked up and smiled at her as she approached.

"Arctic, Heave, sorry to interrupt," Flit said as she settled into a spare space beside them. She had grown up around these two, both around her father's age. Both were greying, but that was where the similarities between them stopped.

"Flit, nice to see you. I hear you've only got a day or two left with us." Heave nodded his nearly bald head at her.

Flit smiled. "Yeah, I'm healing up all right. Gotta get my medical approval from Physie though, and she's tough at the best of times."

Arctic smirked, Physie was his older sister; they had the same round face and warm smile. "I'll have a talk to her for you. You're wasting away with us in the storage vaults."

"That would be great. Although I couldn't help but overhear you talking about the desiccant. You said three bags were missing?"

Heave laughed and shook his head. "No, there's nothing missing. Arctic's just getting senile, is all."

"Me? You're the one complaining every time you get off a seat. 'Oh—my back!', 'Ah, this damp is no good for my joints'."

Flit chuckled at the banter between the two, but she pushed on. "What storeroom was this in?"

"Eighteen. Why?"

"I wanted to see if it was one I counted, but I only did the odds. I figured I could help put an end to your bickering."

Heave and Arctic laughed.

"You are your father's daughter, Flit. I can see where you get your cheek from." Arctic crossed his arms over his broad chest.

"Good old genetics, always—"

The door to the Mess opened and Flit looked up as Scraps, Patch, and Link walked in. She jumped out of her seat, giving Heave and Arctic an apology before weaving through the tables towards them. As Scraps looked up and saw her coming, he smiled and gave a slight wave. Her stomach fluttered, but that was only because she was excited to tell him about what she discovered.

"Woah, Flit, slow down." Link put her hands up as Flit slid to a stop in front of her.

"You'll never guess what I just heard," Flit whispered, leaning in close enough so that the three could all hear her. She stopped, looking around to see that people were watching the fuss. She didn't want anyone overhearing what she had to say. "Come on, let's sit while we wait for the others."

Flit led her way back to their regular table. The four of them all settled down, Scraps opting to sit on Flit's right side while Patch and Link sat opposite.

Link reached into her pocket, retrieving a small glittering black geode that she must have picked up on her patrol, and added it to the pile of carefully curated decorations on the table. With a satisfied nod, she looked at Fit and leaned in close. "So, what's all the excitement about?"

"I overheard something interesting from Arctic and Heave. There were three bags of desiccant missing from storeroom eighteen."

The others just looked at her with blank expressions.

"And that is exciting because...?" Patch trailed off, looking between the others to see if he was the only one not understanding her point.

Flit sighed. "What do we put into the sewage pipes to ensure that the gases don't become too flammable?" Flit bounced up and down in her seat as she waited for the revelation to click.

Patch shrugged. "Um... I don't know, stuff?"

Scrap's eyes widen as he blurted, "Water!" He sat up straighter as he looked down at her with those intense red eyes of his.

She beamed back at him. "Yes!"

"Sorry, I still I don't get it." Patch looked between Flit and Scraps.

"Well, if we add water to the sewage to reduce the flammability, and bags of desiccant are going missing from the storerooms..." Flit spoke slowly, her eyes wide with excitement.

Link tilted her head to the side as she watched Flit more closely. "Flit thinks someone stole the desiccant and used it to soak up the water so those pipes would produce gas. All the extra pressure would cause even the best maintained pipes to burst." Link sighed and shook her head, clearly disagreeing with the line of reasoning she telepathically plucked from Flit's mind.

"What? That's crazy," Patch whispered, looking around to make sure they nobody was listening.

There were people close by, but they were all too busy with their own business to bother listening to what Flit, Scraps, Link, and Patch were discussing.

"No, it is not." Scraps leaned in closer. "When the pipes exploded, they did not leak, did they? If the sewage were in the correct liquid state, it would have gushed out, and you would have returned to the shelter covered in—" Scraps stopped and frowned, not completing the sentence. They all knew where it was going.

Excitement sizzled through Flit. Scraps understood what she was getting at.

"Flit, I know that it was scary, but it was just a maintenance issue. We need not search for more sinister causes. Control had their postcogs look at it. If there was anything dodgy going on, they would have seen it," Link whispered, her words laced with warning.

"I'm not searching for more sinister causes, they showed up all on their own. Come on, that can't be a coincidence." Flit's frustration grew as neither Patch nor Link took her concerns seriously.

"Well, if you're convinced you're right, take it to Posthoc. He'll know what to do about it," Patch offered.

Flit's stomach clenched at the idea and she shook her head. Posthoc would dismiss her faster than Patch and Link had. "No, we need more evidence."

Patch groaned. "Flit..." He slumped back in his seat and buried his face in his hands as he shook his head.

"Flit, the Intelligence team said it was a closed cased. Insufficient maintenance. That's all," Link reiterated, her tone soothing.

Link's comment only aggravated Flit further. With her jaw set in determination, she forged on. "Well, I don't believe them. Those pipes weren't even that old. And what are the chances they exploded right when we were in the sector? They could have gone off any time, but they didn't!"

Patch looked at her through his fingers as if she was a madwoman.

"It is a lot of coincidences," Scraps conceded.

Patch stared at him, wide-eyed. "Oh, come on Scraps, don't tell me you're buying this."

"I investigated a lot of cases in the Hub, and I no longer believe in simple coincidences. I agree that the situation may warrant further investigation."

Flit could have exploded with the pride she felt at seeing Scraps thinking about it.

Patch wasn't so impressed. "Underground protocol dictates that we have to respect rulings made by our superiors."

Flit cocked an eyebrow at the microkinetic, annoyed that he was using Scraps' love of policies and protocol against him.

Scraps looked between Flit and Patch for a few moments before he shrugged. "If Flit had followed protocol that day in the tunnels, Cogs and Heft would be dead. This situation is odd and warrants further investigation. Protocol or not," Scraps explained as he looked at Flit. Their eyes connected and a spark of something sizzled between them. The corners of Flit's lips curled up in victory.

Patch and Link looked shocked. Scraps would never step outside of protocol of his own account. But Flit noticed that he had been different after the tunnel collapse; more willing to push boundaries. It might have been out of character for him to agree that breaking protocol was justified, but he was firm on the matter. He had come so far since joining the Underground.

"Woah, guys, why so serious? You could cut the tension in here with a knife."

Tweak's voice sliced through their conversation as he, Sway, Swipe, and Clarity walked over. Sway slid his arm around Link's shoulder and kissed the top of her hair in greeting.

Link shrugged. "Just a difference of opinion."

Flit was about to argue that it was more than that, but she bit her words back. The more people that knew of her discovery, the more people that may squeal when she and Scraps investigated it.

"Well, that's nothing new in this team." Swipe cast an accusatory glare at Flit.

Flit sat a little straighter, her shoulders squaring. Swipe always blamed her when there was tension around.

"We were just waiting for you guys, sheesh. Now, are we going to eat? Because I'm starving," Link snapped as she got to her feet. She pushed her chair back with a clatter and made her way over to the servery. Sway followed her, slipping his hand into her back pocket and muttering something to her as they walked away.

The others all made their way over to see what was on offer for dinner that night. Flit reached out, taking Scraps' hand and tugging it to hold him back. "I know we're supposed to be watching an old-school movie tonight, but maybe I can pop by your room and we can discuss how we'll get this evidence," she suggested.

Scraps looked down at their joined hands, blinking. "Uh, oh… Sure." He seemed to shake himself out of whatever was bothering him. "That sounds like an excellent plan. Will you come by straight after dinner?"

"I'll grab some things from my room first."

With that sorted, Flit and Scraps joined the others in getting their dinner. When they all sat back down, the conversation turned towards the full group mission they had coming up in two weeks. It was rare they all got sent out together, but one of the mutant bat dens had become troublesome and they needed to clear it out to avoid the creatures doing damage to infrastructure. Missions like that brought them together. The tensions from earlier were all but forgotten.

When the meal was over, Flit was just about to tell Scraps she'd see him soon, when there was a commotion over by the doors. A group of six people had walked into the Mess. All looking a little scraggly and worse for wear, but with broad smiles and shoulders sagged with relief.

Clarity nudged Flit with her elbow. "They're back."

Hawkeye!

Flit teleported over before the others could blink. She landed right in front of Hawkeye and looked up at him, eyes wide. To his credit, he didn't flinch when she appeared in front of him. He must have expected nothing less. She pulled him into a back-breaking hug, hardly daring to believe he was real. His laughter filled her ears as he hugged her back, wrapping his arms around her and holding her close. After Flit was reassured by the staccato tattoo of his heartbeat through his chest, she pulled back and looked up at him, her hazel eyes meeting his green. "Hell, Hawkeye, were you gone long enough?" she whispered, all of her worries about him for the past few months welling up inside her.

"Too long." Hawkeye's expression turned serious. "Far too long… I heard you got hurt in a tunnel collapse. Are you all right?" He scanned her body with a critical gaze, looking for injuries.

Flit waved her hand, dismissing his concern. "Punctured lung, fractured ribs, nothing that hasn't almost healed already."

Hawkeye's expression of concern only grew. "Flit..." The word puffed out, a sound of shock as the true extent of her injuries settled over him.

Flit tilted her head to the side, furrowing her brows at his apparent loss for words. "Hawk?"

"Flit, I—" Hawkeye stopped himself short. He looked down at her, seeming to weigh his words before the clarity of a decision cleared the conflict away. "Oh, fuck it."

One moment Flit was looking up into his familiar face; the next, his lips were on hers. They were warm and sweet, and he pulled her in close. It should have been a delightful comfort to feel his strong body against hers, but Flit's stomach roiled. Without thinking, she teleported two steps back and left Hawkeye there, blinking and bamboozled by her sudden absence. His eyes widened when he realised what had happened.

Flit held up her hand and took a step back towards him. "Hawk..."

Flit looked over her shoulder and saw how many pairs of eyes were on her and Hawkeye, all watching with unabashed interest. One pair, deep crimson, made her heart hammer even harder. "Can we go somewhere private, please?"

Hawkeye's expression hardened, but he nodded and let her lead him out. As they walked, Flit, still reeling, wondered how on earth she could let her best friend down without breaking his heart.

31

SCRAPS

SCRAPS SAT, eyes wide and heart thundering, as Flit took Hawkeye's hand and led him from the Mess.

"Well, that was interesting." Tweak's voice that cut through the stunned silence at the table.

"Not that we didn't see it coming," Clarity said, her soft voice tinged with uncharacteristic smugness.

Patch groaned. "You see everything coming."

The others laughed.

Except for Scraps. He wasn't in the mood for laughing.

"I bet Flit's taking him to give him what he's been wanting for years," Sway said in a low, suggestive tone.

"Sway!"

He shrugged, looking at Link. "It's true. They're probably going back to her room—"

"Sway!" Link's second rebuke was enough to shut Sway up with the added incentive of an elbow to the gut. Scraps looked over at the others, wondering how they could joke about something like this.

"Oh, who gives a shit?" Swipe stood up so suddenly her chair clattered to the ground behind her. She snatched her drink bottle off the table. "I'm out. I have better things to do than talk about Flit's bloody love life."

Before anyone could say anything to hold her back, Swipe stormed out. Scraps could understand why Swipe would walk out.

She and Flit worked together as required to be part of the same team, but even he could tell their tolerance for each other in social situations was limited.

Clarity sighed and waited before Swipe was out of earshot before continuing. "I don't think Flit was happy with Hawkeye's surprise."

Scraps certainly hoped not. It wasn't courteous of Hawkeye to kiss Flit in the middle of a room full of people. Or at least, he didn't think it was. He wasn't well versed on kissing protocol, but he was grateful that Swipe hadn't made her move on him in front of everyone.

"Why wouldn't she be? I'd be happy if he wanted to kiss me," Tweak said, a smirk on his face. The others rolled their eyes.

Sway leaned in. "They've always been inseparable. It makes sense."

Scraps shifted in his seat as he realised Swipe made the right move by leaving. Sitting and chatting about Flit and Hawkeye kissing – maybe more – did not seem appropriate. His stomach churned, and he wondered if there was something off in the food

"Inseparable or not, it didn't look like Flit enjoyed it," Link added matter-of-factly.

"Didn't she?" Scraps asked before he could swallow the question back. All eyes at the table turned to him as he spoke for the first time in a while.

Link bit her lip and shrugged. "If she liked it, she wouldn't have teleported away."

The churning in Scraps' gut settled a little. He pressed his palm against his stomach and wondered whether he should head to the medical wing before bed. Link had a point. Why did Flit teleport out of Hawkeye's arms? And where did she take him? Scraps considered the possibilities so he could contribute to the discussion, but any clear thought eluded his grasp. He was gripping the chair so hard his fingertips hurt.

"You're all incorrigible," Acumen said, sliding over and smirking at the rest of the Blue Team.

"Hey, you're a telepath, and Link is biased. What do you think? Do you think they're going for it?" Sway asked. His casual tone set

Scraps on edge. He wanted to leave so he didn't have to hear the answer, but he stayed in his seat, morbidly curious.

"A telepath never tells," Acumen whispered before shrugging. "Besides, I was too busy figuring out how many sweets Tweak owes you."

Scraps looked between Tweak, Sway, and Acumen. They had a wager on Flit and Hawkeye kissing? Was that even ethical?

Acumen patted Scraps' shoulder. "Buddy, everything down here is up for betting against if someone will pay the price."

"And Tweak owes me. Hawkeye was the one that made the move. Pay up." Sway held an open hand towards Tweak, as if waiting for payment.

Tweak groaned and reached into his pocket, retrieving three sticks of some surface type treat and dropping them onto Sway's palm.

Acumen snatched one stick off Sway. "I believe this is my cut. Good night, gentlemen, nice doing business with you." Acumen tore the packet open and stuck the sweet in his mouth, chuckling to himself as he walked away.

Scraps looked between Sway and Tweak, his lips curling in disapproval. "Isn't that kind of behaviour inappropriate?"

"Yes, it is." Patch shook his head at their antics.

"We gotta entertain ourselves around here somehow." Sway shrugged as he opened a sweet and chewed on it. "Besides, the tension between those two has been growing for years. I bet that they come out of Flit's room tomorrow all loved up."

Scraps' jaw ached, the muscles in it straining as he gritted his teeth together.

"She teleported away," Clarity pointed out again.

"Maybe she wanted him to kiss her, just not in public," Tweak supplied.

"She never had a problem doing that with Rook," Sway muttered under his breath.

Scraps' stomach twisted into a knot so tight that he was about to lose his dinner. Rook? Who was Rook? And why would Flit be kissing him in public? Scraps' head spun with the news and he sucked a breath in through his teeth.

Link looked over at Scraps, her head tilted to the side. "Ok, that's enough. Flit and Hawkeye are our teammates and sitting here gossiping about them makes us shit friends. Good night," Link snapped. She got to her feet, snatched up her tray, and walked away.

"Oh babe, come on!" Sway groaned, jumping up and following her, "We're just having some fun!"

Patch leaned back in his chair and crossed his arms over his chest. "Well... that was interesting." He turned to look at Scraps, head tilted to the side in question. It was the same look he got in the medical bay when he was about to ask Scraps about his feelings.

"I... I have to go. Dinner did not agree with me tonight." Scraps got up and grabbed his tray, clinging to it so tight his knuckles were white. He dumped it at the cleaning station as fast as he could before heading back to his room. Flit said that she would stop by after dinner so they could work on their plan to get evidence. He wanted it to be tidy for her.

Unfortunately for Scraps, Flit didn't come by that night. She didn't send him a message to cancel, and she didn't follow up with an apology for forgetting about him. In fact, he didn't see her until breakfast two mornings after they made their plans. She looked tired, her eyes underscored by dark purple bags. Hawkeye came to breakfast too, looking exhausted. Scraps didn't want to know why. All he knew was that Flit had forgotten about their investigation. About him. He didn't have much energy to think about it; the churning in his stomach hadn't stopped since the operatives came back from the surface.

IN THE DAYS after Hawkeye and the others in the Intelligence team returned, Scraps became more and more unwell. Having never been sick before, he now understood why people would complain about it. There was an immense pressure in his head, like an iron fist had wrapped around his brain. He was always only a moment from a headache, and it made it hard for him to think. The churning in his gut turned to an uncomfortable burn that festered through his veins and made his temper short and his words unkind. With every passing day, it was harder for him to concentrate on a thought long enough to finish it. Each night he collapsed into bed, exhausted, and when he woke, it felt as though he hadn't slept at all.

Even the prospect of investigating the missing desiccant with Flit wasn't enough to get him motivated. Not that she followed up on that. He rarely saw her around. She skipped their training sessions and then updated his schedule through electronic messages. She'd even swapped out their first physical session since her recovery with a hand-to-hand training session with Hawkeye.

As Scraps looked at his training schedule for the following morning, he let out a soft groan. Why did she have to put in a sparring session with Hawkeye? Scraps had no interest in liaising with the remote viewer. He held Hawkeye and the other Intelligence members responsible for bringing down whatever surface virus was ailing him. Even at lunch and dinner, he'd found Hawkeye's playful teasing annoying. He never wanted to punch another person in the nose before, but he had a fantasy of doing it to Hawkeye earlier that day.

Perhaps a sparring session wasn't such a terrible idea.

Scraps set the datapad he was researching on aside and sat up, rubbing his eyes. He was on a comfortable couch in the Residence Recreation Room; the Mess had closed an hour earlier, after finishing up the dinner session, and the Rec Room was abuzz with socialisation. Most people were chatting or playing games, but Scraps wasn't in the mood for any of that. As he looked around the large, warm space, he saw Patch over in the far corner, tucked up on one of the two-seater lounges with Honey. Honey was the mother of the ever-delightful Seeker, and one of the first few people he met in the Underground. Scraps recalled Acumen's comments about her wanting mouth-to-mouth with Patch, and he now understood what he had meant. Although it wasn't mouth-to-mouth so much as intense kissing. Scraps frowned, looking around for Seeker, but the bouncing ball of energy was nowhere to be seen.

Scraps saw Patch that evening just before dinner in the medbay, hoping for some answers about his illness. Patch ran several tests and decreed that there was nothing medically wrong with him. He offered to 'talk it out' with Scraps, but Scraps refused. What was there to talk about? He was sick and miserable, and there was no discernible cause. Patch had given him a wary look, but let him go anyway, promising to check in with him over the next few days.

As Scraps sat in the Rec Room, he wondered whether Patch had been too distracted by the prospect of kissing Honey to run proper diagnostics. He would have to make an appointment to see Physie or Tinker instead. They seemed sensible enough to not let their personal lives impede sound medical assessment.

"Are you too busy being all dark and broody, or can I sit down?"

Turning away from Patch and Honey, Scraps looked up to see Acumen gesturing to the lounge beside him. Scraps pressed his lips together at the comment. He wasn't in the mood to talk, but Acumen had always been kind to him. It would be impolite to refuse him a seat. With a flick of his wrist, Scraps telekinetically cleared the game boxes off the couch beside him.

Acumen grinned as he flopped into the chair with a sigh of relief. He turned his head and surveyed Scraps with his sharp blue eyes. "You look like crap."

"I feel terrible," Scraps agreed, even though he didn't appreciate the delivery of the observation.

To his credit, Acumen leaned over, looking concerned. "Have you spoken to Tinker about it?"

"No." Scraps shook his head. "I saw Patch, though, and he said I was fine. I think I will get a second opinion tomorrow."

Acumen looked between Scraps, and where Patch and Honey were still kissing on a couch. "Well, that explains all the caustic glares you were sending that way... But you know, just because Patch is busy outside of work doesn't mean he was distracted when he saw you. Patch is an excellent doctor."

Scraps sighed. Patch had gone out of his way to be helpful on several occasions. Scraps didn't mean to be disrespectful, but he just refused to believe there was nothing wrong with him.

"Maybe you just need a few days off. Even the best of us get burned out sometimes." Acumen shrugged. "Did you want me to talk to Flit for you? See if she'll give you some wiggle room on your schedule?"

"No!" Scraps froze, looking at Acumen with horror. He could not think of anything more embarrassing than having to ask Flit for time off. She had set a very fair schedule for him. What would she think of him if he couldn't follow it? Scraps shoulders sagged a little. Maybe she wouldn't care. She was too busy with Hawkeye, after all.

"Woah, what happened there?" Acumen asked, leaning in and watching Scraps closer. "You went from tense to deflated in a split-second."

Scraps sat up straighter. "I did not."

Acumen rolled his eyes. "Uh-huh," he muttered, unconvinced. "So, when did this 'mystery illness' begin?"

"When Hawkeye and the others came back. I think they brought a virus with them," Scraps explained.

Acumen's lips twisted into a frown and he shook his head. "Not possible, buddy. They underwent thorough health checks before they re-joined the population. Any surface-type viruses spread like wildfire down here. If one of them had something, everyone would know about it by now."

Scraps sighed. Patch had said the same thing. He understood the process, but it didn't change that he still felt sick, and the return of the mission operatives was the only thing that changed in his life around that time.

Acumen raised his hands defensively. "I'm not here to argue about it."

Eyeing Acumen wearily, Scraps slumped back in his seat. He knew Acumen well enough to not bother telling him to get out of his head.

"You're pretty much shouting those thoughts, you know." Acumen shrugged. "They're hard to ignore. But we're getting off topic. Maybe whatever you have isn't a surface virus. There are plenty of regular colds that go around down here. What are your symptoms?"

Finally, a logical response. Scraps counted them off on his fingers as he spoke. "I feel tired all the time, even if I just woke up. I cannot concentrate. My stomach is always churning, and there is a constant pressure in my head. I have also been in a terrible mood; I am angry all the time, and I do not know why."

Shifting in his seat, Acumen nodded as he took it all in. "Is your nose blocked?"

"No."

"Is your throat sore?"

Scraps swallowed to test it. "No."

"Do your muscles ache? Do you have a fever? Any odd rashes?"

Scraps shook his head. Patch had asked him all those questions, too, and the answer was the same. He had hoped Acumen would give him some answers, but from the look on the telepath's face, he was just as sceptical as Patch. Scraps should have known better. Acumen wasn't a doctor.

Acumen chuckled. "You're not sick, but there is definitely something going on."

Scraps frowned. "What do you mean?"

"The frustration, fatigue, and lack of motivation, without the other symptoms, point to something psychological," Acumen explained. "You've been through a lot in the past six months. It's only natural that you feel—"

"I was coping fine with everything until Hawkeye and the others came back," Scraps snapped, throwing up his hands and telekinetically sending one of the cushions on a nearby couch skittering by accident.

Scraps' entire worldview shattered when he learned of the Underground, but he had gotten used to his new life with them. It was a challenge, but he had risen to meet it, and he liked to think he was doing a good job of it. He had gotten to a place where he was truly happy for the first time in his life. Scraps had been spending his newly improved leisure time with Flit in the VR suites, and they made excellent progress on his training. But now Flit was too busy with Hawkeye to even check in with Scraps anymore, and he lamented the loss of his closest friend in the Underground.

Instead of being shocked or annoyed at Scraps' outburst, Acumen chuckled softly. Frustration boiled inside Scraps and he pressed his lips together, unimpressed.

"Scraps, buddy, you're not sick. You're jealous," Acumen said with a dismissive wave.

Scraps blinked. "Excuse me?"

"Look, I don't like telling people what they're thinking, but you're new to the whole social interaction thing, and I hate seeing you torn up over this, so I'll make an exception." Acumen leaned in closer as he spoke, his voice hushed.

Scraps instinctively leaned closer. "What do you mean?"

"Do you like Flit?"

After discussing that same issue with Patch only a few weeks ago, Scraps thought he had already dealt with it. He blushed at the memory. "She is a good person and she has been an excellent mentor." At least she was until Hawkeye got back.

"I'll take the blush and the non-answer as a yes." Acumen let out a heavy sigh. "The reason you're all twisted up inside is because Hawkeye came back, kissed Flit, and now you think they're spending all their time together... but deep inside, you wish it was you."

"No, I—" Scraps was about to argue when the realisation slammed into him.

When Scraps talked to Patch, he had dismissed the idea of having a romantic attraction to Flit because he hadn't met the criteria of being upset when she spent time with other people. Maybe the issue back then was she was spending time with friends, but Hawkeye was so much more than a friend. Then, he thought of what it would be like to kiss Flit. Touching her in the freezer had certainly stirred more than just his imagination.

Acumen was right.

"So, what is the protocol for this? What do I do next?" Scraps asked. Now he knew the problem, he needed to figure out the solution.

Acumen scratched his stubbly grey beard as he considered his answer. "You should probably start by telling Flit you like her."

"Oh, that should be simple enough." Scraps settled his datapad on the nearby table and got up.

Acumen looked up at him, confused. "Scraps?"

"Yes?"

"Where are you going?"

Scraps' furrowed his brow, he thought it was obvious. "To talk to Flit."

Acumen groaned and shook his head. "Sit down, Scraps."

Scraps frowned but complied with the request.

"You can't just drop it on her like that," Acumen explained. "You've got to do it at the right time. Wait until you're alone with her, maybe during a quiet part of your patrol or something. And make sure she's not in one of her moods. You want to catch her at a time when she'll feel comfortable to tell you she likes you too—"

Scraps blinked. "Flit likes me?"

Acumen winced and raised his hands defensively. "I didn't say that. I was speaking hypothetically, of course..."

Scraps' shoulders fell. "Oh... right. So, I need to find the right time before I tell her. And then what?"

Acumen chuckled. "You just worry about your part, let Flit take care of the rest. She's got enough relationship experience to handle what comes next. You just let her know how you feel so she stops denying what she's got right in front of her." Acumen got to his feet with a groan and squeezed Scraps' shoulder reassuringly. "All right, now I've done my good deed for the day, I'm off to bed. Good luck with everything."

With that brief farewell and a smug smirk, Acumen left Scraps to his thoughts. Instead of feeling reassured by the plan that Acumen laid out, he was more intimidated. He was terrible at navigating the social complexities of life in the Underground, and Flit was tempestuous at best. How was he ever supposed to line up all the variables correctly to act upon his new plan?

32

FLIT

FLIT'S LIPS curled into a triumphant grin as she read the message on her datapad.

> **To:** Flit
> **From:** Cogs
> **Subject:** How do you always find yourself in these situations?
> Hi Flit,
> Yes, I agree, it needs to be investigated. If I get caught doing it, I'll lose my clearance privileges.
> Keep an eye on your inbox. An access code may or may not appear there over the next couple of weeks. It certainly shouldn't be used for sneaking into the storerooms…
> —Cogs
> P.S. For the love of everything good in this world, please delete this message the moment you've read it.

Flit read the message a second time, just to be sure she wasn't dreaming, and then deleted it as Cogs requested. She wiped her deleted files, just to be sure. She had been hoping for that kind of response when she contacted Cogs and told her about the missing bags of desiccant. It was good to have a lead to go on. Something to distract her from the mess her social life had become.

Flit was just about to turn her datapad off and get up to do some stretches when a new message pinged into her inbox. Surely Cogs couldn't have gotten her the codes that quickly? Then, she saw Hawkeye's name in the 'From' field and her stomach dropped. She considered putting the datapad aside, to ignore whatever he couldn't say to her in person, but then she saw the subject line and sighed with relief. She opened the message.

To: Flit
From: Hawkeye
Subject: Training Report
While Scraps has made progress without hand-to-hand specific training, he is not in the correct mindset to be engaging in such sessions. After lacking energy and motivation to engage in routine exercises, he was easily frustrated and failed to pull punches and kicks appropriately.
Scraps' repeated inability to stick to the pre-planned drill resulted in the session being cancelled early, to reduce risk of further injury.
Given his enthusiasm for combat and general physical training prior to my absence, I am not sure what the problem is. I am genuinely concerned for his wellbeing, but do not feel I am an appropriate person to raise this issue with him. Therefore, as per the Mentoring Policy, I have raised my concerns to you so you may investigate if you deem it necessary.

Flit set the datapad down with a frown of concern.
That didn't sound like Scraps at all.

Flit was too concerned about the report to be annoyed by the lack of friendly greeting or sign off in the message. After Hawkeye had kissed her, she took him back to her room and let him down as gently as she could. He was her best friend, and he always would be, but he was like a brother to her. She would never be able to see past it. She tried to explain it all as kindly as she possible, but she could almost hear Hawkeye's heart breaking. Ever since then, he had done his best to avoid her at meals, and she was so caught up in her own head that she retreated into herself. If they were going to skirt around each other, that was fine, but she would not let their issues get in the way of ensuring Scraps was ok.

With a heavy sigh, she checked the training schedules on the intranet to see where Hawkeye should be. Much to her relief, he was on a recreation period. Ever since he had kissed her, he had spent his rec periods holed up in the Residence's VR suites, so she figured that was the best place to start her search. Flit made her way out of her room, heading down in the elevator to find him.

Flit's guess was right. She peered through the small windows in the door of each VR suite until she found Hawkeye. He was inside the small black room, in training shorts and a singlet, bouncing from foot to foot, probably playing a boxing simulator. She watched as he jabbed and blocked, noticing for the first time the way his lean muscles rippled under his skin. She tried to see him as something more than her friend, but even though he was attractive, she just couldn't get into it.

Flit tapped the screen on the door to bring it to life and wrote him a message.

Hawk. Can we talk, please? It's Flit.

In the small, black-walled three by three-metre space, Hawkeye paused. His hand swiped across a menu Flit couldn't see and his body tensed. His hands balled into fists at his sides before his shoulders sagged and he pulled off the VR headset with resignation. He rubbed his eyes and made his way over to the door.

"Uh, hi." Hawkeye scratched the back of his neck the way he did when he was nervous.

"Hey… I was just hoping we could talk about the training report you sent through about your session with Scraps."

"Oh." Hawkeye's shoulders fell. Flit tried not to let it sting when she saw just how dejected he looked. "What do you want to know?"

"What happened? The behaviour you described isn't like Scraps at all. He lives and breathes his training."

Hawkeye shrugged. "That's what I thought, too. At least, he did before I left. But I don't know what's up. He was going way too hard." Hawkeye hung the band of the goggles over one arm as he reached up, tugging the collar of his singlet down. Flit sucked in a breath as she saw the red and blue of a forming bruise.

"He got three punches in before I called it quits. I don't know what his problem is, but I'm not here to be a punching bag."

Flit scrunched her face up with concern. "I'll look into it," she promised. "Thanks Hawk." She turned to leave.

"Flit?"

Hawkeye's plea stopped her in her tracks, and she closed her eyes, taking a steadying breath, before she turned back to him. "Yes?"

"I—Flit, I just wanted to..." He trailed off, scratching the back of his neck again.

"Yes, Hawk?"

"Is that all you came here to discuss?"

"Yes." She refused to let the look of disappointment and pain in his eyes make her conviction waver.

"I just hoped that—" Hawkeye took a deep breath. "You know what, don't worry about it. I'll see you at dinner."

"See you then." Flit fled before Hawkeye tried to say anything else to her, fully aware she was running headlong towards one problem to forget about another.

THREE HOURS LATER, Flit teleported down the corridor on her level of the Residence. The grey duffel bag hooked over her arm was straining at the seams. She stopped in front of Scraps' door and rapped on it with her knuckles. After a minute, it slid open. Scraps looked shocked to see her there and stood, dumbfounded, as she smiled at him.

The moment Flit's gaze fell on Scraps, she forgot why she was there. A fine sheen of sweat shone on his skin, making his singlet cling to his chiselled chest as it rose and fell in ragged pants. She balled her hands into fists at her side as she resisted the instinctive urge to reach out and trace the contours of his muscles with her fingertips.

With a wave of his hand, Scraps stopped the droning, instructional exercise track playing through the speakers in his room. His eyes roved down over her casual cotton summer dress and sandals. His cheeks, already red with exertion, flushed deeper and he gulped as he tore his eyes away from her.

Flit shook herself out of her transfixion and cleared her throat. "Hi." She teleported into his room without being invited. He didn't even complain under his breath about her lack of manners. He just turned to face her and let the door slide shut behind him. There were dark circles beneath his usually bright eyes, and the clear exhaustion in his posture made her heart ache.

"Hello," he replied, looking between her and the door.

"I heard you've had a shit few days, so I came to help." Flit held up the duffel bag on her arm.

"How do you intend to do that?" He tucked his hands into the pockets of his black exercise shorts.

"You and I are gonna have some fun. After you turned Hawkeye into your personal punching bag this morning, I figured I would put you into intense recreation training. I know we started after we got stuck in the freezer, but I let things lapse over the past week. I'm sorry."

Scraps frowned at her. "But my schedule—"

"I've already changed it. Your afternoon is now clear to spend with me." Flit beamed at him, pleased she had the foresight to wipe out that obstacle before he mentioned it. She stepped a little closer to him.

Despite how tired and drawn his face was, Scraps smiled back at her. "That could help, but what will we do?"

"I want to show you one of my favourite places in the Underground. Bring a spare pair of shorts," Flit advised.

"A change of shorts?" Scraps' voice cracked.

"You'll be thankful for it later, I promise." Flit teleported to his door and opened it before he could argue with her.

He evidently trusted her enough to not challenge her secretive instructions. She waited as he retrieved the clothes and then walked out to join her. She took the shorts and tucked them into her bag. Scrap's looked at her with confusion in his eyes, but he didn't ask why she wanted them.

Scraps pointed to the duffel bag. "Would you like me to carry that for you?" His eyes darted between the bag and her ribs.

"No thanks, I've got it." Flit hitched it onto her shoulder.

Flit took Scraps to one of the deepest, darkest sets of natural tunnels in the Underground. The smooth, concrete lined and walls gave way to roughhewn rock passages and hard packed earth floors that were barely wide enough for two people at a time. They walked in silence until Flit could stand it no longer.

"So, I've been getting reports that you don't seem to be yourself lately," Flit said, looking up at him through the red light of the torch in her hand as they navigated one of the steeper descents. The tunnel grew cooler but more humid as they got lower. If it weren't for the gravel laid into the soil, it would have been a slippery journey.

"I've been..." Scraps hesitated, chewing over his words. "Unwell."

Flit's concern grew. "Have you seen someone in the medical team?" Flit asked, glancing at him surreptitiously to assess whether he was up for the trek. Not that she knew what she was looking for. But he was nice to look at, so she pretended it was all about her concern.

"Yeah, I talked to Patch yesterday. I'm fine now, I just need to catch up on some rest."

"Or some recreation."

The look Scraps gave her was overflowing with scepticism.

"Don't give me that look," Flit warned, pointing a finger at him. "When you're not feeling well, it is the perfect time to engage in some self-care. As talented as you are, being tired and distracted isn't good for anyone. Besides, what we're doing won't be any more strenuous than the workout you were doing."

A reluctant smile tugged at his lips as he looked over at her. "I don't have a say in this, do I?"

Flit beamed; it was about time he resigned himself to her expert mentorship. It was nice that he trusted her. While the others were quick to write off whatever her ideas were as brash or flippant, he took the time to listen to them. The game they played on patrol was a case in point. She didn't know whether it was because he was fresh to the Underground and hadn't become jaded to their cause, or because he genuinely cared, but it didn't matter either way. She was grateful he decided to join them.

"You're such a fast learner," Flit teased, bumping her shoulder into him as they walked. When Scraps smiled down at her, she noticed a slight blush on his cheeks, and even though she was sure it was innocent, she couldn't help but smile back.

The dark downward journey levelled out and the gentle whoosh of running water echoed around them. The tunnel opened into a magnificent cavern; one third of it was blanketed in sand-like silt, and the walls and ceiling were large, jagged rock faces that had been carved out over hundreds of thousands of years. Whilst the space would naturally be pitch black, artfully placed lighting filled it with a calming yet unearthly blue radiance, making the water look like the ocean, even if there was no sky above it. Much to Flit's pleasure, the cavern was empty. "Welcome to Sapphire Beach."

"This is unexpected." Scraps spun around as he took his surroundings in with awe.

Flit nodded as she walked over to the edge of the water, looking for the painted markings that showed the water level in the cave. "We're at high-tide now, so we should be safe to leave our things just back there. There must have been a lot of rainfall on the surface if it is up this high, but we'll be safe. This cavern has never filled beyond where you're standing now, not as long as we've known about it."

Flit teleported back over to where Scraps was standing and dropped her bag by his feet. She bent over, unzipping the duffel and pulling out two towels that she settled onto the sand side-by-side. She sank onto one and looked back over at the water. "You know, that's something I miss. Rain." Flit patted the towel beside hers to let him know he should sit.

Scraps sat beside her, his eyes darting around as he took in their gorgeous surroundings. "Rain impeded things."

Flit shrugged. "I suppose, but there is something lovely about it. How it washes the entire city clean. And that smell in the minutes before it starts? I love the anticipation of it. Like, you know something is coming, but without looking at the sky you can't tell how big of a storm it will be."

When Flit looked over at him their eyes met, and he was watching her with interest.

"Is there anything you've been missing about the surface?" Flit turned so she could face Scraps.

The blush on his cheeks deepened and he shrugged as he looked at her. "Apart from the fact I knew how everything worked up there? No. I have found things down here that make my new life here worth more than the predictability and order."

"Oh?" Flit leaned in. "That's interesting. What sort of things are worth more down here?"

"Uh... I've never had so much freedom before; there are so many things that I can think about doing now that I never would have contemplated before. I... I feel human, for the first time in my life."

"Scraps, that is amazing." Flit's heart surged with joy. Every moment that led to his confession, no matter how difficult, was worth it to hear him say those words. "I can't even imagine how hard it was for you to break free of the Government's programming, but you've taken it all in stride, and hearing you say that... It makes me so happy for you. You really are a wonderful person, and you deserve this." She reached out, taking his hands in her own and gently squeezing them. "You've proven yourself to be a valuable team member since you came down here, and an even better friend."

Scraps looked between Flit's face and their clasped hands with indecision in his eyes. Flit let go of him and sat back. He let out a quick breath and turned away, getting lost in his own thoughts. That was what Flit was hoping to avoid.

"Did you get much of a chance to go swimming when you lived in the Hub?" Flit asked him.

He looked over at the sparkling water nearby. "Only for training purposes."

"So, if we go for a swim, I won't have to dive in and save you from drowning?" Flit winked.

Scraps chuckled nervously. "No, I should be fine without your help. However, if I drown, and I need mouth—" Scraps stopped, shaking his head, his cheeks blazing red.

"If you need...?" she urged, cocking an eyebrow at him.

"Nothing, never mind," Scraps blurted, returning his attention to the water.

As tempted as Flit was to make him spill, she didn't want him to clam up. "Great, well, in that case—time to swim!" Flit teleported to standing and kicked off her sandals. She peeled her emerald green dress over her head. Beneath it, she wore a deep midnight blue bikini that hugged her curves as though it was painted on. She slipped a hair elastic off her wrist and tied her brown locks into a loose bun before she looked back at Scraps.

Except, Scraps hadn't changed. He sat behind her, eyes wide. Flit realised that he probably hadn't seen a woman wearing so little up so close before. She didn't mind him looking. In fact, she had an impulse to ask him if he wanted to do more than look. She squashed that impulse down. Instead, she pointed to his shirt. "Come on, we only grabbed spare shorts for you. You don't want to get your t-shirt wet."

Flit turned away from Scraps' wide-eyed stare and made for the water. She braced herself for it to be cold, but it was so much more frigid than she expected. She gasped, her heart hammering painfully hard against her chest and sent adrenaline coursing through her veins. To acclimatise faster, she steeled herself and dived right under, gliding through the water and enjoying the feel of being enveloped in the jolting coolness of it.

When Flit broke the surface, the water was too deep to stand in. She turned around and wiped the water from her eyes. Back at the shore, Scraps pulled his shirt off and waded in. He scrunched his face up with each step he took. Flit's looked lower to take in the well-sculpted body she'd only seen hints of during their training.

"It's cold, isn't it?" Flit laughed. Scraps grinned through his chattering teeth. "Hurry up and dive in already!"

The water was up to Scraps' mid thighs. He frowned but nodded, taking a deep breath before he dived. Flit watched the smooth ripples caused by his body as he slipped under the pristine surface and kicked his way towards her. When he emerged, he was tall enough to stand, even though she had to tread water. He shook the water from his hair and she reached out, brushing some stray droplets from his forehead to stop them from dripping into his eyes.

"See? Much better." She pulled her hand back so she could stay afloat.

"I thought this was recreation. The temperature of the water makes it more like torture."

Flit shrugged. "You just have to keep moving. You'll warm up soon enough."

"Maybe I should do some laps." Scraps looked from one side of the cavern to the other, sizing it up.

Flit laughed. "Of all the things you could do in the water, you want to swim laps?" His decision didn't surprise her. In fact, she found it rather endearing.

"What else would I do?" Scraps asked, perplexed.

"Let's play a game."

"Another game? How many games do you know?"

"Life isn't worth living if you aren't having fun in your spare time. But if you don't want to play games, think of it as a training exercise."

The perplexed look on Scraps' face brightened at the prospect. "I can do that."

"Good. The aim, as always, is for you to catch me." Flit paddled back towards the shore until she could sink her toes into the sand.

"You want to teleport around in here? Is that even safe?"

Flit snorted a laugh. "No way. Not in the water. I may be crazy, but I'm not that crazy." Flit waved dismissively. "We can dive or swim. No powers."

Scraps considered that for a moment before nodding. "I must warn you, I was third fastest in my birth cohort during my aquatic training."

"Good. You might have a chance of catching me for once." Flit pushed forward with both of her hands and splashed a wall of water at him before diving under.

Scraps was fast, but movement was Flit's forte. The two chased each other around above and below the surface of the water until they were both tired and panting. There were several instances where Scraps had grasped Flit's wrist or ankle, but she was just as slippery in the water as she was in the training room.

"Come on, you almost had me!" Flit panted in one of the rare moments where both she and Scraps stopped and stood, waist deep in the water, sizing each other up.

"Almost? You said I had to catch you, not hold on to you."

Flit tilted her head to the side as she considered this. She noticed his eyes dip below her face before they snapped back up, and he pressed his lips together.

"Well, if you don't hold on to me have you really caught me?"

"Do not tell me you want to change the rul—"

Flit didn't hear the rest. She dived, aiming for the spot a few metres behind his right shoulder. She would be in shallower water there, which would give her the advantage to launch herself off solid ground. In the deeper water, his longer body made it much easier for him to catch her.

Scraps' fingers brushed her hip as he reached out to grasp her. She broke the surface of the water. Once he looked like he was about to catch up, she dived back out into the deeper water, gliding just under the level he was swimming on. Her stomach grazed the rough silt as she passed. Scraps put his feet out, his toes pressing against the ground that she couldn't reach, and he flipped and pushed himself back into his own wake. He slipped through the water just above her, and then his muscular arms wrapped around her waist. He kicked at the floor again and dragged her out of the water, her laughter breaking the surface as he did. She tried to squirm out of his grip, but he held on, though not tight enough to put too much pressure on her ribs.

"I've got you now," he panted into her ear, his warm, heaving breath tickling her neck.

A shiver ran down Flit's spine. "Damn it, I thought I'd get another five minutes at least." Flit squirmed, turning around in his arms and looking up at him. She was all too aware of how his wet, shirtless chest was pressed against her bikini-clad body. Scraps' skin was searing hot where it touched hers.

When Scraps looked down at Flit, she caught sight of something she hadn't seen on his face before. "Feeling better now?" Flit asked, trying to catch her breath.

Despite the exertion, Scraps smiled. "Yes. You are very good at distracting me." Scraps' cheeks flushed a deep crimson.

Flit raised an eyebrow. She was about to make a cheeky comment, but she thought better of it. He wasn't one of the Underground lads who lived for suggestive flirting. "And what am I distracting you from? What's been on your mind?" she asked, taking a safer route and hoping he was ready to share.

"Well, you, actually," Scraps admitted.

Flit was surprised. "Me? Why?"

"I don't know. Or at least, I didn't at first." Scraps looked down at Flit but made no move to release her. Flit bit the inside of her cheek gently, to stop herself from talking. He was opening up; she didn't want to interrupt. "But for the last week, I haven't been myself. At first, I thought Hawkeye and the others brought back some kind of virus, but Patch said I am not sick."

"Well, that's something at least. If you were feeling unwell, why didn't you come and find me? I'm here to help, you know that."

"You were too busy with Hawkeye." Scraps tore his gaze from hers and looking at some place past her shoulder as if it were the most interesting spot in the cavern.

"Too busy with Hawkeye?" Flit scoffed. "I've barely spent time with him since he got back and—well... Since he got back. Why would you think I was too busy with him to spend time with you?"

"He kissed you," Scraps blurted. "And then you did not come to my room for our investigation."

Flit's stomach dropped. How had she forgotten that? "Oh, shit. Scraps, I'm so sorry." Flit cursed her own stupidity. "That kiss took me by surprise. He's my best friend; pretty much like a brother to me. I didn't know that he felt—feels—that way about me."

"Oh."

"But I'm not interested in him like that. I just want to repair our friendship."

"So, you are not together?" Scraps asked slowly.

When Flit looked back up at him her eyes widened a little at the intensity in his gaze. "No," she whispered, voice hitching in her throat.

"Good."

"Good?"

"Yes, good. Because I like you... and the thought of you two kissing made me feel—ugh." Scraps' shoulders sagged as the words tumbled out.

Flit bit her lip. Her arms settled around his hips. Her heart skipped a beat. He said that he liked her, but she wasn't sure if he knew what he meant. She had to clarify before she got too carried away. "So, Hawkeye and I kissing made you feel uncomfortable?"

"Yes, very."

Flit's stomach fluttered with nerves. She looked deep into his eyes and threw caution to the wind. "How would you feel if I kissed you instead?"

Scraps took a moment to consider his response in that serious, brooding way of his. Flit's entire body buzzed with anticipation as they stood, bodies wet and pressed together in the frigid water. Finally, he spoke. "I think I would enjoy that."

Flit slid her hands over his hips and stomach, pushing up along the hardened ridges of his chest to settle on his shoulders. She guided him down towards her, tilting her head to one side. He mirrored her without hesitation, but she stopped before their lips touched. "Good. Because I think I would enjoy it too," Flit admitted, her hot breath mingling in the tiny space between them.

Scraps clutched at her hips as he dipped his head and they kissed. Flit shut her eyes as she tasted him for the first time. Her head spun as she tried to calculate all the places their bodies were touching in a mix of flushed skin and cold evaporating water.

It was a soft kiss, a gentle one. Nothing more than a closed-lip test, but one they passed with flying colours. She was tempted deepen it, to taste more of him, but Scraps was new to kissing and she didn't want to push him.

Flit's eyes fluttered open and she looked up at Scraps. "Was that ok?"

"It was so much better than I imagined," Scraps whispered back, meeting her gaze with an intensity that made her flush.

"Would you like to do it again?" Flit asked.

Scraps nodded without hesitation.

Flit smiled and leaned in. Scraps groaned into the kiss. She tilted her head a little more and ran her tongue along his lips to allow him to get comfortable with the unfamiliar sensation. His arms tightened around her, pulling her body more against his. She deepened the kiss and they got lost in each other.

33

SCRAPS

SCRAPS COULD NOT THINK of a single thing he enjoyed more than kissing Flit.

As they stood in the chilly water, holding each other so intimately, Scraps lost track of everything else. All he knew was Flit; her taste, her smell, how she felt in his arms. But most of all, he knew she wanted to kiss him. He had spent their entire swim trying to ignore how her near-naked body moved so gracefully. Her deep blue bikini seemed to disappear when she was in the sparkling sapphire water. Scraps could almost imagine she wasn't wearing it at all.

Scraps had tried hard to catch Flit, although not to prove himself. He wanted to catch her so he could hold her. Seeing her in her swimwear sent shivers through his body. The quick brushes of his skin against hers were like surges of electricity in his veins. He wanted more. And when he got it? The surges turned into roars. His body responded in all the right ways. That is what kissing should be. Not the forced, awkward mess with Swipe. It was consensual, curious, exploratory, and exhilarating.

Scraps had never given much thought to the mechanics of kissing beyond pressing lips against lips; but Flit knew what she was doing. She tilted her face just right, so it was comfortable; she moved her lips and made his breath hitch in his throat. She used her tongue in ways he never thought possible. The act was so much more intimate than he had ever imagined; he understood why people didn't go around just kissing anyone.

Without meaning to, he tightened his arms around her, pulling her body closer to his. The brush of her bikini-clad breasts against his bare chest turned into a firm press, and a groan of appreciation slipped through his lips and into Flit's mouth. She chuckled as one of her hands slid down from his shoulder to his lower back. Her fingertips were like fire against his skin and his head spun as his blood pumped elsewhere in his body.

Flit pulled back. Scraps felt smug at the sight of her panting just as much as he was. She had the most endearing pink flush high on the apples of her cheek. Without thinking, he brushed his fingertips over those warm patches, and she smiled, leaning into his touch. Scraps swore his heart swelled three times its size.

"For a newbie, you're pretty damn good at that," Flit whispered to him, with a trademark mischievous glimmer in her hazel eyes.

Scraps smirked back at her. "Perhaps, but I do not want to rest on my laurels. I am sure I still have more to learn."

Flit chuckled and slid her hands over his shoulders and then ran them down his biceps. Her gaze fell from his face to his exposed chest and arms. There was no mistaking the appreciation in her expression. Scraps had to bite back a groan of arousal as her look resonated with a primal part of him.

"I'm so glad you said that." It was all the invitation Flit needed to close the distance between them again.

It was almost like they hadn't stopped kissing. Scraps fell into it, wanting more. Flit slid her hands down his arms and threaded their fingers together. She moved them from her shoulders, guiding his palms over her own back, over the ties of her bikini, until they settled onto her shapely hips. Her skin was smooth under his, his hands instinctively tightened on her body. He stroked the curve of her waist with his thumbs, wanting to learn more about the shape of her. She moaned into the kiss. The sweet sound stoked the flames of his desire. Scraps made it his personal mission to elicit that sound from her again.

Without warning, Flit pushed back from him.

Scraps' head spun at the sudden loss of contact. "Flit? What is it?"

But then he heard it.

A strange, multi-pitched nattering echoed through the tunnels. At first, he worried it was the rumblings of another tunnel collapse. Or maybe the roar of an incoming surge in water levels. Flit's narrowed her eyes as she peered towards the only walkable entrance and exit into the cave. The echoing got louder; the symphony of tones unwound into the distinct sound of voices. Flit's shoulders sagged in relief. Scraps wanted to be glad, but he was too disappointed at the loss of close contact to celebrate.

"Sounds like we've got company," Flit muttered under her breath, reaching out and pressing a gentle hand against his chest. He nodded as he looked over, wondering who else would come down here in the middle of the day.

"Children, when we get onto the sand don't forget to—"

"Scraps!"

Flit's hand fell from his chest as Scry, a young postcog assigned to tutoring the Underground's children, rounded the corner with six kids in tow. Well, six had been in tow before one golden-haired boy broke rank and streaked towards the water.

Scry groaned. "Seeker, what did I just finish saying?"

Seeker skidded to a stop, his feet slipping on the silt. His shoulders sagged as he turned around. "Yeah, but you said the water would be empty. It's not. Scraps and Flit are here. They're adult supervision, right?"

"By adult supervision, I meant me." Scry dumped a duffel bag at the farthest dry edge of the cavern.

Seeker turned to Scraps and Flit. "I'll be out in a minute." He raced back, dropping his bag on the ground by his teacher's and peeling off his shirt. He looked over at the other kids. "Last one in's a rotten egg," he yelled before he charged into the water.

The other kids were just as excited, shedding their own clothes so they could run into the water with euphoric squeals and splashes.

"Well, if that didn't kill the mood..." Flit grumbled, looking at Scraps and letting out a heavy sigh.

Scraps empathised with the disappointment in her tone. He had been enjoying their interaction. He was about to ask if she thought they could do it again sometime when a loud squawking cut through his thoughts.

"Scraps! I haven't seen you in aaaages," Seeker yelled, having to raise his voice over the sound of his own chaotic splashing. Scraps chuckled and he reached out, offering the child a steadying hand. Seeker took it without hesitation, using it to help keep his smaller body afloat in the water. Scry swam over and pulled Flit aside. Scraps couldn't hear what the man said to her, but the apologetic expression on his face was unmistakable.

Scraps focused on Seeker. "I know, buddy. I have been busy with patrols and training, I—"

"Mum says you were in that last explosion. That's crazy! Was it exciting?" Seeker inched closer, speaking in a hushed, awe-filled tone.

"It was scary, silly," Kindling admonished as she paddled over to them.

Spending time in the garden with Acumen and the children was something Scraps had been missing because of the intense training schedule Flit had set for him. It was refreshing to focus on the crucial, routine labour, and teaching the kids about the systems was rewarding.

"It would only be scary if he died. He didn't die. He's fine." Seeker rolled his eyes.

"If you're dead you can't be scared, dummy!"

"I'm not a dummy!"

"Are too—"

Scraps chuckled and interrupted the bickering before it got worse. "It was scary, but I was just in an emergency shelter when the tunnel collapsed. It was Flit who went out there and saved Cogs and Heft." He gestured towards Flit, but the kids only had eyes for him. "Things like that should scare you a little. It gives your body the adrenaline you need to get through the situation. Being scared isn't a bad thing."

The kids looked at Scraps in awe as they kicked about in the water. "That's so cool," Seeker gasped reverently.

Kindling nodded.

So, they didn't have to disagree on everything.

"One day I'm gonna be in Security too," Seeker announced, looking at Scraps. "Maybe we could go on patrol together."

Scraps chuckled.

"I thought you wanted to work for Control?" Kindling frowned.

"Nah, that was yesterday. Now I wanna be in Security, just like Scraps!"

A sense of pride well up inside Scraps at the admiration in Seeker's words. He'd never had someone look up to him before, and he found it flattering. He had learned during his time in the Underground that children were unabashedly honest. They didn't hide their thoughts or mince their words the way the adults did.

"If all us adults do our jobs right, we'll get back to the surface one day and you can be whatever you want to be," Flit said, turning away from her conversation with Scry, and reaching out to ruffle Seeker's hair.

Seeker's brown eyes bulged with excitement. "That would be… amazing!" he cried out, letting go of Scraps' hand to flail about as his voice echoed through the cavern.

Scry groaned. "Flit, really?" He shook his head.

Flit turned to him, her expression hardening. "What?"

"Don't fill their heads with impossible dreams."

"It's not impossible," Flit snapped. "If we don't have hope for the future, why would they? They deserve to see the sunlight as much as anyone up there."

Scry just shook his head. He didn't bother arguing. Scraps wondered whether it was because he knew Flit was right, or because he knew Flit would never give in.

"If we lived on the surface, we could go to a real beach! With actual sand, and waves, and sharks!" Kindling realised, her eyes wide with wonder.

"Regardless of what body of water you're in, you need to learn to swim properly," Scry reminded Kindling. The kids groaned, faces falling as they were brought back to reality. "Everybody, start your laps now. If we get back early, we can use the VR suite for our lesson about photosynthesis!"

The promise of the VR suite was enough to have the children

splash into line and start their swim up and down the length of the cavern. They were all proficient once they got into the rhythm of it. It made him wonder why Scry bothered to teach them when they were unlikely to use the skill.

"See you two later. Sorry again for interrupting." Scry nodded at Scraps and Flit before swimming off to help correct one of the kid's technique.

"I suppose we should head back up, yeah?" Flit suggested, her eyes trailed after the children. They would get no more privacy in the cavern.

"Sure."

Flit and Scraps got out of the water and dried off. If Scraps was honest with himself, being interrupted was good. He was so lost in kissing Flit that he lost all sense of the space they were in. He hadn't heard the echoes of the kids, and probably wouldn't have until they were right next to him. Being with Flit like that was engrossing. He understood why the Government didn't want Registereds engaging in romantic relationships or erotic acts. Scraps wouldn't be effective in the field with the thought of Flit's touch at the forefront of his mind.

Scraps was lost in thought as they made their way back up to the Residence. The journey was arduous. The tunnels were steep and slippery on the way down. After swimming so much, and the strange way that Flit's body against his had stolen blood from his extremities, it was even more tiring to manage the constant uphill slog. He noticed with amusement that Flit didn't walk so much as teleport every few steps. He supposed it was one of those times that an ability like hers was useful.

It wasn't until the dirt tunnels levelled out that Flit spoke again. The surrounding walls changed back from rock to concrete, and Flit turned off the red-light torch they were using.

"Scraps, what happened down there..." Flit started.

Scraps looked over, but she avoided his gaze. "Yes?" He wondered what she wanted to say. She never hesitated.

"I think it's best we keep it between ourselves for a while."

Scraps let out a breath, crestfallen. He had such an amazing time with her, and he wanted to tell everyone about it. "Oh, uh, I see."

Flit stopped walking and placed a gentle hand on his shoulder. He couldn't meet her eyes. Did she regret kissing him? Had he done it wrong?

"I enjoyed it," she promised, biting her lip. "And I'd like to do it again soon. It's just that…"

Scraps looked at Flit. It was so unusual to see uncertainty on her face. He could tell from the way her mouth opened and shut that she was trying to find the right thing to say. "Flit?"

"It's just… We need time to get to know each other like that before letting others know. Once they do there will be a lot of pressure, and you—or I—don't need it complicating things."

Scraps nodded. He understood. At least, he thought he did. The Underground was a fertile place for gossip and rumours. He didn't know what sort of pressure she was talking about, but he agreed it would be nice to have time to settle into things before everyone else knew. "So, no more kissing?" He tried and failed to keep his voice neutral.

"I didn't mean that. I want to kiss more. But I also need some time to think about it all. The last year has been—" Flit stopped suddenly; her hands balled into fists at her side. She shut her eyes for a moment as she took a deep breath. "Difficult for me. I need to know if I'm ready to be vulnerable again."

Scraps frowned. Flit never seemed vulnerable. He wanted to ask what she meant, but she was sad, and he didn't want to make it worse. "Ok." He shuffled his feet, unsure of what else to say or do.

"Thank you." Flit bit her lip as she took a step closer to him. She reached up, cupping his cheek and guiding his face down to hers. The kiss was soft and tentative, but no less thrilling. She stepped back and they resumed their walk to the Residence.

Scrap spent the rest of the journey working through his confusion. By the time they reached the elevator in the apartment-style Residence building, Scraps thought he understood. Flit wanted to kiss him, she wanted to learn more about him, but she just wanted to keep it quiet. She confirmed his hypothesis when she said goodbye to him and suggested they resume their study for his orienteering test after dinner. When she said it, there was a sparkle in their eyes insinuating they may do more than study, and he was ok with that.

34

FLIT

FLIT WAS serious when she told Scraps it was time to resume studying for his orienteering test. She had been holding off while she tried to figure out what to do about the Hawkeye situation, but after kissing Scraps she realised why she had been dragging her feet. She hadn't allowed herself to see it, but all the signs were there.

Swipe, the bitch, was right.

The look on Scraps' face when she had asked him to keep their relationship private haunted her. She didn't mean to be cruel or dismissive: she just knew they both needed time to find their way with each other. A place like the Underground, with a permanent captive audience, bred gossip at the best of times. It was not something she or Scraps needed as they navigated their blossoming feelings for one another.

Those feelings were a source of conflict for Flit. Whenever she was away from Scraps, guilt ate at her. There had been several times over the days following the kiss she was tempted to call it off. But when she saw him, all her worries slipped away. After Rook, Flit thought no one would ever make her heart flutter the way he did. It was early days with Scraps, but a small forgotten part of her saw a glimmer of beautiful potential.

"Is this uncomfortable?" Flit asked, looking back at Scraps over her shoulders.

He shifted and shook his head, smiling at her. His red eyes took on the look of eagerness they always held when he was experiencing something new. "It does not help my concentration levels, but I see no harm in it," Scraps told her.

One thing that Flit had noticed over their study sessions was that they were both easily distracted. Alone in Scraps' room, they didn't have to hide. They were free to kiss, touch, and explore. So, trying to focus on something as dry as path markers or tunnel geography was difficult. Somehow, no matter how far apart they started, their chairs inched closer until their thighs were pressed against each other, and then it was all over.

Stopping the casual touches was impossible, so Flit decided they needed to embrace it. Instead of sitting on separate chairs, she was on Scraps bed with him, between his legs, with his datapad on her bent knees. It reminded her of how they had sat in the freezer a while back. Except they weren't doing it to keep warm. Flit enjoyed it more than she should. "I would suggest we don't bother studying—"

"But I need to prepare for my orienteering test!"

"Yes. So, let's call this a compromise. A win-win scenario." She tapped the screen on her knees and brought it to life. Scraps' cheek brushed against her ear as he leaned forward to read over her shoulder. When he reached out to navigate the map on the screen, he had to reach around her with his right arm. She found his left and wrapped it around her waist. His hand froze as it settled on the screen and he turned to look at her.

"Is this ok?" Flit asked.

"Yes," Scraps croaked, his body tense against her back.

Over his time in the Underground, Scraps had gotten good at controlling outward signs of his emotions, but lust was new to him and he was terrible at hiding it.

Flit smirked. "Then by all means, continue." Flit gestured to the datapad. She pointed to several places on the screen. "What are these marks here?"

It was a few seconds before Scraps answered. "Those are the tunnel markers. The tip of the triangle points true north, the letter is the sector, and the lines underneath indicate what level the tunnel is."

"Good. Where will you find them?"

"In surface-level tunnels, they are hidden on the side of the lighting tracks."

Flit waited for more information, but she heard Scraps take a deep breath and his hand caressed her stomach. Maybe separate chairs were better after all. "Mid-level?" she continued.

"Along the utility pipelines."

"And the deep-le—" Flit stopped mid-question when Scraps pressed his lips against her neck. Her breath caught in her throat and the hand covering his tightened.

Scraps tensed behind her. "Sorry. Was that inappropriate?" he whispered. His hot breath brushed against her exposed skin.

"No, it was perfect." Flit reached up, cupping his cheek and guiding him towards her neck once more. It had been so long since anyone had kissed her there. A soft moan escaped her lips as his mouth found her neck again.

"I could not help it. It just felt like the right thing to do." Scraps rested his head against her shoulder.

Flit nuzzled her cheek against his. "I'm glad you did it."

"You smell so nice," Scraps whispered with wonder.

Butterflies fluttered in her stomach. Other guys Flit had dated in the past were far less forthcoming with their thoughts and feelings. Scraps had not grown up seeing the rise and fall of romantic relationships around him, so Flit supposed it made sense that he hadn't learned to guard his feelings like she did. Still, it was endearing, and it made it far too easy to feel comfortable with him.

Flit couldn't hold back anymore. She turned her face, hoping to catch his lips with hers, but a loud beeping from the datapad on her lap interrupted them. She jumped, shocked by the intrusion. She looked at the screen to see a message from Cogs blinking at her.

"Oh, shit." Flit sat bolt upright. There was a rush of cool air where Scraps' lips had just been, and the bed creaked a little as he sagged back against it, thrown by the sudden change in pace. "It's Cogs. She sent me a temporary access code for the vaults. She put a loop on the surveillance cameras in storerooms eighteen, nineteen, and twenty."

Flit teleported off the bed and onto her feet to face Scraps.

"Uh... what?" He looked dazed. His eyes dipped from her face to her neck, stuck on what they had been doing a moment ago.

Flit almost wanted to ignore the message, but they may not get another chance. "I talked to Cogs after I heard the stuff about the missing desiccant. She agreed that we should follow up on it. I've been waiting for her to get us an opportunity like this to investigate. We've got to go!" Flit said. She teleported over to Scraps' desk and pulled her jacket from where it was draped over his chair.

Scraps sat up straighter. "We are going down there now?"

"Yes. Well, I am. You can stay behind if you like, but I'd appreciate your help down there." Flit tugged her jacket on and then pulled her unbound hair out of the back.

"Right, of course." Scraps hopped up off his bed. He walked over and grabbed his own jacket, shrugging it on as he looked over at Flit. "Do we need to stop over at the armoury before this mission?"

Flit rose an eyebrow at him. What kind of investigation did he think they were doing? "Armory? No way. We're just going for a poke around. We'll be fine, I promise. Plus, weapons'll only make us look more suspicious."

Scraps nodded. They slipped their boots on and set out.

FLIT WAS IMPRESSED; she didn't even need to tell Scraps the best way to sneak around the Underground. Most people who had she dragged along on her adventures attempted to slink in the shadows, which only made them look more suspicious. The best way to get around in such situations was to own it. Together, she and Scraps strode down those tunnels as if they had a purpose. People wouldn't interrupt them if they thought they were busy and important. Flit and Scraps made it look like they walked down those prohibited tunnels every day, and it worked.

"Ok, eighteen. This is us," Flit said as she stopped in her tracks. She entered the code Cogs gave her into the access panel. Much to her relief, the doors slid open. Flit grinned at Scraps. He gave her a rather dashing, mischievous smirk before looking over his shoulder.

"Well then, let us investigate." Scraps gestured for Flit to go in first.

Once they were both in, Flit shut the door behind them so anyone passing by would not know they were there.

The storeroom stank of a mix of chemicals. There were neat stacks of barrels and sacks on metal shelves that reached from the clean concrete floor to vented ceiling. The Supply team took great pride in ensuring their tunnels and storerooms were tidy, ordered, and accessible, the restricted areas especially so due to all the different substances stored there. In the past, the Underground lost a good chunk of serviceable tunnels and people because the wrong chemicals were stored together, and mixing vapours caused an explosion.

Flit walked around the room, scanning the labels on the various bags and drums. She narrowed her search to the bags and found the desiccant at the back of the room. "Scraps, the bags are here," she called as he experimented with the internal access panel. "Can you please check how many bags there are in the digital inventory? It's in the menu under—"

"Fifteen bags," Scraps said, turning back to her.

Flit beamed at him, pleased he was one step ahead of her. It was like the times in the VR puzzle rooms. They fell into a natural rhythm when they worked together. Flit counted the bags. Fifteen. The stock and record matched, but there was no way of knowing whether it was because there was nothing missing, or because whoever was stealing them had gotten smarter. Flit frowned and straightened up and pointed to a sensor above the door. "If someone stole the bags and walked out that way, the scanners would pick up on the chips in the packaging."

Scraps looked around the vault. The door was the only way in or out. "So, they had to have another way to get them out."

"Exactly." Flit looked up at the extraction fans in the ceiling. Two small grills with spinning blades, all managed by the Supply office. Each storage unit had emergency override functions, but if someone activated them Arctic or Cogs would have known about it. There were so many filters between the storeroom and the vent shafts that sneaking heavy bags of desiccant out that way would have been too much trouble.

Scraps frowned. "There must be another exit." He reached out, holding his hands up and moving boxes and bags away from the walls with his power.

Flit teleported to the opposite side of the room and helped him clear the space. She rolled barrel after barrel of some noxious smelling liquid into the middle of the floor when she noticed how silent the room had gotten. She looked back over at Scraps to see him watching her with an interesting look in his eyes.

"What is it?" she asked, straightening up.

He shrugged, but his cheeks turned red. "Nothing... I just like it when you are bent over like that."

Flit cocked an eyebrow at him. "Well, I'll do it more for you later. But for now? We have work to do."

Scraps' grin widened as Flit leaned over and checked behind the remaining barrels. The panels on the walls and floors were the stock-standard concrete used in these parts. She ran her hands along them. The cool, hard surface was smooth to the touch. Nothing to suggest foul play or tampering. She went over each wall several times but could not find anything suspicious. It was possible, of course, that Arctic was mistaken. With a frustrated sigh, Flit started to push the boxes back against the wall. Now they had no leads, and if they had no leads, then the others would tell her to stop. That there were no suspicious reasons for the tunnel collapse. As much as she wanted to believe them, she just couldn't.

"Flit, look!" Scraps' sudden exclamation broke through Flit's angry musing. She jumped and her head banged against the metal shelving. A can on the shelf toppled over and started to roll away. She reached out to catch it but was too slow.

Instead of a dull thud of can hitting the concrete, it was more of a hollow whack.

"No way!" Flit gasped, pushing the items on the shelf to the side. Scraps came over to join her. "What did you find?" she asked, too busy trying to clear the shelf to rub her aching head.

"According to the computer system, the desiccant was moved to this storage vault four months ago."

Flit stopped. The first tunnel collapse was around that time. She looked at Scraps. "This is getting more and more suspicious."

"I concur. Let's see what is behind this shelf, shall we?" He shifted the last few cans away and gestured for Flit to step back. He reached out with both hands, pulling the metal racks away from the wall and sliding them to the side as if they were as light as feathers.

Once the shelves were out of the way, Flit and Scraps had better access to the panel behind them. With some strategic knocking and tapping, they discovered it was hollow. It took them a good long while, but they found a section on the middle of the left edge where the seam between panels was deeper than the rest. Flit pushed on it and let out an excited gasp as the panel popped back and slid aside. She peered around the corner and looked into the empty storeroom next door—a storeroom that was decommissioned because it was 'faulty'. She turned back to Scraps. "Can I poke around in here for a bit while you put that stuff back? Once I'm done, I'll come and get you and we'll go talk to someone in Control."

Scraps' eyes were shining with the satisfaction of their discovery as he nodded. Flit shimmied past the empty metal shelves. She left the concrete door open a little so she could hear if Scraps found anything new.

Flit teleported to the control panel by the door and played around with it, trying to figure out how long ago the room was decommissioned and if anyone had been in or out since. She found some records showing that someone had accessed the space at least six times since it was closed. She tried to open each file, but they were beyond the access level of the code that Cogs had given them, so she sent them through to her instead.

That was enough proof to show that it was possible for people to steal and sneak out bags of desiccant, so Flit went back to the home page on the control panel menu. Satisfied, she was just about to turn the screen off when she heard voices from the other vault.

"Do you think you.... you can't...."

"I am just retrieving something for a patrol. The team...." Scraps rose his voice as he spoke, allowing Flit to hear what he was saying clearly.

Flit swore under her breath. Someone caught them. Looking

back at the almost closed concrete panel, she winced. She should have shut it all the way. She teleported over and the voices got louder.

"Stupid mule. You can't just come down here and walk around—"

Flit couldn't quite tell who it was yet, but she wanted to punch the guy that owned that voice. She bit her lip and held her breath as she slid the concrete door back into place. It let out a soft click as it settled. She couldn't hang around to see what happened, because she wanted to get Scraps out of there. Fast. She teleported back to the door of the decommissioned chamber, pushed it open, and teleported to the now open door of storeroom eighteen. "Sorry, I was just looking for some—"

Scraps was penned in the rear corner of the storeroom by Tally, an older man who oversaw the storage tunnels. His face was wrinkled with age and surly grimaces.

"Tally, what's going on?" Flit asked, walking in and placing a hand on his shoulder. He was small for a man, about the same height as her, but with a dumpier build and calculating eyes.

He turned his angry glare on her. "I found this Registered snooping about our supplies."

"He's not a Registered, he's one of us. And his name is Scraps, please use it," Flit snapped. "Scraps wasn't snooping around, we came down here to get some stuff for our patrol." Flit was trying very hard to not smack the nasty old bastard.

"Really, then why was he using a retired access code, hmm?"

Flit's eyes flicked to Scraps. "Ah, that would be my fault. Sorry. I forgot the code that Posthoc gave us, so I just went with whatever—"

"Your sweet-talking bullshit may work on some dafter folks, girl, but not on me. No-one can guess a code without raising an alarm for too many failed attempts! You're up to something."

Flit gritted her teeth. She could knock him out, but he would just wake back up and report them anyway.

"What are you doing down here?"

"I told you, we are getting some supplies that—" Scraps begun.

"Not you, you red-eyed freak," Tally snapped at him.

Flit teleported between them, her hands balled into fists at her side. There was a heavy, invisible presence on both of her shoulders and she looked back at Scraps. He shook his head. "You know what, old man, we don't need to tell you shit," Flit spat, crossing her arms over her chest. Behind her, Scraps tensed.

Tally shook with rage. "How dare you!"

"How dare I what? Call you old? Or point out we don't report to you?"

"You wait until I tell your father—"

Flit snorted. "My father? Is that the best you can do, run to my Dad? Ha, some threat."

As Flit continued to goad him, she could almost see steam whistling out from his hairy ears. "That's it. You're both coming with me."

Tally stepped back and pointed to the door. Flit turned to Scraps and winked at him as they stepped out. Tally had fallen right into her trap.

"Don't even think of running away. All of the electronic records'll point to your snooping, don't you worry about that," Tally muttered as he stormed off ahead of them, looking back to make sure they were following.

Flit and Scraps fell into line after him, hanging back a little so they could whisper to each other.

"Was it wise to antagonise him like that, Flit?" Scraps whispered, his eyes darting between Flit and the cranky old bastard.

"Nope, not at all. But don't worry, I've got this. You just need to trust me." Flit winked, confident in her plan. Scraps looked sceptical but went along with her until they turned down the tunnel that would take them straight to Control.

"You think I have no authority here?" Tally growled as he pointed to the security checkpoint. "Then let's see what Harmony and Divvy have to say!"

Scraps gulped, but Flit just patted him on the back, holding back the triumphant smile that tugged at her lips.

35

FLIT

AS FLIT PREDICTED, Tally bypassed his own office and marched them out of the Supply tunnels towards Control. The closer they got to the security checkpoint, the more Scraps straightened his back and set his lips into a serious line. Flit wished she had a chance to warn him about what she was doing so he wouldn't be so worried. As an Ex-Registered, he would associate being marched to his superiors' office as a genuine threat to his safety. However, this wasn't the Hub, and Harmony and Divvy were never heavy-handed with their punishments. Flit reached over, tugging on his sleeve to get his attention "We'll be fine," she promised with a confident smile.

"The penalty for fraud and unauthorised access of that level is banishment from the Underground. Flit, I do not know what makes you think we will be fine—"

"Scraps," Flit interrupted, hearing the panic rising in his tone. "That may be the policy, but they've never enforced it. Besides, we are going to them with important news, not because we got greedy and tried to steal restricted substances. We won't get kicked out. Just trust me, please. I wouldn't do anything that would get you into real trouble."

"You two, stop chit-chatting and keep up," Tally snapped, glaring back at them over his shoulder as he tapped a request into the panel outside the door to Control.

Scraps' shoulders were still stiff, but he didn't look as wary.

That was something. It was a tense few minutes before a clearance flashed and the door to Control opened.

Standing by the door, ready to meet them, was Divvy. She was wearing her crisp fatigues as usual, her red hair down and framing her face. She looked between Flit and Scraps with a frown of concern before turning to Tally. "Harmony is waiting in the meeting room."

That was all she said before she turned on her heel and led them past Mission Control into the rear corridor. The space had changed since the tunnel collapses. There were more people in the room and glass screens were set up on every available surface. They were monitoring all the various system pressures in the tunnels surrounding the habitation area. Flit wondered whether Tally had fought against losing that responsibility, or if he had handed it over willingly given how deadly the explosions were. Perhaps the loss of face put him in an even more foul mood than usual.

Divvy led Flit, Scraps, and Tally into the meeting room that she and Harmony favoured. The circular table had five chairs around it. Tally settled himself opposite of Harmony and Divvy, and Flit sat right next to him to save Scraps the discomfort of doing so himself.

Divvy picked up the datapad on the table and tapped the screen, frowning as she read what was on it. She laid it back down flat and spun it so Flit and Scraps could read it. "Impersonating another individual in to gain unauthorised access to a restricted zone..." Divvy read out loud, looking between them.

"Loitering around the chemical storage vaults, too," Tally added, not wanting anything left out.

Flit stopped herself from rolling her eyes at just how eager he was to further incriminate them. "I assure you, we had an excellent reason."

Harmony looked at Flit and shook her head. "There is never an acceptable excuse for fraudulent behaviour, Flit."

"There is," Flit argued. "But what we have to say is best shared in private." She tilted her head towards Tally.

Tally's watery eyes widened, and his upper body stiffened with outrage. Harmony and Divvy, however, looked at each other with an unspoken spark of curiosity. "Tally, could you excuse us for a few minutes, please? We'll call you back in," Harmony promised.

Tally stared at her. His mouth opened and shut several times before he let out a grunt of agreement and got to his feet. He walked out, muttering something unintelligible under his breath.

Divvy turned her piercing gaze on Flit. "Do I have to remind you that you're on precarious ground?"

Flit shook her head. "No ma'am."

"Good. Proceed." Harmony gestured to Flit and Scraps to let them know that they had the floor.

"A couple of weeks ago in the Mess, I overheard some Supply workers saying some bags of desiccant were either miscounted or went missing from storeroom eighteen. Desiccant has limited uses and it's not a tradeable good. Anyway, Scraps and I figured it could have been put in the pipes to decrease moisture, reduce flow, and increase pressure, which would—"

Divvy sighed. "Flit, I doubt—"

"Hear me out, please," Flit blustered on. Scraps winced beside her as she interrupted their leader. "There is no way that those pipes would explode like that without help. And what are the chances of three incidents happening so close together?"

"Flit, that's enough."

"No, let her speak. You may know what she is going to say, but I would like to hear it for myself." This time, Harmony was the one to interrupt Divvy. She leaned in, looking at Flit. "Go on."

Flit beamed, looking at Scraps. This is what she was hoping for. However, he still looked like a child caught with their hand in the cookie jar.

"So, we investigated. If the bags of desiccant went missing then someone had to have stolen them. But how could they get past the sensors on the doors?"

Harmony leaned in a little closer, invested in what Flit had to say. "And?"

"We found a hidden panel in the back of storeroom eighteen." The words tumbled from Flit's mouth. She grew more and more animated as she spoke. Scraps shrunk further back into his seat. "It slid aside and opened up straight into nineteen, which was decommissioned months ago. I checked on the register, and someone has been in and out six times since it was closed off, all accesses around the dates of the explosions."

When Flit finished speaking, she looked between the two leaders. The room filled with a thick silence as Harmony and Divvy processed the revelation. Flit turned to Scraps, and when she caught his eye, she winked at him, victorious.

Divvy was the first to break the silence. "We need a moment to discuss this in private."

Flit got to her feet, chair scraping against the polished concrete floor. Flit's steps bounced with excitement as she and Scraps walked out. Scraps looked over at her, eyebrows furrowed.

"I thought they said they'd call me back in," Tally grumbled when he spotted them.

Flit shrugged. "They will when they're ready." She was too busy wondering what Harmony and Divvy would say to care about Tally's theatrics.

Flit wanted to say something to Scraps to let him know they were safe. Even if they got into trouble for sneaking around, there was no way Harmony and Divvy would excommunicate them with the information bomb they just dropped. If the leaders wanted privacy, they must have thought the pair were onto something.

It was an awkward five minutes in the corridor before the door to the meeting room opened again. Divvy stood in the threshold, a grim expression on her face. Flit, Scraps, and Tally turned to her, waiting to hear what she had to say. "Please, come back in."

The three filed past and took the seats they had vacated. Divvy cleared her throat. "Tally, as usual, Harmony and I would like to thank you for your diligent service."

Tally shot Flit and Scraps a disdainful glance. Scraps stiffened. Annoyance flickered through Flit and she turned away from the older man.

"I was just doing my job." Tally downplayed the compliment, even though his inflated ego suffocated Flit.

"You stopped a situation that could have been very problematic for the Underground," Divvy insisted. "We will discipline Flit and Scraps appropriately. Thank you again, and have a good afternoon."

Flit's heart seized in her chest, her confidence faltering. Tally narrowed his eyes. His face fell as he comprehended the subtle dismissal in Divvy's tone. Flit figured the grumpy old geezer wanted to see the leaders rake her and Scraps across the coals for their transgressions. Even though his afternoon entertainment was snatched away from him, Tally rose to his feet, nodded respectfully to Harmony and Divvy, and slunk out. The leaders waited until the door slid shut behind him to continue.

"Pulling a stunt like that could be a security risk for the entire Underground," Divvy said, turning her serious gaze on Flit and Scraps. "Why did you investigate this yourselves, rather than taking it to your superiors?"

"That was my call," Flit said, not wanting Scraps to get into trouble for it. "Would you have listened to me if I didn't have proof?"

"She has a point." Harmony couldn't hide her smile. She'd always had a soft spot for Flit. She was the one who spoke up in Flit's favour when she wanted to join the Security team and her mother had tried to stop it.

Divvy sighed and pinched the bridge of her nose before shaking her head.

"Nevertheless, your actions cannot go without consequence. Especially as you dragged Scraps into this," Harmony turned to Scraps, her motherly expression turning sharp. "Flit is renowned for testing the limits down here, but that was not something I expected from you."

Scraps hung his head. "Yes ma'am."

Flit groaned, hating that Scraps crawled straight back to that place of unthinking obedience in front of their leaders. She crossed her arms. "Rules are only good when they help people, not hinder them. Now we know what is going on, we can prevent further problems."

"It isn't your place to make those decisions," Harmony reminded Flit far more gently than Divvy would have.

"Nevertheless, until we can test the validity of your claims, you are both confined to quarters outside of your shifts and meals at the Mess. You will not have access to any other areas unless otherwise given clearance by Harmony or myself. Any further transgressions will earn your more serious punishment," Divvy announced.

Flit let out a sigh of relief. As far as punishments went, that wasn't too bad. She'd had worse in the past. The tension in Scraps deflated as he sat beside her. They hadn't been doing much between eating, patrolling, and 'studying' anyway, so the punishment was unlikely to make much of a difference.

"Thank you for your leniency, I assure you that I won't transgress again," Scraps promised the leaders.

Harmony and Divvy didn't bother waiting for Flit to make the same vow. "Your restrictions begin now," Divvy warned them as she and Harmony rose out of their seats.

Flit and Scraps walked out of the room. Once they were down the corridor and out of earshot, Flit smirked. "And get caught doing so."

Scraps stopped walking and looked down at her, confusion in his scarlet eyes. "Pardon?"

"What you meant to say back there," Flit informed him, "was that you won't transgress again and get caught doing it."

Scraps groaned and shook his head. "Flit..."

Flit stepped closer and poked his chest. "No. Don't do that. Don't get back into that Registered headspace. You made a call today, and that decision might save dozens of lives," Flit said fiercely, looking up into his eyes and poking his chest again for good measure. "Good people die when those in power get complacent. It falls on our backs to make sure they don't forget their first priority is protecting the people they serve. They may let leads slide, but we never will."

Scraps took her hand and held it against his chest. He smiled, nodding as they stood together. "You are right, but let's wait a while before we test the boundaries again. I do not want to push my luck. They won't be so lenient next time."

36

SCRAPS

"WHO IS COVERING Racer and Lift's security shift tonight?" Patch asked between bites of dessert.

Scraps looked up from his dinner and over at Flit. He wasn't aware of any extra patrols.

Flit shrugged. "Not us, we're done for the night." She bit into her wrap.

"We're taking it," Swipe interjected, breaking out of her conversation with Hawkeye. Posthoc had assigned Hawkeye to patrols with Swipe rather than putting him back with Flit. Scraps heard rumours that Hawkeye might be reassigned to Intelligence permanently; he supposed that keeping the patrol partnerships as they were was easier than making constant changes. He didn't mind, he was grateful for the time with Flit.

Flit looked over at Swipe and Hawkeye. "Why does it need covering, anyway?" she asked.

Swipe ignored her, but Hawkeye decided it was worthwhile answering. "They got put on a deep-level patrol with Amber and Lynch. One of the lower tunnels has flooding issues. They upped the number for safety. They told us about it last night in the rec room."

"Which you would have known if you hadn't gotten yourself in trouble—again—and been restricted to quarters," Swipe sneered before sipping her soup.

Scraps frowned at the persistent animosity between Swipe and Flit.

"You're totally right. I mean, I should have been hiding behind my mirror and following beauty tutorials like you. Why bother my pretty little head when there are concerning things going on right outside my door?" Flit mocked.

Swipe's shoulders tensed and she narrowed her blue eyes at Flit.

"Have they determined the source of the flooding yet?" Scraps changed the topic, hoping to defuse the conflict between the women.

"No, but they suspect natural erosion. There's a subterranean river nearby. They'll know more by this time tomorrow. If we lose that tunnel, our best escape route out to the western edge of Old City is gone." Hawkeye leaned forward and put his elbows on the table as he spoke to Scraps, subtly creating a visual barrier between Flit and Swipe. It was the first time that Hawkeye had spoken to Scraps properly since he had returned. Everything else, even in training, had just been one-word answers or clipped statements and requests.

"That path to Old City is one of the best escape routes we have if the Government come down here to smoke us out," Patch added.

Scraps furrowed his brows in confusion. "You would risk going into Old City rather than The Hub? The radiation levels there are off all the scales."

Hawkeye snorted in amusement.

"Sorry, is radiation amusing somehow?" Scraps did not think there was anything funny about the radiation levels in that part of the city at all.

Flit sighed. "No, it isn't." She glared at Hawkeye. "He's laughing because the radiation readouts the Government get are bullshit. There's no more radiation in Old City; not any more than in most parts of the Hub, at least."

Scraps shook his head. "That is not possible, I have seen the readouts myself." The Underground was misinformed. He read the reports and saw the instruments go wild when entering the abandoned metropolis. He knew first-hand the radiation levels were astronomical. If the instruments weren't good enough proof, surely all the mutant creatures were.

Hawkeye sighed, looking tired of the conversation. "The readouts are fake."

"But—"

"We attach geotags to spyware. Whenever Government devices enter certain parts of the city, we feed them false positives," Patch explained.

Scraps was at a loss for words. That level of interference with the Government's readouts was beyond anything he imagined possible.

"If the Government realise Old City is fine, they'll come in and start demolition; use the site for industry. If they do that, they'll be right over our heads. Whatever digging they do will destroy the structural integrity of our tunnels and we can't have that," Flit said.

Scraps sat back, mind boggling at the amount of work a hoax of that size must take. "Well, it is effective."

"The Government restrict their micros with their classification systems. We don't. We have some very skilled, tech-oriented micros that can do all sorts of things." Patch told him.

Scraps looked at Patch, curious. "Can you do that?"

Patch chuckled and shook his head. "I wish. Technology is a mystery to me. Human bodies? I can tinker with them all day and night, but geotags and software and hardware—ugh, no."

"Huh..." Scraps trailed off and the group fell into silence as they finished their meals.

"Hawkeye, we'd better get going," Swipe announced as she put her fork down on her tray and sat back in her seat.

Hawkeye nodded as he started piling his own items back onto his tray. He stopped half-way through to look up at Flit. "Any chance I can drop by your room tonight? I could bring some VR gear."

Flit's eyes widened with surprise. She looked like she was about to answer, but her gaze flicked to Scraps for a fraction of a moment. "Oh, uh, sure. What time?"

"I dunno. G Sector doesn't take long. Maybe two hours?"

Flit chewed it over before nodding. "Sure. Sounds great."

Hawkeye's grin was wider than Scraps had seen it since his return. The tall, sandy-blonde-haired remote viewer got to his feet and picked up his tray. He and Swipe said their farewells and made their way out. Unlike earlier, when he thought Flit and Hawkeye were together, Scraps didn't feel jealous about them spending time together that night. He figured it was because he was the one kissing Flit, and he was certain that she wasn't interested in her friend like that.

Flit, Patch, and Scraps were the only ones left at the table. Flit was more fidgety than usual as she poked at her empty plate with her fork. Suddenly she stacked her things up on her tray. She looked up at Scraps. "I'm gonna head back to my room. Meet you there?" She stood up.

"Are you sure? Won't Hawkeye be coming over?"

Flit shrugged. "Yes, but I don't want to waste an hour of study time with your orienteering test so close."

Scraps smiled. "I will be up shortly." He looked down at his meal. He was almost finished. Normally Flit would wait for him so they could walk together, but this time she seemed eager to leave.

"Great, see you soon." Flit picked up her tray. "I'll get the stuff ready."

As she turned, Scraps noticed how her fitted tights hugged her rear in the most visually appealing manner. More and more often he had been learning what he found attractive. Flit's behind was right at the top of that list. He watched as she walked away, transfixed by the swaying of her hips.

"Scraps? Hello?"

Scraps tore his eyes away from Flit and turned to Patch. "Sorry, did I miss something?"

Patch laughed, his brown eyes crinkling in the corners. "I was just saying that you seem much better. I'm guessing you got over whatever made you feel sick?"

"Yes, I feel great now. Never better." Scraps turned his attention back to his dinner.

Patch rested his elbows on the table. "So, you and Flit, huh?"

Scraps' eyes widened and his heart beat harder as he looked at Patch. "How did you know?"

It was supposed to be a secret. He hoped that Patch wouldn't go telling everyone, he would feel terrible if his distraction was the reason Flit's request for privacy was destroyed. Scraps didn't want to do anything to risk the intimate bond that was forming between himself and the energetic teleporter.

Patch looked victorious. "I'm good at picking it." He shrugged nonchalantly. "So, how did that happen?"

Scraps' sat straighter and shook his head. "Flit asked that I don't discuss it with others."

"Why did she say that?"

"I... can't discuss that either." Scraps pressed his lips together tighter. He wished he could, though. He wasn't sure if things were progressing properly between them and talking to someone like Patch about it would help.

Patch frowned and looked around them before leaning in. "How about we walk back to the Residence together and we can talk about it on the way? I won't tell anyone else. Doctor-patient confidentiality and all that," he promised.

Scraps smiled. "That is a great idea." He used his powers to reach out and take Patch's tray, emptying it on his before he got to his feet and went to put it away. Patch tried to argue, but as Scraps dealt with the crockery and cutlery, the medic sighed and let Scraps work. They left the Mess together, and it was a couple of minutes before the tunnels were empty enough for them to talk with any semblance of privacy.

"So, what's the deal? What happened between you and Flit?" Patch asked.

"A few weeks ago, we went down to Sapphire Beach and we kissed," Scraps admitted, figuring that the beginning was as good a place to start as any.

Patch stopped walking and looked over at Scraps, eyes wide. "How did that come about?"

"Well... You were right about me not being sick. I talked to Acumen and he said that I was just jealous of Flit and Hawkeye."

"Oh, really?" Patch asked, his expression was one of surprise, but there was something in his tone that sounded almost smug. Scraps wondered if he was being sarcastic.

"Yes. I told her I liked her. We kissed for a while before Scry and the kids came down for a swim and we had to stop. When we were walking back up Flit asked me not to tell anyone. She said it would be best if we kept it to ourselves until we knew whether we are both serious about it. Until I know what I want from it."

"Ah." Patch leaned back against the tunnel wall and put his hands in his pockets.

From the look on Patch's face, Scraps thought the microkinetic understood Flit's request better than he did. "But I don't know what she meant by what I want from it. I like her, I like kissing her. It is simple enough."

Patch appeared to think it over as he looked at Scraps. For a moment, something akin to sadness flashed in his expression. "People want different things from relationships." Patch explained slowly. "Some people want to kiss, or touch, or have sex. Others want an actual romantic relationship."

Scraps pressed his lips together as he tried to comprehend it. "There's a difference?"

"There is. It's the difference between wanting to be Flit's boyfriend, and just wanting to hang around with her and fool around without the commitment. If it was just a casual thing, you could explore a little. Kiss other women, or whatever."

The memory of Swipe kissing him came back to Scraps, and he shook his head. "I do not want to kiss other women. Especially not Swipe."

Patch scrunched up his nose. "Swipe's probably not the best example. Are there any other females down here that you think are attractive?" Patch asked.

From Patch's tone, it was clear he was keen on using this example, so Scraps indulged him to see where the lesson would lead. Scraps thought about the women he'd met in the Underground and tried to decide which ones had the same effect on him as Flit. Even though Flit was the only woman he'd thought about lately, he could remember a few that featured in his more daring dreams when his hormones first kicked in.

"Oh, I know," Scraps said as the inspiration struck. He stood a little straighter. "Link is very attractive."

Patch made a choking sound and his face went red. "Er—can you think of anyone other than my sister?"

"I'm sorry, was that inappropriate?"

"Yes, but I left it open ended, so it's my fault. People generally don't talk about their close family members like that."

"Ah, I see. My apologies," Scraps said with a thoughtful nod, filing that information away for later. It was yet another thing he didn't know, thanks to how the Government raised him. "Clarity, then. Will she work?"

"Perfect," Patch spluttered a little too quickly. "If given the opportunity, would you like to kiss Clarity? Would you want to spend more time with her intimately or develop an emotional connection with her?"

It only took Scraps a few seconds to decide. "No, Flit is good. Why would I need anyone else?" Scraps did not see the point in exploring options with other women when he already had the best he had ever met.

Patch smiled and patted Scraps on the shoulder. However, his smile fell at the edges. "Look, I'll make an educated guess here and say that maybe Flit was talking about herself more than you. It's possible she's the one who needs more time to process things."

That made sense to Scraps. "She said that she was not sure if she was ready to be vulnerable again. But I do not understand. Why would she be vulnerable if we were dating?"

A flicker of sadness crossed Patch's face. "When you're in a relationship, you invest more than time and physical energy. You invest your emotions. You allow yourself to be open to the possibility of loving the other person. When you do that, there is always the chance you'll get hurt."

"Oh, I would never hurt Flit." Scraps' tone was full of conviction.

Patch shook his head. "Most people don't intentionally hurt each other." He sighed as he pushed himself off the wall and stood straighter. "It just means that once you've allowed that person into your life so intimately, ending the relationship will be a kind of loss. If you love someone, they become a part of you. It is no easier to lose them than it would be to lose, say, your own arm. Whether you break up, drift apart, or worse... it's painful."

Scraps digested that information and the weight that Patch's tone gave it. He wasn't sure how he would feel if he 'lost' Flit, for whatever reason. "So keeping our relationship quiet buys Flit more time to decide if she is willing to risk the pain of it ending?"

"Yes, you've got it." Patch gave Scraps a bright smile. "Just give her a bit of time, and I'm sure things will be fine."

Scraps understood the concept, but not the logic behind it. Still, Patch told him to give Flit more time, so he would.

For all the hype people made about relationships, they were far too over-complicated.

37

FLIT

FLIT WASN'T sure what made her escape from dinner as quick as she did, but all she could think was that she hadn't been alone with Hawkeye since he kissed her. When she got back to the messy chaos of her room, she had a sudden urge to tidy before Hawkeye came over. It would keep her hands busy and her mind off the situation. She missed his companionship, but she wasn't sure how to act around him anymore.

Then there was Scraps. Flit didn't enjoy hiding things from her best friend, but she couldn't confide in him when she had broken his heart so spectacularly.

By the time the knock on her door broke Flit from her tidying, she had cleared her table and packed her laundry away. She teleported over and opened the door for Scraps, smiling when she saw him. He had a look of resolute understanding in his eyes—it was the expression he wore every time he discovered something new—but it was replaced with shock as he peered past her and saw her room.

"Woah." Scraps put a gentle hand on Flit's shoulder as he stepped past her and turned in a slow circle, taking in his surroundings with awe.

"Oh, come on, it's not that big a difference." Flit mumbled, rolling her eyes.

"Yes, it is!" Scraps pointed to the ground. "Look! You have a floor. I was not sure what was under all those clothes. Flit, this is good. It would almost pass inspection in the Hub." Scraps nodded his approval, his face set with an impressed smile. "Almost."

Flit groaned. One difference between her and Scraps was their tolerance for disordered living quarters. Coming from the life he had, Scraps' room was spotless and organised. He didn't have an affinity for collecting random items like Flit did. Her own room was a museum of artefacts from her life; pictures on the wall, rocks from her childhood trips to the parks in the Hub with her parents, clothing stylishly draped over the furniture so even the simplest items became works of art (or so she told herself to justify not putting them away).

When Scraps looked back at Flit the wonder on his face softened; he used his telekinesis to shut the door behind her as he stepped closer. He reached out, running the tips of his fingers over her reddened cheeks. "You cleared your bed off too. It is good to know that we will not push any clothes onto the floor when we get distracted," Scraps said in a low tone.

Flit looked up at him and smirked. It was an endearing attempt to be seductive. She appreciated the effort. "You mean when we get too caught up studying?" she teased, leaning in and pressing the front of her body against his.

"Yes, that is exactly what I meant." Scraps closed the gap between them. Flit wrapped her arms around him.

SCRAPS AND FLIT did a bit of studying *and* kissing. Flit retrieved her maps and datapads and they settled onto her bed. Time trickled by and, as usual, Flit got bored. She put her own datapad aside and slid up to sit beside Scraps. It was so easy to distract him with light kisses. Light kisses soon turned into deeper ones, and before they realised it they were both laying down together, wrapped in each other's arms, as they explored the delicious chemistry growing between them.

A knock on the door had Flit and Scraps spring apart. Flit, breathless and flushed, looked over at the time on the panel by her door. "Shit," she hissed under her breath.

Scraps looked up at her in question. He was so endearingly ruffled from their kissing that she was tempted to ignore the knocking and just keep going.

But there was more knocking. "Flit? It's me."

Hawkeye's muffled voice destroyed any desire Flit had left and she sat bolt upright, looking at Scraps with panic in her eyes. "Damn it." She brushed her hands over her clothes to ensure they were sitting right. Scraps reached out, patting down her messy hair. Flit bit her lip as she teleported off the bed and gestured for Scraps to stand. She gave her blankets a quick tug to straighten them up and picked up Scraps' datapad. She unceremoniously shoved it in his hand and gestured to her table.

"Flit? Are you in there?"

Flit teleported to her door and gave Scraps a moment to settle at the seat by her desk before pressing the switch for her door and tugging her clothes back into place one last time.

"Hawk! Sorry, we got caught up studying." Flit plastered a smile onto her face as the door slid open to reveal her best friend.

True to his word two VR sets dangled from one of Hawkeye's hands, and a bag of snacks clasped into the other. "We?" Hawkeye peered around the doorframe. His smile fell when he saw Scraps sitting there. "Oh."

"Scraps has his orienteering test coming up. I'm pushing him hard to get him in the record books," Flit said with her usual swagger.

It was enough to convince Hawkeye. He rolled his yes. "Evening, Scraps." From his tone, it sounded more like a concession than a greeting.

"Good evening, Hawkeye."

"I hope Flit isn't working you too hard? You deserve some rec time in the evenings. She shouldn't be forcing you to study every night just so she looks like a good mentor," Hawkeye teased, smirking over at Flit. Even though they hadn't talked in weeks, it was almost as if nothing had changed between them.

Scraps chuckled. "Oh, there is no need to worry about that. I enjoy studying. Especially with Flit. She is an excellent tutor."

Flit cheeks burned and she shot Scraps an exasperated glare. He shrugged innocently. She loved that his sense of humour was developing, but didn't appreciate it quite as much when he used it against her. Flit wasn't sure if she wanted to yell at him or push him against the wall and kiss his smugness away.

"Right. Well, I suppose that is good to know." Hawkeye looked between Flit and Scraps uncertainly.

"So, you got the VR sets. You're my hero. I've been missing the VR suite because of this stupid house arrest." Flit took the sets from Hawkeye to check that they had the right attachments for her screen.

"Yeah but I've only got two…" Hawkeye trailed off, looking over at Scraps pointedly.

Scraps furrowed his brows and Flit could see him trying to read between the lines of Hawkeye's statement. She knew he understood it when his eyes widened.

"Oh, of course." Scraps jumped to his feet and pushed the chair under the table. "I should do some independent study before bed anyway. Goodnight, Hawkeye." Scraps tucking his datapad under his arm. He then turned to Flit and smiled. "Goodnight, Flit."

Something in his voice made Flit's knees feel weak. "See you in the morning," she muttered. It felt wrong to wish him goodnight and watch him walk out of her room without a proper farewell. She didn't have long to linger on it though. Hawkeye waited until Scraps shut the door behind himself. He walked over, relieving Flit of the VR sets and taking them to her built-in screen to connect them.

"So, you think it's a stupid house arrest, huh?" Hawkeye asked.

Flit rolled her eyes. "Well, yeah. Scraps and I were only trying to follow some leads and find the cause of the tunnel collapses. No one got hurt, and hell, we only broke one stupid rule."

"You know Control and Intelligence are running their own investigations, right?"

Flit snorted with contempt.

"It's true. I know you had a lead, but you can trust them to follow it up. You shouldn't put yourself in danger."

"Danger? We were in a Supply tunnel! It was hardly an adrenaline-pumping experience."

"All the same, you need to take a step back."

Flit's crossed her arms over her chest and she narrowed his eyes at him. "You've gotta be kidding me. This is the first time we catch up in weeks, no— months—and you're grilling me about my investigation?" Flit threw her arms in the air, her hand shaking with anger. "Who sent you?"

Hawkeye sighed and turned around. Setting the second, not-yet-connected headset down on the end of her bed. "It doesn't matter who sent me. Even if they hadn't, I'd still be concerned."

Flit was unimpressed. "Why?"

"Because you always get yourself into trouble, Flit. I know your recent adventure was safe enough, but what if you stumble on something—or someone—who is dangerous, hmm? What then?" Hawkeye faced her square on, the look in his green eyes telling her he would not back down.

"Then I'll take them down!" Flit snapped. Hawkeye rolled his eyes. She took a deep breath, balled her hands into fists at her side, and glared at him. "Why don't you ever trust me?"

Scraps hadn't questioned her hunch or their need to investigate. Yet, here was Hawkeye, born and raised in the Underground, and he didn't give half a shit about protecting it.

Hawkeye sighed. "It's not that I don't trust you." He sat down on the end of Flit's bed and leaned against the wall as he eyed her tiredly. "It's just that you don't have all of the information. Look, I shouldn't be telling you this, but..."

"But what?"

"When I was in the Hub for that mission, we were investigating leads on the initial collapse. One of our covert agents went AWOL, so we thought maybe she was captured and interrogated. Maybe she spilled important information and the Government came down here to take us out."

Flit walked over and sat down beside Hawkeye, her frustration lost in the excitement of his revelation. "And?"

"And nothing. We couldn't find her, but we also found no record of her being captured. There was no evidence that she, or anyone else of value, were taken."

"Interesting," Flit muttered, her mind spinning.

"That lead went cold. I have a feeling that many other leads went about the same way. It means we have to stop looking out and start looking in."

Flit leaned in even closer. She knew it had to be an inside job. "They think it was one of us?"

Hawkeye shifted uncomfortably. "Given the depths of the tunnels and the fact no one has seen any strangers since Scraps arrived, it makes sense."

Flit stiffened at the thinly veiled insinuation. "You better not be implying what I think you're implying," Flit warned, shuffling back so she could watch his expressions as they spoke.

Hawkeye shrugged. "I'm not saying anything. I heard you've been spending a lot of time with Scraps lately and I need to know you're safe." Flit glared at him and he raised his hands defensively. "I'm not the only one who's concerned. We all think—"

"We? Who's we?"

He shook his head. "It doesn't matter. The point is, as his mentor, you're best placed to notice if he's acting weird."

Flit crossed her arms. "Are you seriously asking me that?"

"Someone has to. I mean, have you?"

"Hawkeye!"

Hawkeye sighed. "Fine, whatever." He shook his head. "Just keep your eyes open, yeah?"

"I am not spying on—"

"Flit—"

"No!"

Flit's hazel eyes met Hawkeye's green and they stared at each other, stuck in a stalemate. When Hawkeye refused to capitulate, Flit narrowed her eyes at him. "Is that all? Have you interrogated me enough or did you actually come here to try and repair our friendship?"

Hawkeye tore his gaze away from her and his face dropped, lips falling into a frown. He ran a hand through his hair. "I didn't know it was broken."

"Isn't it?" Flit asked. They sat together in silence as the divide caused by the kiss yawned between them like a gaping chasm. The guilt of being with Scraps and not telling Hawkeye also weighed on her. It wasn't like them to keep secrets from one another, but in all fairness, Hawkeye had kept the mother of all secrets from her. Still, she wanted things to go back to the way they were before the kiss.

"I hope not. Even if you aren't interested in me like that, I still want to be your best friend." Hawkeye reached out a hand, bridging that seemingly insurmountable distance with an offer of hope. A chance to get back the friendship they both valued.

Flit took Hawkeye's outstretched hand without hesitation and sniffed, tears stinging her eyes. It might take a while for them to fully heal their relationship, but it was a start. She forced a smile onto her lips and cleared her throat. "Good, because I haven't whipped your arse at Hover Race for soooo long."

38

SCRAPS

SCRAPS DIDN'T HAVE many goals when he joined the Underground. He had few expectations. The only thing he wanted was to figure out how to catch Flit.

They stood at opposite sides of the training room. Scraps was crouched at the ready, panting as sweat rolled down his face. Flit had a fine sheen of perspiration over her face and neck, but her plain grey tank top didn't cling to her body the same way Scraps' stuck to him. She wasn't even short of breath. For the last hour, he had run himself ragged trying to catch her. She fluttered about and dodged his every attack with infuriating ease.

"I've used every technique the Government taught me to deal with teleporters and I still cannot catch you," Scraps puffed.

Flit had a playful smirk on her lips as she prowled back and forth, hands in her pockets. She wasn't even teleporting. She was just messing with him. "Oh, come on. I know you can do it," she tutted. Then, her smile turned wicked. "Maybe I just haven't given you the right incentive."

Scraps pressed his lips together and stood straighter. "The right incentive?"

Flit stopped pacing and shrugged. "Higher stakes to encourage you to succeed." She slipped her hands out of her black cargo-pant pockets and tugged her singlet down by the hem. The movement pulled the scooped neckline down to reveal a tantalising hint of the deep valley that ran between her breasts.

"Oh." Scraps gulped. "You meant t-that kind of incentive."

"Yep, and there's more where that comes from." Flit winked.

Scraps' legs shook and his heart thundered in his chest as his body reacted to her implication. He cleared his throat. "Now I am at even more of a disadvantage."

Flit let out a dramatic sigh before she disappeared and snapped back into place right in front of him. "Catching me means I no longer have any advantage over you." She looked up into his eyes.

Scraps shoved his hands into his pocket so he couldn't reach for her. "At least it would put us on an even playing field." He took a deep breath, inhaling that sweet, intoxicating scent of hers.

"Not getting caught is what keeps me alive. If you knew how to catch me, all it would take is one clench of your fist and you could strangle me." Flit's voice was so low that he had to lean in closer to hear.

"I would never do that to you," Scraps promised. Even the thought of someone else hurting her made his stomach churn and temper roil.

Flit's face set with grim determination. "There's a reason I've worked so hard to get this good. I don't want to be caught by anyone. Ever. If you get caught, you're under someone else's control."

"Getting caught is not so bad. It led me to you," Scraps whispered. He pulled his hands out of his pocket and cupped her cheeks. He leaned down and kissed her. Flit let out a soft moan that tingled through his lips and deep into his chest.

When Scraps pulled back Flit looked up at him, biting her lip. She took a step towards him so that the tips of their toes were touching. "Don't resist," she whispered and wrapped her arms around him, pressing her warm, curvaceous body flush against his. She settled one hand against his lower back and the other on the back of his neck.

Flit gave him a second to register the position they were in before she teleported them both to another part of the room. Scraps couldn't get his bearings before she teleported them again and again and again. He held her tighter as vertigo made his head spin, his stomach lurching as they flitted around the room faster than he could blink.

"You—"

Jump.

"Need—"

Jump.

"To—"

Jump.

"Keep—"

Jump.

"Me—"

Jump.

"On—"

Jump.

"The—"

Jump.

"Move—"

Flit stopped long enough for Scraps to get his bearing before she continued teleporting them around at a punishing pace that made him regret having lunch before training.

"Don't—let—me—stay—in—any—one—spot—long—enough—to—catch—my—breath." She punctuated every word with another teleport.

Flit landed them right back where they started, and Scraps stumbled. Her small hands wrapped around his biceps to steady him. She looked up at him, beads of sweat rolling down her face. "Make me move. Wear me out. Make me dizzy enough I fall right into your arms. Then," The intensity in Flit's eyes as she spoke made his breath catch in his throat. "Then, Scraps, I'm yours."

Flit squeezed his arms affectionately and stepped back. Scraps was cold and unsteady without her embrace. It was like the life was sucked out of him. He took a step towards her, but she teleported back, not letting him get close.

"Catch me," Flit breathed.

Scraps' heart hammered in his chest; she had given up her advantage. She revealed her weakness, and in doing so, made herself dangerously vulnerable. He would never hurt her, he knew it with every part of his being, but he had to know he could catch her.

Scraps nodded and reached out, sending a rushing of energy her way. She teleported to his left. He sent another wave in her direction, but not so strong. Forcing her to remain in place just wasted his energy. Instead, he focused on keeping her on the move. Again and again, he threw his power at her the moment she landed. At first, he was slow, but he soon learned the tell-tale signs of her movements: feet hitting the ground, a gasp half-breathed between locations, a rustle of clothing.

It wasn't long before the tide turned, and Flit was the one dripping with sweat.

On and on it went as he wore down his tireless companion. At least, she seemed tireless until the sound of her popping into place was marred by a scuffle and a muttered curse. Scraps reached out, sending a force to steady Flit as she almost tumbled into one of the metal training benches. She wobbled in the air at an alarming angle before he set her right, keeping her in his grasp. He held her on the spot and she watched, panting and wide-eyed, as he strode over. She didn't teleport away; she was too busy trying to catch her breath. Sweat plastered her hair to her face, and her skin was flushed with exertion.

"Have I got you now?" Scraps bit his lip as he looked down at her. She had never looked more attractive than she did in that moment.

Before Scraps knew what was happening, Flit wrapped her arms around him and slid her hands up to the back of his neck. She pulled his head down to hers and kissed him. He groaned at the taste of her and took her in his arms, lifting her up against his body and into the kiss. She scraped her nails along his flushed skin and he gasped into her mouth. She slid one of her hands down to his arse and pulled their hips together. The moan that slipped from her made him forget about everything else.

There was no training room, no Underground, no Government. Nothing.

Just Flit.

The kiss went on. He barely noticed when Flit teleported them over the other side of the room so that her back was pressed into the corner. She slid her arms around his shoulders and used the corner to support her as she wrapped her legs around his hips. Scraps was certain Flit could feel the effect her kiss had on him.

"Fuck, Scraps," Flit moaned. Scraps had kissed her enough to know she was swearing because she liked it, not because she was angry. "We should stop..."

"We should?" Scraps groaned as his lips caught hers again and he used his body weight to press her harder into the corner. His hand slid between them, over the fabric of her tank top.

Flit broke the kiss. "Scraps..."

When she said his name like that, he didn't want to stop. "Yes?" He trailed kisses over her cheek to reach the delicious spot behind her ear he found a few nights before.

"Now that you know how to catch me, will you..."

Scraps stopped kissing her and pulled back to look into her eyes. They were shining with an emotion that he had never seen in them before, something that spoke of utter vulnerability. "I will never control you," he promised in a reverent whisper.

Flit's eyes filled with gratitude. "Good."

It was Scraps' turn to smile when he dropped his attention back to that spot and drew a toe-curling moan from her in response. One of her hands covered his as she guided it under the fabric of her bra and against her soft skin. If Scraps died in that moment, he would die a happy man. He'd never gotten down to skin level before, but now he could see why anyone with a sex drive would want to.

A booming knock echoed through the room. Flit yelped and teleported away. Scraps' threw his hands up, his telekinesis saving him from slamming into the concrete corner. He turned around to see Flit standing by the door panting, her cheeks flushed. She tugged her tank top back into place and smoothed her hands over her hair before looking at him and gesturing to the door in question.

Scraps straightened up and ran his hands over his clothes to smooth them out, wincing when he brushed down his pants. The insistent throbbing there would not dissipate in a hurry. He reached his arm out, using his ability to summon his towel over from the hook by the door. He patted some sweat off his brow and held the towel in front of him to cover himself and then nodded to Flit.

She smirked at him before she pressed the panel on the door and it slid open.

He wanted to wipe that mischievous smirk away with a kiss.

At least, he did, until he saw who was waiting at the door.

Dressed, as usual, in casual grey utility gear, Harmony and Divvy walked into the training room. Flit stood back, looking just as surprised as Scraps felt.

Harmony smiled at them. "Sorry to interrupt your training. We have an update for you both. I wanted to stretch my legs, so I figured we'd come to you."

"That is very considerate, thank you," Scraps said politely as he walked over, trying not to stumble as he waited for the blood to return to his legs.

"We get so caught up running the Underground that we don't make it out of Control often. I've always found that rather ironic." Divvy's tone held a hint of amusement. She looked between Flit and Scraps. "Either way, we've come here to let you know we investigated your lead. We can safely assure you there was no foul play involved."

Relief washed over Scraps. Even though Flit's hunch was a logical explanation, he would rather know there weren't any traitors in his new home. When he looked over at Flit, his smile fell. He recognised the expression on her face. She didn't believe a word of what Divvy said.

Flit crossed her arms over her chest. "Really?" She cocked an eyebrow. "Missing chemicals, dodgy doors in the back of a storeroom, access to an out of comm—"

Divvy waved a dismissive hand at Flit. "I know how it looks, but we found some documentation that was misfiled. It checks out. The engineers have assessed the circumstances of the collapses and determined it was due to negligent maintenance. We appreciate your enthusiasm, but you don't need to worry any more. Do you understand?" Divvy looked at Flit rather than Scraps.

"Oh, of course, sure." Flit replied.

Everyone in the room knew she was lying.

"Now that's sorted, you're no longer restricted to quarters. Please don't make us regret giving you back your privileges." Harmony fixed Flit with a warning look.

"We won't, thank you for your leniency." Scraps stepped up beside Flit.

Divvy looked at him. "I know you won't, Scraps." She patted his shoulder. Scraps beamed at her level of trust. When he looked over at Flit, he swore he caught her at the tail end of an eye-roll.

"How is your training?" Harmony asked, looking between the two of them.

"Excellent. Flit taught me how to catch her." Scraps was glad for the change of topic.

"Really?" Divvy cocked an eyebrow at him. "I've heard that is difficult."

Scraps smiled at Flit. Memories of pressing her into the corner only moments before tumbled back into his mind. "I've only managed it once, but it shouldn't be hard to do it again."

Flit snorted. "Care to put your money where your mouth is?"

Harmony and Divvy chuckled.

"I suppose we should let you get back to it then." Divvy gestured to Harmony and they both made for the door.

Scraps snapped to attention. "Yes ma'am. Thank you, ma'ams." Harmony smiled back at him as she followed Divvy out of the room.

Once the door slid shut behind them, Scraps relaxed his posture turned to Flit. "You are going to keep investigating, aren't you?"

Flit rolled her eyes. "Obviously."

"They said—"

"I know. I don't believe them. No one has been held accountable for what happened, and we need to find out why." Flit balled her hands into fists at her side, and Scraps knew she was serious.

Even though it meant going against the leaders' direct command, he was glad she still wanted to follow up on their lead. He had thought they were on to something, and he had enjoyed working with Flit. He wasn't ready for it to be over. Scraps steeled himself with a breath before speaking again. "I understand."

"Good." Flit looked at him, eyes flashing with approval. "People are getting desperate and they're looking for anyone to blame. They won't stop until they find a scapegoat. It isn't right." Flit's voice, laced with frustration, rose as she spoke.

Scraps might have been terrible at reading social cues, but he knew Flit well enough to read between the lines of her comment. "They are blaming me, aren't they?" Scraps' stomach dropped.

Flit pursed her lips together. He thought she may not answer, but eventually she nodded and sighed. "Yes, and it's bullshit. I'm going to find the idiot that did it, and they'll have no choice but to see you the same way I do. You're a good person, Scraps, and I won't have anyone saying otherwise." Flit jutted her chin out in defiance.

Scraps' entire body felt warm and light and he stepped closer to her. He thought back to the moments before she showed him how to catch her and the vulnerability in her eyes as she gave away her deepest secret. She did that, knowing what the other people in the Underground were saying about him. She did it despite knowing his past. She did it, even if it meant she may one day be at his mercy.

Flit trusted him.

Genuinely, and with the full force of her insurmountable conviction.

That meant more to Scraps than anything else ever would. For the first time, he knew he wasn't alone.

"Then I guess I will have to come with you to keep you out of trouble," Scraps said with a sideways smirk, hoping to lighten the mood.

Flit blushed an alluring shade of pink and muttered, "Keep me out of trouble? Ha! I'd like to see you try." She teleported to the opposite side of the room, sank into a ready position, and bounced between the balls of her feet.

All amusement drained from Scraps as he watched her. His mouth set in a grimace of determination and he narrowed his eyes. With the speed of a cracking whip, he swiped his hand and sent a dumbbell from a nearby rack rocket towards her. She had no choice but to teleport out of the way.

Scraps was done playing around. He would catch Flit again, and he would prove he was worthy of her trust.

39

FLIT

WHEN FLIT STUMBLED BACK to her room that night, she was looking forward to tearing her clothes off and having a nice hot shower before falling into bed. After Harmony and Divvy left, she and Scraps trained for another hour. He took her advice on how to catch her to heart, and he caught her; again, and again, and again. She would have been annoyed, but each time he caught her, he held her close and kissed her until she was dizzy. She only teleported away when she feared they were getting too hot and heavy for the training room. By the end of the session, she let him catch her because she was tired of running from his kisses. She wanted them.

After training, she and Scraps patrolled some mid-level tunnels. It was an easy but long route that took them right up to dinner time. Then, after dinner, the Blue Team celebrated their release from house arrest by inviting them to the VR suite. They even threw in some restricted moonshine to sweeten the deal. Scraps didn't drink, but Flit decided to have a couple of shots for old time's sake.

Flit groaned in relief as she reached her door. She slapped her palm sloppily against the reader and the door slid open. Just as she was about to teleport in, she stopped and let out a loud yelp. "What the fuc—"

"Sorry to surprise you like this." Harmony stood from where she was sitting at Flit's desk and gave her an apologetic smile.

Flit remembered her manners and pursed her lips shut. She

reached behind her head, scratching her neck. "Ah, sorry about the language. You scared the crap out of me." Flit stepped forward enough to let the door close behind her.

"That wasn't my intention, although the look on your face was hilarious." Harmony winked. "I think it's time that you and I have a private chat."

Flit didn't feel so tired anymore. "Oh?" She kicked off her boots and teleported over to her bed. She sat down on the edge of it and looked at the leader of the Underground with unabashed interest.

"It's about the lead you found," Harmony conceded "You won't stop investigating, will you?"

Flit considered lying for about two seconds. Then she shrugged. "No. There's more to it. Divvy's explanation was too clean-cut."

Harmony looked at her through narrowed eyes. Flit refused to shift or squirm under her intense scrutiny.

When it was clear Flit wouldn't back down, Harmony nodded. "Good. Because I agree with you."

"Look, I know you and Divvy said—" Flit froze. "Wait... what?"

"I agree with you." Harmony sat up straighter. "The evidence was too tidy. But my hands are tied. I can't be seen following up on leads which didn't pan out when we're already so stretched for resources. The last thing I need is for people to think I don't accept the outcome of the investigation."

"You don't accept it?" Flit's eyes widened and she sat straighter.

"We had our team look over the access records to storeroom eighteen and nineteen. There was nothing suspicious about the accesses, but I still feel like we're missing something."

Flit sat in captivated silence. She didn't want to risk talking in case she stopped the revelations tumbling from Harmony's mouth.

"I shouldn't tell you this, but while we were going through the patrol records for the junctions in the affected sectors, something felt off. Shadow and his team investigated the areas but didn't find anything. I'm still not convinced. I just get this feeling, you know?"

"Oh, I understand completely." Flit's stomach was swirling with excitement at the confirmation that she hadn't been imagining things. "The collapses couldn't have been accidents."

"I'm sorry." Harmony shook herself out of her thoughts and

looked over at Flit with a heavy sigh. "This is nothing more than the rambling of an old woman. Divvy and I are working far too much and not getting enough sleep. I must be imagining things. Please forget I said anything. Just... be careful, ok?" Harmony got to her feet and smoothed out her trousers.

Flit was so lost in her own thoughts she didn't realise that the older woman was about to leave until she was standing by the door.

"Good night, Flit," Harmony said.

Flit jumped to her feet. "Good night Harmony. Thank you for coming by."

"Thank you for hearing me out. We need more people like you down here to keep us on our feet." Harmony gave her a half-salute, half-wave and stepping into the hallway.

As soon as the door shut behind Harmony, Flit collapsed back onto her bed, her mind racing. There was so much to take in from the conversation that she knew she wouldn't be able to sleep.

"UGH, I NEED A BREAK!" Flit groaned and threw herself back on Scraps' bed. She unceremoniously dumped her datapad on his pillow.

Scraps looked up from his own datapad and sat a little straighter at his desk. "Still nothing?" He put his own study down to give her his full attention.

"Nope. I've been looking for a whole week and can't find a thing. But I know what Harmony meant, there's something there. There has to be!" Flit glared at the ceiling. Footsteps sounded through the room and the bed sagged beside her left hip.

Scraps' large, warm hand settled over her stomach. "If anyone can figure it out, it's you," he said with an encouraging smile.

Flit's heart warmed at how much faith he had in her, even if her own confidence was flagging. "I hope so, but for now... I need a distraction. If I look at those maps again, my head will explode."

Scraps chuckled. "Well, that will not do. Maybe I can distract you."

Flit propped herself up on her elbows to look at him and smiled as she saw his light smirk. "Oh?"

"I can tell you some interesting facts I read."

It was a sign of how desperate Flit was for a break that she agreed to listen. It wasn't the distraction she was hoping for, but she couldn't be picky. "Sure. Shoot." Flit sat up and crossed her legs.

Scraps put his hand on her knee and she covered it with her own. "While I was studying, I learned that the naming conventions used down here are a mirror image of the ones used for the grid-pattern of Old City." Scraps' smile was so wide that it almost split his face in two.

Flit didn't know anyone who would be nearly as excited about that revelation, but she was glad it made him happy. "That's interesting." Flit had never given much thought to where the naming conventions came from. All that mattered was they worked.

Scraps frowned. "You are not impressed." He drummed his fingers drummed on her knee as he thought. "Oh, I know. Do you remember when you told me that Sapphire Beach got its name because of the blue lighting?"

Flit nodded. "Yes, that's right."

Scraps expression turned smug. "Actually, it is not. According to the public archives, and there is a much more interesting story behind it."

"Ok, you got me," Flit conceded as she sat straighter. "Continue."

Scrap got that cocky look in his eyes he got whenever he was right about something. It made her feel like kissing him.

"When the Underground was first mapped for habitation, the explorers stumbled across the beach. They thought found a deposit of blue quartz, but it turned out to be sapphires. They couldn't mine much without destroying the integrity of the tunnels, but they sold what they did get on the black market in the Hub, and then used the funds to fit out the habitation tunnels."

"Well, shit. Who knew?" Flit hummed, genuinely impressed.

"Everyone could if they cared to look in the archives."

"Pft!" Flit rolled her eyes. "I'd rather play in the VR suite."

Scraps laughed and shook his head. They would just have to

agree to disagree on worthwhile past-times. "If you think that is cool, I have got an even better fact for you."

"You can't possibly top that last one, but I'll listen." Flit winked, humouring him.

"The classifications of surface-, mid-, and deep-level tunnels have changed three times in the history of the Underground. At first there were just surface- and deep-levels. The first refugees wanted to get as far away from the city as possible. The second time was when the Government abandoned Old City. The Underground introduced the mid-level tunnels as the new habitation zone to reduce the strain on the resources it took to keep the deeper levels hospitable."

Flit sighed. "And the third time?"

"That was when the Government transitioned to fully wireless communication tech. They reclassified the tunnels based on whether they had the old wires in them. That is why the surface- and mid-level tunnels are not all the same depth, but the deep-level tunnels are relatively consistent."

Something in what Scraps said tickled at Flit's mind and she perked up. "Say that again, please."

"From the beginning? Ok." Scraps shrugged. "The naming conventions for—"

Flit shook her head. "No, not that bit! The bit about the transition to fully wireless whatever."

"Oh, well, the reason that the surface- and mid-level tunnels are all at different depths is that the Underground reclassified them when the Government stopped using wired communication tech. The Underground reclaimed some surface-level tunnels as mid-level, based on the amount of protection afforded from wireless communication tech, thereby giving them more growing space."

"Is there a map of the tunnels that were reclassified?"

"Yes. Would you like to see it?"

Stomach fluttering, Flit nodded. "Yes please."

Scraps used telekinesis to summon his datapad. He tapped the screen a few times and brought up a 3D matrix map of the previous tunnel classifications before handing the device to Flit. Flit did a quick search and brought up the newest map, transposing it over the old one.

Flit's eyes widened as excitement welled up in her. She bounced forward on the bed, catching Scraps' face between both of her hands. "You're a freakin' genius!" she squealed excitedly before kissing him, hard and passionate. At first, he was too shocked to react to the kiss, but he soon softened into it.

When Flit pulled away, Scraps chuckled. "Well, I am not the one who reclassified them, but if that is the reward it gets me, I will not claim otherwise." He caressed Flit's cheek.

Flit rolled her eyes and shook her head. "But you are a genius. I spent the whole week trying to find a link, and you did it for me!" Flit reached for the datapad she had flung aside in her eagerness to kiss him and showed him the map. "Here, look. The tunnels that collapsed are here and here." Flit pointed to them on the map, "Both were changed from surface-level to mid-level in the reclassification!"

Scraps took the datapad and turned it so he could see the map easier. His expression changed from interested to impressed. "That means they all hold old wired communication cables."

"Scraps, thank you." Flit teleported the datapad back onto his desk. She was too excited to do it with any finesse and it landed with a soft thunk that made him wince.

Flit looked up into his eyes, unable to describe just how grateful she was for his help. Without his dedication to learning and studying, she never would have found that link. Something inside her clicked when she saw it. She needed more time to figure out how it was connected to the blasts, but she knew beyond a shadow of a doubt that they were on the right track.

He brushed off her thanks. "It was nothing."

Flit got to her knees and moved closer to him, gently resting her forehead against his. "It is everything. You're amazing. You need to stop doubting how wonderful you are." She brushed her lips against his as she spoke.

Scraps closed the distance between them to kiss her properly. Flit shifted and draped her arms around his shoulders, pressing herself up against him. He sagged against hers, his face tilting to deepen the kiss. She fell into him as just easily as she did every time they kissed; affection and arousal swelling in her heart. It was a long time before they came up for air, and by the time they did, Flit's mind had moved onto something far more sensual than tunnel maps. From the look on Scraps' face, his thoughts had too.

"I have been thinking about our last training session all week." Scraps confessed in a low, husky voice.

Flit laughed. "That kiss made you think of training?"

Scraps shook his head. "Not the training itself, the part where you teleported us against the wall."

"Ah, that makes a lot more sense." Flit was relieved the kiss left a bigger impact than their training. "It was fun. Would you like to do again?"

"Yes!" Scraps spluttered.

His enthusiasm made Flit laugh. "I was hoping you'd say that."

Flit pushed him back on the bed, kissing him the whole way down. His warm hands settled on her waist and once he was laying down, she straddled his hips and kissed him harder. The moan that rattled from his mouth reverberated right down to her core. She tightened her grip on his chest, bunching up the fabric of his shirt in her grasp.

"We may not be against the wall," Flit said as she trailed kisses from his lips to his jawline, "but the bed is so much more comfortable." To prove her point, she rested her weight against him.

Scraps grasped at Flit's waist to hold her in place. "I like this much better." He kissed his way over to her neck and nipped at the soft skin there.

"Good." Flit cupped the back of his head to hold him to her as she tentatively rocked against him. The groan that rumbled from deep in his chest inspired her to do it again. She slid her free hand down his side, feeling the contours of his firm body. She roamed lower until she brushed her fingers over the hem of his shirt. "Can I take this off?"

Scraps clung to her tighter. "Yes."

Flit smiled as she skimmed her palms over his taut stomach and chest, pushing up his shirt along the way. Scraps sat up just enough so she could tug it off and cast it aside, not caring where it fell.

Slowly but surely, the rest of their clothes followed in the way of

Scraps' shirt. They got closer to each other than they ever had before. The heady sensation of skin against skin was enough to make Flit dizzy and remind her of the pleasures she had forgotten. She gasped with need as his lightly calloused hands ran over her body. She was caught between begging for more and willing herself to be patient. Flit wanted to give Scraps the chance to explore her, and she wanted to learn all about him.

Flit and Scraps kissed and touched until the only barriers between them were their underwear and their threadbare restraint. When Scraps' hands stalled over the clasp of her bra, Flit pulled away from the kiss and smirked at him. "That's a lesson you can learn another day. Tonight, I just want it gone."

Flit reached behind her back and unclipped her bra with one hand, letting the moulded cups cling to her breasts so Scraps could remove them. His fingers shook as he held a hand towards her. With two simple flicks of his wrist, he telekinetically slid the strap off her left shoulder and then her right. He reverently traced his fingertips over the skin he had revealed, his eyes wide with admiration. Flit's breaths came in short, sharp puffs as she looked into his eyes. He had no idea he was driving her wild with his slow, sensual exploration as his hands dipped from her shoulders to the swell of her breasts and peeled the bra cups away.

"Wow," Scraps breathed, transfixed by what he revealed.

Flit laughed softly, even though the cool air of his room made her skin ache for warmth. Luckily, Scraps had the same idea as he reached out and cupped her breasts in his big hands. He leaned forward, pressing his lips against her neck in hot, needy kisses as his hands squeezed and explored.

"They are so soft," he marvelled.

"And yet, you are so hard." Flit ground her hips against his for emphasis.

Scraps sat up and kissed her neck. "You have that effect on me."

Flit laughed softly and nuzzled her cheek against his. "Are you ok with this? Can we keep going?"

Scraps stopped kissing her. "I would love to, but I do not know what to do," he warned.

"You're doing good so far," Flit promised, pulling back so she could look into his eyes.

He didn't look convinced. "When we first started kissing, I did some research. I understand the biological basics, but a content warning came up on some videos I found, so I stopped looking… I want to make you feel good, but I do not know how."

The insecurity in Scraps' words were another sign of how corrupt the Government was. They didn't let him develop those sorts of skills purely because he was a Derivate. Still, it wasn't the right time to get angry about it. Flit cupped his cheek, her heart melting at the look in his eyes. "You're an adult, you can ignore those content warnings," she told him before she sighed and shook her head. "But that doesn't matter now. Would you like to know the best way to learn how to make me feel good?"

"How?" Scraps perked up at the prospect of learning something new.

"You let me teach you," she whispered, brushing her lips against his.

Scraps gulped as he looked between her eyes and her breasts. "Should I get the datapad so I can take notes?" He tore his gaze away from her to see where the device had gone amidst their frolicking.

"No, your hands will be too busy to type."

To prove her point, Flit took his right hand and guided it down over her belly until it settled against the junction between her thighs. "Explore whatever you like. I'll let you know when it feels good."

Scraps, always a good student, did not disappoint. He circled, stroked, massaged, and teased her through her underwear, using her moans and whimpers as a guide. He seemed content with what he was doing, but Flit took the initiative to let him know it was time to move on. She reached down and pulled the thin fabric aside.

Scraps groaned as he tentatively pressed his fingers against her bare skin. Flit gasped at the pleasure that shot through her body. She looked down, about to beg for more, when a memory flickered past her eyes and she was in a different place at a different time. Instead of Scraps touching her so intimately, it was Rook.

Rook. With his deep brown eyes and messy black hair, his naturally olive skin and square-set jaw. She used to love it when Rook touched her like this. They spent any spare time they had in his room exploring each other. With every touch of his hands or lips, Scraps' affection replaced the sense memory of Rook's loving caresses.

Soon Flit would forget what it was like to be with him at all.

And Flit's memory was all she had left of him.

Flit gasped. "Shit!" She teleported off Scraps and to the other side of the room. Her lips trembled, and her eyes stung as they filled with tears.

Scraps blinked, shocked. "Flit?" The instant he saw the state she was in, he was on his feet, looking around to see if there were any threats before he stepped towards her. "Flit, I am sorry. Did I do something wrong?"

The look of guilt in his eyes severed the last thread of restraint Flit had on her emotions. Tears sprung from her eyes and trickled down her cheeks. "No. Y-you're amazing. I—" Flit stopped, looking around for her clothes. She found them by his desk and teleported over. She snatched up her pants and stumbled into them as she shook her head. "Sorry. I-I can't do this." She tugged her tank top over her head without even putting her bra on.

Scraps took another step towards her, holding his arms open. "Flit, what is it?"

"Don't!" Flit staggered back. "I just—" She shook her head in frustration, unable to finish the sentence. With another teleport, she was standing by the door. She slammed her hand against the access panel. As it opened, Scraps, almost naked, dived for cover.

Flit made jump after jump until she was in her room. She shut the door and fell back against it, sliding down to the floor. The emotions she had bottled up for the past few months tumbled out.

She thought she was ready to move on, but she was wrong.

40

SCRAPS

IT WAS A LONG NIGHT.

Between the pent-up desire and the uncertainty surrounding Flit fleeing his room, Scraps didn't sleep much. When morning finally came, he hoped to see Flit at breakfast, but she wasn't there. Scraps sat with the Blue Team, listening to them chatter about their plans for the day. After pushing his eggs around on his plate until they were cold, Scraps decided to find Flit. He was just about to get up to leave when a soft, warm hand grabbed his arm. He frowned as he looked down at Swipe.

"Where are you off to, stud?" she asked, furrowing her brows in concern.

"To find Flit and—" Scraps stopped, wondering if he should tell Swipe more. The last thing he needed was to upset Flit further by giving away their relationship.

"You're not scheduled for training with her until later."

"I, uh, I need to clarify something about my orienteering test," Scraps lied.

Judging by the way Swipe narrowed her eyes, she didn't believe him. Still, she took her hand off his arm with a sigh. "That test isn't the be all and end all, you know. Don't freak out about it so much." Swipe's face softened. "I'll see you in training. An hour, yeah?"

"Sure."

Scraps left the Mess, dumping his tray in the scullery on the way before he set out to find Flit.

THREE-QUARTERS OF AN HOUR LATER, Scraps had no choice but to go to training. Flit wasn't in her room, the VR suite, or even in the Residence Commons. She was nowhere to be found. He was concerned about her; the way she left the night before was so abrupt. She went from enjoying what they were doing to backing away from him in a matter of moments.

Scraps' training session with Swipe went well. After significant improvement on his fine control since his arrival in the Underground, Scraps and Swipe were working on his telekinetic strength and speed. By the end of the session, Swipe was satisfied with his progress, and she predicted that, with time, he could easily match her abilities.

"You would progress faster if you weren't so distracted all the time," Swipe said before she took a long drink from her water bottle. "What's going on stud?" She leaned against the observation window and looked him up and down.

Scraps observed Swipe using pet names for many of her friends, and even though 'stud' felt a little too intimate for their friendship, he had grown used to it. But that did not mean he wanted to confide in her. "I am not distracted. I just did not get much sleep last night."

Cocking an eyebrow at him, Swipe asked, "Really, was something keeping you up?"

Thanks to his relationship with Flit, Scraps picked up on the flirty nature of Swipe's tone. He had no intention to return the suggestive banter, but the problem was, her comment wasn't too far from the truth. So, he skirted around the issue: "I am just concerned about my orienteering test."

Swipe narrowed her eyes at him. "Flit should be helping you with that."

"She is helping me. I just..." Scraps trailed off, not knowing what to say to that wouldn't land him in more trouble.

When Swipe crossed her arms under her breasts, Scraps' eyes

were drawn to the way the pose propped them up higher. He caught himself staring and looked away, blushing. Swipe smirked when she saw him look away and slinked closer, her eyes alight with suggestion. "Well, if you need any help, don't be afraid to ask. You know where to find me."

"He'll be fine, thanks."

Eyes wide, Scraps looked around as Flit's voice came through the speakers on the walls. The door opened and Flit walked into the room. She had deep purple circles under her eyes, but she had enough energy to give Swipe an acidic glare.

Swipe didn't even look at Flit. "You have your own voice, Scraps. Don't let Flit take it away from you like that." Swipe patted his chest before winking at him and walking out.

The tension in the room was palpable as Swipe strode past Flit, turning her nose up at her along the way. Flit watched Swipe like a cat about to pounce until the door shut behind the blonde woman. When Flit turned to Scraps, the anger in her eyes dissolved into something that made him want to hold her. Her shoulders sagged as she leaned against the wall. "I'm sorry about last night. I shouldn't have run out on you the way I did." Her voice cracked as she spoke, and she looked at her feet as she shuffled them around.

Scraps walked over and took her hands in his. "Are you ok? I worried about you all night." He just wished she would look at him.

"I'm fine."

They both knew it was a lie.

Flit sighed. "I had some stuff going on in my head. I do want to teach you everything I promised to, I'm just—" Flit stopped talking and sucked in a deep, shaking breath.

Gently squeezing her hand, Scraps asked, "You're just?"

"I don't know, Scraps. I'm a mess." She shook her head. Flit rested her hands against his chest as a tear slid down her cheek.

Scraps reached up, wiping the tear away before kissing her forehead. "You are not a mess. And you have nothing to be sorry for. I have enjoyed every moment I have spent in your company, last night included." Scraps stepped back to give her some space. "Except for when we got caught investigating the storage vault. That, I could have done without." He winked at her.

Flit's eyes widened as she looked at him, and for a moment he thought he may have judged the situation wrong. But it passed, and she laughed through her sniffles. "You get funnier every day." She playfully swatted at his chest.

Scraps caught Flit's hand and kissed her knuckles. She shivered and looked up into his eyes. She leaned in to kiss him, but just before their lips met, Flit seemed to think better of it. She stepped back, clearing her throat. Scraps wasn't pleased about the loss of contact, but her laughter was a sweet relief.

Flit scrubbed her tear-streaked face with her hands and cleared her throat. "So, I uh, I have news for you." She squared her shoulders and tried to look serious and professional. It was the same stance she used around their team members. "Your orienteering test is this weekend."

It was the last thing Scraps expected to hear from her. "Ex- excuse me?" he stammered, thrown by the change of topic.

"Your orienteering test. I set the date for this weekend."

Scraps' stomach dropped and he shook his head. "No, Flit, I am not ready. I need more time to study. I have at least two more weeks of study scheduled." Scraps pressed his lips together as he recalled the timetable he set up, checking off what was essential and what he could do without. "I still need to cover chapter three of the advanced navigation manual, and sections E through L of the deep-level tunnel schematics. If I don't pass this test—"

"Woah, Scraps, slow down." Flit put her hands on his chest and shook her head. "No one studies as hard as you do. You know more about this place than most of the engineers down here."

"But I had a plan, I am not ready for the test yet. I cannot possi—"

Flit's lips collided with his. All the fight went out of him and he sank into the kiss. It was sweet, it was slow, and even though it lacked the fire they shared the previous night, it had a wonder all its own. He wrapped his arms around her and held her close, taking reassurance in her confidence. She was right. With her help, he would get through the test. She wouldn't lead him astray.

When Flit pulled away from Scraps, she looked up at him. Despite how tired she was, her eyes sparkled in the clinical light of the training room. He caressed her cheek. "Do you know what to do about that lead we found?" Scraps asked. It had to be on her mind.

"I have an idea," Flit admitted, "but don't worry about that. You just focus on the orienteering test."

Knowing better than to push, Scraps changed the topic. "Will I see you this afternoon, after your training?" He asked. It was one of the few days they had off from patrols. Yesterday he had hoped to spend it in his room kissing Flit; now he was just hoping he could be by her side.

Flit shook her head. "After dinner. I have to sort out the finer details of your test and submit them to Control."

Scraps could use the time before dinner to study, and then maybe she would talk to him after and let him know why she ran away. "I am already looking forward to it," he said with a smile.

"Great." Flit got to her toes to kiss him before she walked out.

Scraps was about to follow her when he noticed Swipe's water bottle sitting on the windowsill. He reached out, summoning it into his hand. Swipe was out on patrol until the evening, so he would just have to give her the bottle at dinner.

SCRAPS GOT a lot of study done in his room before he went to dinner. Not having Flit around meant he had no distractions. Not that he would ever complain about the way she distracted him, of course, but it was much easier to study without getting distracted by her sweet scent or feeling the desire to lean in and kiss her smooth neck.

When he arrived in the Mess, Scraps went to the team's usual table in the back corner of the room. Patch, Tweak, Link, Sway, and Flit were already there. As usual, Sway's hands were on Link, rubbing up and down her back in slow motions. Scraps wondered for a moment what it would be like to touch to Flit so openly, but he pushed the thought away. He was content with what they had. He would wait as long as it took for her to feel comfortable enough to share their relationship with the others.

"How's the study going, mate?" Sway asked as Scraps sank into the empty seat beside Flit.

"I made good progress tonight." Scraps said with a smile, flicking his eyes to Flit as she smirked over at him.

Sway chuckled. "That's good. Are you gonna beat any records getting back here? I mean, with all that study you must know these tunnels better than the back of your hand."

Scraps was hoping to, but saying so would just sound cocky. "I might have studied a lot, but you guys know this place. It is your home." Scraps shrugged as he set Swipe's water bottle onto the table.

"Right, well, I'm gonna get my dinner. Scraps, do you want to come up and see if your favourite chilli-stew is on the menu?" Flit asked. The others chuckled. Everyone knew Scraps was not fond of spicy food.

"Sure, sounds great." Scraps got to his feet and fell in beside Flit as they walked to the servery. It was the standard fare for the middle of the week. None of the meals had too much 'kick' to them, so he could pick anything without worrying too much about burning his oesophagus.

"So, the study went that well?" Flit asked as she heaped food onto her plate.

"Very much so. Having no distractions really helped." Scraps winked at her.

"Is that all I am? A distraction?" Flit asked.

Scraps smirked. "I did not say it was a bad thing."

Flit smiled at his comment as they moved further down the line towards the drinks. "So, can I still come by tonight, or will I be too distracting?"

"Probably." Scraps shrugged. "But I would still like you to."

"Well, I can't say no to that." She smiled up at him and it melted his heart.

Trays piled with food, they turned and made their way back to the table. The others at the table sorted out their own dinners, and soon everyone was eating and chatting as usual.

Halfway through dinner, Swipe and Hawkeye returned from their patrol and went to get their own meals. When Swipe looked over, Scraps smiled and waved, pleased he remembered her water bottle. She narrowed her eyes at him, and he had the unnerving feeling she was angry at him. He wasn't sure what he did to earn her ire, but he would probably find out.

Hawkeye looked exhausted when he set his tray on the table and slumped into a seat opposite Flit. Meanwhile, Swipe snapped the chair across from Scraps out with telekinesis, letting it scrape against the floor with a hair-raising screech.

"Wow, rough patrol?" Link frowned and put her fork down as she looked between the latecomers.

Clearing his throat, Hawkeye looked at Swipe. "Uh, yeah. You could say that."

With a viscous stab of her fork, Swipe speared a piece of steak and gave Scraps a pointed look. Scraps no longer had any doubt that he had done something to annoy her.

Luckily, Scraps had something to improve her mood. "This might brighten your night." He slid her water bottle across the table. "You left this in the training room. I thought I'd bring it out for you."

Throwing her cutlery down, Swipe glared at him "I know I left it there," she snapped. Her tone was so acidic that the others looked over warily. "I went back to get it, but you and Flit were making out by the door and I didn't want to go anywhere near you."

Scraps' jaw dropped as all eyes turned to him and Flit. There was a tense silence at the table as Flit's cheeks reddened and Hawkeye choked on his food.

"Swipe, I-I... Uh..." Scraps stammered, not sure what to say. He looked at Flit, hoping for some guidance. He didn't want to give up their secret, but he couldn't call Swipe a liar when she was telling the truth.

"Oh sure, now you're at a loss for words. Surprised someone caught you, huh?" Swipe banged her fist on the table and the plates rattled. "I thought you were better than that, Scraps. But you're not. You get your hormones back and you go after the first thing that throws itself at you."

Scraps pressed his lips together, bristling at how Swipe referred to Flit.

"Don't you dare talk to him like that." Flit's words lashed

through the tension, sharp as a cracking whip. The anger simmered off her as she leaned forward. "You might be jealous, but that doesn't give you the right to be a bitch."

There was a sharp, collective intake of breath from their friends. The buzz of conversation at the surrounding tables stalled as the other diners turned to see what was going on. Scraps saw Acumen, Posthoc, and Bookworm sitting at the table behind Hawkeye. All three had turned away from their meals to watch the brewing tension.

Swipe's expression sharpened. The plates and glasses on the table rattled as her control over her powers slipped.

Acumen pushed his chair out from the table. "Okay, that's enough."

"Is it?" Swipe stood up. "Because I'm just getting started."

Scraps winced as Flit got to her feet beside him. She was at least a head shorter than Swipe, but the disparity wouldn't make her back down.

"Ladies, sit back down," Acumen warned.

"I'm not sitting at the same table as that tramp!" Swipe slammed her hand down on the table.

From the way Flit's hands balled into fists and her shoulders hunched, Scraps was glad there was a table between the two women.

"Shut your mouth—" Flit started.

"Or what? What could you possibly do to me, Flit? You already got my best friend killed—"

"Don't. You. Fucking. Dare," Flit hissed.

Scraps put his hand on her arm. She shook it off. He looked at the others, but they were all frozen, watching the drama unfolding before them.

"What, tell the truth? Shit, Rook's only been gone a year and you're already fucking around?" Swipe threw her hands up in the air and all the plates and glasses on the table rattled. "Did you even love Rook, or were you just messing around with him like you do with everything else?"

There was no warning. No lead-in. One moment Flit was

beside Scraps, the next she had teleported to the other side of the table.

Flit's fist collided with Swipe's face. Swipe fell back into Hawkeye, crying out in pain as she landed on his lap.

Acumen got to his feet. "Flit!"

Almost everyone in the Mess jumped up to see what was going on.

Swipe leapt up, throwing her arm out in a broad sweeping motion. The plates, cups, cutlery, and Link's table decorations all hurtled towards Flit.

"No!" Scraps pushed his own energy out to divert the trays from Flit.

Both Swipe and Scraps were too slow. Flit teleported behind Hawkeye and grasped Swipe by the collar. Then the two women disappeared. When they reappeared a nanosecond later, Flit slammed Swipe against the wall and pulled her fist back, ready for another punch. Before she could release it, her arm froze, and she let out a cry of frustration as Swipe held the strike back telekinetically.

"Get off me!" Swipe grunted. She tried to push Flit away with one hand as she gestured with the other. Two dining chairs flew towards Flit.

Flit teleported before the chairs hit her. Swipe had to dive out of the way to avoid them herself. She tumbled to the floor and rolled, only to have Flit appear over her, straddling her waist. Flit went to throw another punch, but Scraps broke out of his shock and scrambled over the table, launching himself at Flit to hold her back.

Sensing his motive, the others jumped into the fight. Hawkeye grasped Swipe's arms and held them back as Scraps tried to drag Flit back by her hips. Tweak and Sway grasped her hands. With so many people holding onto her, it would be difficult for her to teleport away. Or so Scraps hoped.

"Flit, don't hurt Swipe. Don't teleport away," Sway ordered. Flit's body stiffened and she froze at the command in his tone. Scraps hadn't seen Sway use his telecoercion before, but if Flit was unable to resist his order in her heightened emotional state, he was strong.

Flit shook with rage. "Let me at her!"

"You want me that bad, break the fucking coercion," Swipe taunted as Hawkeye pulled her to her feet.

With a primal yell, Flit spat at Swipe. The thick globule of saliva splattered against her cheek and dripped down her neck.

Flit may not have been able to hit her or teleport away, but she still got back at her. As alarmed as he was by the fight, Scraps found Flit's tenacity and creativity inspiring.

"Bitch." Swipe grunted and snatched her arm from Hawkeye's grip. She tore a nearby screen off the wall and sent it hurtling towards Flit.

Scraps thrust his hands out, stopping the expensive device from hitting Flit and the others. It shattered into a million pieces, the glass shards showering down on them like rain.

"That's enough!" Posthoc yelled as he and Acumen waded over, standing between the two seething women.

Scraps held Flit's rigid trembling body against his chest tightly, giving her just enough room to breathe. The raw pain he saw in her eyes earlier was enough to make him feel like he was the one who was punched in the face.

Sway leaned closer to Flit. "Go. Get out of here," he urged.

Flit, frozen in place by his orders, sagged as he released them.

"Don't you dare!" Posthoc barked, but free of the telecoercion, Flit teleported away.

Scraps saw her flicker at the door long enough to open it before she was gone. He went to chase her, but Acumen's hand settled on his shoulder. Scraps watched in dismay as Hawkeye ran out after her instead, not caring that Swipe tumbled back against the wall as he abandoned her.

"I should—" Scraps started, shrugging off Acumen's hand.

"I know, buddy, but Hawkeye understands what she's going through. She needs him more," Acumen whispered. Jealousy surged in Scraps' chest.

"You're better off without her. You don't need her drama," Swipe snapped.

Scraps turned back to her. "What?"

"Swipe, if you don't shut up, you'll be spending the night in the brig," Posthoc warned, stepping between Scraps and Swipe.

"That's not fair, she hit me first!" Swipe whined, dashing some blood off the corner of her lip with the back of her hand.

Posthoc crossed his arms over his broad chest. "You deserved it."

Swipe growled, outraged. She looked around, hoping someone would speak up on her behalf and tell Posthoc it wasn't her fault. The members of the Blue Team looked away. No one wanted to intervene.

"This is bullshit!"

"We're done here. Get out before I change my mind," Posthoc snapped.

Swipe looked like she might argue, but she let out an indignant huff and pushed past Posthoc as she stomped out of the Mess. Sensing that the drama was over, the people who had stopped eating to watch turned back to their meals to gossip about the events in hushed tones. The Blue Team remained on their feet, their plates and glasses upturned, the contents splattered over the table and floor before them.

With a heavy sigh, Patch leaned over and started collecting the scattered trays and bowls. As much as he wanted to go after Flit, Acumen had warned Scraps against it, and he had to trust him. Scraps joined in the clean-up effort with the others. No one in the team spoke for the longest time.

The awkward silence broke when Sway slid over to Acumen. "You were right. They hooked up. I guess I owe you," Sway whispered, smirking between Scraps and the mind-reader. Sway patted Scraps' shoulder as he stood there, shocked. Scraps was about to say something when Acumen spoke up.

"Sway, you have no tact. Just shut up and clean." Acumen shoved a tray into Sway's hands. Sway rolled his eyes, but Acumen ignored him, then guided Scraps to another table and urged him to take a seat. Scraps felt deflated and overwhelmed as he sank into the chair. This was not how his night was supposed to play out. He stared at the door, struggling to process what happened. It was a good ten minutes before someone slid a drink to him across the table. He looked up to see Link smiling at him tentatively.

"Tonight's drama aside, I'm glad you and Flit are together," Link told him as she pushed her dark curly hair behind her ear. "I haven't seen her this happy in the longest time.".

"She does not seem very happy to me. I think I have made things worse for everyone." Scraps took the glass and swirled the water around as he glowered at it.

Link sighed. "What happened tonight wasn't your fault. Those two had a history long before you got involved."

"I do not understand. Why can't they just be civil to each other?" Scraps pressed his lips together in frustration.

"People don't act sensibly when they're in pain."

"What pain?" Scraps put the glass back down on the table. "Why is it that everyone else knows what is going on and I do not?" He looked at Link, wishing she would give him something. Anything.

Link reached out and held his hands. "It isn't up to me to tell you that. Why don't you head back to the Residence and wait for Flit outside her room? She'll need someone who cares for her when she gets back."

Scraps wasn't happy with that answer. Between Flit's insistence they keep their relationship quiet, the way she ran away last night, and the fact she punched someone only minutes ago, Scraps was confused. He thought he understood Flit, but none of those things matched up with the confident, caring woman he knew.

With a heavy sigh, Scraps got to his feet. If Link said Flit would need him, he would be there for her. Even if he didn't know why. The reason didn't matter, really. He hated seeing Flit so sad and angry. He would do anything within his power to help.

41

FLIT

FLIT BOLTED.

She kept moving until her body and emotions gave way and she collapsed on the hard floor in a torrent of tears. Swipe's accusation replayed in her mind, exacerbated by the guilt that had risen inside of her over the past few weeks.

The worst part was that Swipe was right.

Rook was dead because of Flit's selfishness.

Over and over, those thoughts assaulted her. The tears were a downpour. Each breath she took felt like daggers were being driven into her lungs. Her heart ached so much she swore it would burst.

She loved Rook with every fibre of her being. She always would. Flit would do anything to take back what happened to him. To keep him safe. Yet there she was, falling for Scraps, letting him fill the hole in her heart that belonged to Rook. It was so selfish and gluttonous to think she deserved another chance. She shouldn't be able to live a full, happy life without him. That wasn't their plan. They were supposed to live that life together.

"Flit?"

A familiar voice broke through the hurricane of fear and despair in her head, but she pushed it away.

"Flit!"

A pair of warm, strong arms wrapped around her and held her tight: a physical anchor in an emotional storm.

"Go away." Flit struggled, trying to pull herself away.

But she didn't have the energy.

"No, I will not go away. I don't care what Swipe said, I will not let you go back to that dark place. Not now, not ever."

Flit opened her eyes. Even in the dim reserve lighting of the abandoned training room, she could see the stubbornness in Hawkeye's steady gaze. She gritted her teeth, perhaps hating him in that moment more than she ever had. "You don't u-understand! I d-deserve this! I'm so f-fucking stupid for thinking I had a r-right to be happy," Flit spluttered and shook her head as she tried to squirm out of Hawkeye's arms again.

"It was not your fault, Flit. Do you hear me?" Hawkeye growled, taking her chin in his hand and forcing her to look at him. "None of it was your fault."

Flit tore her face from his grasp.

"You've spent so long just surviving day to day. You have denied yourself so much while you mourned. You can't do that anymore. Rook wouldn't have wanted it; he would have wanted you to enjoy your life. All he ever wanted was for you to be happy."

Flit's hands balled into fists and she glared at Hawkeye. "You don't know what he wanted!"

"Yes I do." Hawkeye slammed his hand down on the concrete in frustration. "I know because he loved you, just like I do."

Flit winced as she looked up at him, her red-rimmed eyes wide with shock.

"I know because I love you so fucking much that I know when to let you go. Rook would have too." Hawkeye paused, taking a slow, shuddering breath. "If that is because of Scraps, then so be it."

Flit's heart hammered against her ribcage so hard it took her breath away. She shook her head, hating that she had hurt so many people. "Hawkeye—"

Hawkeye held up a hand to silence her. "Don't, Flit. Don't apologise. Don't try to make me feel better. I love you, but I never want you to lie to yourself. I... I just want to see you live a full life. If I'm not in it, then that's something I have to come to terms with."

"Hawkeye, you'll always be part of my life." Flit shook her head vehemently. That was the way it had always been. They had grown up together, they had been inseparable their entire lives. When Hawkeye's parents had died of a nasty virus that made its way into the Underground, Flit was there for him. She had picked him up when he stumbled, and in return, he had been her rock when Rook was murdered. Flit would be nothing without Hawkeye.

Hawkeye sighed and nodded, pulling her into his arms and resting his chin on the top of her head. Flit sagged into his familiar embrace. The tears streamed down her face, and Hawkeye held her through it all.

A COUPLE OF HOURS LATER, Flit and Hawkeye made their way back to the Residence. Flit was physically and emotionally exhausted. Her body hurt in places where Swipe had got in a hit. She would have more than a few bruises in the morning. Hawkeye sensed her weaknesses, and without asking, he slipped an arm around her waist to help her stay steady as she walked on her shaking legs.

When Flit and Hawkeye exited the elevator and turned the first corner, Flit stumbled to a stop. "Scraps!" Flit's heart melted at the sight of him crumpled on the floor, sleeping against her door.

Poor Scraps woke with a start. His eyes snapped open and he looked around, disoriented. He scrambled to his feet and brushed the wrinkles out of his t-shirt and cargo pants. His red eyes flicked between Flit and Hawkeye. There was a wariness in them, but it faltered when he saw the state she was in. Her hair was messed up, and her eyes were red, and her face was puffy and covered in splotches of dried tears.

"Flit." Scraps stepped closer, but seemed to think better of it when Hawkeye straightened up beside her.

Hawkeye took his arm from around Flit's waist and stepped back, nodding at Scraps. "You two have a lot of talking to do," Hawkeye said, giving Flit a serious look. He turned to Scraps and added, "Please take care of her."

Flit's shoulders sagged with relief at Hawkeye's words. Scraps nodded with a solemn expression and reached out to take Flit's hand. Before Flit took it, Hawkeye pressed a gentle kiss on the top of her head and turned to walk away.

"Hawkeye?" Flit called, stopping him in his tracks. He turned, looking back at her over his shoulder. "Thank you."

Hawkeye nodded. "Any time, Flit. If you ever need me, you know where to find me."

And with that, Hawkeye walked away.

Flit bit her lip as she turned back to Scraps, relief radiating through her worn body as he wrapped a reassuring arm around her shoulders. She turned and looked up at him, biting her lip as she tried to figure out what to say to him.

"I just... I just wanted to make sure you were ok," Scraps explained, still looking dazed from what had to have been an uncomfortable nap against her door.

Flit was overwhelmed by how lucky she was to have him. "That is sweet, thank you." Flit squeezed his hand. Scraps smiled and threaded their fingers together. Flit looked at the door to her bedroom, and then at him. "I don't know what time it is, but it must be late. Are you... are you too tired to talk?"

"With you? Never," Scraps said quickly.

"Good, because I haven't been fair to you. There is something you need to know about me if things are going to work between us," Flit explained, her voice wavering as she looked up into his trusting eyes.

"If you are too exhausted right now, I can wait," Scraps offered, smoothing some of her messy hair down against her head.

Flit leaned into his touch and sighed. "No. I've held on to this for too long."

Flit reached past him, pressing her palm against the scanner outside her room. The door slid open and they both stepped inside. Scraps' breath caught in his throat as he took in the state of her room. Her living space had gone from 'organised chaos' to 'complete and utter pandemonium'. Everything in her wardrobe had been torn out and flung around as she searched for what she buried in her most recent clean up.

"We can sit on the bed." Flit led the way, stepping expertly on select patches of clear floor. He followed each step to avoid treading on her belongings. When they got to the bed Flit stopped. There was a metal chest nestled in her blankets that was a metre long and half a metre wide. When Scraps noticed it, he gestured towards it, and lifted it off her rumpled bed covers.

Flit covered her hand with his and shook her head. "No, leave it." He lowered it down and she gestured for him to sit on the pillow end of the bed while she settled onto the foot. She kicked off her shoes and bent her legs, wrapping her arms around them and hugging them to her chest. "You can open it." Flit jutted her chin towards the box, tears shining in her eyes. The items in there would help tell her story better than her words alone ever could.

42

SCRAPS

SCRAPS WATCHED Flit as she curled up on her bed, her eyes filling with fresh tears. He ran his hands over the cold metal of the box and frowned at the idea of opening something that would spill those welling tears. It was a standard archive-style box used by Supply for storing important records and information. The smooth, dark grey metal was scuffed with wear, showing it had been opened and closed many times. He didn't ask Flit what was in it. If she wanted him to open it, he would see for himself.

With a gentle tug, Scraps lifted the lid off the box. Inside, a folded shirt cushioned a datapad, several handwritten letters, and digital photo album. Scraps furrowed his brow as he picked up the threadbare fabric. It was the top half of the standard-issue long-sleeved fatigues handed out by the Underground. Why would she have that in a box? Scraps lifted it from its resting place, the neat folds unravelling to reveal its significance.

"Oh."

Stitched just above the front left chest pocket was a single name.

Rook.

Scraps had heard Rook's name a handful of times since he joined the Underground, always connected with Flit's. The argument between Flit and Swipe earlier confirmed his suspicion that Flit and Rook had been on intimate terms. Scraps shifted uncomfortably as he held the shirt of Flit's ex-lover. Scraps folded it neatly, making sure the crease lines matched up, and set it on the bed beside the box, looking at Flit.

Flit nodded to the digital photo album in the box. "Keep going."

When Scraps picked up the album, the screen flared to life and he was greeted by a striking male face. The man's jawline was so finely chiselled it looked like it was carved of stone. His dark brown hair was cropped close on the sides, but the top was longer and artfully ruffled. His tanned olive skin complemented dark brown eyes that flashed with mischief, even in the still frame of the photograph.

Scraps looked at Flit. "This is Rook?"

"Yes." Flit's eyes dipped down to the photo, her neutral expression strained with emotion as she took it in.

Scraps nodded and swiped to the next photo. It was a younger version of Flit. If he had to guess it was at least four or five years ago. She and Rook had their arms draped around each other and were reclining on the sands of a real beach on the surface. The next photos showed them kissing by the water at Sapphire beach. Another was a candid shot of them holding hands as they ate dinner in the Mess. There was a group shot of Flit and Swipe and the rest of the Blue Team, all looking much happier and much younger.

Faster and faster, Scraps swiped through the photos and videos that were stored on the device. There were so many. So much evidence of an entire life Flit lived before she met him. Indisputable proof that she had loved before him. Scraps stopped as Flit reached out to take his hands. He hadn't realised how fast he' was swiping until she did that, or how much his fingers were shaking. He looked up at her, heart hammering in his chest as the images of Flit hugging and kissing Rook flashed through his mind.

"I'm not showing you this to hurt you," Flit whispered, taking his hand from the album and pressing a soft kiss against his knuckles. "I just need you to know why I've been holding back."

Flit gently took the album from him and settled it, face down, on top Rook's shirt. But it didn't help. The smiling faces from those photographs were emblazoned on his mind.

Taking both of Scraps' hands in hers, Flit asked, "Can I tell you about Rook and I?"

When Flit spoke of her and Rook like they were an item, an icy fist plunged into Scraps' chest and grasped his heart. Was it normal to feel jealous of someone who was no longer around?

Still, Scraps took a deep breath and nodded. He needed to know what sort of situation he was dealing with. He also needed to know how he could help Flit through whatever she was dealing with.

Flit pushed the box against the wall and scooted forward. "This tunnel network hasn't always been the only base held by the Underground. When the resistance first started, there were half a dozen outposts in other cities. The Government slowly rooted us out, one by one, until about seven years ago there was just us and a settlement in a forest outside of Longbeach. Somehow, the Government found out about them too. They recalled everyone there to this base. Rook, Swipe, and their families were part of that group."

It surprised Scraps to hear there were more resistance bases in the past. If the Underground, as he knew it, was the last remnants of resistance, how long would it be before the Government found them too, if they hadn't already? Is that what the tunnel explosions were, warning shots from the Government?

"Even though having our last outpost disbanded was worrying, it meant that we got a whole heap of new people. That doesn't happen often, but everyone settled in well." Flit took a deep breath and hugged her knees closer as she continued. "Rook and his family were like mine; his parents were the only agents that escaped from Longbeach without their Citizen aliases being compromised. He lived with them in the Hub during the week and came down to the Underground on evenings and weekends like I did. He understood what it was like to live that double life."

Flit reached out and settled a hand onto Rook's old shirt. She brushed her thumb over it with such tenderness that Scraps was captivated.

"Rook was three years older than me. He was part of the Security team in Longbeach and slipped into the same role here well. He had a real knack for navigating the tunnels and everyone seemed to love him. He was such a joker; it was hard to stay angry at him for long. Even when he deserved it.

"Rook trained me in Security. All my early patrols were with him. As you know, all the time you spend alone with your patrol buddy means that you get to know each other pretty well."

At that point, Flit let go of the shirt and reached across the box, taking Scraps' hand again. She gave him a weak smile. Scraps was grateful for it. Even though he could hear the pain in her voice, she still reached out to comfort him.

"So that is how you two got together? On patrol?" Scraps asked, wondering about the parallels in their relationship.

"Yes, but after a year he got reassigned to Control. That's when Hawkeye and I became patrol partners. Not that I complained, Hawk has always been my best friend. I was just worried Rook would forget about me. But he didn't. Instead of hanging out with his new Control buddies, he spent his spare time with the Blue Team. He said he missed me. When he finally asked me out, I was so excited."

Scraps caught how the air seemed hitched in Flit's throat with every breath she took. She blinked rapidly as she looked away from him. He held her hands a little tighter as he thought about the time frame that Flit mentioned.

"The people from Longbeach moved over seven years ago and Rook asked you out after he transitioned into Control a year after that. That means you were together for around five years?" Scraps asked. It seemed like a long time for someone Flit's age.

"Five years and one day," Flit said, looking back at the album. She gently extracted her hand from Scraps' and reached into the box, fingers shaking. She tapped the screen and swiped until she found the photo of her and Rook hugging on a beach.

"Our double lives meant we got to live our relationship down here and in the Hub. While we were up there, I could almost pretend that things were normal. We were like any other couple, living day to day... Just with a rather dangerous secret." Flit gave a little shrug and chuckled to herself, shaking her head. She turned the screen off and looked back at Scraps. "But it was our double life that got him killed."

Scraps knew it had to be coming, but the words still felt like a punch to his guts. Even though he never met Rook, the thought of losing anyone from the Underground to the Government was reprehensible.

Flit shifted the photo album to the side of the box and pulled out a tiny purple velvet pouch. She turned it over in her hands, fingertips fretting over it as she continued. "Rook and I were inseparable. I loved him more than I ever thought possible, and he loved me... We saw our futures in each other. So, on our fifth anniversary, Rook took me to the training room where he first kissed me, and he asked me to marry him."

Flit reached into the pouch and pulled out a ring. It was a simple gold band with a modest diamond that sparkled as it refracted every possible ray of light. Flit's fingers shook as she settled it onto his palm. If Rook asked Flit to marry him, Scraps could only assume that they were very much committed to each other. When he looked back at Flit, tears were streaming down her cheeks. He wanted to lean forward and kiss away her pain, but he didn't dare interrupt. Instead, he took a deep breath and handed the delicate ring back to Flit, not wanting to drop it or damage it by accident. He wasn't used to handling such precious things.

Flit sniffed and dashed away her tears with the back of her hand. "I said yes, of course. I don't even think he finished the question before I agreed." Flit's trembling lips curved into a smile as she tucked the ring away. "But getting married in the Underground wasn't enough for me. I wanted it to be official in the Hub too. Rook didn't care either way, but I insisted. The Underground falsifies records all the time, and they had done it before for other agents so they could get married. So, I told Rook to head back up to his apartment and tell his parents. I hung around to speak to Digit in Intelligence, so she could fudge the forms."

Flit rubbed her eyes with the heels of her hands and sighed. She kept her head in her hands as she continued speaking, her shoulders shaking. "I went home that night and sent him a message, letting him know I sorted it out. He didn't reply. The next day, after work, I went to his apartment to check on him and get the Government forms started. But when I arrived..."

Flit stopped, pain rattling every breath she took. Without thinking, Scraps put Rook's shirt back in the box, set the lid on it, and floated it over to a clear patch on her desk. He shuffled forward and wrapped his arms around Flit, pulling her onto his lap as he held her close.

"It was an Active Investigation Scene. There were government seals all over the hole in the wall where they had blasted the doors away. Inside... I-inside, I found Rook's father on the floor in the hallway. They hadn't even taken his body. They just left him there. The entire apartment was riddled with bullet holes. There was a trail of blood leading into Rook's room... but he wasn't there. I searched the entire apartment, but neither h-he nor his mother were there."

"They took them..." Scraps breathed.

Before he had been taken in by the Underground, Scraps had just been promoted to a unit tasked with apprehending lawbreakers and dragging escapees back to the 'safety' of the Hub. If he was given the order back then, he would have dragged Rook and his family into the Government's clutches without a second thought.

Flit looked up at him. He could tell from how her expression softened that she knew what he was thinking. She reached out, her fingers brushing his cheek. There was no resentment behind her eyes. No hate. No burning need for revenge. Just an overwhelming sense of loss and pain that made him want to fall into her warm gaze.

"Yes, they took Rook and his mother, Fortune. About a month later Digit called me into Control. She found a report on the Government's database. CAA-7XX."

Scraps was stunned into silence. It had been a while since he had heard a designation; it was something from his old life. He pursed his lips together as he decoded it. CAA meant Rook was the highest level of telecoercionist. Scraps heard rumours of Derivates that powerful, but to have confirmation that they existed in the Underground was a surprise. From the number, he knew that Rook was only a year older than himself, but the XX was something he had never come across before. Knowing what he knew now, he figured that it had to be an acknowledgement that Rook was not born as part of the regular Derivate breeding crop. It was the only explanation that made sense.

"Did Digit find more information than just his designation?" Scraps asked. Perhaps if they could figure out where Rook was or what they had done with him, they could get him back.

"Yes. They noted that he was male. Twenty-six years old. One-hundred and eighty-five centimetres. Dark brown hair and eyes. Guilty of espionage." Flit sagged against his chest. "Even with a control chip inserted, he tried to escape several times. Destroyed a shit-load of Government property in his attempts, too." Pride tickled the edges of Flit's words at that revelation. It sounded like the kind of behaviour Flit would endorse. "Three weeks into his captivity, they determined he was too much of a risk. Unrecoverable, apparently."

Scraps winced. He had seen the Government assign that label to the select few Registereds who broke their rules. He knew what came next. "They terminated him."

The words sank between them like a lead balloon. Flit nodded. Her entire body shook in his arms as she sobbed.

Scraps didn't know what to say or do to ease her pain. "Flit, I—ah, I'm... I..."

"It doesn't matter," Flit said miserably, burrowing her face into the crook of his neck. "Nothing that anyone says can ch-change it." Her voice broke on a fresh wave of tears.

Flit was right. There was nothing he could do to fix it. No matter how much it hurt to realise that he was also responsible for destroying other people's lives in this way, he couldn't change the past. It made Scraps wonder what would have happened to KD-035 if he had retrieved her before the rats did.

Scraps was so lost in his own musings he was startled when Flit pulled away from him. He looked down at her, her face shining with the evidence of her loss.

Flit reached up and cupped his face in her trembling hands. "You need to understand how dangerous life is for us. How potentially heart-breaking relationships are. One moment you're planning your life with the person you love, and the next you're attending their funeral," Flit whispered. "I like you, Scraps. I have for a while.

I didn't ask for more time because I wasn't sure if I wanted to be with you. I know I do. I just don't think I could survive losing someone else."

Scraps looked down into her eyes, unable to fathom the pain she was feeling. "Do you still feel that way?" Scraps asked. If being with him would break her like that, he did not want any part of it. He wanted Flit, and not being with her would be hard, but he could not bear to cause her any pain.

Flit shook her head, thinking back to what Hawkeye said earlier. "No. I'm tired of holding back. I've been trying so hard to avoid getting hurt that I forgot to live."

Flit's words were firm and full of determination. She sounded less like a mourning lover and more like the woman Scraps knew.

Sitting up straighter, Flit took a deep breath before she spoke. "No matter how I look at it, I'm falling for you. I don't want to deny it anymore."

Heart full to bursting, Scraps leaned in and pressed a soft kiss against Flit's forehead as he held her close. He had barely learned to crawl when it came to relationships, but he knew he wanted to be in one with her. Scraps didn't care about her past, or that part of her heart may always belong to a ghost. The present was the only thing that mattered, and he wanted to spend it with Flit.

"Good, because I have never wanted anything in my life as much as I want to be with you," Scraps whispered against her hair.

Flit looked up at Scraps, her eyes wide and full of appreciation. She slid her arms around the back of his neck and pulled him down for a soft, slow kiss. Scraps melted into her.

When Flit pulled out of the kiss she whispered, "I'm sorry I didn't tell you any of this earlier."

Scraps shook his head. "You have nothing to apologise for." He kissed her cheek and she sighed, resting her forehead against his shoulder.

Scraps wasn't sure how long he held Flit for. All he knew was that her breathing became slower and quieter against his neck. Her shaking eased. Every part of her began to relax into him. Eventually, she let out a soft yawn.

"I'm sorry for keeping you up. It's so late. We should get some sleep." Flit's voice was raw and sleepy.

Scraps was so exhilarated by her trust and affection that he could have held her like that all night without getting tired. But he hadn't gone through the same emotional rollercoaster she had. He took a deep breath of her sweet-smelling hair before he made to move away from her. "You are right. I should let you sleep. I will see you tomorrow at breakfast," Scraps promised as he gave her one last hug.

When Scraps went to pull away from Flit, she grabbed his arms and held him close. "Stay?"

There was no suggestion in Flit's tone. No cheeky wink following her words. Scraps looked down at her bed. They had already established it was big enough for two, even if it was a tight squeeze. It just meant he would need to sleep close to her. Perhaps she would even let him hold her all night.

"Of course." Scraps stretched his legs out and used telekinesis to untie his laces and ease off his boots, thankful for the fine control he had been practising.

When his shoes were off, Scraps sat back and watched as Flit settled under the covers of her bed, holding them open for him to slide in. He laid down on his side, his head on her pillow, as he reached out and trailed his fingers over her cheek is soft fluttering strokes.

"What are you thinking?" Flit whispered, her hazel eyes catching his.

Scraps was so caught in her gaze that he couldn't have looked away, even if he wanted to. It felt good to be laying there with her, her sweet breath mingling with his between them. "I am thinking about how grateful I am that you were the one to find me. I did not want to be here at first, but you have shown me a life I never knew I could have. No matter what happens, I will always be grateful for that, Flit."

Flits face softened and she leaned in, kissing him softly. "Goodnight, Scraps," she murmured as she tucked herself against him.

Flit's breathing slowed and her body relaxed more and more into Scraps as she drifted off to sleep. Seeing her relaxing after such a tumultuous night filled him with relief. At least if she slept, her mind would get some rest. Allowing him to hold her as she slept reminded Scraps of just how much Flit trusted him. Asleep or awake, she laid her vulnerabilities down in front of him. That level of trust was the most intimate honour Scraps could imagine. Even more so than the times they had come close to intercourse. Scraps had never slept with another person before. But as he held Flit's body against his, he decided he never wanted to sleep alone again.

43

FLIT

FLIT'S ALARM blared through the room, rousing her from the best sleep she had in weeks. Only, she hadn't had enough of it yet.

She buried her face in her pillow. "Off!"

The piercing wail continued, undiminished.

Flit groaned. "Off. I said off!"

A warm body shifted beside her, and her eyes snapped open. The emotional turmoil of the previous night flooded back, but it was muted. Somehow, sharing it with Scraps halved the load. He proved he was there for her, in the tough times and the fun ones. He didn't resent her for keeping her past from him, and he wanted to continue with their blossoming relationship.

"Do you always yell at your alarm?" Scraps' dry and husky comment was accompanied by a sleepy laugh.

Flit sighed. "Only when it doesn't listen to me the first time." She pulled her face out of her pillow and turned her head to look at him. She was lying on her stomach, her left side lined up along Scraps' front. He had one arm under the pillow, and the other draped around her hips.

He yawned. "Loud noises confound the voice recognition software."

"I know, but it's satisfying."

Scraps chuckled. He raised his head and peered over Flit's shoulder to check the time on the panel near her door. His face fell, and he held her a little tighter. "I should get up. I've got training with Sway."

Flit waved a dismissive hand in the air. "I'll send him a message and cancel it. You've got your orienteering test in a few days, no one will argue with that."

"So, can we study instead?" Scraps sat up, sliding his arm from under the pillow so he didn't jostle her.

Rolling her eyes, Flit said, "No, we'll sleep some more." She wrapped her arms around him and pulled him back down onto the mattress. To make sure he didn't run away, she slung a leg over his. As she did, the top of her thigh brushed against something that made her eyes widen. "Oh..." Flit looked up at him, biting her lip.

Scraps shifted his hips away from her and blushed. "Ah, sorry. It happens in the mornings," he blurted, looking away from her. His entire body tensed.

Flit put a hand on his chest and propped herself up to look at him. "Sorry? There is no need to apologise. I think it's a particularly fun way to wake up." The heat of his skin radiated through his t-shirt and warmed her palm.

"That is because you are not the one waking up like this. It is a nuisance," Scraps grumbled.

Flit furrowed her brows. "A nuisance? I don't know if I've heard it called that before."

Scraps shrugged. "It takes a long time to go away in the mornings."

"You wait for it to go down?" Flit propped herself up on one elbow so she could look at him.

"Well, I distract myself by reciting policy and procedure." Scraps blushed as he looked away, his pressing his lips together as Flit giggled.

"Bloody hell... No wonder you like studying so much," Flit sighed. Scraps narrowed his eyes at her. Flit leaned over and kissed his scowl away. "Sorry, I shouldn't tease you. Why don't you let me show you a more efficient way to deal with it?"

Scraps looked down at the lump in the sheets and then back at her. "Please do."

Flit smiled and pressed the full length of her body against his.

She put her leg back over his thighs and used her right hand to unbuckle his pants and ease them down. When she brushed her fingers over him, Scraps groaned with delight.

It was the permission Flit needed to make good on her promise to educate him on the finer details of intimacy. She taught him how good it could feel to indulge his natural instincts. Scraps had so much guilt and shame around the concept because of the way the Government raised him. At first, he held his doubts, but he placed his trust in her as surely as she placed hers in him. Those doubts soon turned to trembling warnings that it felt too good. He was getting too close.

Flit brushed her lips over his cheek and nipped at his earlobe, murmuring, "Stop thinking, just feel."

So he did. When he allowed himself the freedom, he stopped warning and started begging; please keep going, never stop. Flit leaned in and kissed that warm, musky skin at the crook of his neck as she granted him the powerful release he had been craving.

When it was over, Scraps collapsed back into the bed and looked at Flit with such awe and satisfaction in his eyes. She smiled back at him, her heart aching with affection. She reached out, caressing his cheek as he yawned and struggled to keep his eyes open.

"You lay back and relax. I'm gonna have a shower and then I'll come back to bed, ok?" she whispered with a gentle kiss.

"I'll shower after you," Scraps muttered, words slurred.

Flit smirked. From the way his body sagged against the bed, she knew he'd be fast asleep by the time she got out of the shower. She didn't blame him.

FLIT WOKE for the second time that day to the sound of banging on her door. She looked at Scraps sleeping peacefully beside her as she slipped out of bed. Pulling on a fluffy purple dressing gown, she tied it tight around her waist before teleporting to the door. She opened it to see Acumen standing there.

Acumen's expression went from a smile of greeting to wide-eyed understanding in a heartbeat. "Oh." Even though Flit had been sure to stand in the doorway so he couldn't see past her, he gauged the situation immediately.

Putting a finger to her lips, Flit stepped outside her room and let the door slide shut behind her. "Good morning."

"Apparently so." Acumen nodded towards her room. "Although it's more like mid-afternoon than morning."

Flit rolled her eyes. "What do you want?"

"I just wanted to check in and see how you were doing after last night."

Flit frowned, wrapping her arms around herself as she looked past Acumen. The previous night was painful to even think about. "I will not apologise for punching her, no matter the consequences. I'd do it all over again, given the chance." She looked up into his bright blue eyes, refusing to back down.

Acumen put a reassuring hand on her shoulder. "I don't think you should apologise either. I'm obliged to tell you not to do it again —I know, I know!" Acumen raised his hands defensively as Flit thought about telling him where to shove his request. "There's no point, so I won't. I just hope she learned her lesson, because she's got one hell of a bruise."

Flit grinned, a smug sense of satisfaction rolling through her. Even though she was in no rush to see Swipe, she wondered whether bruise-blue would suit her complexion.

Acumen sighed. "And how is Scraps? Did you tell him about Rook?"

"Yes." Flit's throat constricted as those emotions crept back.

"I take it from the pleased sleepy daze radiating from him, he was okay with it?"

"Yes, he was... And now that he knows, I've got nothing left to hide from him. And I'm done hiding from myself, too."

Acumen smiled and squeezed her shoulder. "Then I'm happy for you."

Flit nodded and looked back over her shoulder at her closed door. She was just about to thank him for checking on her when he spoke again.

"I can take a hint, you know," Acumen chuckled, using humour to deflect the growing emotional nature of the conversation. "Before I go, there's one more thing. I don't want you to say your answers out loud though, ok? Just think them."

Flit pursed her lips, curious about what he could ask that would need to be kept silent. Nevertheless, she nodded.

Acumen took that as permission to proceed. "I've heard through the gossip-chain that you've brought Scraps' orienteering test forward."

Mmhhhmm? Flit cocked an eyebrow at him. That was common knowledge.

"Posthoc showed me your planned starting point. Why did you pick that tunnel?"

I spun the three-dimensional network map around on my screen and picked a point at random.

Acumen rolled his eyes. "You can't lie for shit when you speak. You're even worse when you're thinking them."

Flit jutted her chin out and crossed her arms over her chest. *Maybe I picked it for a reason. Is that going to be a problem?*

Shaking his head, Acumen said, "You shouldn't take that route."

Why the hell not?

"It's too dangerous to be close to the surface right now. If you don't change it for yourself, change it for Scraps. You don't know what it will do to him, being that close to the world he left behind."

Flit gritted her teeth at the insinuation. *You don't know Scraps like I do. He's ready for it.*

"Flit, please." Acumen rolled his eyes. "I'm a bloody mind-reader. I can't go into details, but this is important. Change the starting point. You may not care what anyone else thinks, but Scraps is a good guy. I don't want to risk losing him to the Government."

Acumen didn't wait for a response. He turned and walked away. Flit sighed and slumped against the door, rubbing her eyes. She was doing the right thing. She chose the starting point because it was in the sector right beside the one with the reclassified tunnels they discovered. No-one in the Blue Team had been assigned a patrol in that area since Tally caught her and Scraps in the storage tunnels. It was beyond suspicious. They uncovered something important; she knew it. Now they needed to follow up. Everyone warning her away just made it more important. She refused to believe that Scraps wouldn't be able to handle being that close to the surface, that he wasn't ready. They just didn't know him like she did.

44

SCRAPS

THE NEXT FEW days passed in a blur of training and study for Scraps. News of his and Flit's relationship spread through the Underground like wildfire, as did some very embellished recounts of Flit's fight with Swipe. Swipe had done her best to avoid them, but they spotted her at meals sporting colourful bruises and a look of pure annoyance. She had taken to sitting with the remaining members of the Green Team and would talk to Heft or Oculus any time any of the Blue Team members looked her way. Given Scraps' run-ins with Heft, he tried not to take the slight personally. Flit was his priority: as long as she was safe and happy, he could ignore Swipe's unfriendly behaviour.

Scraps' orienteering test arrived faster than he thought possible. He stood in the armoury wearing his grey fatigues and running his hands over his utility belt to double-check that he had everything. For once, Flit didn't throw in any words of caution or encourage him to take extra grenades. She stood, leaning against the door frame with her arms crossed over her chest, her lips pursed together.

"I am ready to go," Scraps announced, confident he had everything he needed.

Flit tugged her black backpack a little higher on her shoulders and gave him a firm nod. "Good." She teleported to the spot just in front of him. He had seen the momentary flick of her eyes as she assessed the space, so he wasn't surprised when she landed so close. "I went to the medbay and got some anti-nausea medication for you. We'll be teleporting out there. I can take it slow, but it'll still knock you around a bit." Flit reached into one of the many pockets of her grey fatigues and pulled out a small foil packet of pills.

Scraps reached out, closing Flit's fingers over the packet and pushing her fist back towards her. "I will be fine. Having your arms around me negates the side-effects of teleporting." Whether it was all the extra practice, or the distraction of having Flit's body so close, Scraps found that teleporting didn't bother him as much in training as it used to.

Flit smiled as she rested her hands on his chest. "If anyone else said that, I would laugh. But not you, I can tell you mean it." Flit grasped the collar of his jacket and pulled him down for a gentle kiss.

For a blissful moment, Scraps wished that they didn't have the orienteering test, that they could just head back to her room and spend the whole day together.

Flit tucked the foil packet into the top pocket of his vest. "I'll just leave them here in case you decide you need 'em. We'll be doing long range teleporting, so it will feel different. I'd rather you take these than vomit on my shoes. Or my face." She winked at him.

It never ceased to amaze Scraps that Flit could find a joke in every situation. His stomach churned as he thought about the test ahead. He had studied hard for it, but the labyrinthine tunnel networks were impossible to know by heart. He had never felt nervous about any of the tests he did for the Government. It could have been the natural emotional response previously inhibited by his chip, but the stakes felt higher in the Underground.

"Scraps?" Flit's voice broke through Scraps' musings and she gently cupped his cheek. "You've got this."

Scraps just nodded and readjusted his pack on his shoulders. He took a deep breath. "You are right. Everything will be fine. Let's go."

Scraps and Flit left the armoury and made for the tunnels that led to the northern exits. Flit caught Scraps by surprise when she slipped her hand into his, but he didn't pull away. After watching so many other couples in the Underground be open about their affection, it was nice that Flit wanted to do the same.

When they reached the edge of the habitable tunnels, Flit pulled her hand from Scraps'. She ferreted around in her pocket to retrieve a visor, then gestured for him to lean down. He did, and she set the visor over his eyes and pressed a sensor on the side. His world went black. She wrapped her warm arms around his waist and lined the front of her body up against his. Scraps took a deep breath; she was touching him because of the teleporting, but it was hard not to think of her sexually when she was so close to him.

"Sorry 'bout the visor. I need to begin the blackout so that you can't see where we are. Let me know if you need a break—and don't forget to breathe, ok?" Flit reminded him.

Scraps nodded. Flit slid one hand behind his neck and the other onto his lower back and she teleported them away.

IT WAS A LONG TRIP. Scraps wasn't sure if all the teleports were necessary, or if Flit was required to add extras to confuse his senses, but by the time they stopped, his head was spinning and his stomach churned. He kept both of his hands on the smooth curves of her waist as she reached up and took the visor off him.

"Have we reached the starting point?" Scraps asked, peeling his eyes open and allowing them to adjust to the flickering reserve lighting in the tunnels.

"Yes." Flit watched him carefully. She kept her arms around him to steady him; Scraps was grateful for that. "You ok?"

He swallowed down a wave of nausea as his brain and body struggled to comprehend the fact they had stopped moving. "Yes, I just need a moment to regain my bearings... and my balance."

"Well, you did it without the meds. I'm impressed." Flit rubbed her hands up and down his back.

The point of contact helped Scraps focus and push away the lingering threat of bringing up his breakfast. "That is my new mission in life, to impress you," he told her with a smirk, even if he did regret not taking the pill.

Flit cocked an eyebrow at him. "Scraps was that... was that a joke?"

Scraps shrugged noncommittally. Flit laughed. The vibrant sound bounced around and chased away some of the dreariness in the dank concrete tunnels. Scraps liked how Flit could bring colour and life to any space just with a laugh or smile.

"You're learning, Scraps." Flit patted his shoulder before she stepped back. She straightened out her jacket and hitched her backpack up a little higher on her shoulders. Her face was more flushed than usual, and beads of sweat dotted her hairline. It was rare that she got this flustered, even in training. The trip must have taken quite a bit out of her.

"I am. But what I need to figure out is how to get back to the base." Scraps looked around with a wry smile as he tried to pick out the hidden details and markers in the tunnel, ready to get started.

"Not yet, you need to get some energy back in you after all the teleporting." Flit stepped back. She shrugged her pack off her shoulders and sank onto the ground in a cross-legged position. She patted the ground beside her.

Scraps frowned. "We should get started. I do not want to waste time."

"We'll waste more time if you pass out because you're were hungry and dehydrated. Sit."

Flit had a point.

Scraps took his pack off and sank to the floor too, finding it more difficult to fold his significantly longer legs under him with the same graceful ease that Flit did hers. He rifled through his pack and pulled out some spare clothes and his canteen before finding the rations he packed.

The pair ate in silence. For once, Flit didn't fill the space with chatter. Scraps wouldn't have noticed if she did. He was too busy looking around and trying to figure out where they were. He discovered something new about the tunnels with every bite of his dry rations. Up in the corner, along the edge of the lighting track was a symbol; a triangle with an uppercase F inside it and one line underneath it. The tip of the triangle was tilted diagonally to the upper right, meaning they were in a north-easterly running tunnel. The letter indicated that they were in sector F, and the line highlighted that they were all the way up in the surface-level tunnels.

Down lower, Scraps saw a grate in the floor with the small indentation patrollers used to register a checkpoint. He did all the calculations in his head and realised just how close they were to the surface exit tunnels. "I haven't been this close to the surface since that day you found me."

Flit looked up from the dry roll she was munching on and a wide smile spread on her face. "You already know where we are?" She asked, sitting straighter as she set her roll aside and watched him, hazel eyes sparkling with eagerness.

"Surface level, sector F, a north-easterly tunnel. The checkpoint is down there—" he pointed to the grate. "Once I see the Underground symbol, I'll get a better idea of which tunnel we're in." When he took another breath, he realised that the markings weren't the only sign. The air smelled fresher here; less stale, with a taste of more movement.

Flit beamed at him. "I told you you'd be fine," she said with a wink and a decisive bite of her roll.

"DO ORIENTEERING tests always begin in a surface-level tunnel?" Scraps asked as they walked along, constantly scanning for the signs of a manhole that they could use to get down to the level beneath them. They walked for almost two hours, and thanks to the markers he found and the direction of the arrows in the checkpoints, he had a reasonable idea of where they were.

"Not always. Sometimes they start in the natural systems, like deep enough that you need headlamps."

Scraps supposed it wouldn't make sense for everyone to start in the same place, given how people in the Underground gossiped. He had always appreciated the predictability of the Government's standardised testing, but he understood why the Underground used different methods.

"Who picks the route? Was it all you, or did you need to have it approved?" In the flurry of study, he hadn't asked Flit for much information about her side of the process.

"There are some guidelines. I figured out a route using those. It was approved easily enough. For once, I stuck to the rules." She winked at him.

"I am glad you picked this region. It is good to get a whiff of fresh air again." Scraps pointed to the ceiling as they walked under a sewer grate that had shafts of warm yellow sunlight beaming through the rusted metal bars. Just as they had passed under it a breeze passed by and whistled down the tunnel, caressing their sweating faces with refreshing coolness.

"Me too. I—"

"Oh." Scraps stopped, pointing to a manhole cover a few metres further down the tunnel. He jogged over to it and used telekinesis to lift it clear. He got down onto his stomach and leaned over the edge, peering down into the ladder-well. Flit kept quiet and waited while he listened for any signs of creatures or people in the tunnel below. After a minute he stood up and brushed his pants off.

"You go first," he offered. Even though Flit would never admit it, the manhole covers were far easier for him to move than for her. They were the old style, made of cumbersome iron. Letting her go first would relieve her of the responsibility of having to replace it as she climbed down.

"No being a gentleman today, Scraps. You have to take the lead for the whole test," Flit told him, shaking her head.

His shoulders sagged. "Ah, of course." The rules of the test stated that Flit was there to watch his progress and only intervene in emergency situations. Nevertheless, after he started climbing down the ladder, he used telekinesis to pull the grate over far enough that Flit could just crawl through, and then easily pull it back into place.

Once Scraps hopped off the ladder, he looked back up just in time to see Flit settling the manhole cover into place. They lost some light from above, but he looked around as his eyes adjusted, making sure it was safe for him to join him.

"All clea—"

Scraps didn't have time to finish before Flit popped into place beside him. He should have known that she would rather teleport down than climb the full way. Scraps shook his head, wondering how she stayed so fit when she rarely used her own legs to get around. He looked left and right to decide which way would be best. Either direction would get them back around the same time. If they went left, the tunnels would be more level, but they'd have to go through an area prone to bat infestations. The right twisted and changed elevations, but rarely had any mutated pests. Given a choice, Scraps would prefer to avoid running into bats, even if it meant walking more. The trade-off in energy and time it would take to fight bats was not worth it. So, Scraps turned to the right and started walking.

He stopped a few seconds later when he didn't hear Flit's footsteps. He whipped around, hands at the ready, but saw her standing where he had left her with a sheepish smile.

Brows furrowing, he asked, "What is it?" The dull reserve lights flickered and buzzed above her head.

"Well... I was hoping we could go this way." She jutted a thumb behind her. Toward the bat-infested tunnel.

Sighing heavily, Scraps shook his head. "You're not supposed to be guiding me..." He looked at her seriously, astonished at her lack of resolve when she had only just refused to let him move the manhole cover for her.

"I know, it's just... Well, you know. I kinda picked this route for a reason."

Scraps looked around again and made a mental map of the tunnels in his mind. He thought about where the bat tunnels would take them, and everything fell into place. He sighed. "Flit..."

Flit teleported to stand right in front of him and she put her hands on his chest. "I know, I know. This is your orienteering test and I gave away our location. But we need to go that way to see if the outdated comms lines have been activated between sectors E, F, and G."

"But my test—"

"Fine," Flit interrupted with a frustrated huff. "What happens if we go that way?" She jabbed her finger in the direction he had chosen.

"We will come across a large junction. The middle fork will be a descending tunnel. We should be able to get a decent way down before we have to rest for the night."

"And if we start out early tomorrow, when will we get back to base?"

Scraps did the calculations in his head. "Just after midday?"

"Right. Now, if we go that way"—she pointed toward the direction she wanted to investigate—"for just a little while and look around, we should be able to find an emergency shelter to rest in for the night. If we start early enough, then we'll arrive back at base tomorrow by what time?"

Scraps tried to figure out a rough route in his head. If they didn't run into trouble with the mutant creatures, and if they only spent an hour or two investigating, they would still return to base later. "Mid-afternoon?"

"Only a couple of hours difference!" Flit waved a hand dismissively. "It'll be worth it, I swear. We may not get to investigate this area again. Have you noticed the only team assigned to this sector lately is the Green Team? Someone in Control doesn't want us here, Scraps, which is exactly why we need to do this."

Scraps frowned as he looked back down the tunnel he had chosen. "But the record—"

"Screw the record. You'll still make good time. Better than pretty much everyone in our team, at least. Besides, what point is a record if there is another tunnel explosion because we didn't investigate, huh?"

Flit had him there.

Scraps looked down at the lively woman in front of him and sighed in resignation. She was right. With all the death and destruction that had happened, they needed to take this opportunity. The safety of the Underground came before his desire to prove himself to his new comrades.

Without another word, Scraps stepped around Flit and started walking in the direction she suggested. He didn't need to look over at her to know that she was grinning from ear to ear.

45

FLIT

EVEN THOUGH FLIT knew the tunnels well, she always underestimated the sheer sprawling size of the network. All the tunnels that exploded or collapsed in the past six months were in different sectors, but only just. They bordered the edges of their sectors at different levels, following the jagged line of reclassified passages. It was the reason it had been difficult to pick up on the connection between them at first.

Thanks to the collapses, Flit and Scraps had to transverse a mix of old transport tunnels and dank sewers to get where they wanted to go. The explosions had taken out key parts of the transition routes between zones. Despite the arduous trek, Flit was grateful they didn't run into any mutant creatures in the dark recesses of the more cavernous junctions. If she had peeled away from Scraps, Flit could teleport to the places they needed to check much faster, but given the recent history of the area, it was safer to stick together. They had to do their investigation properly, not quickly.

"I think the communication lines ran behind those covers," Scraps said as they reached the starting point they were looking for. He gestured high towards the narrow line of metal panels running along the top corners of the tunnel.

Flit squinted at the panels. The tunnel was high enough that it receded into the shadows behind the flickering lighting, making the covers hard to see. They blended in well with the dirty concrete walls in the darkness. Flit shrugged her bag off and pulled her visor out of it. She settled it over her braided hair like a headband and turned the attached headlamp on. When she looked back up, the dusty metal of the covers glinted as the focused beam of light shone on them. "I'll concentrate on following the communication lines if you keep your eyes out. I'm not sure what we're looking for, just anything that seems out of the ordinary," Flit suggested as they continued with renewed purpose.

Scraps and Flit spent the next two hours walking through the reclassified tunnels. Flit grew more and more restless and disheartened as time dragged on. The tunnels were just as musty and disused as any of the others in lower levels. Flit and Scraps well overshot the tunnel they needed to go down to get back on track for the test, but still found nothing. They agreed to make their way back to the nearest emergency shelter for the night when Flit saw something.

At first it was just a flash in her peripheral vision, a place where the grease and grime on an otherwise dull panel had been smudged off to show the stainless steel beneath. Flit stumbled as she saw it. Her eyes widened. "Scraps, look!" Flit tugged on his arm and pointed the smudged panel. "We need to get closer."

They retraced their steps back to the panel in question. It was at the top of a corner of a junction that had four tunnels feeding into it. At the opposite side, there was a ladder that led to the level just above them, which used to be a train line and one of the key routes when Old City was still operating. An important junction in the old days, but not something that she or the other Security team members would ever pay much attention to.

"It's too high up, I can't see a bloody thing," Flit muttered. The panel ran along the corner of the wall that met the three-metre high ceilings.

Scraps took a step back and looked up before shaking his head. "I cannot see it either." After a moment he turned back to Flit. "I can lift you up so you can get a closer look."

Flit frowned as she looked at him. He was strong, but they'd been trekking through the tunnels all day and her legs were feeling weak.

Scraps stepped up beside her and put his hands around her waist. "I'll put you on my shoulders," he suggested. "Jump on three. One, two, three."

Flit bent her knees and pushed up. Given how controlled the movement was, Scraps had to be using his telekinesis to help lift her. As soon as Flit was high enough, Scraps' hands left her waist. She let out a squeak of surprise at the lack of physical support, but a subtle force guided her back. She hooked her knees over his shoulders and steadied herself before his telekinetic hold dissipated.

"There you go." Scraps reached up and placed his hands on the small of her back to help her stay balanced as he stepped forward.

Flit chuckled and shook her head. If there was one thing she could say about Scraps, it was that he always got the job done. From her perch on his shoulder, she was at the perfect height to reach the panel. Flit ran her fingers along the edges of the metal where clean streaks criss-crossed over the thin film of sticky grease. Finger marks, maybe? She figured that had to be it but was distracted as her own fingers caught over some strange bumps along the lower edge of the panel. Leaning forward, Flit's eyes widened.

"Scraps, I left my multi-tool in my bag. Would you mind passing it to me, please? It's in the outer front pocket." A few seconds later he levitated the tool to her face level. "Thanks." Flit patted Scraps' head before she reached out and snatched the tool out of his telekinetic grasp.

She flipped through the different screwdrivers and tools on it with a frown. Every now and again she held one up against the bumps in the panel and shook her head. She tried attachment after attachment until Flit slipped the edge of a thick file under the dent.

"Well, shit." It fit. She stuck her tongue between her teeth and tilted her head to the side, concentrating hard as she levered the panel up. She did the same thing in all five the indentations. With a quiet pop, the panel fell off and clattered to the floor.

"You found it!"

"Someone's been here recently," Flit muttered, too busy trying to figure out the clue in front of her to claim victory just yet. She ran her fingers over the circuit board beneath the panel. Red, blue, and yellow PVC-coated wires ran off to either side of it. On the left they were connected to a new switch with a port compatible with modern datapads.

"That is the right connection for our tech," Scraps said excitedly, confirming Flit's own theory. Relief and dread flooded her at finding what they were looking for.

Flit bit her lip as she looked down at her bag. "Scraps, can you get my datapad too, please? It's in the back pocket."

Scraps shook his head. "I can get it, but I do not think we should. What if you connect to that terminal and set off an alarm? Technology is not my area of expertise, but if I were someone who was using this for nefarious purposes, I would have protected it from tampering."

Flit frowned. Scraps was right. She was tempted to try anyway, alarms be damned, but they may only have one shot at accessing the terminal. They needed to get someone with the right skills to look at it. Flit let out a heavy sigh. "Ugh, you're right. Maybe just pass me the datapad so I can get a few pictures of it for Control and Intelligence?"

Flit loved that Scraps trusted her enough to search through her bag and float the datapad to her without further argument. Anyone else on her team, even Hawkeye, would refuse to do so until she made a dozen promises saying she wouldn't tamper with it. Scraps, though, knew when she was serious and when she was playing around.

Once she had the datapad, Flit took photos from several angles, and one video recording of the panel and the area they were in. When she was finished, she passed it back to Scraps. "That'll be enough evidence to get some attention. We should find a shelter and get an early night so we can get back on track first thing in the morning."

As she grabbed Scraps' shoulders, Flit was about to warn him she was going to teleport when a shudder-inducing scrape of metal against concrete made her heart leap into her throat. Her entire body tensed, but she realised that Scraps was just floating the discarded panel up, holding it against the wall.

"We should put this back, just in case someone comes by." He levitated the panel to line it up with the gap, but it shook, and he couldn't push it back in alone. Flit leaned forward, careful to not throw him off balance, and pressed it into place with the back of her jacket-covered wrists.

Scraps' hands settled onto Flit's hips just as she was about to teleport down. She considered teleporting anyway, but she enjoyed the familiar caress of his telekinesis around her waist and let him help. With the same level of control as earlier, Scraps lowered her back to her feet.

"Thanks." She smiled at him, reaching up to push some of his sweat-dampened hair off his face.

Scraps leaned in closer. "Can I see the pictures, please?"

Flit sighed and swatted his chest. "Here I was thinking you were leaning in for a kiss." She passed him the datapad.

Scraps swiped through the pictures, a frown creasing his lips. "That tech looks very modern." He tapped the device screen to turn it off and handed it back.

"I agree." Flit tucked the datapad into her pack. "They'll have to listen to us now. Even if it's not related to the tunnel collapses, someone's using the comm lines for something dodgy."

Scraps nodded in agreement as Flit pulled her backpack back on. "So, where was that emergency shelter again?" Scraps asked, looking at her for guidance.

Flit smirked and shrugged. "We're back under testing conditions now. You're gonna have to find it yourself."

Letting out a low groan, Scraps shook his head and turned back the way they came, muttering something about the inconvenience of her selective rule following.

"WELL, YOU LOOK EXHAUSTED," Flit laughed as Scraps collapsed onto one of the three beds in the emergency shelter. She shrugged her pack off and threw it on the bed opposite to the one Scraps had claimed.

"I think it has something to do with the four-hour diversion we took," Scraps groaned as he shifted just long enough to pull his backpack off and throw it onto the dust-covered concrete floor.

Flit walked over to a panel near the grubby looking door and slid her finger over the screen. It flared to life without a hitch, and Flit was pleased they had found one of the better shelters. It had three beds, a functioning bathroom, and a drinking water connection. There were so many in the Underground that it was impossible to keep them all in top shape, so finding one this good was rare. It was updated enough that it worked on retina scans rather than passcodes. The retina scan was swift, and once the menu was open, Flit flicked to the communication screen and sent a message back to Control.

18:46. Flit and Scraps. Sector F, Emergency Shelter 39. All is well.

"Are you telling them about the communication terminal?" Scraps propped himself up on his elbows and looked over at her from the bed.

She shook her head. "Anyone in Control could receive that message. I don't know who we can trust. We're taking this straight to Harmony."

The panel flashed a 'message sent' confirmation before the screen returned to its normal blank state. Flit started the process again, and this time accessed a different part of the menu with several options in it. She selected one and there was a dull grinding sound as a section of the rear wall sunk backwards and slid into a cavity, revealing the small but functional bathroom. According to the stats, it even had hot water.

"Lucky for us, you found us a shelter with a shower." Flit grinned at Scraps. "I don't know about you, but after today I'm eager to get cleaned up before we eat."

Flit teleported to her bed and rummaged through her pack for her soap, shampoo, and clean clothes.

"Does teleporting short distances like that take less effort than walking?" Scraps chuckled.

Flit nodded. "Across that distance, it's as easy as blinking. And way less boring than walking." She stripped off her socks and flak jacket and then tucked the bundle of clean clothes under her arm. When she turned around, she noticed Scraps watching her closely. She wasn't sure if he was expecting her to strip off completely, but she just winked at him as she looked over her shoulder and teleported away.

Flit didn't bother shutting the door when she went into the bathroom. The shower was against the same wall as the door and was therefore out of view. She reached over and pressed the buttons to turn the water on and enjoyed the fresh smell of warm steamy water as she peeled off her clothes.

The water was hot enough that the shower screen fogged up within minutes. Flit relished the way it burned clean tracks down her grimy skin and washed away the dirt and fatigue of the day. She hadn't expected the orienteering test to be so tiring. However, she *had* done an extensive amount of double teleporting before their long trek. It made sense she was exhausted.

Despite how tired she was, Flit's mind was abuzz with an odd mix of excitement and dread. There was a certain sense of satisfaction that came with knowing that her gut instinct was right, and the others were wrong to call her crazy. Finding the confirmation was a step in the right direction, but she hated that it meant that there was a traitor in their midst. She hoped there was a good reason for it all, but the knot of unsettled nerves deep in her gut only twisted tighter.

Conscious there would be a limited supply of hot water, Flit let out a heavy sigh as she turned the flow off and stepped out. She looked around the bathroom and then cursed under her breath. She brought her toiletries and clothes, but nothing to dry herself with. "Ah, Scraps... Can you do me a favour please?" Flit called out. "I forgot my towel. Can you please get it out of my pack for me?"

There was silence for several heartbeats before Scraps stammered, "Oh, uh, sure."

There was a creak as he got off the bed and a scuffle as he rifled through her bag. She winced sympathetically, realising Scraps would have had to go through her underwear and other personal items to get her towel. Flit didn't mind, but she could just imagine how much he would be blushing as he went through her things.

Goosebumps prickled along her limbs as the steam from the shower dissipated into the room beyond. She wiggled her toes and bouncing on the balls of her feet to keep warm, wrapping her arms around herself.

"Here you go—" Scraps' poked his hand around the edge of the fogged-up shower screen, the towel hanging from his grasp.

Letting her wet fingers brush over his warm skin as she took the towel, Flit smirked. "You didn't have to get out of bed to give me this, you know. One perk of telekinesis."

Scraps' awkward laugh bounced through the room but stopped abruptly as Flit stepped out from behind the opaque shower screen, wrapped in nothing but a towel.

46

SCRAPS

SCRAPS GULPED as Flit stepped out from behind the shower screen. She stood in front of him, her very wet, very naked body only a handspan from him. She said something, but the words were lost as Scraps' eyes traced the path of a stray droplet of water sliding down her neck and between her soft, round breasts.

"Scraps?" Flit's voice snapped him out of his reverie.

Scraps cleared his throat and dragged his eyes away from the droplet. "Ah, uh. Yes?"

Rolling her eyes, Flit reached out and patted his shoulder. "You didn't hear a word I said, did you?"

"Uh... No," Scraps admitted, blushing.

Flit laughed. She grabbed the collar of his jacket and pulled him into a deep kiss. Scraps groaned into her mouth, his hands reaching for her towel-clad hips. His palms just touched the soft microfiber when she disappeared.

"You better get clean before we get too carried away," Flit chimed from behind him, where she leaned against the bathroom doorframe.

"You are right." He walked over and skirted past, taking care not to brush against her. He retrieved his towel from his pack before returning to the bathroom.

Scraps had the fastest shower of his life. He always enjoyed the relief of the hot water after a long day but being alone and naked in the shower meant his arousal refused to abate. He figured seeing Flit when he got out, fully clothed and waiting to eat dinner, would help him calm down.

Scraps wrapped his towel around his waist and walked out of the bathroom to retrieve his clothes. "For dinner I brought—" Scraps stopped mid-stride as he looked for his pack.

Flit sat on his bed with her legs crossed, towel tucked between them. She had set their dinner out in front of her like a picnic. Her hair was still wet enough that droplets of water were trickling off the ends and sliding over her chest. Scraps swallowed. His earlier hopes were dashed by the fact Flit was still in a towel.

"Yes, time for dinner." Flit leaned forward and patted the bed on the other side of the food. The top tuck of her towel strained, and Scraps just wished it would unravel. "Are you hungry?"

There was something in Flit's tone that made Scraps' legs weak. He was hungry alright, but not for the dried rations he brought along.

"According to the rules, I can't share any food with you, but I don't think anyone has to know about these." Flit slid two foil-wrapped bars of chocolate across the bedspread for his inspection. "I knew you'd bring dinner, so I thought I'd supply dessert."

Scraps smiled at Flit as he settled onto the bed and floated a bar up to his eye level, turning it this way and that. "Chocolate does not fill enough nutritional requirements to qualify as survival food."

Flit snorted. "Scraps, when you're with me, chocolate is the only survival food." Flit winked at him as she tore her rations open.

Scraps laughed and shook his head as he let the chocolate bar fall to the bed cover. He opened his own rations and they sat together in companionable silence as they ate their meals. When they finished, Flit let out a loud sigh and relaxed back against the wall at the head of the bed as she looked at him. She unfolded her legs and settled them flat on the mattress. Scraps' eyes wandered up the smooth, exposed skin; all the way to the top of her thighs where the towel hid the most tantalising part of her anatomy.

"Catch!"

Scraps jumped as Flit grasped a chocolate bar and threw it towards him. His hands were too slow to react, but he caught it with a flick of telekinesis and redirected it onto his lap. He peeled it open and took a bite of it before he leaned back and looked over at her. "I have never eaten dinner dressed only in a towel before. It is a rather odd thing to do," Scraps admitted, looking down past his bare chest at the towel still wrapped around his lower half. Thankfully, eating eased his arousal, but if he looked at Flit as she reclined like that for too long it would be back in full force.

"That's a pity. I could watch you eat dinner dressed in a towel any day of the week." Flit's eyes drifted down to his chest. She took a decisive bite of chocolate and rolled it around in her mouth before chewing.

Scraps gulped. Something about her look made him feel like she was devouring him rather than the chocolate. Scraps rested his free hand on Flit's knee. She looked up at him through her lashes, her bow-shaped lips curled into a smile dripping with mischief. Scraps was wary. He'd seen that look before, and while he trusted her, he was aware of her penchant for playfulness.

Flit reached out, grabbing the discarded foil wrappers of their rations and teleporting them into the corner of the room. She leaned forward, getting onto her hands and knees and crawling towards him. Scraps swallowed his mouthful of chocolate to avoid choking on it as his towel stirred in response to how hers barely constrained her assets. The bed sank on either side of his outstretched legs as she crawled over them. "Flit?" His voice trembled with a hint of wariness.

With a laugh, Flit plucked the remainder of the chocolate bar out of his hand and put it on the bed beside him.

"I-I thought chocolate was an important s-survival food," Scraps stuttered, unable to speak fluently with her warm and almost naked body hovering over his. She smelled fresh, feminine, and utterly enticing.

"It is... but I've got something better for you," Flit whispered.

Scraps frowned, confused. "What could be better than chocolate?" He knew of her preference for the creamy treat, and there was only one thing she would pick over chocolate. "Unless you brought ice-cream?" Scraps smiled and sat straighter in anticipation. He liked ice-cream.

Flit's smirk grew wider as she continued to crawl up his body. Maybe he was on to something.

"I did not see a cooler pack in your bag earlier. Surely, you couldn't ha—"

Scraps spluttered to a stop when, with a deft flick of her fingers, Flit brushed the twist that was holding her towel together undone. Quicker than a flash, she teleported the hanging towel off her body and straightened up so she was straddling his thighs, completely naked.

Scraps' mouth flapped about uselessly as he took her fully naked body in for the first time. His hands opened and closed at his sides as he tried to figure out to do with them. He had been fantasising about this moment for weeks, and now it was happening, he didn't know where to start.

Scraps' breath caught in his throat as Flit leaned forward. He could feel the heat radiating off her naked body, and it turned the blood in his veins to liquid fire. His arousal hardened and he couldn't do anything to hide how it tented his towel.

"I think this is better than ice-cream, but you'll have to decide that for yourself." Flit's sweet-tasting breath fluttered over his lips and he let out a strangled groan. He didn't have long to imagine what she meant when her lips pressed against his in a deep, passionate kiss.

Scraps sat beneath Flit, hands grasping onto the sheets beside his thighs. He didn't know what the rules were for this encounter. They had kissed and groped before, but they had always been wearing more clothes. The last time he got so close to touching her naked skin, she fled the room and left him in a state of confusion.

"Touch me, please," Flit breathed into the kiss as one of her hands slid up his bare chest. Her fingertips scorched his skin and he arched his back, pressing himself against her palms.

"Where?" The word trembled as much as his fingertips.

"Start here…" Flit met his eyes as she slid her hands over his shoulders and down his arms. She took both of his hands in hers and settled on the alluring curves of her hips.

Scraps groaned. "How is it possible for your skin to be so soft?" Wonder and arousal laced his tone.

"It gets softer," she promised, guiding both hands up over her waist and across her stomach.

Up, higher and higher. Scraps' eyes followed his hands, and he didn't know which part of him was luckier; his hands for touching her, or his eyes for being allowed to witness the show. "Flit..."

Scraps' didn't know what else to say. There was so much he wanted to convey; how grateful he was to have met her, how beautiful she was, how he had never wanted anything as much as he wanted her. None of it mattered, though, as she slid his hands up to cup her plump, firm breasts.

"H-how will I know if I'm doing it right? I don't have criteria to work with." The last time he touched her, their session had been cut short. Since that night, she had been the one touching and teaching him about his own pleasure.

"Oh, I'll let you know."

And she did.

Scraps soon learned that words fell short when it came to touching Flit. There were so many instances where a gasp or moan told him things that he would never have understood in any other way. As his hands roamed her body, he was in total awe of her; he had never enjoyed touching something as much as he enjoyed touching Flit. He loved that he could reduce her to a puddle of moans and whimpers with the slightest flick of his finger.

It turned out Flit wasn't the only one rendered speechless by infinitesimal movements. As Scraps discovered more about her body, she continued to map his. She used her fingers, her palms, her lips, and her tongue. She dragged her teeth along his sensitive skin, blew soft, cool breaths over his hottest parts in ways that made him tremble. Flit unlocked a universe of potential in his body and showed him just how deeply one person could feel pleasure.

Scraps couldn't have completed a sentence if he wanted to, and for once, he didn't try.

There were no words that could describe how she made him feel as she laid him down on the bed and settled herself over him. With a groan, Scraps' met Flit's eyes and he lost himself in her completely. The way their bodies joined was the perfect physical translation of all the emotions he felt for her. Every undulation of her hips, every gasp through her parted lips, every searing glance; he consumed it all. This changed everything. He never wanted to go back to what he was before, and he knew that from now on, he wanted Flit by his side.

THE NEXT MORNING, Scraps woke with great reluctance. The only reason he peeled his eyes open was because Flit shifted in his embrace. He groaned, not ready to get out of bed. "Morning Flit." Scraps cleared his throat, his voice rough and gravelly with sleep.

"Morning. Sleep well?" Flit whispered as she burrowed her face into him and pressed a soft kiss against his bicep. She squirmed a little, rolling over in his arms and looking up into his eyes. Her hair was messy, her cheek red where it had been resting against his arm.

Scraps caressed that warm spot as on her cheek and smiled at her. "That was the best sleep of my life." He leaned down and captured her lips in a soft kiss.

"Here I was thinking shelter cots would make it one of the worst," Flit teased when the kiss was over.

Scraps chuckled and pulled her tighter against his body, burying his face into her sweet-smelling hair and sighed contentedly. "The cot had nothing to do with it."

Flit chuckled. "You enjoyed last night that much, huh?"

"Enjoyed is not a strong enough word."

"Shall we go again?" Flit's hand drifted down between them.

Scraps groaned as Flit wrapped her fingers around him. "Can we just never stop? I could stay in bed with you forever." He leaned down to kiss her, but his eyes snagged on the panel by the door. The screen flashed, indicating the time. Scraps' sat bolt upright. "Oh no!"

"What is it?" Flit looked around for threats as she sat up too.

The rough sheet covering them fluttered down her naked body and Scraps' eyes dipped to her breasts. Groaning, he closed his eyes. "It's almost midday." Frustration dripped off every syllable.

Flit furrowed her brows as she looked over her shoulder at the door. "And?"

Scraps looked down at her, gulping deep, his hands balling into fists at his side. "I want to stay here with you and, well... you know"—he nodded towards her naked body— "but if we do not leave now, we will get back late, and I want to make good time." Scraps stopped and, unable to help himself anymore, traced his fingers over her breasts.

Flit sucked in a breath and closed her eyes.

"I want to stay here though."

Flit smiled, capturing his hand in her own and she looked into his eyes. "It's ok. We'll have every night together, but this is your only orienteering test. Let's focus on that, yeah?" Flit suggested as she held his palm against her breast, right above her hammering heart. She peppered a trail of kisses from his lips to his left ear. She tugged on his earlobe with her teeth before whispering, "Besides, the faster we get back, the sooner we can do this again."

Scraps shivered at her words. He supposed that was true. He leaned back, took a deep steadying breath, and nodded. "Let's get this test over and done with."

DRESSED, armed, and ready for the day, Flit and Scraps made their way through the nearby tunnels. It didn't take long for Scraps to pick up on the various markers around the shelter. He worked out a new pathway back to the base and, even given their late start to the day, he was confident that they would make good time.

The pair walked along in companionable silence, their footsteps echoing up and down the tunnels behind them as Scraps focused on finding the right turns. Despite the silence, they shared glances that spoke of the night they had together. Scraps blushed every time he saw the look in her eyes.

After only half an hour of travel, Flit stopped walking. Scraps was about to ask what was wrong, but she held up a hand in a 'stop' gesture. He clamped his mouth shut and settled his hand over the pistol on his utility belt. Flit narrowed her eyes and peered down the tunnel ahead.

"Hide," Flit hissed.

Scraps dashed to the side, dragging Flit with him. They ducked into a nearby alcove and he pressed her into the wall, shielding her with his body as he peered around the corner. His heart seized in his chest and he took his gun out of his holster as adrenaline flooded through him.

47

FLIT

FLIT STOOD, back pressed to the wall, her heart hammering as Scraps peered around the corner. "I saw movement down there," Flit whispered, "but there shouldn't be any patrols out here."

Scraps nodded. "It looks like a group of people."

Flit's eyes widened and she squirmed between him and the wall, poking her head out of the alcove. In the distance, the shadows shifted between the stray beams of light streaming through the grates. "Shit, your eyesight is good."

He shot her a frustrated glance and wrapped a protective arm around her, but he didn't pull her back. The blob of people grew closer and wider. What was one wobbling shadow fanned out into a group of wavering silhouettes. Nearer and nearer they drew, bypassing all the turnoffs and junctions, their footsteps growing from a distant pitter-patter into a relentless march. Scraps' hand tightened on her arm. His breathing was steady and when Flit looked up at him, she recognised the familiar look of concentration on his face. After the wonderful night they had shared, she'd been hoping for more action today... but not this kind.

"Those aren't Underground fatigues," Flit murmured.

Scraps narrowed his eyes with concern. "They're not Government-issued either."

Flit and Scraps both took their pistols out of their holsters and held them close.

Who were these people, and what were they doing in the tunnels? Adrenaline surged through Flit as the reality of the threat grew. She trained her eyes on the group and noticed that they were all dressed in nondescript black cargo pants and dark grey flak jackets. There were four of them at the front, with another row of feet behind. It was hard to discern exact numbers.

Scraps gently grasped her arm, tugging her back into the shelter of their side tunnel. He leaned down, pressing his lips against her ear. "There are too many. We need to find a shelter. Report to Control."

Flit bit her lip. She hated letting a group of strangers walk around their tunnels. It compromised the safety of everyone she loved and cared about. "We can't just let them—"

Scraps interrupted her hissed comment with a kiss. It shocked Flit to silence.

"We won't," he promised as he pulled away. "We will get back-up."

Flit saw the plea in his scarlet eyes. She hated walking away, but he was right. If anything happened to Scraps because they bit off more than they could chew, she would never forgive herself. She was falling for him, hard. The previous night proved that. She'd be damned if she let anything happen to him. Peeling away from him, she leaned around the edge of the tunnel again. They were getting close. The low buzz of clipped conversation echoed down to them. She and Scraps had to move soon, or else they would be found.

Flit slid back into the alcove and pulled Scraps down to her. "There's a turn off just to the left. I can see the corner. I'll teleport us there. We'll have to go closer to the surface, but there's another shelter nearby."

Scraps nodded and wrapped his arms around her. Flit held onto him and edged back to the main tunnel. The spot she picked took them closer to the group, but the only alternative would leave them wide open down the straight tunnel they had come from. This was their best shot.

Within the space of a blink, Flit teleported Scraps and herself to the new tunnel, just on the corner. As they landed, their feet clattered against the concrete.

"What was that?" a gruff male voice muttered.

The footsteps around the corner stopped.

Tension bloomed in the tunnels, a silence that spoke of both side's awareness of the other. The group didn't want to move in case they missed another sound. Flit and Scraps couldn't move, or they risked making one. Flit looked up at Scraps, her heart racing. He tightened his arms around her, not taking his eyes off the tunnel they had come from.

The next instant something shot around the corner and flew past Flit's face.

"Grenade!" Flit gasped. She grabbed Scraps' shoulders and teleported them just as—"Ahh!"

The force of the explosion slammed them against the far wall of the main thoroughfare. With a sickening crunch, Flit was crushed between Scraps and the concrete wall. Jarred by the impact, her pistol skittered across the floor. Flit's head spun as agony lanced through her arm.

"Flit!" Scraps held her close as they sank down. He used his other hand to buoy them up with telekinesis.

"That's them!"

Through a haze of pain and adrenaline, Flit watched the newcomers sprint towards them. A familiar face bobbed behind them. "Heft?" Flit whispered. Beside her, Scraps froze as he recognised the man too.

"Get her first, she's a teleporter!"

"Fuck." Flit cried out in pain as she wrapped her arms around Scraps. She gritted her teeth and pushed past it. She took a deep breath and prepared to teleport.

The deafening blast of weapons fire filled the space. Scraps threw up his hands, diverting the bullets with a surge of telekinetic power. They hit the wall and it exploded in a shower of concrete and flames. The forced knocked Flit and Scraps to the ground. A piercing ringing filled Flit's head, the proximity of the explosion deafening her. She couldn't hear the tunnel collapsing around her, but she saw it. Scraps jumped to his feet. Flit was about to jump up too, but a broken slab of concrete from the ceiling slammed into the ground between them. Flit rolled to the side to avoid being crushed.

"Flit? Flit!" Scraps' voice was muffled by the ringing in her ears and the concrete slab, but the panic in his tone was loud and clear.

Flit's heart seized in her chest. They were separated, but... he was safe. Behind that wall of rock, he had a chance to escape. She could exploit that; she would fight and buy every second she could for him to get far away.

"Follow protocol, retreat!" Flit screamed, pushing herself to her knees with her good arm and scrambling to the side as the dust settled around her. Determination to protect Scraps thrummed through her. It gave her energy to force her shaking body to its feet. Flit turned to face the thugs. They emerged from the fog of debris, weapons raised, as they moved in to surround her.

"Zach, the gun!" a thug at the front barked.

Off to the side, a man reached into his holster and retrieved a gun Flit had never seen before. It had a large clear cannister at the back with a throbbing purple glow emanating from it. She didn't know what it did, and she didn't plan to hang around and find out.

Flit's hands snapped to her belt, retrieving a dagger in her left hand as she took a fire grenade out with her right. She teleported behind a man at the back and lashed out. Like the others, he was dressed in thick plated body armour. She sliced her dagger along the arm-join of his suit and blood spurted out of it. He screamed. The others turned towards her. With her position blown, she lobbed the fire grenade at the guys on the opposite side to distract them. She teleported as it exploded, drowning them in blistering flames.

"Fuck. Get her!" the one who ordered the use of the weapon yelled as he dived aside. They ducked and rolled, but the flames caught on the hem of a few sets of cargo pants. They were briefly distracted trying to put the flames out as Flit teleported between them in several short hops, her dagger whirring, blood spurting, as she severed whatever joints she could get to through the cracks in their armour.

Flit reappeared in the middle of her circle of destruction. "Heft," she panted, looking the man she had known as an ally. "You're not a traitor, don't do this."

Heft's glazed eyes met hers. "You started this when you brought that mule down here." Anger and scorn dripped from his words. He turned and looked over his shoulder at the people Flit didn't recognise. "Get her!"

Rage swirled through Flit, colouring her world with a deep crimson haze. She teleported further down the tunnel behind Heft, but there was smoke and dust everywhere. She couldn't jump far enough to make a quick getaway.

The resounding boom of a gun firing echoed through the tunnel. Instead of a normal bullet Flit could dodge, a shower of purple sparks sprayed into the smoke and dust, lighting it up like fireworks on a cloudy night.

Flit cried out as the glowing crackles of power hit her.

She tried to teleport again, to escape to somewhere she could recover from the pain. A wave of vertigo swept over her and she tumbled backwards.

Was it the ground that she slammed into? Or the ceiling?

"Did it work?"

Footsteps surrounded her like a swirling vortex. A lethal trap she could not escape. Her fingers shook as she reached for her utility belt. Aftershocks of agony rippled through her in rhythmic pulses, violent echoes of that first purple blast. She wondered where Scraps was. In her own mind, it felt like she had been fighting for an eternity, but probably only a couple of minutes had passed. She had to buy him more time to get to the shelter. Flit flipped the lid on the pouch that held her fire grenades as the twirling carousel of bodies slowed and she could see straight. She would get behind them, blast them with the grenades, and high tail it out of there.

Flit tried to teleport again.

Every cell in her body exploded with excruciating pain. It was like claws had pierced into the very building blocks of her being. Her screams reverberated through the tunnels. When the spasms stopped, she wrapped her fingers around a grenade and flipped the safety off. As soon as it was armed, the grenade was sucked out of her grasp and cast aside. She barely felt the tunnel shake as it exploded, unable to see or feel further than her own body.

She had to get out of there.

Flit tensed, willing herself to move.

Her body resisted.

She pushed harder.

What small semblance of focus she gained dissolved, smothered by an obscuring tide of purple nausea.

"It's working!"

The faces of the thugs swirled around her in a grotesque, shifting fog of disjointed facial features.

"Put the inhibitor on."

"No!" Flit wailed and thrashed as she ordered her body to move. Once more her cells refused to comply. Her head exploded with agony as a heavy set of hands pushed a cold metal ring around her head. Then—

"Ahh!"

A blow to the back of her head threw Flit into the unforgiving concrete wall like a rag doll. As she slumped down the wall and lost consciousness, she hoped she'd bought Scraps enough time to get to safety.

48

SCRAPS

THE BANG of concrete slamming into the ground was nothing compared to the roar of blood in Scraps' veins as he watched the tunnel collapse between him and Flit. He flung his hands out. He tried to push the concrete out of the way. The weight of the slab made him stagger. It was too big for him to move. He groped for the fire-grenades on his belt, but he hesitated. He didn't know where Flit was. An explosion could crush her under the debris or bring the entire tunnel down on top of them.

With a grunt of frustration, Scraps stopped trying to move the concrete and pounded his fists against it in frustration. "Flit. Flit!"

"Follow protocol, retreat!"

Protocol: regroup at the nearest shelter. Send a Code 1A to Control. Wait for reinforcements.

The part of Scraps that would always be KC-847 had him turning on his heels. His footsteps echoed in time with his racing heartbeat as he ran down the passage. He came to the first junction and turned left towards the nearest shelter. He skidded to a stop.

Screams of agony echoed through the tunnel. Scraps felt like a bucket of icy water was dumped over his him. His heart seized in his chest and his mind ground to a halt.

"What am I doing?" Scraps hissed to himself, looking back over his shoulder at the concrete separating him and Flit.

He gritted his teeth.

Flit had risked her life to rescue him, an enemy, from one of the most dangerous parts of the Underground. When E-09 collapsed, she went out to save her comrades. He stayed behind and she almost got killed. If the situation was reversed, Flit would never leave him to fend for himself; he couldn't do that to her. Not anymore. She wasn't just a colleague. She was Flit. His Flit. He would not leave her to the mercy of a traitor and his cronies. She was fast, clever, and strong, but that didn't mean she could get away on her own.

Instead of turning left, Scraps veered right. He made a mental map of the tunnels. If he was correct, this tunnel would take him to the level below. From there he could climb up through a service shaft and come up behind them.

More screaming reverberated through the tunnels and pushed him to run harder and faster than ever before.

SCRAPS DIDN'T FIND the thugs where he expected to. The tunnel he came up into was empty. It didn't take him long to figure out which way they went, though. Not with the trail of glistening blood they left behind. He didn't even allow himself to entertain the idea that it was Flit's. It was more likely she got a few strikes in with her dagger.

Scraps followed the trail higher and higher through the tunnels, shocked by how far ahead they had gotten. Why did those guys bother coming down if all they were going to do was retreat? What was their plan? And why was Heft with them? He was horrible, but even he wouldn't turn against his own kind.

Angry voices and heavy, thudding footsteps were the first sign Scraps was gaining on them. He slowed his own steps, keeping his footfalls quiet, hoping to sneak up on them. He had his pistol in one hand and a fire grenade in the other. They transitioned out of the mid-level tunnels again and into the surface-level, where no emergency lights were set up. He pulled on his visor and set it to night-vision. By using night-vision instead of a torch, he would be harder to detect.

When Scraps found them, the group had gathered in one of the larger network junctions. Seven tunnels fed into it, three of which led to the surface. They were so close to getting out. He was certain that they would have a vehicle waiting for them at the exit; this was his last chance to stop them. But where was Flit?

"Don't do this, girl. Come nice and quiet like, and we'll treat you right."

The dull thud of a strike connecting with flesh echoed through the junction.

"Bitch!"

"Fuck you!"

Scraps' heart seized at Flit's furious comeback.

Through the emerald-hued world of his night-vision goggles, Scraps saw Flit. She was a mass of flailing limbs, surrounded by a circle of menacing bodies. One thug launched forward, grasping her by the ankles and pulling them under his armpit. Out of the eight outsiders, it was taking six to restrain Flit. She may be small, but she was hard to subdue.

"Let go of me!"

Scraps' hands balled into tight fists. Why wasn't she teleporting?

"Flit, stop. They won't hurt you if you stop resisting," Heft snapped, hovering around the outside of the circle of thugs.

Flit flailed and squirmed harder. She turned to face Heft, trails of blood streaming from her ears and nose. Her face was flooded with disgust as she jutted her head forward and spat at his feet. There was a glint as the metal of the inhibitor on her head caught the light. "Traitor," Flit sneered.

With a sickening crack, an agent smashed his fist into Flit's face and knocked her out cold. Her body went limp in their arms and one of them sighed with relief.

Scraps flipped the switch on the fire grenade. Fury surged through him. He had always thought fury would feel hot and fast. But this? It was ice cold steel casing his nerves. His mind worked overtime as he calculated the best way to bring those thugs down. Starting with the bastard who punched Flit.

"I thought you liked the mouthy ones, McKinley," a man to the left sniggered. The one who had punched Flit laughed.

It was a repulsive sound in this context.

"Oh, I do... but this one's a live wire. I'd need to sedate the bitch before I got near her."

Another man shrugged and smirked. "Well, she's out cold right now."

"This wasn't part of the plan," Heft argued.

"It wasn't, but you mules don't have any feelings, do you? Well, how about you watch and learn—" the puncher's hands went to his belt and the others cheered and whooped.

"Not on my watch," Scraps hissed under his breath as he lobbed a small metal ball just behind the group.

"What th—"

The grenade exploded. The agents dropped Flit and ducked for cover. Old subway tiles and rusted shards of piping hailed down around them. Scraps threw his hands out. In an ice-cold rage, he wielded his powers with deadly precision. Bones snapped, flesh tore, blood-splattered everywhere. The group dispersed, racing for cover to escape his attack. He pushed his abilities to their limits as he raced in, not stopping until he was standing protectively over Flit's body.

One of the thugs raised an odd-looking weapon at him. Before he could fire it, Scraps tore it from his hands and sent it shattering against the wall. The man's eyes widened in fear and Scraps struck, throwing him into the wall just like the gun. Scraps heard the cocking of a weapon and turned just as another agent fired. He deflected the round back at the man and it exploded in his face, sending the contents of his skull splattering against the wall. Scraps took out the next man that ran at him with nothing but raw telekinetic power tearing him limb from limb.

On and on Scraps went. He was so lost in the adrenaline-inducing fight for survival that he didn't realise it was almost over until only Heft was left standing.

Heft raised one hand towards Flit, another at Scraps. His eyes were wide as he looked around; wary and confused. Scraps panted heavily. Each breath like a knife to his lungs as Heft backed away.

"Do not make me fight you," Scraps warned, stepping over Flit and placing himself between his lover and the traitor.

"Y-you... you ripped them apart!" Heft stammered, his eyes flicking around nervously. Blood and flesh splattered over the walls and there was a soft gurgling wheeze as one of the thugs took their last breath.

Scraps felt no remorse. "You were going to let them rip Flit apart!" The words heaved from Scraps as he shook his head. "Why would you do this? Why would you betray the Underground? They are your friends—your family!"

The confusion on Heft's face intensified. "Me? I'm not the fucking traito—" Heft's denial was cut short as a bullet shot straight through his throat. He fell to his knees, any words he might have said drowning in the blood gurgling out of the exit hole. Scraps spun around. One of the dying thugs behind him collapsed back to the ground, the spent weapon clattering out of his hand. Whatever clue Heft might have given about what had happened in the Underground were dying with him, and there was nothing Scraps could do to stop it. He let out a yell of frustration, flinging his arms out and making the cavern rattle at the impact of his telekinetic tsunami.

There was a small groan from just behind his feet that made Scraps look down. Flit stirred, her pale face beading with sweat as her chest rose and fell in unsteady shakes. Scraps took one last look around, sub-zero adrenaline still pumping through his veins. He made sure that none of the thugs were moving before he leaned over, scooping up Flit's limp body in his arms and taking off at a run.

SCRAPS DID NOT STOP RUNNING until he found a shelter. He slammed his hand against the access panel, smearing it with blood. The door slid open with a groan, dust in the tracks billowing up as he stepped through and set Flit onto one of the beds. He fell to his knees and leaned over to listen to her breathing.

Slow, ragged, but steady.

Good.

Scraps looked around, seeing the emergency first aid kit on the wall. He wrenched it free and it sailed through the air into his hand.

He tore the packet open and got to work, knowing every second could mean the difference between life and death.

As soon as he had done everything he could for Flit, Scraps sent an alert to Control. They responded immediately, letting him know that the first round of reinforcements would be there in two hours. He would have to hold out until then.

Scraps went back to Flit's side and collapsed onto the ground beside her. His entire body ached as the adrenaline waned. He leaned forward, pressing his forehead against her shoulder and taking solace because she was still so warm.

When Scraps looked up at Flit, memories of her in the grip of those thugs flooded back to him. He came so close to losing her. To seeing her dragged off and having her worst fears realised. And the things those men said about her, about what they wanted to do to her...

Obliterated.

That was what he had done to them. Utterly obliterated them. He would never forget the sight of their torn and bloodied corpses on the floor around him. The fight replayed in his mind, a sickening tableau of death and destruction.

Be he would do it all over again to keep Flit safe.

49

FLIT

FLIT WOKE WITH A GASP.

Her body was on fire. Her head pounded so hard it threatened to split her skull in two. As she looked around, it felt like she had a thick layer of sand between her eyes and her eyelids.

And then the memories hit her.

Leaving the shelter with Scraps, running into the group of thugs, being hit by a weird weapon, the thugs dragging her towards the surface.

"W-what... Where—" In a panic, she tried to sit up. The moment she pressed her elbows against the bed, pain lanced through her left side and she cried out, falling back.

"You are injured. Please do not try to move."

Scraps' familiar voice draped her in a warm sense of relief. Flit turned her face to the side and to find him leaning against the concrete wall of... a shelter?

"Where are we? What happened?" she croaked.

"Safe in the Underground."

Her eyes fell on the bloody splatters that dirtied his shirt and matted in his short hair. "What happened?" Flit repeated impatiently. Her tongue felt thick and furry, making it difficult to talk.

"I brought you back to the shelter. You suffered some injuries. I think your left elbow is broken. You probably have a head injury as well; you were bleeding from your ears and nose."

Scraps sounded tired. Flit stretched her shaky right hand out to him. When he saw what she was doing, he pushed himself off the wall and walked over to take her hand, threading their fingers together.

"Where are the others?" Flit asked, only breaking eye contact with him to look around. When she talked, she felt the trails of dry blood on her face cracking and stretching her skin taut.

"The others?"

"Back-up from Control."

Scraps' pressed his lips into a thin line and he shook his head. Flit's stomach churned with anxiety.

"I called them after I brought you back here, they should be another half hour away," Scraps explained.

Flit frowned at him. "Didn't you call them when the tunnel came down?" She was so confused. That was the protocol. That was what she told him to do. She thought they were in the shelter while the others were investigating.

"When I heard your screams, I could not return to a shelter and just wait for the others!" Scraps snapped.

"But... protocol! Scraps, it's what I can trust you to do; follow protocol."

There was conflict behind his eyes as his brows furrowed. Then, his face hardened, and he squared his shoulders as if he had made a grand decision. "Fuck protocol."

"Scraps!" Flit's scoff turned into a painful splutter. She'd never heard Scraps swear before.

Scraps straightened his shoulders as he looked at her, not backing down. "Is that not what you would say?"

"Well, yes, but—" Flit stopped, trying to pinpoint why Scraps shouldn't be saying it. She groaned as the thinking made her head hurt even more. She collapsed back into the pillow and rubbed her eyes. "I told you to go. I was buying you time to get back to the shelter. Scraps, I thought you were safe."

"What point is there in me being safe if they drag you to the surface?" His fingers scraped against the scratchy mattress as he balled his hands into fists. "Do you know how close they were to taking you, Flit? Do you know the things they wanted to do to you?"

Flit saw rare, simmering rage welling up in Scraps. She took a slow, steady breath. She was furious with him for putting his own life at risk, but she would have done the same thing for him. She *had* done the same thing for him. She couldn't be angry at him for it. If anything, she was immensely grateful he chose that moment to decide protocol was a guideline rather than an absolute requirement.

"What happened to those guys?" Flit could still see their faces taunting her. She didn't ask Scraps what sort of things they wanted to do to her. They made plenty of threats while she was awake; she didn't need to hear the hate that would have poured from them when she was unconscious and at their mercy.

"Dead."

Flit sucked in a breath. "Heft, too?"

Scraps nodded and looked away, his face red. "I do not know what came over me. I should have set my gun to stun and used that. But..." Scraps took a shaky breath. "I didn't. All I could see in my head was what they would do to you. My vision turned red, and I did not stop until—" Scraps' tone grew more frantic as he recounted the fight.

"Shh... Scraps, it's o—"

"No, it is not ok! Flit, I killed them. All of them except for Heft. I would do it a hundred times over if it meant saving you." Scraps shook his head vigorously. "What sort of monster am I? What sort of person wants to kill others repeatedly? Who would trade a dozen lives for one or two? The numbers don't work out. It makes little sense!"

"It's not about mathematics, Scraps. It's survival. Instinct." Flit reached out, pressing her palm against his chest. She looked into his eyes. "Emotion."

"I do not act on emotion—"

"No, KC-847 did not act on emotion. Scraps does," Flit whispered. "You want to kill them again and again? Good, because I'd want to do the same if anyone ever tried that with you. It's what you do when you care for someone."

Scraps shook his head and looked down at his hands. His knuckles were white from where he was grasping onto the sheets.

They shook, and he struggled to catch his breath. "The Government was right. I am dangerous."

The blood in her veins turned to fire. Flit grabbed one of his hands and pried it off the sheets, holding it in her own. "You stopped them, Scraps. You got me back here safe. I know you feel like you can't trust yourself right now, so trust me," Flit whispered fiercely, catching his gaze with hers and holding him captive. "You are not dangerous."

Scraps maintained eye contact. He held it until that facade of rage and fear dissolved. Until his chest stopped heaving. Until his hand softened in hers and their fingers threaded together.

Finally, Scraps let out a sigh and leaned over, resting his forehead against her shoulder. Flit groaned, making him shoot back up.

"Flit? What was it?" He scanned her appraisingly to see what was wrong.

She shook her head. "Everything hurts," she muttered. "They had a weapon—" Flit's eyes widened, and she sat up, ignoring the pain sizzling through her body like electricity. Scraps slid an arm around her back, his concern deepening.

"The weapon, Scraps! Did you get the gun?"

"What gun?"

"It was a- a- a..." She tried to think of the best word for it, but her head ached and words were hard. "A large pistol! It shot out a shower of purple sparks and I couldn't teleport through it. It's how they got me. It was like"—Flit flinched, her body flaring with pain at the memory of her failed attempts to teleport—"like my mind wanted to go but my body refused to move. I've never felt like that before. It hurt so much. Like claws digging into every cell in my body to keep me put."

Scraps' brow creased in confusion as he watched her. "You mean, they put the inhibitor on you, and you could not teleport?" He glanced over at the broken inhibitor on the floor by the door.

"No, it was the blast from that weapon. I couldn't teleport at all." Flit stopped. She couldn't teleport back then, but surely she could now. She took a breath and tried to make a jump and that now-familiar pain lanced through her. A scream tore from her lips.

"Flit!" Scraps leaned over, taking her in his arms.

Trembling and terrified, Flit shook her head. "Scraps, I can't teleport. Shit, what did they do to me?"

She tried again with the same result. Flit collapsed back onto the bed, her body seizing in agony. It was impossible. Inhibitors were the only way to interrupt a Derivate's powers.

"Flit, please stop. You'll hurt yourself," Scraps begged, laying her back on the bed. "I took your inhibitor off. This is probably temporary. You just need to rest."

The world spun around Flit and she wondered what it would be like to live without her powers forever. They were such an integral part of her identity. What would she do without them? Who would she be? Even her name represented her ability.

"I did not see any special weapon, but there was something odd about Heft."

Flit's mind ground to a halt as she remembered that aspect of her encounter. "You said you didn't kill him. Where is he?"

"Dead. One of the thugs—"

"Scraps, Flit!"

The door to the shelter slid open and the sound of feet and voices echoed in from the corridor. A swarm of people flooded into the room, led by Acumen and Shadow. Patch was there too. He pushed past the others and dashed over, falling to his knees beside the bed. His cold hands pressed against Flit's temples as Acumen pulled Scraps aside. She tried to push Patch away, to see where Acumen and Shadow were taking Scraps, but the medic was in the way. She was about to call out to him when Patch shushed her.

"Flit, you're injured. Stop squirming. Let me assess you," Patch ordered.

But she didn't want him to assess her. She wanted to stay with Scraps, to make sure he was ok. She tried to teleport away, but her attempt was blocked again by the aftershock of that weapon. Through a fog of pain and dissociation, she watched Scraps being led out of the shelter by Shadow and Acumen, where a throng of Underground members were waiting for him.

"Scraps, no," Flit cried, twisting away from Patch's hand and pushing herself back up against the wall.

"He'll be fine, I promise. They just need Scraps to take them to the scene. Please just lay down and let me work," Patch murmured as he reached for her again.

She shook her head and scrambled as far from him as she could, every part of her body protesting the effort. "No, you don't understand," she tried to argue. If Heft was dead out there, they would blame Scraps, but he didn't do it. She believed him. But they might not. What would they do to him if they thought he had killed one of their own?

"Charm?" Patch called out over his shoulder. A middle-aged woman with bouncy red curls stepped forward; she was one of the Control workers. A telecoercionist. When her blue eyes met Flit's, they held an unspoken look of apology.

Panic turned Flit's vision red. "Don't you dare—"

But Charm interrupted her. "Sleep."

That single word was enough to fling Flit into the prison of her own slumber.

50

FLIT

"ARE YOU SURE ABOUT THIS?"

Flit turned to her mother, her eyes narrowed. "If I don't get out of this room soon, I swear I'm going to lose my shit."

Beside Flit, Scraps cleared his throat. He slid his strong arm around her waist to help her stand as she slid off the bed. There was reproach in his eyes for talking to her mother that way, but she ignored it.

"Don't you dare go too far. I know you want to stretch your legs, but you're still in recovery. And no—"

"No teleporting. I know." Flit sighed and shook her head. She sensed her mother's concern in the way she was fretting about the walk. As much as Flit wanted to teleport far away from the sterile medbay, she knew better than to push her luck.

It had been three weeks since the fight in the surface-level tunnels. For the first two weeks, Flit faded in and out of consciousness. If the severe concussion, fractured skull, and broken elbow hadn't been enough to take it out of her, she also had to recover from the effects of the mystery weapon. The medical team refused to let her out of bed until a few days ago. She had taken short walks around the room and visited the other medbays, but she never left that section of the tunnels and she was restless.

The only thing keeping Flit sane was the fact there was always someone at her bedside. Whether it was her parents, her Blue Team buddies, or someone from Control wanting to get some more details, she never lacked for social stimulation. Most of the time, though, it was Scraps. If she pretended to be asleep and peeled her eyes open just the slightest, she could catch him studying on his tablet while he sat dutifully beside the bed. It made her heart swell to see him in those sweet, stolen moments. Whenever he noticed she was awake, he would tuck his datapad away and devote all his attention to her. He was instrumental in convincing her mother to give her leave to go for a walk. He promised he would not leave her side, and after he saved Flit's life, Tinker had grown a deep respect for the Ex-Registered.

"I will make sure she follows the rules," Scraps promised Tinker, his eyes scanning Flit for signs of weakness as she straightened up and got ready to leave.

"Traitor," Flit muttered under her breath, earning a chuckle from her mother and her boyfriend.

"You have an hour, Flit. Do not make me send out the search parties." Tinker gave Flit a warning glare and Scraps a grateful nod. Flit marvelled at the favouritism her mother was already showing towards Scraps, but she couldn't begrudge either of them for it.

With an excited smile, Flit said, "Let's get out of here." After being bed ridden for so long, her muscles were stiff, and her balance was a little off. Scraps tightened his hold around her waist as he sensed her disequilibrium. She smiled at him in thanks.

Just as Flit and Scraps reached the door to the medbay, it slid open to reveal Shadow and Acumen. Flit's shoulders fell and she barely managed to suppress a groan.

Acumen snorted. "Lovely to see you too, Flit."

"We're just about to go for a walk. You know, away from this place I've been caged up in for the last three weeks." Flit rolled her eyes.

Shadow gestured for Flit and Scraps to take a seat. "We won't keep you long."

Flit bit the inside of her cheek to stop herself from complaining as she turned around and sat on the nearest bed.

Clearing his throat, Shadow looked at her mother. "Tinker, may we have the room, please?"

Tinker frowned but nodded before tucking her datapad under her arm and leaving the room.

This wasn't Flit's first visit from Shadow or Acumen. They had stopped by to see her several times since she woke up. When they were there, she knew it was time to talk. The two were full of questions, wanting to get her side of the story. There wasn't much to tell, no matter how many times they asked the same things. She tried to fight, she got shot with that weapon, and Scraps saved her arse. Yes, she was sure Heft was with the group of thugs from the start of the fight. Yes, he attacked her. No, she hadn't seen the others before. Did they seem like they wanted to harm her or Scraps? She had rolled her eyes and told them that the evidence was clear enough from her injuries.

From what the other Blue Team members told her, Scraps was taken in for questioning straight after the incident. He was confined to a jail cell for twenty-four hours while they brought in an entire team of postcogs and telepaths to ascertain the truth of his story. Word had gotten around about what had happened and, even though he was cleared of any wrongdoing, some of the residents of the Underground were still suspicious of him. Flit hated to think about it, but she figured there would always be someone who was unable to see beyond his past, no matter how much he did for them. For the most part, though, people were too caught up on Heft's betrayal to linger long on Scraps' part in it all. The investigation then turned to Heft's team, and all the slip-ups in protocol and awareness that allowed so much death and destruction to befall the rogue group of Derivates. The Green Team, so low on numbers, was disbanded while Control figured out what to do with the few remaining members.

"To what do we owe the pleasure of this visit?" Flit asked once she was settled, looking between Shadow and Acumen. The bed sagged as Scraps settled beside her. She took his hand, holding it tight. She could sense the tension in him every time someone official came. He wouldn't admit it, but she could tell he was terrified their scrutiny would return to him.

"We came by to let you know that Harmony and Divvy have closed the investigation into the fight in the tunnels, and the preceding explosions," Shadow announced, cutting straight to the point. Flit appreciated that about him; he didn't waste time on pleasantries.

Scraps sat straighter. "Are you able to share the final findings?"

"Heft was behind it all. Oculus and the other members of the Green Team were unaware of what was going on," Acumen explained, giving Scraps a grim nod.

"And the communication line in the junction?" Flit pushed, wanting as much information as she could get out of them.

"It was accessed twenty-four hours before each incident. The receiving addresses were encrypted. Our micros could not trace them, but we are sending out teams to ensure the lines won't be used like that again," Shadow informed them seriously.

Flit had more questions, though. "How did Heft get in touch with this group? Do you know anything about them or the weapon?"

Shadow and Acumen both shook their heads at Flit's questions.

"There was no identification on their bodies. Any information they might have had died with them." Shadow's eyes settled on Scraps as he spoke.

Scraps tensed at her side. Flit leaned into him, annoyed that Shadow was making him feel bad for protecting himself. Those guys weren't down there to share details over a cup of tea. They were there to kill.

"Why did they kill Heft, though?" Scraps asked, his tone pained.

Shadow gave a small, noncommittal shrug.

"Because they didn't want him telling us anything either," Acumen supplied, earning him a reproachful look from Shadow. "Or at least, that's my personal opinion. Which you most certainly will not find in the report."

Flit smirked at the sass in Acumen's comment. Shadow huffed, the only sign of annoyance he was likely to show. Although they hadn't answered all of Flit's question. "And the weapon?"

"We have a lot to address with scarce resources," Shadow hedged.

Flit narrowed her eyes. "And you don't think the weapon is a priority?"

"I didn't say that."

"Yeah, but you didn't say it was."

Scraps' settled his hand on her thigh. Shadow and Acumen looked at each other for a moment, the silence between them thick with unspoken truths. When they turned back to Flit, she had a feeling they were going to lie to her. Again.

"The investigation into the weapon is ongoing. With your security clearance, I'm unable to say any more than that." There was a finality to Shadow's words, but Flit ignored it.

"Like, a proper ongoing investigation, or like the early one you guys did into the tunnel explosions?"

"Flit..." Scraps warned under his breath.

Flit shrugged. "What? It's true. If it's given the same level of care as the initial investigation into the tunnel collapses, we'll end up with an army of the bastards marching down here with those weapons in no time."

"I assure you, we are taking this weapon very, very seriously," Acumen promised her.

Flit pressed her lips together, unconvinced, but she nodded. "Well, if you need someone with good instincts to look into it, you know where to find me." Flit's offer was not entirely sarcastic.

The corner of Shadow's thin lips turned up into a rare smile. "I'll keep that in mind." He turned his steely gaze to Acumen.

Something silent passed between them before Acumen nodded. "Right, well, I'm sure you two are eager to go on this walk. We won't hold you up any longer. Flit, just promise us you'll behave, yeah? I'm tired of telling your folks you almost died." Acumen got to his feet and brushed his camo pants down. Flit chuckled. There was no way she would make that promise, and he knew it.

All four of them walked to the door together. Acumen and Shadow turned left to head back to Control. Flit took Scraps' arm and tugged it to lead him in the opposite direction.

"So," Scraps begun after they had been walking for a few minutes, "where are we going? We could go to the park or cruise by the training rooms. I am sure some of the teams will be hanging in the Mess Hall if you would like to socialise for a while."

"I was thinking of heading to my room."

Scraps furrowed his brows as he looked at her. "I thought I brought you everything you needed a few days ago?"

"Oh, you did. The only thing you couldn't bring me was privacy. That is something we can only get there." Flit tilted her head to the side as he processed what she said.

Scraps' staggered to a stop and turned to her. "I, uh, I thought you wanted to stretch your legs?"

Flit's lips curled into a mischievous smirk, her hazel eyes sparkling with suggestion. "I did say that, didn't I?" She pressed her hands against his stomach and slowly slid them up his chest. The heat of his skin radiated through the plain cotton t-shirt he was wearing. "But why stretch only my legs, when I can stretch my whole body?"

Scraps' eyes widened. "Surely we do not have enough time for that."

Flit grasped the collar of Scraps' shirt and tugged him down to her level. She brushed her lips against his in a soft kiss that was full of promise. "How much time do you need?"

His low groan shook the narrow space between them.

She chuckled. "I thought as much. Come on, we don't have a second to waste."

Flit linked her arm with Scraps'. She took her first step, tugging him along with her, but stopped when he refused to move. She rolled her eyes as she turned back to face him. His look of surprise had been replaced with an expression of concern. "Flit?"

"Yes?"

"What they said about that weapon earlier... You will not let that go, will you?"

Flit looked into Scraps' crimson eyes. She didn't want to lie to him. Not after they had been through so much together. He had shown himself to be quite the investigation partner; there was nothing to be gained by hiding the truth. "No."

Scraps' muscular shoulders sagged, and he shook his head.

Flit gently patted his chest. "But that is tomorrow's problem.

For now? We have less than an hour to visit Tunnel Forty-Two and get back to that prison cell they have the nerve to call a medbay... Are you in? Or do I have to take care of myself?"

Flit offered Scraps her hand.

Scraps' expression of concern changed into one of amused endearment. He reached out, taking her hand and brushing a kiss over her knuckles. "I'm in," he promised. "For whatever crazy adventures you want to go on, I'm in."

TO BE CONTINUED...

COMING SOON

2021

For more information and bonus content, visit:

www.livevans.com.au

Lightning Source UK Ltd.
Milton Keynes UK
UKHW010721091020
371301UK00001B/37